The History of Light Book 2:

THE BOOK OF SOUND

KEVIN HINCKER

THE HISTORY OF LIGHT

VOLUMES 1 THROUGH 5

THE QUESTION IN THE DANCER'S KISS

THE BOOK OF SOUND

THE HISTORY OF LIGHT BOOK 2

KEVIN HINCKER

CONTENTS

A WORD ABOUT THE CITY

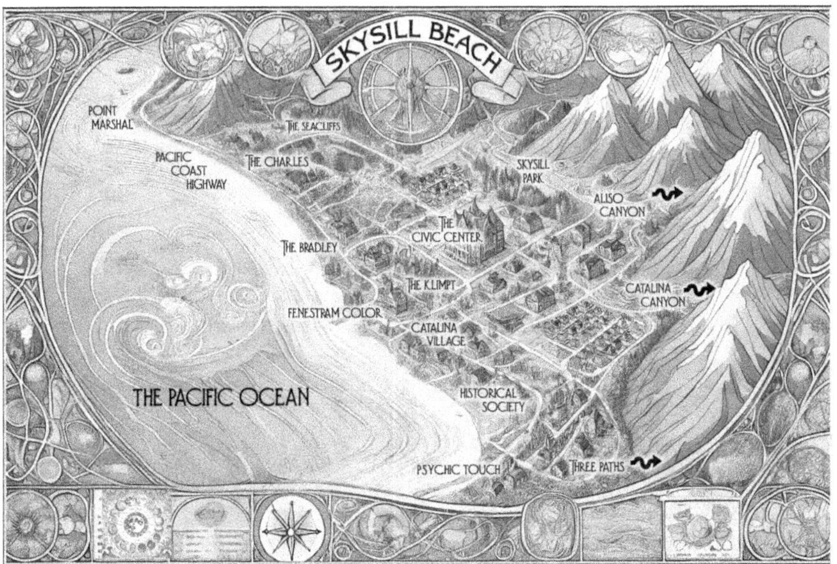

Skysill Beach Master Plan

Skysill Beach is an art colony on the Southern California coast. It is stylish and quaint, wholly dedicated to taking money from tourists, and hosts a multitude of art galleries that *compel* shoppers to buy, using special ultraviolet paint. This is a town where ghosts and psychics and magic *light* are the pressing mysteries. Ringed by high coastal hills, resting in a bowl tilted toward the Pacific, it feels at once wild—filled with parks, pressed against the sea, separate from the outside world—and oppressively controlled. An unseen power oversees the painters of Skysill, who have lived for generations, trapped without knowing it, in a city they can never leave.

THE FIVE FAMILIES

~

1. **ASPECTU** *sight* [*The PAINTER*] *
2. **AUDITUS** *sound* [*The MUSICIAN*]
3. **SAPOR** *scent* [*The HUNTER*]
4. **NIDOR** *taste* [*The ALCHEMIST*]
5. **TACTUS** *touch* [*The DANCER*] *

* Prime

THE THREE PSYCHIC PATHS

1. The offspring of either Prime and AUDITUS - _The Path Before_
2. The offspring of either Prime and NIDOR - _The Path Beneath_
3. The offspring of either Prime and SAPOR - _The Path Behind_

THE HIGHER COLORS

1. **choke** - *accumulation / dissipation*
2. **compulsion** - *attraction / repulsion*
3. **reason** - *transparency / obscurity*
4. **crush** - *large / small*
5. **farewell** - *beginnings / endings*
6. **wander** - *near / far*
7. **bleed** - *destruction*

CHAPTER
ONE

I made my plan to warn Caroline of all my dangerous character flaws just as we were jumping in my car to go get drunk. It was a plan made on the fly, so it wasn't very thorough. Plus I was still confused by Caroline's mind-blowing kiss, and Samantha's ghost on the sidewalk. But all that—lack of time, confusion from kissing and ghosts—those are just excuses. The truth is, my plans are mostly placeholders for whatever else was already going to happen.

A thorough plan would've taken Caroline's appointments into consideration, and all the murdered bodies I'd seen, and her psychic skills and the various crimes I might or might not be wanted for. But I was in no condition to juggle a plan that complex. So I decided I'd issue a simple warning—*be aware, I have bad judgment and unpredictable seizures and melted a steering wheel with my hands a few days ago*—which I planned to deliver and after that let the chips fall. I still hoped we'd end up getting drunk.

But a hundred yards into our drive to the bar we stopped for breakfast burritos, which I hadn't planned for. Ordering burritos somehow led to a round of runaway kissing in the drive-through line. Her mouth was warm and sweet like her lips were dripping churro sugar, which I knew was unlikely. I tried giving my seizure warning at that point but the taste of her derailed me, then people started honking, then we drove away and forgot our burritos. For a few hours I completely forgot I had any dangerous flaws to warn anyone about, while Caroline kept looking confused, coming back to my mouth like she was surprised she hadn't got tired of it. The whole day passed that way.

At four in the afternoon we were still making out like high school truants. Just intoxicated, inexplicable, endless sweet kissing. It was impossible to stop, bordering on obsessive. I'd skidded my car into a safety pullout along the Pacific Coast Highway. At that point I still hadn't warned Caroline of my bad judgment—though some of that had to be obvious by then, I felt—when a police cruiser pulled off the highway and stopped behind us.

I was wanted at the precinct for questioning, I was informed. The officers had been searching for me all day and it hadn't left them feeling generous. I had to tail them to the station, and I brought Caroline with me because they hadn't told me what else to do with her. She took roadside questioning by law enforcement as a matter of very little concern. She seemed to enjoy it. I started wondering if her judgment wasn't even worse than mine.

Getting out at the station car yard I offered my keys to her but she said she'd walk home. Together we strolled toward the gate and the impatient cop there. It'd grown cool. The sky was a slanting canvas of clouds on fire. With the day almost over I felt leaving her this final image of me as a person of interest in ongoing murder investigations made me look more murdery than I really was. And still she hadn't been warned.

"Here's a question," I said, watching as she walked, her tongue on her lips like a memory, "I guess I'll just say it—I feel like I have things some people would call issues, which, well, everyone calls them that, which in the name of full disclosure you should hear about, also for your personal safety, but now I have a problem. I don't know if this is the perfect time to bring it up, in a police impound lot. What do you think?" I said it really casual and charming, in my way.

"You're wondering does revealing these safety issues to me here at the police station put them in the worst possible light?" she asked. I nodded. She really understood me.

"No," she shook her head, "because early on I factored police visits into my idea of you, since you kept showing up trailing crimes I could see you hadn't committed. I don't understand half of what's happening to me. I don't know why I feel like this. I swear you taste like a coke float and usually I don't like a coke float, so how come I like it when we kiss?"

An idea came to me in a flash—the worst ones always come that way, you'd think I'd learn—to ask her to meet me tomorrow morning at the office of *Asher Gale: Authentication and Investigation*. If she saw they'd officially put my name on a door I thought I might appear even more law-abiding. It's not something I'm used to worrying about so I didn't know if it was an incredibly bad idea or not.

She considered the idea as we ignored the cop who wanted us out of his impound *faster*. We'd stopped kissing for the moment. We strolled through that end-of-days tangerine sunset shimmer, among confiscated getaway cars and drug cartel panel trucks, making memories.

"I'm sorry," she said after a second, "I forgot your question. I got lost picturing you in an office. What's *that* like?"

I admitted I didn't remember.

"I know there's a reception desk," I said, "and—oh, my forgeries are there. I mean the forgeries aren't mine. Or I don't know. It might be a grey area."

"There's forgeries! There's a little bit of everything. This isn't forgeries they called you in for tonight, though, right?"

"No. Tonight it's the other thing. The murders of Waylon and Tobias."

She took my hand. We let our fingers bridge the pieces of us. It felt structural and undeniable and almost totally insane.

"It's been a long time since a boy brought me on one of his police interrogations," she smiled.

"For a lot of people those are too personal. But nothing's too personal for me. And honestly, this might not be those murders, it could be a parking ticket I probably have or it might be that cryptocurrency or those hitman Brazilians who vanished from that beach where those officers found me covered in blood. Any of that."

"Or it could be money laundering," she said, remembering Waylon. "Don't forget money laundering."

"Right, the laundering. Anything. It could be Samantha committing suicide. So, do you want to come to the office?"

"Oh," she said, and took a sad breath. "That poor girl."

We kept walking slower. I wished I hadn't brought suicide in. And listing all the crime I'd witnessed the last few days probably emphasized whatever questions she might have had. Would she want to see more of me?

She stopped walking. She turned, and her brown eyes were overfull of all her worst judgment, and it was so beautiful. I was sorry I'd ever doubted her.

"I'd like seeing your office of forgeries," she told me. "They keep coming up so I should probably get familiar. You have my number. Let me know where to come find you."

Then we started making out in the impound lot. Neither of us planned it, it was just what we did whenever there was some spare time. The cop got sick of waiting and chased Caroline away. I tried to watch her go but they wouldn't let me.

In the station, they sat me in a hard chair and pitched questions, the same ones from the day before but at different velocities. At the beginning we were friends. They were sure I'd done something murder related, I was sure I hadn't, they encouraged me in different ways to confess anyway. I just kept reminding them of the Brazilians who'd donated the blood evidence on the beach, and the knife used in Tobias's murder where I said there had to be Brazilian DNA, but none of mine, plus at Waylon's scene there was *his* blood was everywhere but *I'd* swabbed clean, plus all the other exonerating evidence. I pointed out it had actually been me who called the police at these murders, and it was also me who reported the Brazilians breaking into the Klimt. Then I joked it seemed like me doing their entire job for them, which we all thought was funny. I pointed their whole case out because I told them it seemed like they hadn't really been paying attention, and we laughed.

Yes, they agreed, they had all that evidence, but what they really wanted was a story they liked that accounted for a man, naked on a beach beside a murder victim, covered in blood but it's *his own blood* but he doesn't have any wounds. I told them I sympathized and shared some of their questions.

What I didn't tell them was, they were asking the wrong questions. The questions they should have been asking were, *did it seem like you died, stabbed by two Brazilians, who then vanished except for a piece of one shoe while you became a ghost or something, before returning to your body with no stab wounds to find Veronica Night offering you an internship—on the beach where she also might have healed your stab wounds with magic light or maybe you healed yourself or maybe it was a hallucination?* If they'd asked me that, I would've admitted everything. That's why it's important to know the right questions.

They had their own theories anyway. Since they'd recently had a few extraneous beach dwellers go missing, they started putting pressure on the wild coincidences they continued to see in my story: all the crimes on beaches, all the murders, all the missing people and break-ins not to mention suicides, and me in the middle of everything, just innocent. I admitted it was all very hard to understand.

Hours later they released me onto their sidewalk.

That night in my living room, in moonlight through my bay windows, I ate cold pad Thai and observed my final, unfinished painting. After I ate I sat in front of the easel and touched a brush to the canvas, a moth weight, tracing the long abandoned strokes of

Higher color. I ran the soft filaments up-down, back-forth, but without paint. I don't own paint.

My mind surprised me picturing the bristles sliding inside Caroline's open shirt, between her breasts and down the middle of her. Her lips pulled open, she whispered. Then because my mind darts around a lot I wondered if I shouldn't go to Asher Gale's office early the next morning before Caroline got there to make sure her visiting wasn't an incredibly bad idea, since it had started to feel like it might be an incredibly bad idea.

And that is why, jogging across PCH in the damp of that Skysill Beach dawn, mounting the Bradley Building steps and hurrying across lobby marble to the elevator, unlocking Asher Gale's door, and charging into his office, I didn't see the ghost until it was too late.

CHAPTER

TWO

She floated, ultraviolet streamers of dayglow fusion fire, five feet down the entry hall, right in front of the door to the office bathroom. Samantha Goodman, translucent, complete, with *dominion* tendrils spinning above and below, welding her in place.

I wondered why there was a ghost in Asher Gale's office.

And then my fingers crabbed into claws. Behind me the office door eased shut. I realized I was going *chromatic,* right in the hallway, and I couldn't even see what the trigger had been, it made no sense —no acquaintances in emotional distress, no breathtaking art, no eclipses. Only the ghost, and ghosts, I felt, were pretty unremarkable these days for this kind of reaction.

I braced for *chroma storm* insanity but it didn't come. The Colors didn't rampage, no ice behind the eyes, just my fingers clenched in bone balls. My skin got slippery loose and it felt like wet paints all over my body, and that was new. I reached my arms turned my head, my muscles cocked, and I froze.

I felt I had an outer body, and a different body inside that.

The inner body shivered.

I felt a tab pop in the space between my ears. A jerk. And then I hung behind, slightly above the back of my own frozen flesh, just as I had the day before in front of Psychic Touch. And I became the thing some people, including only me, were calling a ghost.

Through ghost eyes I saw straight ahead—only straight ahead. My flesh head had frozen while turned one way in unhappiness, and he was very uncomfortably *locked tight*. The cheek he left facing me needed a shave. His hair needed cutting or combing. Good lord, who was supposed to be taking care of him? He needed a gardener.

I saw I had ghost arm pieces sticking into view. My whole ghost body was bonfiring all seven Higher colors and *dominion,* spinning around me in a fishbowl tornado. The ghost body was numb, numb as a bucket of cold water.

The world was quiet. It stayed that way while the three of us—ghost me, flesh me, Samantha—waited stacked in that little hallway for how long I do not know. I hoped to suddenly find myself back in my flesh like I had the day before. Samantha still held her shining goblet drilled with holes where *dominion* dipped and ran. She still had her lack of expression and her pantsuit. *Dominion* made her utterly blank face expectant.

Caroline would arrive, it occurred to me. Then the hallway would be very crowded. She'd discover my flesh body frozen dumb. She'd see no ghosts. Just my flesh, drooling a little bit. It wasn't exactly a murder scene but it wasn't the picture I'd wanted to paint of reputability. I tried moving my ghost body but there weren't any nerves to do it. I tried screaming.

I heard a ghostly pseudo sound.

"Hey you!" I ghosted at Samantha, while the mouth on my flesh body twitched and let more saliva out. He looked really pained.

"Samantha, what the fuck?" I ghosted out, in my charming way, "what're you doing here? Are you doing anything anywhere? Do you have any idea what's going on?" Flesh me moaned louder, trying to push out the words I ghosted.

"I'm expecting someone any minute," I told her, "you know her, it's Caroline, you met her yesterday. You live on her sidewalk. She's on her way. You know I think the two of you might like each other. You'd be surprised the things she likes. Though I don't know how long we can go like this, I think I'm acting unbalanced, more unbalanced than usual, like marginal and unpredictable but not in the good way—the police keep getting involved, so what she thinks of me I don't know, I have to say it hasn't been a problem so far—but still I don't want her seeing me this way in the hall, because look I'm drooling, she's not judgey but she's got to have limits, I just don't know what they are. She cuts the bullshit... I have no idea why I'm telling you this." Making words in long streams is easy as a ghost since you don't breathe air. Flesh me mangled and moaned every word.

"Are you here about your goblet?" I pressed Samantha. "If so then okay, I guess, I'll keep trying to help, though I have to be honest I've got *no* idea what to do—if *you* have ideas let me know—the fucker who made you commit suicide died in a house fire or I'd ask him, and listen, right now I can't stay frozen up here. I'm just thinking out loud. What if you're not doing this to me but I'm doing it to myself? You see my hands?" I appreciated Samantha listening so well. For me it was easy, I long ago got comfortable talking to things that weren't there. She and I were bookends. We faced each other across flesh me like he was our coffee table.

"I'm having a *chroma storm*," I continued, "see? A new kind of *chroma storm*. Do you think? See my body, see how he moans when I talk—it's awful, to tell the truth, don't look—he's connected to me, what if I got him on his hands and knees somehow and crossed his eyes, I could try to get out of this. Out of this hallway. What do you think, I'm open to ideas. And I don't say that often."

She didn't have ideas. I tried mine; my flesh body was like a Novocain flesh puppet, thick and far away and forming gibberish words, but connected to me enough to want to talk. So I started puppet-mastering him to have closed eyelids. Drop down eyelids.

Close god damn eyelids. I did pulling, pushing, all the strings, it was the slowest puppet show in human history but the lids closed, they finally did, and I felt victorious and exhausted.

Next I puppeted his eyes crossed toward his nose. Just by feel, I couldn't see his face. I had to keep a focused thought going, *cross cross cross*, for many seconds to get a result, which is not one of my strengths, and his eyes kept slipping out of control but at last I got them pinned.

The next step was, get him kneeling. I was feeling the pressure. Caroline could open the door any second. I urged one of his knees to bend two inches, it took forever and sapped me but then flesh me was tilted, precarious, so I bent his other knee and got him leveled, like posing a Barbie.

But then flesh me started tipping. At that point there was nothing I could do. I'd bent one knee a quarter inch too far, leaned him somehow—with no inner-ear feedback I had no idea what was going on over there. I did know he was going down, face first, to eat his teeth and break his nose. I felt terrible for him.

He went slow at first, then very fast. I couldn't even grimace. He fell in the direction of transparent Samantha—and then instead of falling through her, he hit her. And bounced.

He bounced again, in a thick-flesh way, then jerked to a stop in the air leaning on her shoulder—a shoulder made completely of light, I wanted to protest—then he slid, cheek against her ghost arm, and I thought he'd roll off but he rolled *over*, sideways, to hit the wall with his face and get wedged against the paint.

I couldn't help amazement. It was amazing. He was propped sideways in the air pinned to the wall by nothing, supported by light off a ghost. His back shivered, spasm straight, arms at sides and legs stiff as fence poles. He was pitiable.

No way I'd get him to his knees from there, he was stuck. I decided to skip the knees step and I really started muscling his eyeballs, puppeting without remorse. The energy required for puppeting was heating up that flesh body. I watched him sweat puppet pools like he was running wind sprints. I pulled delicate muscles in his pupils to press his tiny, massy moon eyes, until our strength was about to expire.

Suddenly ghost me sucked down and in toward flesh me, dizzying, titling through the air, angling toward his back propped against the wall, and then ghost me just... slid into flesh me.

We weren't attached, though. Just co-occupying space. I saw through both sets of eyes at once, which meant paint on the wall, and I felt his flesh nearly interacting with my ghost, sliding like poled magnets. I viced my pupils further. My body bucked, burning —pain kindled up from him, rising fast, volcanic pain, and the seven Higher colors of ghost me faded from sight leaving only a pulsing corpus of *dominion.* It buzzed and throbbed, a heat-pressure sun knot, still not tight enough to press my bodies together, my two bodies crushed in a vice. The *dominion* corona popped the hall, spun out through it—flesh me screamed—ghost me screamed.

The fever crush broke something.

I almost had time to worry, then I saw that the broken thing was only me uncorking pressurized *dominion,* so it tubed down flesh me's right arm, scalding, into his fist, to disappear. My two bodies Lego-snapped back together. It really felt like the right time to pass out, but that was just me with my wishful thinking.

Back in one body propped on the wall, suddenly Samantha was just ghost vapor. Nothing held me suspended off the floor and I dropped through her, right out of mid-air toward the tile, where using ninja reflexes I badly strained my wrist and bounced, and then lay, tender and insulted. I found that my hands did open. That meant the *storm* was over.

I flexed them both to give me confidence. The right one dropped something that sang like steel when it hit the floor. I sat up and saw a fisted metal nugget, shocking *dominion* into the air like fifty cherry bombs in a mirror factory. I batted it away down the hall and cursed and braced against the wall and got to my feet.

But then I was standing up right inside Samantha. It felt

perverse, or at least rude, so I pushed from the wall and stumbled to the reception desk and sat. I rubbed my wrist and rolled my shoulder, then faced back at the hallway. Samantha pivoted all the way around to glow at me, as though nothing had happened.

"That *sucked*," I told her, rechecking my body in case it's been violated while I was elsewhere. As I did, I fired ideas at Samantha, because now I was in the habit.

"I feel like shit. I bet I look like shit—in fact I know I do, I just watched myself—and I still have my problem, my real problem, which surprisingly isn't turning into a ghost, it's the girl coming to the office, who I'm thinking about too much, and I still don't know if having forgeries and an office is going to seem more normal or totally less normal to a girl like her, like, my mind just goes right back to her even though—I just escaped being a *ghost*, I barely even know her—*why do I care so much? What's happening to me?*"

I panted. Sitting at the desk I stacked business cards with my name, feeling sore.

"It doesn't seem normal," I complained, "I'm obsessed. You know, all we do is kiss? And it's not like *she's all I can think about boo hoo*, that happens several times a year, it's just it's literally, except incidental contact, all I did or wanted was kissing, that's all, obsessively, and just, I don't know, *chit-chatting*. What am I *doing*? Something's got to be really, badly wrong, don't you think?"

It was pretty rambly, but true. There was extra height and glint to the world when I thought of Caroline, like a person had never looked before—and I'm a person who's really given to blinding, self-destructive attachments, so why hadn't I ever felt anything like this in the past?

The office door rattled, the knob started turning. I stopped breathing. I didn't feel ready. I could only watch, right down through the center of Samantha's Higher swirling torso, as the door swung open.

And through it stepped a man in dirty white pants, without shoes, in a torn white waiter's top. Peter by The Beach.

He came down the hall, passed into the back of, then through, then came out the front of, Samantha, as if she wasn't there, which was unsettling. He moved up to the desk and saw my neat pile of Asher Gale business cards and added one more to the top, with a solemnity it didn't deserve. His card was bent and a little stained but familiar—it was the one I'd written on when I'd suggested he come live at Asher Gale's office. Yesterday? Maybe. The yesterdays blurred.

Saying nothing, he went past the desk, and I turned in my reception chair to follow him. He forged back into the part of the office where I kept thinking they should put a Pilates studio and sat on the tile, then lay on his back on the floor, spread like a snow angel, half in slanting window sun, half in shadow.

When I went over he blinked up desert island eyes.

"Hi Peter," I told him, "you can have a chair."

"No," he barrel voiced, "I still have tonsils, the floor is brute force." The sun had baked almost everything out of him but a voice.

"How about water?" I asked, thinking Caroline would be proud of me.

"Live on the floor now, live here, live on the floor where it's starting to happen." He patted a place beside him, urging me down.

"I'm going to let that be your thing," I told him. I pointed to the inner office, where the Admiral had his desk. "There's a bar in there, if you want booze. They left a lot of booze."

"The highest pass is the place to look back where you've been," he agreed. His hair spread above his face, and over the floor around his neck, long like fraying twine, wild as a hedge.

"I'm glad you made it," I told him, and since he liked it where he was I left him and sat in the swivel chair, thinking how it seemed like a lot of foot traffic for one morning for an office no one used. Crowds, even crowds of three with one-third of them ghosts, discomfort me, so I retreated to the Admiral's bar myself and got vodka. My cloudy thinking about Caroline, whether she'd approve the things I did, why it mattered if she approved, hadn't grown clearer, though thinking about her at all was thrilling and distracting.

I caught a flash of movement from the reception room.

I took my drink back to reception and saw Peter, fast as a wraith, heading for the door. He transited Samantha again, which got more unnerving the more I saw it, and reached the door and pulled it open, then stood aside, holding it like a palace guard. It was an empty door. He had an awkward way of moving. You wished his joints would bend more than they did, but he was fast and utterly silent.

I sat in the reception chair for a better view and saw the flinty tip of a walking stick appear in the door, and then watched the whole stick come through and then Lady Damely appeared as the driver. She wore a black hat whose pearls knew they were the best ones, a beaded clutch just as certain of its beads, and she'd given her black buttoned business suit a gothic air with lace gloves and the duck-handled walking stick.

She swept in like the door had been opened for her arrival but stopped when she saw Peter holding up the wall. Her pearls clutched their throats. Peter's head lolled an inch or two, it was odd, I'll admit it, and his free hand scratched inside his clothes. Damely and I watched him let go of the door, which swung closed behind her, then come toward me, and I swiveled my chair to watch him lay down again in the Pilates area.

Footsteps approached behind me. I swiveled back, drinking vodka, and saw Damely moor up at the desk. These chairs really paid for themselves, I thought, all the back and forth.

"Hello Asher, you look horrible," Damely intoned. She grudged her stick at Peter on the floor. "Your man let me in."

"So *that's* what he is," I said.

"Why do you have him on the floor?" She sounded suspicious.

"Isn't that just what they do?" I swiveled again, and we both watched my alert, greasy, dew-eyed man ignore us. "I never had one before. Maybe he's sick. Do you think he's in pain?"

"Possibly. In my experience some are born to service, but most suffer."

"Maybe you'll lie on the floor with him. He likes that. He tried to get me before but I have a date." I pulled in a deep breath. "Well, okay. You know, make yourself at home I guess, sit anywhere. You're meeting somebody?"

"What?"

"Not my business, let's do that. There's booze in there," I pointed to the Admiral's minibar. "There's nothing to eat, I already looked. I'll get out of your way as fast as I can." I wanted Caroline to show up right then and see me being so civil, because it doesn't happen every time.

Damely's pearls looked less and less happy, misgiving me my vodka and the man I had behind me on the floor. Out of all the things those pearls hated, you could tell, not having any idea what was going on was what they hated most. But welcome to my world, pearls.

"Asher, stop this, I am here to engage your services." She said it slow, like I might be a child, which helped. "I do not have much time. There is a canvas I must have authenticated. It is very pressing, and unfortunate. What is your rate?"

"Six drinks an hour but I can't, I'm meeting a girl."

"Your *fee*, Asher, good lord!" She arched a look down her high, thin septum. Was this worth the effort, she was thinking? It was a look I knew. "What do you charge for your services?"

"Lady Damely," I said, and stood from the swivel chair and watched her, and drank more vodka, then sighed, "there's some mistake. I don't have services. It's the truth. It's a fact. I can't authenticate your painting."

"Well of course *you* can't authenticate my painting, Asher! It is in *Los Angeles!*"

Her voice got quiet, husky and paranoid, like *Los Angeles* was a planet where demons ate ladies with pearls like hers. So, just the usual. All Fenestram painters—other than me—refuse to leave the city. They pale at the very idea. For myself I'm perfectly comfortable with the idea of leaving Skysill Beach, traveling to Los Angeles or anywhere, though I've never done it. In my case that's just lack of curiosity, but for Damely and the others not leaving always struck me as a kind of pathology. *My* Los Angeles's a normal city wasting megalopolis-resources a hundred miles north. Damely's LA is one of the gateways to hell.

"You cannot travel out of Skysill," she said with a weak shudder, "of course. I have come to you for a recommendation, from among your northern authenticator brethren. Surely you have a network of some kind? Who among those in Los Angeles can you recommend? My man there has gone missing!"

"I'm no good with men, Lady Damely. Look at mine. Ask someone else."

"Indeed I will not. I will ask you! I know you, Asher Gale, and I knew your parents, I was your father's patron, for heaven's sake. I want to help you, now that you have traded your career as a promising artist and taken up shopkeeping. I feel I owe you."

"That feeling passes if you give it a few minutes."

Her bringing up my parents from nowhere slid me breathless, with an urge to run someplace, and it distracted me to silence while Damely started floating out her case.

"Here are the details," she said, the handle with its duck bill circling like a soup mixer. "I presume you are recording this. I do not see you taking notes. There is a woman I have worked with for some years, and she occasionally alerts me when art of the sort I collect becomes available."

She checked that I was listening and got the wrong impression so she kept talking.

"Earlier this year," she said, "this woman informed me of a painting, The Dancer's Kiss, 1490, Niccolo Filippi, a *sighted* Florentine master of the High Renaissance, little known in his time, that would soon be available in a very private auction. You see?"

"You saw a pretty picture and you liked it," I shook it out.

"No, I never saw the picture," she told me, "no images were made available. But the woman assured me it was a masterpiece. For her own reasons she implored me to acquire it, though I would have done so in any case. An undiscovered Filippi to add to my collection! I put the funds into escrow, she facilitated the sale with her connections in Italy, and the painting was shipped to a law office in Los Angeles, where it now waits in escrow until its provenance can be confirmed."

She really got her money's worth out of a sentence. It was like a lecture from an audiobook. I wondered how many pictures she'd had trouble with before this, to be so organized laying it out.

"Now then," she said, rowing us out into the middle of her problem, "I have an appraiser I always use, whenever a piece must come through escrow out of Los Angeles. A talented man, not *sighted* but an extraordinary eye. He agreed to authenticate The Dancer's Kiss, and to contact me with his results. Some weeks passed. Other projects occupied me. I recalled, finally, that I should have heard from him. After that I tried for some time to make contact. He returned neither call nor email. He had vanished."

"Some are born for authentication, some suffer. That's the point you're making?"

"My point is the *escrow*. The escrow window is nearly closed. If I do not certify this piece in the next two days, the sale is dissolved and the canvas shipped back to Italy. I need someone to authenticate The Dancer's Kiss by Monday morning, and it will take a very talented, discerning eye."

"Just have the seller extend your escrow," I said, because I don't know when to leave well enough alone. She really sucked you in with a predicament, one problem layered on top of the next.

"That is precisely the problem," she layered higher, "I cannot extend! The purchase was negotiated blind, as many of this sort are, and the only person who knew both the buyer and the seller was the woman who presented me the piece in the first place! And, sadly, I can no longer ask her to intercede. She is ... no longer available."

"She disappeared with your appraiser? Consider the possibility you're being conned."

"No Asher, she did not disappear. She committed suicide. Five days ago."

Everything in me froze other than the part still drinking vodka, which kept doing that, and I thought to myself, that's funny, I know a girl who committed suicide just a few days ago. My mind disappoints me sometimes. The things it's supposed to forget but never does. I did some suicide math. I didn't get the answer I wanted.

"What was this woman's name," I asked, "who killed herself? The one who set up your deal?"

"Her name was Samantha Goodman."

I looked past Damely into my hallway at the ghost flashing there. Damely watched me finish my drink and put down my glass, then get up and go to Samantha, both of us wondering what I was doing. Samantha pivoted in silent inches as I came, to face me square.

"I knew *a* Samantha Goodman," I meditated out. "What if she's the same Samantha Goodman as yours?" I examined my Samantha and held my hand up to her transparent, swirling head. "Was yours about this tall?"

"I would say."

"Small nose," I said, close on the ghost, "heavy face, sexy and wouldn't mind kicking the shit out of you if you needed it? Hair curling out?" I leaned further, as close as I could before she got smeary and turned to nothing but a Higher blur. "Deeper smile lines than you'd expect? A blend of hate and hilarity?" I'm no wordsmith. I do what I can with the few I have.

"Yes, that sounds like Samantha," Damely agreed. "You knew her? It was she who brought me the Italian connections. So you see my problem."

"Did you ever know Samantha to have a goblet?" I asked. I looked at Samantha's goblet. "Say, yay big? Holes drilled all over?"

"No. Why, pray?"

My phone rang. I looked—Caroline calling. Now? Why calling?

She should be walking in the door. I felt chemicals ramp up picturing her walking in a door, any door, like a science experiment to see if electrifying blood and impatience created happiness, which it doesn't.

"Hey!" we said simultaneously when I answered.

Right away she cut in front, talking fast in a bad news voice, saying, "Ash, I'm sorry, I can't get to your office this morning. It's a work emergency."

"Really? They're having a parade here." I smiled at Damely. She eyed me. She didn't think of herself that way.

"I love parades," Caroline said, "but I have too many appointments backed up."

"But... it's Saturday," I lamented, which isn't anything I *ever* do, "don't psychics take days off?"

"We do! You remember those appointments I rescheduled yesterday so the two of us could spend all day necking in pullouts?"

"I remember necking, yes. The appointments... oh. So... you rescheduled all your appointments from yesterday to today? Is that what you're saying?"

"You catch on fast. It's real attractive."

"I'm just naturally attractive, but I almost never catch on."

"I've never met a boy with your self-confidence yet so neurotic," she discovered out loud, making me sound fascinating. "You're like a beautiful broken unicorn."

"You said I was the cat from your bedroom."

"The dead one, I know, and the way you switch around is honestly breathtaking."

We took a second having our breath taken, trying to figure out what we were talking about. To me the subject was a spinning, blood-sugary mix of confusion and desire, so I hoped she had a better handle on it than that.

"I think you want to tell me what you're wearing right now," she purred, without any handle at all.

"Your self-confidence is even slicker than mine," I said. Damely was looking more confused, not even pretending she wasn't listening.

"Slicker's a great word," she tested it, breathy, "now say what you're wearing. Pants?"

"The logical thing would be come confirm that yourself. You should really come."

All my worrying what she'd say when she got here, and now me complaining she hadn't arrived yet—I like allowing myself room to be complicated. Caroline sighed. I thought I felt warm breath on my neck. I'd gone twenty years not fantasizing anyone breathing on me. I wasn't used to it. I couldn't make it stop.

"I just can't," she moaned, "and believe me I want to come. Ash, I have to ask... that was a lot of... just nothing but kissing yesterday, right? Like... *so much?*"

"I think," I said, "it was *maniacal.* Ridiculous amounts of... what's going on with this?"

"I don't understand," she admitted. We soaked for a moment in warm confusion before she told me, "I'm going to be at a party tonight, will you come make out with me there?"

"Yes," I told her, and as I did, Peter went by on my right, heading back to the door. Damely watched him along with me. Only one of the three of us saw him splash through Samantha, then he reached the door, pulled it open, and stood to the side, holding it empty.

"There he is," I heard a hidden, reedy voice insist from the hall. A finger stabbed past the door frame. Just one finger. "Homeless! Homeless! I *told* you!"

"I have to go, Ash," Caroline was saying.

"Can I call you in a little bit?" I asked, but was distracted, there was a finger.

"He's right there!" screeched the finger's voice and it trembled. Damely began by looking at the finger but ended up by looking at me, pearls almost unconscious, in case I knew what was happening at the office we were in.

"Don't call," Caroline said. "Just meet me at the party. I'll text the address."

After she hung up my attention shifted door-ward full time, and I watched the finger become my neighbor Phil, who stood in Hawaiian shorts, supporting a bowl of fruit salad in the hand that wasn't pointing. He'd backed as far from the doorway as he could until he leaned against the far wall of the outer hall. It made him look even smaller than usual.

Phil's eyes kept shooting to someone out of view in the hall, and then that person moved into the doorway and filled it, floor to frame and down both sides, with police uniform. My friend Hennessy the omnipresent.

His rolling eyebrows pinned his face in a move called *I do not want to be here Gale.* He used that move all around the inside of Asher Gale's office, from the door.

Phil's little head appeared around Hennessy's side.

"That's him," Phil confirmed at Peter

I rose and started their way. Damely fanned herself with the top of her cane, which couldn't have moved much air but was all she had.

"Wait here," I told her as I passed. It wasn't clear if she heard. I moved on, hesitated getting to Samantha, and put my hand out to make sure she still wasn't solid, then hurried through, then nodded to the blockade at the door.

"Hennessy," I said, "I mean, what're the odds?"

"So. Here we are where you work," he informed me.

"I don't work," I said. "You're thinking of someone else. Is there a problem?"

"Another day, another crime," he shrugged. "And you, present at every scene."

"That's the crime, right there!" Phil announced about Peter. Peter let go of the door so it started swinging shut while he headed back into the office, I presumed to the floor he liked. Hennessy stopped the door with a tank tread boot.

"What's the problem, Phil?" I asked the balding head.

"There're homeless people in the building," he snapped, "that's the problem!"

Hennessy looked down, with regret and disappointment, at the thin head of hair sheltering at his belt. He spent a moment just watching, wondering about his life, and when he looked at me his deep disappointment faded to general cop disinterest, and I understood suddenly that he liked me better than many other citizens he encountered. It was an uncomfortable thought.

"So, Gale," he told me, "talk to me about your bum. Do so fast."

"This isn't what you think," I said.

"No," he told me, "it is *always* what I think, and that is the tragedy."

"Okay then, do you think that's Peter by the Beach? Because it is," I said. I looked back into the room to find Peter in the swivel chair behind the desk. He'd put on the wireless receptionist headset. He had his hands on the armrests. He stared at us.

"What is the reason Peter is here?" Hennessy snarled.

"He's the receptionist," I guessed out loud.

"That's insane!" Phil shrilled. "Look at him!"

"Gale," Hennessy hammered, "my time has limits, your leash is short."

"Ask him," I insisted. How much worse could it get? "Peter," I called, "are you the receptionist?" He appeared a little blurry seen from this side of Samantha, but he looked comfortable.

"I have pet manta rays," he called back, "in my hallway. Don't trust the eels. The mantas watch my stuff for me."

"And there you have it," I said, turning back to Hennessy, "receptionist."

"You know anything about this?" Hennessy barked at Damely, who startled, like she'd forgotten she was in the room, or had been caught trying to forget.

"Oh no," she assured us, "oh no no, no."

"Mystery solved," I announced. I looked at Hennessy's boot. It was the only thing standing between us and the rest of our day. After a minute of thinking, his eyebrows went back to their corners.

"No concern of mine who you hire," he decided to me. "Please make *very sure* I am never called here again. And by please, I do not mean please."

I nodded, he took his boot back, the door finished closing. I heard Phil arguing his case, and Hennessy ignoring him and walking away. And then it was just the four of us again and the room was quiet. Cozy. Like the Donner Party. We looked at each other, all except for Samantha who never looked anywhere but at me, and Damely and Peter who could only see me and not Samantha.

Skysill Beach had filled with things people wanted to involve me in, and I suddenly, badly, desired a different tempo, my old tempo of not doing anything and no one caring. I wanted out. Someplace no one knew me. I went to Damely, who had a vacant look and whose pearls had been humbled to chalk. I got her a drink from the admiral's office.

"So you need an authenticator in Los Angeles," I told her and handed her the glass. She took it and grimaced when the sting hit her throat but didn't put it down.

"That's right," she said, "by Monday morning."

"Because there's a painting," I continued, "1490, by a *sighted* Florentine master named Niccolo Filippi, that Samantha Goodman convinced you to buy for reasons she didn't share before she committed suicide. And you had an authenticator you usually use, but he's disappeared. Is that it?"

Damely nodded, just as surprised as I was to find I'd been paying attention. I drained the last of my own vodka.

"Okay," I said. "I'll do it."

"Do what?"

"Go to Los Angeles and look at your painting."

"But that's... in... Los Angeles. Los Angeles is..." she was reduced to waving in the Los Angeles direction.

"I know where they put it," I said. "I guess I need names.

Addresses. Is any of it written down?" She said it was. The world had started going sideways for her the instant Peter'd ushered her into the office. Now a Fenestram artist was volunteering to go to Los Angeles for her. Tomorrow maybe it would rain cellos and fried chicken. She gave up. She took a card from her clutch and set it on the reception desk. Peter saw it, reached for it, but I got it first. I could see I'd have to watch him.

"I'll be invoiced, I presume?" she quavered.

"It wouldn't surprise me," I said. "Almost nothing surprises me." I looked at Peter. "Will she be invoiced?"

"Deeper and deeper, but the bottom never comes," he rumbled. Damely gave the sharp small sound a pigeon makes in pedestrian traffic, then held her hand out to shake. I shook it because she needed help balancing, and after that she tugged her gloves tighter and chaperoned her cane back through the middle of Samantha. At the door she paused, but since Peter'd been promoted she was forced to let herself out.

"I'm going to give you my office key," I said, turning back to Peter to find he'd left the desk and was spread on the floor again, still in the wireless headset. I hadn't heard him move.

I felt my pockets for my keys. I didn't find them there or anywhere on me, and I went to the admiral's minibar but didn't see them there. I came out, back to the reception desk, but they weren't beside the monitor or on the floor. I remembered unlocking the door and coming into the room with them. I did remember that.

"What'd I do with my *keys*?" I protested out loud, as I did more and more these days. My voice took an empty room bounce. I was standing and failing to remember when Peter padded past me again, heading for the door. That's when I realized Samantha had vanished, sometime while I'd been failing to remember or been drinking, or getting a drink. The place was emptying out.

Peter grabbed an object off the floor in the hall by the door. It clinked. It was about the size of a lighter. The object glared *dominion* at me from between the fingers of his fist. He started back. He set his find on the reception desk and continued to his spot and then lay on his back. I thought maybe I should get a water bowl for him over there.

He'd found my keys. That much, it wasn't hard to see. He'd probably seen them in the hall answering the door so many times. But now they were fused in a metallic fistful. I saw key colored outlines in wavy silver, with some green from Samantha's office key. *Dominion* fell off the lump in all directions, spiraling, dimming, vanishing a few feet out: *dominion* infused in the metal.

The same thing had happened with my steering wheel after pulling myself from the *storm* outside Felicia's house. *Dominion* passed out of me, into my car. It'd ruined that car. Now it'd melted the only key I had to my second car. It was getting to be my most self-destructive habit.

The admiral had one extra office key in his desk drawer, I found using searching—along with a lot of envelopes addressed to Asher Gale that smelled like bills. I shut the drawer. What should I do with the one key? I thought Peter needed it more than me. This office was bad luck for me. I should never come here. I kept accepting assignments.

"I'm leaving you a key, here at reception," I called to Peter on the floor.

"Not so loud," he instructed, subsonic, "I'm close now, too close, then I sink."

"Sure," I said, thinking receptionists were actually a lot of work. "I'll check on you later."

"There was timpani sunrise all around. But we never saw, never even saw," he sorrowed, his voice deeper than ocean pipe. He lolled his head toward me. "Be careful you know. Everything might say what it means pretty soon."

"I'm going to have to take that chance," I told him sadly. "There's carpet in the other room if you want softer floor."

I went to the door. Peter could take care of himself in his new home. He'd been doing it for years so I wasn't concerned. My wrist hurt turning the knob, sore from falling through Samantha onto the floor when she'd stopped being solid enough to hold my body up. That was something not to think about. Because how could you? I had bigger problems. I needed to learn to hot-wire a car so I'd have someplace to make out with Caroline, which was all I had in mind doing. The last thing I saw as I left the office was the key gobbet, banging out *dominion* on the desk.

CHAPTER
THREE

In the end the most efficient thing was to buy a third used car. I got one with extra keys, which I put in different pockets. I stopped and bought new clothes. Then I drove around, dropped by the train station, avoided going back to the house I didn't have a key to at the moment. When the stars were out I followed Caroline's directions, roping around a canyon road up and out, onto a high shoulder of coastal hill where I parked. Before getting out of my car I combed my hair. My ghost view of my flesh head had persuaded me to make an extra effort.

Eucalyptus menthol hit my lungs in a night breath. Where the road ended, trees shielded me from the lights of Skysill upcoast. A wrought iron fence stood, tips high, some yards back from the turn-around, the serious kind of fence you put around your parliament building. From somewhere beyond that, beyond a dark, complicated garden, I heard music, and voices, and saw the eves of a tall building.

They'd put three small gates in the parliament fence, side by side. Above them in iron work was spelled out, *Three Paths Manor*, and there was a seal with three thrones. Copper fancywork twined the gates patina green, green like old money. And above each gate, a silver word; *Behind*, above the left gate, *Beneath*, above the middle, *Before*, above the right. Each word had a throne.

I choose the middle gate, which wasn't closest but felt least like a commitment. The hinges swung, Teflon smooth, and I stepped onto a path of fine white gravel. That went ten feet ahead then slid between high hedges. I followed, and was hedged around a corner, then found myself hedged down many long and tight leaf passages turning at random right angles, so at first I suspected a maze, but there were now branching paths inside paths. It was just a badly designed trail. I lost all sense of direction. I'm no explorer. Finally I was disgorged onto a courtyard in front of a dark building.

The party sounded from inside, swallowed and indistinct, because this building was old and had deep bowels and that's where it kept its parties. Four mortared stories of it rose to block the stars. Two wings spread from a central turret. The windows were small and naked looking—the kind of manor house dukes buy for vacations then forget they own. From the walls, ivy draped tired gargoyles.

Castle quality double doors filled the foot of the turret, but I found them locked, and no one came when I announced myself. Over the doors were carved the words *Behind, Beneath, Before* with the seal of thrones, so I knew I was in the right place. I pounded harder. I couldn't see the iron knocker you usually find on keeps this size. I only got a sore hand. I would've gone home at that point if it had been any girl but Caroline.

There was a Caroline-nearby feeling forming. It raised shivers of anticipation and confusion. I made my way right, along the foot of the building to the corner and around that, and in back I saw a third wing joined to the turret, and an open door that let out party light. The light fell on a wide stone porch. Someone stood and smoked there, under a banner where *Happy Birthday!* had been painted. The stroke of the B was off, making the letter look like the number 3. Someone's 3rd birthday?

I hurried to the porch, where, through the door, I saw a long, wide hall run right and left, with an arched ceiling, baroque and inlaid. The floor was ancient rugs, the walls dark wood panel, rooms or chambers with arched entrances and no doors opened all the way down. The lights were not bright. The hall was filled with party people.

Friendly techno beat in glassy waves, stirring the crowd but not shaking them. They moved, grouped and separate, all ages, both inside the chambers and in the hall, gyrating, laughing, some of them sleeping on floors, in chairs, reading, and despite the party streamers and thrumming music there was something domestic to the scene too. In some of the darker chambers people lay in groups, eight or a dozen together with shaved heads, murmuring or motionless. I didn't see Caroline anywhere. I had no instructions for finding her.

I stepped back and tapped out a text, and had to wave my phone around, and couldn't get a signal.

The man on the porch watched, cigarette flaring, beads strung on a thin neck, loose linen shirt, black hair tied, Aztec emperor eyes practicing sympathy and antipathy both. His wide lips uncurled smoke.

"It's no use," emperor-eyes told me, "you can't get reception."

"I'm supposed to meet someone," I complained.

He started to reply but was interrupted. Somewhere deep in the building a voice stuttered up a cry, which became a hollow, rhythmic ululation. In the hall others joined, here and there, so the chorus rose louder than the music. After a minute it faded, and music took the night back. Emperor-eyes and I listened and watched each other. Only one of us seemed surprised.

"My name's Jorge," he told me, since apparently we were ignoring the ululation. Jorge gestured off the porch, around, out over the sea. "Welcome to Three Paths."

Now I saw, sparkling on top of his head, a crooked tiara with the words *It's My Birthday* in glitter. So Caroline'd invited me to Jorge's birthday party, but she hadn't told me. Wasn't that surprisingly negligent for a person concerned with appointments like she was? I thought so.

"Happy birthday," I told him, for Caroline's sake wanting to appear gracious, but Jorge shook his head.

"Happy Threes-day," he said. Then shrugged. "Three of us."

"Okay. I'm only looking for one girl, her name's Caroline." I said it too hurried, a bit needy, but the Caroline-is-here feeling was getting stronger and so was my jumpiness.

"Everybody's inside," he pointed, then faced back into the night.

I waved my phone some more because I'm an optimist and I've got limited problem-solving skills. Then, from the doorway behind me, I heard a shuffle, and a dreamy voice saying, "I don't know who that is."

I turned. Jorge went by me gentle but fast. "It's okay, Li Wei," he said, "it's fine."

Li Wei leaned in the doorway, lacking much focus, but what he had, he turned on me. He looked papery, wafty, thin. He shook his shaved head.

"I don't know the Path he's on," Li Wei wafted out. "I don't know it. Not the broken Path. Is he on the Broken Path?"

"Caroline invited him," Jorge said in *calm down, Li Wei, it's okay* tones, which made no sense because Li Wei was the calmest person I'd seen in weeks. Doper calm, in fact, though I didn't see open evidence.

His calm didn't last.

"I don't care *who*," he exclaimed to Jorge, voice forcing a sudden shriek, "he shouldn't be here. I don't know who's seen his Path. I don't know!"

Other revelers appeared behind Li Wei, surrounded him, and pulled him gently back into the general swirl, and though he stayed twisty in their arms for a moment, he soon floated sideways into a diorama of others like him, shaved heads like chicks in a box, and lay down.

It just, I thought, moved the *that's-funny-what's-going-on* meter one tick too far. I wished it hadn't.

"Okay," I said, turning to Jorge, who used a little of his sympathy and some antipathy on me, "normally I'd never want to know what goes on anywhere. Normally I'm fine ignoring *everything*, any hooting, shaved people—normally you know I'd leave, hit the bar, none of this intrigues me the *slightest*, but tonight I can't do it. Honestly I'm unbalanced, I'm meeting this girl, doing things I can't explain—I combed my hair—so it's at least one third your birthday, I'll tell you, it feels a little culty here—no judgment—but induction rites, spiked booze, I'd prefer you told me before I went in. I am still going in."

Jorge took a few seconds to smoke, watched me, sighed. "Information wants to be free. But it also wants the right question at the right moment."

"So it *is* a cult."

"One answer can be true for many questions," he said, like an apology.

"That's confusing, you're saying it's many cults?"

After more smoking, which finally wore thin for both of us, he killed his butt and shook his head. "Okay, well, let's see if we can go find Caroline."

He moved fast after he made up his mind and I had to hurry after him through the door, though he stopped to look at me once more, before saying, "I just hope she knows what she's doing."

I went in feeling less confident than I liked. I was hit with sudden humidity and the smell of snack food. I heard people drinking birthday wishes to Jorge as he wove us down the hall. We passed a stairway with so much traffic I wondered how many people had been invited to this party or if this wasn't where most of these people already lived, and the party started up around them.

I looked up the stairs, sideways into every diorama opening, behind and among the swaying congregants, for a girl with brown eyes and blond hair and boots. I knew she sometimes wore Marvin the Martian socks. Mainly I recalled her voice. I seemed to have that voice in my head. I'm barely used to hearing myself there, so it was disorienting.

Jorge seemed to have a good idea where he wanted to go. Halfway down we peeled into one of the chambers. This room looked a little like an alpine ski lodge after an avalanche. There was a bar, drinking horns mounted on the walls, a card game in one corner and beds and dressers and pizza boxes everywhere. People ate and studied under reading lights or birthday danced with glow sticks, and I saw a clutch of shaved heads in a pillowed pile.

"I don't see Caroline here," I noted. Jorge ignored me.

From the card table a bellow came, "Suck it, losers!"

A woman stood in regal triumph. She wore a lot of extra weight like it wasn't any extra weight at all—she was huge and nimble and ready. She scooped money off the table with hands sized to make the rest of her look even bigger.

"Phyllis," Jorge called.

"Jorge! Happy birthday to me," she purred, approaching us. On her head sat the same silver tiara Jorge wore, *It's My Birthday*! She wrapped Jorge in a hug and he vanished for a second, then she showed him again.

"I don't know who this is," she speculated at me then. She said it a lot more personably than Li Wei had, but it still wasn't normal.

"He's looking for Caroline," Jorge told her, and they both examined me.

"I don't know," she said, and turned to Jorge with surprised eyebrows. "I hope she knows what she's doing."

"My name's Asher," I told them so they'd stop talking about me like I wasn't there, and because I'd forgotten to say it earlier. It came out a bit surly. "And happy birthday," I said, to take the edge off.

"Well, relax somewhere," Phyllis told me, gesturing vaguely at the pizza and the floor. "I'll go see if she's here yet. Just..." she didn't finish her thought, shared confusion with Jorge again, and off she went, bouncing people sideways.

When I turned back, Li Wei had wafted near. He stood behind Jorge.

"He shouldn't be," Li Wei dream shuffled in my direction. "No one knows his Path."

He'd brought friends this time. They swayed indecisively behind him, a corps of roughly shaved drifters with unfixed eyes. Jorge, moved by something sad, I felt, raised his hand to touch Li Wei's cheek. Li Wei shook him off, looked at the floor, the ceiling, spoke in a rising tone.

"The rules!" His voice had spiked kite ways, high and moving higher fast. "He's strange here. He doesn't know the Paths. He doesn't know the Paths!"

A murmur rose from the crowd behind him and as their agitation mounted Jorge's emperor-eyes shifted, a flicker of concern behind a wash of confidence, like Caesar meeting Brutus in an empty hall.

"Of course he knows the Paths," Jorge said, low and easy. "All of you, listen."

He was saying it to Li Wei, but staring at me, like giving me an important message, though if that was true I'd almost certainly fail to understand it. You need to come right out and say things to me.

"Listen, people. This is Asher. Caroline invited him. I'm sure Asher knows the Paths, otherwise Caroline wouldn't have brought him. She knows the rules. Think, Li Wei. Asher certainly knows the *Path Before*—the path ahead, the path through the future." More direct staring, right at me. I didn't get it.

"He knows the *Path Beneath*—the path underfoot, the path through the present. And he's Caroline's guest so he knows the *Path Behind*—the path the world has taken, the path of the past." He looked to me, deliberately, slowly, and said, "I'm sure he knows to ask only the right questions in the right moments."

There was pregnant silence. It took me a second. Then I got it.

"Ohhhh," I said, all simple and happy. "Past, present, future—are you all... psychics? There's, like, hundreds of you—why didn't somebody tell me? *Now* it makes sense. No, that's going too far. But—it's a psychic party—Jorge, you're psychic too? Is everybody here psychic?"

Sometimes I get a better grip on big conclusions when I come to them like this, out in public, occasionally staggering under their weight. But Jorge didn't like it. He just had time to narrow his eyes, frightened, imperial, very disappointed in me, before Li Wei started an ululation that spread to the crowd around him and down the hall. The ones behind me inched inward. I turned to measure my free space. When I turned back, Li Wei had a revolver.

"He asks questions," Li Wei moaned, "questions at Three Paths!"

Like a punchy boxer fighting gravity his gun and his half-closed eyes wandered, but they kept finding me again.

"Li," Jorge said, "I don't know where you got a gun, but I know you don't need it."

Li Wei came a step closer, and someone stepped behind me so I had no escape. Li Wei aimed the pistol into my eye, eight feet back.

"I'm just meeting a girl," I tried, dry tongue, the way you try when there's a gun and a person and he's crazy. Li Wei wasn't listening though, he was aiming, and Jorge had his arms spread my way and toward Li Wei, but Jorge was out of position, he had no angle. No controlling this. Li Wei began to squeeze.

And this, I complained to myself, is what comes of kissing psychic girls.

Immediately after that I went *Gray*.

It grabbed me in the middle of a breath, so cool and soft, such a tranquil greyscale, crushing all color from the palette. I moaned with satisfaction.

Things got slow. My shoulders eased, my belly tightened, my grimace softened out. That grimace—so funny—I had a grimace! The humid air, my brand new pants, everything felt glorious on my skin. I was a rung bell. I felt *fantastic!*

Grinning into Li Wei's bruised eyes made me laugh because grinning didn't change Li Wei's plans for his gun or even get his attention! So many things could happen next! I might let Li Wei shoot me

—it might feel *unbelievable.* Or it might be disappointing. I saw his finger tighten.

I'm fast when I'm *Gray.* Usually not faster than a trigger finger. Usually not fast enough to cross eight feet and grab a pistol someone's firing, but now? I thought I could do it. It felt *amazing* in my body! A twist, a leap—I pictured it—whip the gun free, break Li Wei's arm when I took it—how would that feel? I'd shoot him, that might be *fantastic*! I tensed, greyscale glittered...

"... the Path Before is broken..." Wei Lui was screaming, "... no one can see his..."

"*I have seen!*" yelled a voice from the crowd.

A new voice? Not brand new. Familiar but I couldn't place it. Awesome mystery!

"Move. You. I will go there," the voice muttered, pinched and guttural.

I decided I'd delay breaking Li Wei's arm and or killing him. Both of us wanted to see who was coming through the crowd. And out of the wall of bodies behind Li Wei, Nikita Thomasonian stepped, very slow—not from her old age, I thought, just from a contempt for wasted movement. In a grey shirt spreading over a grey peasant skirt she looked cadaverous but tidy. She turned her sideways goose-eye stare back at the crowd, who watched without a word, then she turned to me.

"This one," she gave me the back of two fingers in the silence, "is a sensitive. I have seen it."

"He asks questions in the house!" Li Wei cried. "He won't say his Path!"

"Possibly he does not know." She shrugged. "He is sensitive, but not bright."

So much was happening, I kept forgetting Li Wei's gun. And part of me was now suggesting a little color might do the scene some good. Li Wei was looking unconvinced and wavery about his pistol, like he'd forgotten what he wanted it for. Jorge flashed some *listen to me* at the crowd, and that was amazing to see.

"You heard Nikita," he said, mostly addressing the shaved heads. "She's seen Asher here at Three Paths. So let's just lower the volume. Calm. Everything's groovy. Li Wei, I'll take that."

I cajoled my own brain to ease myself from the *Gray*. It gave me up reluctantly this time. Color watered back in, along with uncertainty and sweat-soaked clothes.

"You're a shifty old crosspath," yelled a voice from the crowd. A clear voice, not wavery. "Why should we listen to you?"

Nikita pulled herself straight.

"Eh," she flicked, "believe, do not, you will have the answer soon. I am crosspath. Yes. But I am here. I still *practice*. You—*pfft*," she pointed, you had to admire the disdain she got out of almost no motion, "you never leave, confused and stupid like vulture babies. I might not walk one Path, but I know truth when a Path shows it. This one," she pointed me out like a medical examiner at the morgue, "belongs at Three Paths."

As unexpectedly as it'd started the gun crises passed. Jorge eased the pistol from Li Wei, general merriment churned back up as if no one had ever waved a gun in my face at all. I kept the color really low to help ease my post-crisis shakes. I asked for liquor. Jorge left, following Phyllis, telling me not to move. I sat with Nikita at the card table.

"You do not look well," she appraised me, "though your clothes seem cleaner."

"I think it's this psychic hospitality. You people really have a welcoming way."

"You asked questions, out loud, so everyone gets like my rats in their bag of razors."

I drank brown alcohol, breathed moist air, and pictured her rats.

"Who are the shaved..." I started, then rerouted the question. "I'm now thinking I'm not supposed to ask questions. Though it's not easy to know for sure without being able to ask a question. I don't know who the shave headed crazies are, but they sure are fucking crazy. And believe me I know crazy."

"Yes. They walk the Path Before. Their Path has many problems. A thing with time, we do not talk about it." She flicked at the long hall. "But you know the old saying: the fish dies from the head."

"That's not the saying. I'd like to know what you mean I belong at Three Paths."

She opened her mouth, started something, stopped, maybe she realized it was a question. Instead she shrugged. "The Paths cross in me. All three of them. I find *this* truth in the past, *that* in the future. Sometimes I am confused. I am old woman. Ask Phyllis and Jorge."

"I wonder if Phyllis and Jorge really like me."

"Who knows. Phyllis is Monarch of the Path Before. Jorge is Monarch of the Path Beneath. They are in difficult position. Also they are idiots. Like, little broken idiot dolls."

"A royal Monarch birthday party," I said. "It's like a BBC special in here."

And then Jorge was back with Phyllis, interrupting, and I could tell they'd talked the situation over and decided on a strategy to handle me. I sympathized, and wanted to tell them those never work, for me or anyone else, but they were hurrying. They'd found Caroline. They wanted me out of my poker chair.

Nikita stopped me, her hand over mine.

"It is just... one thing," she said. "In my shop..." she threw a glance at Jorge and Phyllis, then back to me. "You said you had something, in a paper bag. From a ghost."

"Nikita, no ghost stories now," Jorge said. "Just let the Path carry us."

"What about ghosts," I almost asked but then rephrased the questions with, "I don't know why you'd mention ghosts."

"My family have stories, thousands of years," Nikita said, then flicked the Royals again. "But *they* will say no, no ghosts exist."

"Oh Niki, not now," Phyllis said, irritated, and leaned several hundred of her pounds into dislodging me from my seat.

"Now? Yes, no ghosts, they do not exist now," Nikita said. She pushed my hand on the table, holding me. "I am from the old country. My family is Wayweirds, unbroken generations. And they say, hundreds of who knows thousand of years, more than that, *then* ghosts roamed our world. Or some other world. Wayweirds can be vague. But the whole place was ghosts, and from you I felt..."

"I'd like to know what you felt," I encouraged. All she could do was hold her hands up and not have an answer, and then I'd been hooked from behind and started down the long hall, between my birthday escorts who weren't giving me much choice about the service.

"I'm told you're Monarchs," I said as we rolled, being conversational.

"Think of us as wardens," Jorge said. "Game wardens."

"Don't think of us," Phyllis told me, her tiara low and unwelcoming.

"I don't think I know why you're all packed into one psychic dormitory this way," I tried. It felt like an awkward way to get information.

Phyllis looked grim, but emperor-eyes took a breath.

"To escape," he said softly, "from the Paths. To buffer time away. When enough of us come together, the Paths can't find our feet. For some, it's this or madness. For some, it's already madness."

"No more half questions," Phyllis snapped. "We'll take you to Caroline, keep your mouth shut."

I wanted taking to Caroline. Phyllis hauled us down and through an archway so we stood inside a stone silo with a ceiling a hundred feet up; the turret where the three wings met. I saw the back of the castle door I'd knocked, and two more archways where halls of carousing psychics refused all questions and danced the night away.

We went up an iron staircase to a high balcony grappling the round walls, then stopped in front of an ornate wooden door with *Before* carved in sumptuous floral detail. Phyllis opened it and kicked her shoes in and sighed. I saw a worn but respectable presidential palace inside and a suit of armor, then she saw me respecting it and slammed the door. We continued circling the balcony and halfway around came to a second door, with *Beneath* set into wood with turquoise and jewels. This hung open, bachelor style, and Jorge closed it as we passed, and then finally we came to the last door. *Behind*. It hadn't been carved or motifed, but the finish shone a spectrum so broad I dialed my color, just to appreciate it.

Phyllis shook the handle and called, "We're coming in, hon."

In we came. And there she was. Under the sparkle of a tiara. Caroline.

"Happy… birthday?" I asked.

"You combed your hair," she told me, happily.

She wore a long red dress which fit her, thigh to shoulder, close as mare skin, an arterial color that glowed her cheeks and throat, and she had one boot on. It was a million-dollar dress and she wanted me looking, tight and provoking, but all I could think, looking at the dress, was zipper or hooks? Because it had to go. And though my mind is as graphic as anyone's, more than most probably, I was still surprised at the pictures it started making of her, stepping out of her dress, coming to me. I felt I was not in control of the pictures my mind was making for me.

She stayed in her dress but started my way.

"Your slipper came off," I pointed.

"I left it in the bathroom."

"You shouldn't have brought anyone," Jorge argued as she passed.

"Okay," she said and came closer.

"What the hell's up with you?" Phyllis demanded, in outright, question asking rebellion. as Caroline passed her.

I spread my arms. Caroline stepped into them.

"I'd have brought frankincense," I told her tiara, "if I'd known you were a Monarch."

"I know, I didn't want you wasting time shopping," she said, leaning in, chest on mine, dress thin as shower water, and then pushing nipples gave a shock when I realized they were my nipples, it was hard to tell and delirious. Her lips were taking a shape that wasn't a question but a statement as we pictured each other picturing each other in our minds—

"*Caroline!*" Phyllis yelled, only just getting our attention, so Caroline gave my mouth a butterfly landing and smiled and turned to Phyllis.

"Hi honey," she said. "What is it?"

"This is causing problems we don't need," Phyllis explained, pointing at me. "Downstairs, I mean."

"Well I know that. I'm real sorry. I don't know why I did it. He's here now, though. Isn't he beautiful?" She turned back at me. "Since it's Threes-day, think of him like my present. I want to dance!"

She was reaching for my hand, looking at her door, still missing her boot.

"He can't go down there," Jorge insisted. "Li Wei almost shot him."

"Fine. We'll stay here, plenty to do," she said. She stepped close to smell the side of me and so I could smell her sweet soap.

"People need to see us together," Phyllis insisted. "All three of us."

"Yes! Then let's go dancing—hey, we should take this year's picture! Take it for us Ash?" she asked, then turned without waiting for my answer and let her hand brush my crotch as she went while my own hand lingered on the side of her breast, and I watched her smile, and then they were gathered in the middle of the room. I thought, my brain is not usually doing this kind of animal lust, while for the first time I also noticed the room. Eclectic and palatial in an Elizabethan, gold accented, library slash modern home theater way, deep enough for the archery range it also had. Other doors—kitchen, bedrooms, spa—opened on the archery range, which seemed pretty dangerous unless you lived alone or your roommates were psychic.

I got out my phone for the picture. Caroline pulled the Monarchs together and posed them, all crowns and teeth, Caroline's face blissful as desert rain, the other two not blissful, and just when they were closest together I snapped it. It was a good picture but I thought I could compose a better.

I didn't see the ghost in the picture because photosensitive computer chips don't register Higher light. But when I looked up to frame another, because composition is essential, there was Samantha, floating, lit with star fire, between me and the royals. My fingers started curling a *storm*.

"Got it," I managed to force out for the trio by the chair. Then it hit, a *chroma storm* without the crazy. I had just one second left before seizing solid so I eased my knees a little, hands toward pockets, straightened up and arranged my features in less terrified confusion.

Then I was stuck.

"Go on down, you two, I'll get my boot," Caroline said to the other two, "then let's meet in Behind."

She dashed over the archery range. I couldn't turn my eyes to watch her. I started feeling Russian doll bodies. My inside body slipped around. The outside body watched Jorge and Phyllis through the light of a swirling ghost girl.

"This is crazy," Phyllis said.

Jorge wasn't sure. He looked at me. "Nikita did say she sees him at Three Paths." I could tell they were just going to talk like I wasn't there. It was going to work out for everybody.

"Jorge. You know Nikita makes things up," Phyllis complained, "and the way the figura are pouring off the broken Path, the fighting we've been—"

"The Path goes where the Path goes," Jorge stopped her. "We just walk."

"Fuck the path," Phyllis said. Then she sighed. "Come on, I'll get dancing shoes."

As they left, my slippery inside-body shook a few times, like a wet dog, and faster than before, so fast, I popped backward through the space between my ears and became one of the only two ghosts in the room.

"Oh god dammit *Samantha*!" I ghosted out, furious. My slobbery flesh body went galloping to the mouth races, trying to keep up. Samantha had her goblet in the air, which I knew was the point of it all.

"Now? *Now?* Stop showing up like this! You have to give me some space. I'm doing the best I can. Jesus Christ I'm going to Los Angeles for you, which, I have to tell you, should feel a lot more nerve-wracking than this since I've never been out of Skysill Beach, a lot more nerve-wracking, but this girl just blots out everything. I can't think straight. I want to blame you somehow but that's just a bad habit I have. Her hand touched my dick just now, it was like my leg was on fire—this is much, *much*—and she feels the same way! I'm not supposed to be here, but she invited me here, this is a private psychic party, where all the psychics hallucinate and eat dinner. She's more off balance as me. God dammit. I don't want her to see me frozen like this."

My flesh body gibbered, you couldn't make out words but his mouth was moving pretty fast. He seemed a bit more coordinated than the time in the office. I tried puppet mastering him a baby step forward and it wasn't graceful but it worked. I didn't feel I could risk kneeling. But maybe I could walk him to the chair where the Monarchs had posed, sit him, eye cross him, and live through another eternity of *dominion* agony before Caroline got back.

I feared tripping though. I remembered a low, bolstered footstool in the room. Walking the body from behind, baby steps, my view ahead was blocked. We could trip and topple.

"You know what'd be convenient, Samantha?" I asked her. "If you'd say something. Wouldn't that solve a lot of our problems? You could tell me about your goblet. You could tell me what's on the floor in front of his feet. Is there a footstool? If I could see through my flesh eyes I'd look myself..."

And then I *was*. I was seeing from my flesh body. Inside, it felt just as chilled and immovable and not real as my ghost body, but my senses were louder. My body no longer blocked the view but I couldn't turn my head down where I needed to look. My neck wouldn't bend a micron. In some ways I'd liked it better in my ghost body, there at least I had puppet mastering.

And I popped back. It was as easy as complaining about it. Both the bodies felt like frozen gas, but from my ghost I could bend my flesh head forward and down, and when the angle seemed right I jumped back over to him and looked out my eyes at my feet where there was no stool. Back in my ghost I baby-stepped him. Back and forth I checked his feet. I was pretty happy with myself. I aimed us to the side, around Samantha, because I knew she'd be a problem if we hit her.

My flesh body wasn't Gene Kelly. That's why he tripped on the edge of the carpet. I was in the flesh body when I noticed we were tipping. We were going over and it was even more sickening watching it happen from inside. The room tilted. No Samantha in front of me to break the fall. Where's a ghost when you need one? I wanted my *own* ghost in front of me. That would actually be something useful.

And there it flashed. Right there, facing me, four inches off, so my flesh chest bounced softly on my ghost chest, and there I leaned against me. It felt very precarious. I shifted back to my ghost. The ghost view faced flesh me from the front, looking back the way I'd come over the top of my hair, which did look better combed, I thought. And I thought I saw what was happening.

I jumped back into my propped up flesh. From my flesh, I found, I could move my ghost. I used the ghost like a tractor to slowly plow my flesh body vertical, so I was balanced again, then I backed the ghost off a few feet and stared at it from flesh eyes. It was very me looking. I was a swirling ball of Higher screw-reality, streamers of semi-transparency, my right hand out, palm up, holding something. But empty. I jumped back to ghost, facing my flesh.

Samantha had rotated as I'd walked my body past her. Now she hung, just at the edge of my ghost peripheral vision.

"So that's it?" I demanded. "I can move my flesh when I'm in my ghost, I can move my ghost when I'm in my flesh? Can you tell me who designed this system? Do you know what the point is, of any of this? I mean *any* of it, psychics, paths—can you—tell me this—is Caroline supposed to be a queen, what would it be, queen of the Path Behind? Queen of the past? Will that make it harder for me to get her to take off her dress? Do Monarchs like it if you take off your own clothes first? Because all I want, Samantha, all I want is to get with her tonight but instead I get hedge mazes and *oh*, buy a new *car*, and don't shoot my fucking face fucking crazy man, and ghosts, and all the royal disfavor from the other two—why's it have to be this *hard?*"

I would've kept complaining—it turns out all I'd ever needed was a captive audience—but I heard Caroline coming back.

The chair was out of range, what they call an aspirational goal. The floor was where I was headed. I kept my ghost positioned like a spotter, and I dropped flesh me to his knees. I snatched my eyes with imaginary puppet hands, closed them and pulled them crossed, straight from zero to one hundred, because time was short. My ghost body swooped, dropped, slipped-inside my flesh, so we cohabitated, roommates in a tiny loft, and then the temperature started going up.

Sunburn torture doesn't touch it. My flesh body poured sweat like a broken main. One by one the Higher colors went out, *choke, compulsion, reason, crush, farewell, wander, bleed,* and then ghost me was nothing but *dominion,* and *dominion* made the heat worse. *Dominion* compacted a ball in Caroline's suite. Squeezing. Really? Is this the only way? Samantha? Someone? Multiplying pain. Mixing two of me in one.

Again I felt something snap.

Dominion drained away, down my arm into my curled fist, and disappeared. And then flesh and ghost were one. One sweating, groaning, teeth clenched pile of *hi Caroline, I'm your date Asher* for her to find laying on her Elizabethan home theater floor.

Which she did, and the moment she reached me she knelt.

"Shh," she said, her hand on the side of my head. I tried to sit up but saw I'd need to wait a few minutes. She speculated at my face and touched my forehead, and her hand had a little blood. Her face swam around.

"Can you hear me?" she asked.

I nodded. "I'm totally, totally fine."

"Just lie still," she told me. "Do you need a doctor?"

"I need a drink," I decided.

"That's the worst thing for a concussion," she nodded, "so I'm not surprised to hear you want it. What happened?"

I peered down the long barrel of that story. "That's too hard," I admitted.

"How'd you hit your head?"

"There was a ghost. I hit my head on that."

"Okay, I'll get you a drink," she decided.

She rose. I wanted to follow, but this two-body reunion had leveled me like heavy timber, and Caroline was right, my brain felt faintly concussed. I did manage to sit up, my preferred drinking position, while Caroline poured. I saw something fall onto the floor out of my right hand. A melted fistful of glass and aluminum and battery, all run together and glowing *dominion.* I saw that the night was just getting more complicated.

Caroline shifted her dress up to sit beside me. She left a lot of leg showing but neither of us felt compelled to do anything about it. It was a nice change. She handed me a glass and drank from her own. She pointed.

"What's that?" she asked.

"I accidentally melted my phone," I told her. "It's a thing I do sometimes. It's recent."

Her face made a *hmmm,* shape, and she picked up the little artifact and turned it. It had recognizably once been a phone, but also looked like something splashed from a lava flow. What could possibly have done that, a reasonable mind would wonder. That's what I watched Caroline's mind do. After a moment she put the phone on the floor, had a drink, shrugged.

"You can't get reception up here anyway," she said, turning to me. "You look real bad, Ash. Maybe let's get you a doctor."

I shook my head, then wished I hadn't.

"I'll be fine," I assured her. "So this is a nice place you've got. I like the regal thing going on. I love how you wanted to surprise me with all this. It's super unpredictable behavior, one of my favorite things. I made some great friends downstairs. You'll probably hear about me. What's the deal with the Paths? Those are new."

"Not tonight," she said.

"Are you a Queen? Are you the Monarch?" I sounded demented, but that never stops me.

"That's one of my titles."

"You could have told me."

"We don't talk about it. Not outside."

"What do you do, as a Monarch?"

"Some other time, Ash," she said.

There was a low fire across the room, behind her, and it lit the perfect planes of her, the comedy and sex of her, the expanding depths—at that moment all I wanted was to lie beside her and take a long nap. I leaned in, we did kiss, I looked in her eyes, they swam for me, but the crazy was squeezed out of us. Both of us. For now.

"Maybe it's better if I leave," I told her. "Just this time, I don't want to make a habit of it."

She nodded. "It's funny. I've been thinking of you undressed most of today, but now I'm just... your eyes are amazing, your lips are sure cute. But it's like... a hot tide went out."

"Yep, calling it," I said. I stood, slow, a cute lipped grandpa. At least I had keys. I reached into my pocket, confirming, and found the train tickets, which I pulled out.

"I meant to ask," I said, doing sober thoughtfulness though I'm not sure it's my best look, and probably didn't fool anyone with it, "tomorrow is Sunday, which maybe is a psychic day off? Maybe you'd like to take a day trip with me to Los Angeles and back. I have to go look at a painting. I thought we could talk, in public, like on a train, we could try this locked together in a moving train where maybe we can focus and talk a little bit... there are some things for you to know about me. Some of them you must have guessed by now." I handed over her ticket. "Does that sound like a fantastic offer?"

"It sounds wonderful," she told me, genuinely surprised I'd had any doubt. "What time do we leave?"

I showed her details on the ticket, then gathered my strength. She gave me back my melted phone then helped me out her door, circled me around her balcony and down her stairs, and finally sallied up to her castle portico, which she swung outward as slow as whales dreaming. I stood in the portal, feeling the cool night a few yards away, looking at the girl I'd wanted to see for the last 24 hours, a curvy psychic cowboy Queen of the Path Behind or whatever, and saw her frown. I knew what she was thinking. The actual words.

"Does it worry you, Ash?"

I wanted to double check.

"You mean how despite everything, my melted phone, my problems with ghosts, me associated with crimes, murder interrogations, and with you hardly knowing me, despite all that you just said yes I'll ride off alone with you someplace on a train, like none of that mattered?"

"Yeah. Does that bother you?"

"Not until you made me say it out loud," I admitted. "Train station in the morning?"

She nodded. Her tiara sparkled. I tried to shut her castle door but she had to pull it closed herself, I lacked the strength.

CHAPTER

FOUR

We stood in streamers of morning fog on the platform, wrapped around each other, and all I could hope was that when the train finally did arrive and we got inside, our sense of public propriety might have a pacifying influence on our lust, so I could finally warn her about some of my dangerous tendencies. In the meantime Caroline and I engaged in what had become our brazenly personal style of heavy petting. I felt her breath and her waist and she had her hands inside my shirt up and down the back of my pants. I felt our hot tide rolling back in. The clock for warnings was ticking fast.

And then the train arrived. I found that all I could do was look at it. The moment had finally come to leave Skysill Beach.

"It's a real pretty train, Ash," she said, after a moment waiting. "Are we getting on?"

"I just didn't think it'd be this weird. Trains are normal, right?"

"Aw. Is that what this is? We're here confronting your fear of trains?"

"It's leaving Skysill Beach," I admitted. "I've always wanted to leave. I thought I did."

"You're a *virgin*," she discovered, with a tongue tipped smile, then took my hand very gently. "Don't worry honey, we'll go slow. You'll like it I *promise*."

She encouraged me into the stairwell by going first—who wouldn't follow her?—and then I was standing on the stairs, by the door, like a dream, watching the train begin to leave the city I'd never left before.

"Let's go back to the last car," we each said at exactly the same time, startling both of us, then we gave toothy romantic comedy laughs which was even *more* startling and disturbing, then started walking down the train.

She led, one car after another. The train picked up speed. I was walking back toward Skysill but losing the race to the city limits. I took the opportunity to watch Caroline walk. Her hair swished, pony-tailed. Her belted jeans hung low, cinched with a leather braid like a bridle, the end dangling. Her hips moved her pockets.

I was controlling my anxiety as best I could, my fear that crossing the Skysill city limit would mean dying. I regretted the feeling, surprised it had any hold on me. I'd thought I was immune, but here I was, departing, and bonds of apprehension were pulling me. I dialed the color down, trying to mute my emotions, though it produced less effect than it once had. If this was anything like what Lady Damely had felt just *thinking* about the trip, I had sudden sympathy.

Caroline slid us into a sunny pair of seats on the ocean side of the last car on the train.

"What's going on?" she asked. "Hey, you really are nervous leaving, aren't you?"

"Maybe," I told her. Admissions like that usually lead to advice I can't use, so I make them sparingly.

"Ash," she said. She leaned and gave me her lips. We must have been kissing when I crossed the Skysill city limit for the first time in my life. Suddenly there were unfamiliar waves beaching out the window, and then more and more of them whipping by. Through the glass I saw hills without buildings parading out behind us. No more Skysill Beach. It was done.

I leaned out of Caroline range just to clear my head and marshal my ideas, because I need all the help I can get.

"I like your brand new top," she complimented my t-shirt.

"Thank you. How do you know it's brand new?"

"Some people take off the tags. Your way's easier."

"I see, yes, I bought it before you came, from the gift shop."

"You got there early? That doesn't sound like you."

"It's a funny story. I wanted a clean shirt to impress you."

"Mission accomplished."

"I know. So I spent the night in my car in the parking lot until the shop opened." She looked impressed and curious to hear the rest of that story. "I did that because I can't get to my usual clothes, because something happened to my house key."

"What happened to it?"

"Nothing. Well, just some melting."

"I see. Like your phone." I nodded. She thought about my predicament. "You don't have a spare key? Under your welcome mat?"

"I always thought welcome mats sent the wrong message."

The train took a turn inland. I felt the burn of our desire start again, coming up off my arm where she was running her fingertips.

"Look," I said, "the other day you said you were trying to figure out how crazy I was."

"Doesn't matter. Your crazy doesn't scare me."

"You haven't heard the details," I said. "You might be surprised."

"Crazy people never feel surprise," we startled each other by saying together, in exactly the same rhythm, at exactly the same time, then watched as we made more words in perfect synch one after another, "crazy people just expand their minds to accommo-date new facts, and they move on."

It stopped us. For one thing, what the hell did that even mean? And for another it was a very complicated sentence to come out so concurrent, syllable by syllable. Then we laughed. We did that at the same time too. She whispered in my ear, "Okay, go on, tell me exactly how crazy you are."

I started her off with how every stipend artist in Skysill Beach can see ultraviolet light, because that was the least malignant crazy in my portfolio. I found that saying it out loud drove a crystal rush of amazement through my veins. I'd wanted to say it, to someone, for so long. But no one wanted to hear it. Caroline listened, easy-fast, co-conspirator in everything I said. I cut right to the dangerous stuff then, how I'd been melting certain items, I warned her to watch my hands, check for fingers sticking straight out because when I go *Gray* I stop thinking of people like living creatures and think of them as puzzles, with solutions which are often cruel or dangerously unpredictable. I mentioned *chroma storm* seizures in case she saw me in one, just so she'd know what was happening. I went through my newest ghost behavior, and popping out of my body. I covered it all.

"It sounds like a lot of crazy to live with," she agreed, kissing my neck. "You're doing real good, considering."

"I gave up painting," I told her. "I'd *storm* so much I couldn't eat, couldn't sleep. I think about painting every single day. It's the only thing I'm good at. I've never said that to anyone."

"And you feel better now?"

"I wouldn't go that far."

"I mean *right* now?" She had her hand inside the t-shirt she liked, fingertips dancing in the tiny hairs on my chest. I answered by unbuttoning her blouse while thinking how my optimism about our sense of propriety had been a miscalculation. Caroline didn't respect common decency any better than I did. I wondered where all this was going, and how we could get there faster.

"This is going to be fantastic," we both said at the same time.

Then we laughed at the same time. Exactly.

Then we said, "That was weird," at the same time.

Her lips came up off my neck. Her eyes met mine.

"Listen," she rushed out, "I know all about crazy. I don't tell people this either. I spent a lot of time, until I was sixteen, institutionalized. Mental hospitals I guess. A lot of time in little gardens. Doctors wondering if they could fix me, since I thought I was psychic and they didn't. And also I was crazy, totally batshit crazy."

As she admitted it all to me, her fingers dropped from my chest and returned to razoring the hem on her shirt. Just slaying the fabric to strings. I understood. I lifted the fingers to my mouth. The tips. I kissed them, then sucked them.

"This feels *amazing*," we both *thought* at the same time.

"Wait, what, did we just *think* that?" we *thought* at the same time.

Her eyes spun wide. Like my eyes.

"It's like I hear what you're thinking," we thought at the same time.

And then, on a train that carried us north up the California coast, through a morning filled with sun burning off the last of the coastal fog, time stopped. Space vanished. We fell through each other's eyes. A stomach twist and a plummet, a plunge like two pendulums, a collision swinging in and then, somehow, we didn't collide, though something in me badly wanted a collision, and we arced up opposite sides them swooped back down, back and forth like an unwinding clock, until our pendulum was done we found ourselves swinging on a bench, together at the side of a wood, fifty feet from the drop of a cliff, looking out.

Beyond the cliff there was an immense Amtrak carriage. In that, a giant-slow Asher and a giant-slow Caroline, dinosaur sized—vast as moons— ponderously tore each other's clothes off. Caroline and I on our swing sat watching it like enjoying a drive-in movie. One of the other giant passengers in the Amtrak car got up, in slow motion disgust, and moved off screen.

"So Caroline," I telepathed, wondering at my own calm, "what's this thing we're doing now? It's a psychic thing?"

Caroline was equally calm and baffled. I knew she was. We spent a moment watching the giants performing beyond the edge of the cliff. It wasn't clear if we'd be expected to do anything with them, intervene or offer advice. They seemed perfectly fine on their own, but I didn't trust them.

"This isn't psychic, Ash," she said, sounding sure.

"Well, I don't know, it seems pretty psychic. This is telepathy right? Isn't that psychic?"

She shook her head.

"Being psychic's only about *time*," she telepathed, "but this isn't time. I don't know what this is."

A wave of pleasure from the giants rocked us then. I'd been vaguely aware of the smooth feel of giant Caroline's fingernails on giant Asher's arms, little pleasure points, but then the two of them uncovered matching erogenous zones on each other, and the sensations were feeding back. We all felt it. For a moment the two of them in the carriage froze, just like Caroline and I in our swing. Another passenger lumbered up and off in unhappiness. I wondered if our slow motion giants were making noise. They looked like they might be.

"Could this be something to do with your Paths?" I asked, when the pleasure let up.

"Absolutely not. With the Paths, you start on a mountaintop. And you're traveling. And even if you step off the Path you always feel it. You'd better. But this is like... this is like I'm living inside my own head. Maybe it's one of your *chroma storms?*"

I tried exposing the Highers, but all color perception was locked in whatever state it'd been when I'd last used my eyes on the train, latched onto Caroline's pupils and falling. So, just ordinary sight.

"Who knows?" I told her, and gave our swing a little push, because I liked seeing the way it took her hair across her cheek. "Going *chromatic* used to be so simple, back before there were ghosts. But look at giant me's hands out there. And here beside you. No fists."

"Well whatever this is," she moaned, in my mind, getting wild again, "it feels amazing, like... *I never shared anything this amazing amazing—*"

"—ah," I cried in my own brain, "there's so much of you inside—"

Giant me now had giant Caroline's shirt off and was working her bra. The two of them were golden and god-sized in afternoon light, on a train moving hours eating space down spinning planet... and all of it somewhere silent. Giant Asher took giant Caroline in his ponderous arms, she ponderously worked to jam his pants down past his ankles where they'd got snagged on the shoes he'd untied but hadn't taken off. The feel of giant Caroline's skin pushing on giant Asher's belly came down around us on our swing in a convulsive shower, so again we froze, and they froze, mouths wide. Helpless in it.

"*How* is this not freaking either of us out?" she protested weakly. "Are we that fucking crazy?"

"Nothing ever felt this—"

"—pure. I *am* you, feeling can... me oh, now *that's* funny isn't it?"

I looked. The edge of the cliff where we sat had been crumbling, little by little, as we'd conducted telepathy, and now it fragmented with a vengeance, sections cracked and slid down. Dust rose. The edge was nearer. The cliff face was coming for us. It was shadows. It was cold wind.

Out in the Amtrak car the giants had gotten themselves laying sideways across the seats, hardworking lustful giants, while the coastal scenery slow boated the window behind them. Giant Caroline rode giant Asher, while he reached for her breasts, maybe the most beautiful sight I've ever seen, and she bent, so slow, until her breasts pressed his chest and there they wrapped each other, ecstatic, liquid skinned.

The cold wind blew the swing harder. It *tore* us.

"We've been heading to this moment since the first second we met," she thought, and we held hands and watched the cliff collapse closer.

"From that glass of water on the sidewalk," I agreed.

"We're too blissed out."

From far away we felt a hint of something deep in our mind. Despair. Then the giants ground their sweet spots together and it was rapture.

"What's coming won't be bearable," I thought at her. The cliff had almost reached us.

"I'm going to lose yourself," we thought.

The giants vanished.

The world got simple, two minds, a swing, one cliff, facing darkness, and a wind which was the force of me, my black hole gravity, ripping her, her white hot sun, to shreds, and her doing it back. An earthquake rattled the...

Something slammed me in the side.

It happened again and someone was shouting.

My side really hurts, I thought in darkness. What's going on?

A shocking cold cascade of *nothing* pimpled me...

...I gasped up, back in my normal, very uncomfortable body. Caroline gasped too, rising away from me. We were sideways on two seats and sweating, like our giants had been. Caroline's breasts were bare and there was a black baton across her chest, pulling her backward so she stood and blinked sweat and cast for her bearings. She got them. The baton withdrew. I saw my pants around my ankles, my cock and balls still ready for action.

"Like a couple god damn dogs in god damn *heat*!"

Above us stood a woman from train security, showing us her baton. We were a little hypnotized by it. Then she used it to jab my side again, which didn't seem necessary. I understood she was going to keep doing it.

"You got ten seconds to *get* the hell *off* my *train* or I'm calling LAPD—*one* more time now—*Los Angeles, Union Station! Get the hell out!*"

My energy was post-coital dreamy. Caroline was the first to figure out that the guard was mad because she wanted us off her train, because it had arrived in Los Angeles, but some of our clothes were not on our bodies. I got my shirt off the floor and also got Caroline's bra. She'd already put on her own shirt. I got my pants to my thighs and staggered a little going down the aisle but my pants were fully raised when we emerged out onto the station platform. It was sweltering out there.

We stood buttoning and zipping but from the carriage window the security lady frowned and then tapped her baton and pointed—she wanted us to move farther away from her train. You couldn't blame her. She seemed shocked.

"I think, let's get off this platform," I urged Caroline, handing her the bra.

We moved further down, saw luggage come off the train. We were the last passengers.

"So that was… some trip," Caroline said, searching for some other words that didn't come. She looked puzzled. "I don't remember much of what just happened."

"I think me too," I admitted. I glanced back at the train. The pictures were fading. The way dreams go, really hot, erotic dreams. We'd just had a really hot, erotic dream. Did that sound likely?

"Hey," Caroline asked, like she was trying to recall someone's name, "did we just have sex?"

"I don't think so. Your pants were on. Mine got down somehow."

"My top was on the floor."

"It wasn't sex. But we did have… I sort of remember giant…"

From long experience I know better than to spend time worried about my brain, and the ways it fails to be conventional. It's wasted effort and I usually drink my way around it. Caroline seemed pretty comfortable compartmentalizing too. She was looking better and better..

"I feel like I just had a refreshing nap," she gushed. "I notice you got the tag off your shirt."

"I think it got ripped off in the dream we just had. I'm trying to put that behind me."

"What dream?"

We trotted off the platform, both of us sweat-damp. Caroline passed a trash can and dropped her bra in because she said she hadn't liked it much anyway and now it had gum on it from the train floor. She seemed at ease with or without a bra. She just seemed at ease. Her comfort matched the comfort I felt myself. And later on, it was clear from a promise we made glancing at each other, we'd get back to our steam and heat full speed. Whatever that thought meant.

"When we're home this afternoon, you want to come up to Three Paths?" Caroline asked as we headed in a tunnel.

"I'm not sure I'm welcome up there."

"We can't go to your house. You have a key problem. We have to go somewhere."

"I could get a new house. I did it with my car."

"We'll figure it out. Why don't you tell me what you're doing in Los Angeles? We seem to keep getting distracted."

"I know, it's confusing. Well, there's a painting I'm supposed to look at. Samantha the ghost, the girl who's still haunting around? She wanted this picture pretty bad." I pulled out Damely's card to make sure I had it, because of the many things I'd already lost. "It's on Wilshire Boulevard. We can Lyft over. I'll see whatever I see, which will probably be nothing, then let's eat."

I could tell she was analyzing my plan.

"So you already got a new phone since last night's melt job?" she asked.

"I did not," I admitted. She really had a gift. "So then I won't be Lyfting over. I know, we'll get a taxi. They have taxis outside train stations in all the old movies."

"I'll get the Lyft, you got the train tickets," she said, opening her purse for her phone. We turned from our tube of tunnel into an underground concourse where many other tunnels connected, leading up and emerging into the middle of Union Station. It looked like a church for trains, coved ceilings, panels of heavy glass on the walls floor to eave. There'd never been anything like it in Skysill Beach. I gawked involuntarily.

Then Caroline said something I didn't hear because when I

looked down I saw, coming toward us through rows of wooden benches, a familiar figure, a figure in white canvas painter pants and shirt, with lady aviator white hair.

"Hey Ash, I need the lawyer's address," Caroline repeated to me —oh, that's what she said, why is Veronica Knight here?—and from fifty feet off Veronica waved at me, a wave that said, *can you believe this coincidence?*

"What the hell?" I muttered out loud.

"What is it?" Caroline asked.

Veronica dropped her wave and smiled and came toward me, it was a large wide smile with red gums and genuine warmth, so it was almost unrecognizable. Apparently we'd become best friends while I was asleep in the parking lot last night.

"Don't look now," I said, turning to Caroline, "but here's a lady I know." But Caroline was already looking. On her face she wore the frown that complicated her brow the way I liked.

"Veronica?" Caroline said to Veronica.

I turned back, and now that Veronica was closer I realized her genuine affection hadn't been intended for me at all, which made me feel safer. Ignoring me entirely Veronica stopped in front of Caroline. They hugged and laughed like people who'd seen each other just a few days before and liked remembering it.

"What a nice surprise," Caroline said to her. "What are *you* doing here?"

"Me? I'm meeting Mr. Gale, of course," Veronica said, not looking at me.

"That doesn't sound right," I complained, still recovering from the smile.

"How do you know Asher?" Caroline laughed. A wonderful coincidence.

"He's my intern," Veronica said. Then amended, "We're working out the details."

"Well, it was nice seeing you," I said to Veronica not meaning it, but before I could get Caroline away Veronica put one fact beside another in her mind.

"*Ohhhhh* I see. Mr. Gale, you haven't checked your messages?" she asked. Her black eyes hadn't been restocked with pity since the last time she'd used them on me. She looked closer at me, then back and forth between me and Caroline, damp with sex sweat like we seemed to be, and she observed, "Maybe you've been otherwise occupied this morning? Well. I think you ought to check your messages now."

"I don't happen to have my phone anymore," I said.

"Of course you don't," she shook her head. She turned to Caroline. "What are your plans today?"

"I don't know," Caroline smiled, "I'm here for the ride."

"How has that been?" wondered Veronica. "Bumpy?"

"Real exciting," Caroline said. "Ash didn't tell me we were meeting you."

"We aren't," I insisted. "Do you know this lady? This... paint sales lady?"

"I do know her," Caroline said.

"I'm one of Caroline's clients," Veronica said. "She's a very gifted psychic, you know."

"Really," I said, "I hadn't heard."

"She's been helping me with a project."

"Not that much help, I'm afraid," Caroline said.

Veronica was dialing her phone as she spoke, which at first looked like an opportunity to escape while she talked until she lifted a hand to me, *wait,* and put the other to her ear with the phone, and Caroline waited so I had to. After a moment someone answered Veronica.

"Judith? It's me. I did. He's lost his phone. Perhaps a seal ate it, I have no idea. Would you like to speak to him?"

Veronica held her phone to me.

"Who's this?" I demanded.

"It's Judith," Veronica told me. *I don't know any Judith*, I used my suspicious frown telling her. She understood. "Lady Damely," Veronica sighed, like talking to me was one long disappointment for her.

"You know everybody I guess," I complained.

"I play bridge with Judith." She urged the phone to me. "I played with her last night."

Very faintly from the phone I heard a little voice, "Asher? Asher… hello?"

"Take this."

I took the phone, gave Caroline an apology, which she accepted happily, and snarled, "Hello?"

"Asher," Lady Damely said, "I have left you several messages."

"Why are we talking?"

"You made it to Los Angeles. Please say nothing about it to me."

"What was it you said in your supposed messages?"

"I want Veronica to accompany you while you examine The Dancer's Kiss."

"When I work," I explained, "which I'm doing just this one time, I work alone. So no."

"But Asher," she said, using her self-evident voice, "you've already lost your phone, you barely know how to be *civil* for goodness sake, it simply occurred to me you would be safer if you had a partner."

"A partner?" I eyed Veronica. "Whose idea was this, Lady Damely —yours or hers?"

Veronica took the phone before I heard.

"Hello Judith, it's me." She listened and smiled at me. "Well, all right. I'll try to keep him from harm's way. Like a child. I know. Cheers." She hung up.

"And there we are. So I understand," she told me, "that we are expected at the escrow lawyer's. It will be easier if we all go in my car." Without waiting for an answer she led the way to the parking lot, continuing to tap her phone. Sticking to my plan to take a taxi even though Veronica had a car going to the same place seemed petty, which normally wouldn't have stopped me, but I thought I'd continue building on the good impression I'd started with Caroline taking her shirt off in public earlier, and I'd experiment with cooperation.

"I don't know how she found me," I apologized as we walked. "We'll get rid of her fast."

"I don't mind," Caroline said. "She's kind of formal but sweet when you get to know her."

"She doesn't like me. From the moment we met."

"Do you think you might have a small problem making first impressions?"

"I didn't know first impressions were still a thing."

"Well, I met you throwing up on my sidewalk and look at us now, so some things there's no explanation for. But Li Wei wanted to blow your head off after his first impression of you."

"After you get to know me you don't want to shoot me as badly."

"I *have* found that to be true."

For a moment I felt as if, with a little effort, I could have read her mind, and vice versa. The thought was scalding and chilling in layers, a combination I was trying to understand as we followed Veronica into the hard, hot sun beating a full parking lot flat. Veronica headed for a midnight shadow Suburban she'd hired somewhere, with both doors open and a man in a black suit on the curb. He offered her a nod, she slid in the front seat, and Caroline and I got in back. The suit closed all the doors, then we were gliding into traffic. The driver's screen mapped a seven minute ride. I hoped it would be over faster.

"How do you like the art museums in Los Angeles?" Caroline said to Veronica. You could see her working her psychic curiosity on the situation.

"Not at all," Veronica said. "I don't care for art. I'm only here for Judith."

I'd decided not to speak and avoid dignifying things, but then I did it anyway.

"This seems like a lot of trouble, doesn't it?" I asked. "Renting a car, driving hours, tracking me down—I'd like to know how you found me. What am I missing?"

"Many, many things," she smiled. "For instance, I am not renting a car." She was leveling Caroline and I a long, careful appraisal. "Oh my. Look at you two."

Caroline had unbuckled her seatbelt and slid beside me and put her hand under my shirt to play with my nipple. It was very casual, the way you'd scratch your favorite dog on the ear while you watched TV. I pushed my hand down to fondle between Caroline's thighs, equally blithe. We looked politely to Veronica. Well, Caroline was polite.

"My, my, my," Veronica took her time saying, watching us not caring that she was watching us. Then we'd arrived at the glass and steel showpiece where Taylor and Earnest had their lawyer offices. We all got out and Veronica told the driver she didn't know how long we'd be because I'd refused to give an authentication estimate purely out of spite. The driver told her yes ma'am. It seemed polite for a Lyft. We got inside and the elevator went up. Caroline and I were leaning for full body contact. I felt a hormone tsunami gathering to boil. We got to the floor, Veronica cleared her throat, Caroline and I stumbled out.

At a desk we identified ourselves.

"Yes," the receptionist said, "The Dancer's Kiss. We have it ready. This is your last permitted authentication I'm to remind you."

"First and last," I said, "but who's counting?"

"We are," he said.

"You're counting what? Someone else already authenticated The Dancer's Kiss?"

"I'm afraid I don't have that information."

It was puzzling, but I forgot it when we discovered that only

Veronica and I were on the list, and Caroline wouldn't be allowed beyond the desk. I felt cheated. Caroline was gracious. We kissed while they fetched a guard to escort us.

"This feels like falling out of a plane, doesn't it?" Caroline murmured to me.

"Like falling out of something, for sure. It's amazing. I don't think it's normal."

"We have to be careful," she said in my ear. "Something's happening to us."

Then the guard came. I watched Caroline as I went around a corner, looking every inch Monarch powerful, but also like a regular girl wearing a translucent blouse and no bra, in either case someone I wanted to sleep with. When she was out of sight it was easier to stop thinking about her.

A guard took us down a beige hall past large offices, then conferred with a second guard at a metal detector. We got approved. The back half of the whole floor was organized as a warehouse— goods on shelves, lockers, safes, racks of all kinds of items. He stopped for a moment at a shelf to remove a draped canvas, then carried it until we came to a small room, three chairs and an easel, where he set the painting without undraping it.

Veronica turned to him. "Thank you so much," she said. "Please wait outside."

"I leave when you do," he said, polite enough, but you saw he had less customer friendly ways he could talk if he needed to. Veronica smiled.

"It is okay to leave," she told him.

When Veronica said *it is okay* she held her fingers near his lips, and a spidery matrix of tangled *compulsion* grew off them, spread between them, then vanished. Without a word, the guard turned and left the room.

She turned to face me and caught me baffled. Usually I try to hide that. After a moment of staring she nodded.

"So you saw it."

"This time you can't deny it," I hissed. "The *compulsion* trick. Yeah I saw it."

"I've no intention of denying anything." She never took her eyes off me. She went to one of the little chairs facing the draped painting, tuned it to face me and sat in it.

"Not paint," I said, flaring the Highers to scan her, bearing down on her fingertips, not a sign of Higher pigment. "Just light. I saw you do something…"

"It's called an eminence," she explained. We watched each other decide what to say next. She decided first. "There are things I could teach you."

"People try. I can't stop them. Is there a story that goes with your sparkle fingers?"

"Can you sit?"

"No, I have a trick spine."

"Fine. But we do not have a lot of time. Listen then. I am Aspectu, Mr. Gale. So are you. So is every Fenestram painter in Skysill Beach, however improbable and dangerous that fact might be. Does this mean anything to you?"

Something familiar, something circled—then I had it.

"Aspectu. I saw that word on the city map at the Historical Society. Aspectu Prime."

"Very clever. Aspectu are a family. There are Five Families." She showed me the number with fingers, which seemed condescending. "You and I, Lady Damely, all the other painters. Anyone who *sees* ultraviolet light is Aspectu."

"Cut the crap," I said suddenly. "The Latin, the finger families one two three. Before, you said you were here for Judith. Now I have my own theory." I went briefly on the offensive because it takes less ability and planning. "What if you did your *compulsion* crackle on Lady Damely, you're controlling her, and maybe you're here to steal this painting?"

"A *crackle* is called an *eminence*," she explained again.

"Are you crackle controlling Lady Damely or are you not?"

"Aspectu like us resist *compulsion*. We resist it in pigment and in light."

And then even my simplistic offensive skills were tapped. I slipped back into confusion, where I've had more experience. "What do you even want?" I protested.

"I wish I knew. There is so much I don't understand. Your mysterious parents. The trick you did as a boy with your paintings. I only had suspicions you were involved until recently. But the afternoon by the beach changed things. I found you laying on the beach. Do you recall?"

"Yeah, like a vacation postcard."

"Yes. I'd been waiting there quite some time before you woke up. Your... whatever you were doing, it called me there. I reached you in time to see you laying on the sand at the feet of two men who had assaulted you. And then a ball of seven formed around you—*around your body*—blinding me, and disappearing. When it had gone, the men were gone, the sand was gone. But *you* lay there. You woke up! Confused, at a loss for words, so quite normal. But you are without awareness, you see? Untapped!"

I shook my head. I did not see. She continued.

"Two days later Judith mentioned you were leaving Skysill Beach on her errand—which I'd understood that none of you wanted to do, or were able to do, it's very mysterious—and I wondered, why leave now, after so many years in one place? Was it the picture itself? Was your trip related to the incident on the beach? Who are you, really? And then, what should I discover when I get to LA, but you've gone and involved Caroline? Who is much too good for you, surely you realize, and whose life you are about to ruin, whether you know it or not—it really is quite astonishing. Sleepwalking through your days while problems fountain up around you, wherever you go. Don't you find?"

"Actually," I told her, stepping around her toward the draped painting on its stand, "I find my worst problems walk up in train stations. I was doing fine before you got here. Is it me, or does it seem like the only thing you want is to muddy the waters of my life, out of, I don't know, boredom? You like mud? But my waters don't need your help, I can't see anything as it is. All I'm doing is trying to help a dead girl—a girl I never even met before she committed suicide, I don't know how this shit keeps starting up—and you're interrupting me, and you're interrupting my road trip with all your stalking around doing hypnosis on security guards—so let's cut the crap! Can we? Just... *goodbye.* Take your sparkle fingers and go *home.* I'll due diligence this painting. I'll find nothing. I'll get back to my road trip ruining Caroline's life—*not.* And you tell Damely you tried to help me but it was all too much confusion and people fountaining prob-lems for you to handle!"

It was a long speech, and I was tired at the end of it. I turned my back on her and faced the easel, which felt too dramatic. I was sorry to give her the satisfaction. My hopes had never been high that I'd find anything to help Samantha here, from the painting, and now I wished I'd just skipped it. Still I yanked the drape down. I got my first look at The Dancer's Kiss.

I heard Veronica make a puzzled sound.

In 1492, likely in Florence, Niccolo Filippi had painted two men, from a viewpoint suspended above them, as they lay head to head on the stone floor of a cold and candle lit room. One man, on his back in a loincloth, was languorous and dark-skinned. The other faced down, his head suspended over the first man's and obscuring the face. You couldn't see, but it was hard not to think they were kissing. The dancer was the one on top. He had garlands in his hair, his arms and hands were twisted in multicolored lace.

The style was High Renaissance and it was a masterwork, full of luminous juxtapositions, tone and form in classical proportions, but sacred in a way they'd just been discovering, in its simple reverence for human shapes. Just as Damely claimed, Niccolo Filippi had been *sighted.* The Dancer's Kiss was alive with sub-shades, the sisible spectrum colors you need extra sensetive eyes to see. But no Highers.

They hadn't had ultraviolet paint in the High Renaissance, but Filippi had created a matrix of interdependent colors-between-the-colors in The Dancer's Kiss and it gyrated and spun.

"It can't be..." Veronica whispered, and came slowly forward.

The man facing up off the stone floor had a kohl black tattoo over his heart. The image of an eye, styled a little hieroglyphic. Instead of a single iris, the open lidded tattoo had five small circles, the largest in the middle. Superimposed in the center was a thin, five pointed star. It was this tattoo Veronica couldn't tear her gaze from.

"This... shouldn't be," she breathed. Just from her tone of voice, the temperature in the room dropped. "No. It can't." She looked at me. "Who has done this?"

"Go be flabbergasted someplace else," I told her. I was immersed in my inspection. The canvas was riveting, beautiful. Heartbreaking too, in a strange way.

"You don't understand," she protested with a whisper. "This... tattoo, the umbra eye, it is *ancient*. Mr. Gale... hundreds of thousands of years, and more terrible..." She opened up her phone and got a picture, and had to take a few more because her hands were shaking.

"We decided you were leaving," I reminded her.

"This is not a game! This is shocking. The umbra eye has never been drawn, painted, sculpted. Not like this. It shouldn't be here. It's... what does this mean?"

I liked this new, imploring Veronica. I liked having things to tell her she'd never be able to understand. So I nodded professorially, though I've never met a professor so who knows what I really looked like. It felt awkward so I stopped.

"High Renaissance," I told her. "It's a masterpiece, honestly. Florentine. Religious iconography, this gold leaf, reminds me of Giotto's Madonna Enthroned, recently shipped from Italy. Held here in escrow. You know any of this?"

"Judith told me some. Who painted it? When was this painted?"

"That's complicated. Niccolo Filippi painted The Dancer's Kiss in 1492." I leaned in close to really admire the brushwork, the artistry.

"But if you're asking when *this* canvas was painted, I'd say anywhere from three days to a week ago."

"Mr. Gale, please be as clear as you are able. Can you try?" she asked slowly, though I thought I'd been pretty clear.

"It's a copy," I told her. "This is a forgery."

CHAPTER

FIVE

Five hundred year old paint fluoresces in very distinctive wavelengths. From the pigments they used, from the oxidation, you can't hide that from me. But this fluoresced like a movie of the week. It was a forgery, and the thing about forgeries is how they piss me off. Forgeries used to get me up Waylon Goodman's crooked hillside over and over, when nothing else could have done that. So even if this one hadn't been associated with Samantha it would have gotten my attention.

And something in The Dancer's Kiss reminded me of a forgery I'd seen before, somewhere else. Something from Waylon? I thought through the canvases on the walls of Asher Gale's office. All the prizes Waylon had saved from our dysfunctional partnership. I tried to remember if any of those liars had been Florentine, which felt like a weak thread since forgery's pretty stateless.

Veronica was still trying to fit the pieces together.

"So," she said, "the umbra eye, this millenniums old sigil, appears, for the first time in *history*, on a forged painting in a law office warehouse?"

"I know. It's one thing after another, am I right?" I almost sympathized. "My whole week has been like this. You'll get used to it. My question is, did Samantha know that what Damely was buying was a forgery? Maybe that was why she wanted it so much? Or did this get switched on her?"

"Wait. Who is Samantha?" Veronica asked. She was trying to dig in against confusion. It was funny to see. I liked watching her playing catch up.

"Samantha was a girl, she killed herself," I explained. But then out of fairness to Samantha I added, "A painter name Julian did a *compulsion* mural and left her no choice. The usual story."

I left out any mention of her current condition. Why confuse things further? Veronica sensed me doing it.

"What else?" she asked.

"Samantha talked Damely into bidding on this painting in the first place. So, did she want it because of the forgery, or is the forgery unrelated, or what?"

"Did she ever say anything about the umbra eye? The tattoo?"

"I never met her," *while she was alive,* I added inside my brain, "but one thing I do know—whoever painted this is at the very top of the game. A *sighted* forger. You just don't see that. The style... this style's familiar—it's the most authentic feeling forgery I've ever looked at—it'd be very hard to spot if you..." I started having a thought, a complicated one that kept me from talking.

"I see," Veronica said, having the same thought. "Someone already came to authenticate The Dancer's Kiss. I heard the receptionist. Probably Judith's authenticator. Perhaps he saw this forgery and was eliminated."

"That's kind of chillingly casual. But I doubt it. If it was Damely's guy, we know he wasn't *sighted,* he'd miss all the sub-shade color, and I doubt he sees pigment fluorescence like I can. But something happened to Damely's guy—she can't get ahold of him. I'm sure it's just a coincidence."

Veronica took more pics of The Dancer's Kiss, then, as if she couldn't stand the sight, she pulled the drape back over the canvas.

She opened the door of our little workshop. Our security drone appeared.

"We're finished," she said. "Thank you very much."

He nodded, clear eyed and unfriendly as ever. He carried the wrapped painting, replaced it as we worked our way back through the warehouse past other art, books, packaged treasures everywhere. We arrived at the front desk. Caroline was nowhere to be seen.

"We left a girl out here," I reminded the receptionist. And suddenly I was wading right back into the middle of the only really important question. "Where is she?"

"Down the hall, Starbucks," the receptionist told me. "You'll catch her on your way out."

"So I have another question," I said, and he immediately braced. He threatened to raise an eyebrow. "You said another authenticator was in looking at The Dancer's Kiss."

"That is not what I said."

"How many chances does my client get to look at the painting?"

"Three."

"You said today is our last authentication."

"Yes. Those are the escrow terms."

"Right. So when did the first guy come in?" I was tired of words, which happens fast, it's one of the reasons they never offered me a late night talk show. But the receptionist had a show. He had a lot of stamina.

"I'm afraid I don't have that information," he said, defeating me.

"Yes you do," Veronica said, stepping up. "Tell us, dear."

Up came her fingertips, and this time I was closer and saw many tiny *compulsion* lightning strikes flash among her knuckles and reflect in the receptionist's eyes. Veronica's eyes had closed.

"Here it is," he said after a quick trip to the keyboard. "Dancer's Kiss... inspection list... most recent inspection... Whitney Lamb. He and his assistant, let's see, two days ago."

"Two days?" I turned to Veronica. "Whitney Lamb. Find out if that's Damely's man. She's got a few of them, you'll have to be specific."

Veronica dialed. While it rang, the receptionist continued, "And the first inspection, also Mr. Lamb and assistant, was three weeks ago."

"He came twice? Three weeks apart? What'd he look like?"

"We see many authenticators."

"So, you don't remember?"

"I'm sorry," he said, "I'm afraid I don't have that information."

I saw we'd come to the end of Veronica's sparkle friendship at the same time Veronica handed me her phone.

"Asher," Lady Damely lamented. "I hear the piece is a forgery? How certain are you?"

"Absolutely. They only finished painting it a few days ago."

"How unfortunate." I heard her sigh. "I suppose it was too good to be true."

"I hear that happens. Listen, could you and I chat about Samantha some time?"

"Of course. You are always welcome here. I would ask you to leave your man at home."

"Sure," I said, "he'll be heart broken."

I hung up.

"Whitney Lamb was her authenticator," Veronica said.

"He was in there with the painting two days ago. And three weeks before that."

I was stumbling, the facts all jumbled. That happens to me a lot, but I knew it was serious because I saw the same thing happening to Veronica.

"What can this forgery," she said with a soft voice, "have to do with the umbra eye?"

"Maybe Samantha knows… knew I mean. Maybe it's connected to her cup."

"Cup?"

"I'm trying to find a cup," I admitted, picking out a small piece of the story so we could chew it, "it's a goblet, it's full of holes. Don't ask, I don't know. But Samantha knew something about this cup, and now here's your ancient tattoo... I don't know. I think someone should talk to Whitney Lamb. Maybe he *did* find out The Kiss was fake."

I saw Caroline step around the far turn of the hallway, down where they'd embedded the Starbucks. She had coffee. I stopped talking. An underwater sensation floated up from my ankles, and sounds got a little distant and *all* my interest in Whitney Lamb or tattoos or any of Veronica's families or sparkle nonsense blanked out of my mind. I felt my knees loosen, watched Caroline swaying toward me, took fortifying breaths. Veronica stared at me.

"She's like starlight on beaches," I said to Veronica, pointing at Caroline.

"Hm?" she asked. She didn't look convinced. Then I was strutting fast down the hall, and Veronica came after me, mentioning my name a few times but I wasn't turning, and then I had Caroline in my arms.

"Everything's like underwater," we both said at the same time.

The underwater echo was really pronounced when we were together. Then we laughed at the same time, and said, "This is weird," at the same time. My stomach tightened up and I had a clear thought, just for an instant, that it was dangerous, what we were about to do again. But what *are* we doing I wondered right after that?

"What'd you find about... your painting?" she asked, pushed close, struggling to recall.

"It's fake," I said. "Also other stuff. I don't know."

"The way you feel next to me," we said at the same time, locked eye to eye like survivors of a terrible accident, amazed at our luck. A thought forming in Caroline's mind, *Asher...* I couldn't tell...

"I have an idea," Veronica said suddenly. I noticed her putting away her phone. "No need for either of you to worry. Why don't we take my car? I've called Mr. Lamb and left a message. He keeps very particular hours. His office opens for one hour later this afternoon. I'll take us somewhere to wait. Shall we go now?" I heard her voice as if from the bottom of a swimming pool. We let Veronica coax us into the elevator. Thrills ran over our bodies where we pushed them on each other. The buttons on her shirt felt hot. Somehow we found ourselves outside, Veronica's driver waiting right where we'd left him, doors open. Caroline and I beelined for the back seat so we could crush in together. Caroline slid in first and then the driver bumped me and I wobbled and then Veronica was slipping through the door into my seat beside Caroline and the driver had slammed the back closed. Veronica locked the door. I saw her point to the front seat, smile helpfully. I got in up there.

We slid away into downtown Los Angeles. I hardly noticed we were moving because I'd turned to stare at Caroline. Now I wasn't touching her, the underwater feeling had dimmed. But I wanted it back.

"So," Veronica said after a moment. "How long have you two known each other?"

"A few days," Caroline said without looking from me.

"I see," Veronica nodded. "It was... love at first sight?"

"We were made for each other," Caroline said into my eyes.

"You took my seat," I complained to Veronica. I unfastened my seatbelt and tried crawling back between the front seats but the driver yelled and shoved me, the car swerved, and soon after that we were parking.

Veronica stepped out the back and I scrambled out my own door. We'd parked before the palm framed front entrance of a double hotel tower reflecting cityscape. Red jacket bellhops hurried up. Veronica waved them back. She was hurrying.

"Tell Alison to open the penthouse," she called to a man whose red jacket had authority over the other ones. Caroline was unsnapping and clambering across the seats. Veronica called, "and get the Winter Suite ready!" The bellhops scattered, moving fast.

"You keep a room here?" I asked Veronica, watching for Caroline. "They sure jump when you snap."

"Yes, astonishing, isn't it?" she said.

Then Caroline flowed through the car door. She stood. Our eyes met.

Hi beautiful, she thought to me.

I want to be inside you, I thought back.

Me too. No one else can hear what we're saying.

No one ever had what we have.

We're perfect.

Veronica, oblivious to our conversation, motioned her driver, then came to my side. She was sprinting now, like someone was timing her. The driver scurried and got between Caroline and me, offering her his chauffeur assistance, and Veronica had my arm, pulling us toward the front doors.

"Come, Mr. Gale," she insisted, "you're in danger, it's going to be a very near thing."

She was straining with effort. For just a moment I looked away from Caroline, wondering where Veronica's danger was, and while I was distracted Veronica got me through the front doors—opened by footmen—it was getting harder and harder to focus. Veronica took us through a second set of doors into a massive, open, topaz and gold lobby.

"Let's wait for Caroline," I said and stopped. The underwater feeling had been replaced by a buzz. A really horrible buzz.

"We must keep you moving," she told me. She pointed at a bank of elevators. A woman groomed in sheer competence and high heels crossed the lobby to us, fast and precise.

"What will you need?" the woman asked as she came up.

"Hold an elevator," Veronica said. "Mr. Gale, *Asher,* come," she was pulling me again but I wanted Caroline. The buzz was worse. Much worse. I got free of Veronica with a jerk, but then two sets of XXX blue jacket walkie-talkies crowded to either side and each took an arm. I tried resisting but they knew what they were doing. They turned me and hurried us all across the lobby, following Veronica headed for the elevators. I looked back. I felt Caroline coming. I felt the underwater, the buzzing faded.

The front doors flew open. Caroline shouldered through with loose hair trailing, boots and blue jeans and momentum, sliding to a stop sideways like a speed skater—she swiveled the lobby, spotted me and came on, dashing. It was beautiful the way a deer is beautiful, fleeing a lion.

Through our eyes we found each other.

I wonder why they're trying to keep us apart, she puzzled.

Telepathy with you is amazing, I thought back.

It's like sex.

I never had telepathy with anyone.

Seriously why are they trying to keep us apart?

She slammed into me and the sounds all went underwater again, slow motion—it was shuddering pleasure colliding with her. She wrapped her arms around me. *Do we really feel that?* we thought. Tiny breath ecstasy, we clung, kissing, while other urgent hands pulled our shoulders.

"Move, *you*," I heard Veronica, it wasn't clear who she meant, "Alison get everyone clear, hold the door," someone shoved us, "come, you two, inside!"

Caroline and I staggered when someone pushed and we were in the back of the elevator with Veronica where a busboy stood, surprised beside his loaded food cart. Several XXX blue jackets leaped in and pushed the busboy against the wall and then the doors closed.

"Get them apart!" Veronica shouted.

Hands took us each by shoulders, and waists and legs and pulled, but we were strong, we were touching, we were never going to stop touching, no one could change that now. I watched Caroline's deep honey eyes, I didn't want to and never could look away from them again

Veronica sounded desperate. She saw the large tureen on the busboy's cart. "Hot or cold?" she demanded.

"Cold," the busboy said, shaky confusion. "Gazpacho."

With one hand Caroline now hung on my neck, bronco style, pulling my forehead and hers together while her other hand started opening her pants and I circled her waist one-handed while getting my own pants open, like circus gymnasts, our legs entwined, while hands still pulled to part us.

Oh god this time it's happening we thought, an idea with good points and bad points, but beyond any control.

It's too fast, one of us thought.

It's too late, one of us thought.

Before we got farther with our pants, orgasm circuitry shuddered our bodies. We shared indiscriminate hot steam public pleasure in private, with our despair, our longing, stretching our limits. It was like the train, but this time we'd skipped the swing and the pleasant telepathic banter. There was a cliff below us though, we embraced at the edge, it yawned black and deep. We both recognized the place, despite being bliss soaked. I felt like we rose up, and out over the chasm then. Up and up and out over the black.

There came a moment of apogee, a heart stall, the moment every beautiful wave finds, before it curls just before falling. A second. We heard shouting, voices in the elevator. People still trying to pull us, while from that cresting transitory summit we looked back at all the broken roads we'd taken getting there, each of us becoming the people we were, and marveled how those roads had brought us, perfect, together. We saw everything we were. Everything.

A wind struck us and we fell.

In the elevator Caroline's body in Asher's arms burned hot, and his in hers. The end had been coming and now it arrived. They ringed burning arms and legs and minds and *we remember giants* thought at the same time *sitting by a cliff* thought at the same time *we will never have us like this again* and thought *we are vanishing... oh—my—god—feel so good—that what we feel, we...*

Her brown eyes closed. On came death -

- the air was riven by a flash of Higher light and Veronica's voice.

A spectacle spread through the cabin and Veronica, arms down with threads of *crush* strung between them smelling acrid—the cart with its tureen hit Caroline's legs and the tureen levitated to the ceiling, shrouded in *crush*—and twenty-five gallons of freezing gazpacho soup avalanched down over my head and Caroline's head and our faces and we were choking, gasping, and even in the middle of losing your absolute fucking ever-loving mind your body still likes to be able to breathe, we discovered. We released each other, wiped, we spluttered cold slippery and spicy—I instantly slipped feet up in tomato goop but didn't fall because a blue jacket caught me.

"Oh... god," gagged Caroline, "what...?"

"Are you..." I tried to ask her if she was okay but choked soup, coughed, remembered our telepathy. A failing memory. I tried, but remembered, I don't know how to do telepathy. I also remembered, the shreds of a memory, sharing her soul. Ecstasy. Giving everything. Her face was slick and she wiped red sloop, I suffered a wild, reckless, inconsequent urge to *connect* to her, before that impulse faded too. A tide, slowly waning, but unstoppable, as far as I could see. Bound to return.

CHAPTER
SIX

The busboy was the first to speak.

"That was totally weird," he quaked. "Do you want me to call housekeeping?"

"Are you hurt?" Veronica asked Caroline. Not me. Caroline was trying to clean her face but without a lot of success.

"I never saw a tureen do that," trembled the busboy. "Does anyone know what just happened?"

"No one knows," Veronica said to him, "but these guests have a suite upstairs, I'll get everything situated, all will be well soon enough—ah," she said as the elevator stopped, "here we are."

I noticed that a few jackets now stood between me and Caroline. The doors opened and Alison in competent heels stood outside, already positioned with other new friends. The busboy was expelled. In the span of a mascara flutter Alison took it in. She frown-smiled and grabbed Caroline, hair to pants soaked tomato red, out of the elevator. I tried grabbing Caroline's hand but the soup slipped her away.

"Ash," she called, still blinded.

"Caroline!" I yelled. One big jacket put his arm across my chest. I pushed, but slipped, and then the elevator door closed.

"Hckkk," I protested as soup went up my nose again.

We rose one floor, to the top, and the doors opened again. This time they opened into a little vestibule of marble and glass and sunlight, and beyond that a step down to a room for enjoying a vault of clouds. The golden haze of Los Angeles was visible all the way to the sea.

The big jackets disappeared fast for employees of their size, I thought. I stood dripping in the elevator. Veronica stepped out. I waited for the doors to close, which they did not do.

"I want to know what's going on," I said, spitting soup.

"Yes, come," Veronica urged.

I'd noticed a buzz in the air again, in my ears and elsewhere, which I hoped was just tomato soup and not a burst vessel. It was loud. I shook my head.

"Come, *now*," Veronica said. "Time is short. Take this."

She held out a necklace. I did not *at all* like how fast things were going. I never like it fast, and that's all I'd been getting for weeks.

"What's that for?" I asked about her lure.

"Take it."

"Take it yourself! Somebody needs to hose me off. This—this was a brand new shirt!"

"You don't have time—"

"You spilled it on me, you hose it off!"

"Just... enraging. Like a child. Yes then. Quickly. This way."

She got a folded shirt and pants from a jacket person. I followed. I couldn't say a hundred percent, but I thought the buzz was getting louder. I had a moment of vertigo getting to Veronica's washroom while I tried to remember what had happened with Caroline. I took the clothes. I made a mess of the brilliant porcelain bath, shedding red water. The pants fit perfectly. The shirt fit okay but had no buttons in front. Under the pants and the shirt I found her silver necklace, where a thin blue crystal hung.

I took it with me on my way out to wring Veronica's neck.

She stood up when I came into her living room in the sky. "Where's Caroline?" I demanded. My buzzing got louder.

"In good hands," she said. "Clean now? Listening to reason?"

"I've got tinnitus like a jackhammer, but I hear. Explain."

"The necklace. Put it on."

"Those are instructions. I want *explanations*."

"Put the necklace—"

"Where's Caroline? Explain what's happening!" After I yelled I sat on one of her cloud couches and held my head, moaning at the buzz.

"You're infuriating!" she burst out.

"Yeah. You're late to that party. You're keeping me and her apart. Why?"

She saw how I was. Like she was just now figuring it out.

"As quickly as possible then," she decided. She leveled a doubtful look at me, which was the most familiar thing that had happened in the last twenty four hours. "Are you paying attention? Don't make me repeat this. You don't seem to be...all right, look at me. Do you remember, I told you there are Five Families?" I nodded. It was a lot of work getting lectured by Veronica, looking, listening. I hoped this was going to be worth it. "You remember, you and I belong to the Aspectu Family. You, I, the painters in Skysill Beach. We see ultraviolet light."

"What the fuck *Veronica*, my head... the point..." I swayed to the edge of the seat and made the buzzing worse.

"Stop interrupting," she snapped. "There are four *other* Families also."

"Five families, I can count, get on with it!"

"Auditus who *hear*, Nidor who *smell*, Sapor who *taste*, and Tactus, who *touch*. Think of them as sense tribes."

"What does that even *mean*? A smelling tribe?"

"The thing you must understand," she rushed on, "is that the Families have certain relationships but Tactus and Aspectu are the opposites. They are Primes. You are a Prime. The Primes are like magnetic poles, between which the other tribes exist. Aspectu and Tactus are poles opposing each other... oh my god, are you listening?"

I was listening, through my mental fog, deciding if Veronica's sense tribes were more or less outlandish than ghosts. I didn't know. I thought probably less.

"So what's the *point?*" I shouted, and wished I hadn't.

"The point is, there is attraction and repulsion between the Primes. Between Aspectu and Tactus. Like the poles of magnets. Sometimes an Aspectu and Tactus are so perfectly balanced against each other, they... bond. And those who bond this way rip each other apart. It's a short circuit. They empty into each other, then they die."

I stood up, practically buzzed blind, trying to follow it, staggered, "Spell it out!"

"This sex romp you've been having with Caroline you fool! Caroline must be Tactus—I suspected it the moment I saw you together. Such bad luck, bad timing, I don't even know how it could be possible considering her own...somehow you are precisely in opposition, destroying each other! Now please! Put on the necklace! This is what civilized Tactus and Aspectu do. The Sapor make this, it's called a neutral crystal. Asher. Do this now—if you and Caroline are not neutralized you will kill each other."

Could neutralizing be any worse than what was happening in my head? I could barely think. Neutralized, though. Something in how that sounded...

"What if we just stay away from each other?" I pleaded.

"You absolutely won't."

"Do they always die? The Tactus and... Aspectu?"

"Yes, for god...ninety-nine point nine nine nine percent of the time, yes you *die!*"

I almost dropped the chain. My hand was shaky like a junky relapse. Veronica stepped farther back as I raised the loop and watched it swing.

"If I put this... will you take me to her?" I begged.

"Yes."

The chain fell cold around my neck. My unbuttoned shirt let the crystal fall against my chest. And over the course of that first full second I didn't notice anything, just my steadily building buzz. Veronica watched.

Until something came. Like a cloud forming, gassing out from the crystal. I couldn't see it but I felt a heavy mist in the air, accumulating in wet beads all over me, like condensation on an ice pitcher: but this cold wet was sadness. A cloud of pure sorrow. The bad kind, where you can't stop it even if you tried but you don't try because you know you deserve everything you're about to feel.

Usually I'm protected from sorrow. The *Gray* takes me when I'm threatened, I swim around until it doesn't matter anymore and usually then the *Gray* lets me go. So as this sorrow began weighing thicker I wasn't really worried. But the clinging mist built up, heavier, pulled me down so I dipped into some of my minor sorrows— like how I knew I should be nicer to innocent strangers, or pay more attention to my health—the commonplace regrets.

And beads kept layering on. My arms and chest and face got thick with it. Weighing and weighing until I bowed forward and then sank into some of my very uncomfortable sorrow, like the sadness of being such a stupidly difficult brother, my failure to give my life any meaning by living as an artist, how I should go see Tante Celine more. And still it built, layer after layer of cloud until suddenly I got pulled close to my one forbidden sorrow—the sorrow of my parents. My gaze dropped to my hands. Okay *now*. I stared and waited for my fingers to stiffen. The *Gray* would never let me suffer the sorrow of my parents. It hadn't ever before.

There on Veronica's chiffon chaise, I felt my mouth convulse and twist, I heard myself cry out, and Veronica watched, lips pressed tight, as I was crushed under the weight of it. I didn't get the *Gray*.

Instead I remembered, me a maniacal little head case, a child, savage and mind-broken and unfixable, so deplorable I actually drove my parents to abandon me. A detestable and disgusting and abnormal boy who could never be loved or even tolerated. My parents escaped because I horrified them, my inability to be normal, to fit in, to function—their shame about me and themselves drove them away, which was contemptible of them but the shame—they weren't strong enough—the shame was, I knew that a better son, *a slightly better son*, could have saved them. From themselves. My only parents! Saved the family. But I'm not the slightly better son. I'm the unforgivable one who drove them away.

And that used to be my very worst sorrow. The king of them all. But now, I saw, it was no longer. And I was broken under it all and I slipped to the floor at the foot of the couch curling to contain the pain, which in the end only makes it worse, everybody knows that, but only ever in hindsight.

My final sorrow was now the sorrow of Caroline. The glad promises we'd never vow. The love we'd never make. A life we wouldn't build together and a child we wouldn't raise—a family never started, never conceived. Old age, no one to share it, then dying, and sadness missing teeth, sadness missing hearts, sadness missing each other, headless sadness, vacuum sadness. Caroline sadness. The pure acceptance of another person gone, to never come again.

I might have passed out.

I went somewhere while the sorrow cloud layered and layered. Finally I was saturated. And out from my bones, through my flesh, my skin, into the air, the cloud lifted off and I'd never been happier to see anything leave.

I came back slowly. Laying on my back. As I did I heard a whisper. Someone whispering. A name made to sound like an apology. A hand moved under my head. My body uncurled. I opened my eyes.

I lay in front of the couch. Veronica sat on the floor with me. She had my head on her lap, with her hand in support. She watched out the windows of her stratosphere conversation pit, and she was older than I'd realized, seen from below. Her hand was cool when it brushed my forehead. Her eyes were damp. She didn't look at me. She stopped moving when she realized I was back.

"Who're you talking to?" I whisper croaked.

"You lived," she observed. I wanted to argue, but that was going to take a minute. She eased her lap away and laid my head on the floor, and from there I levered myself upright. I took a few seconds assessing. It didn't help.

"It just never slows down, does it?" I finally asked. "So I guess it's true. The Five Families. Me and Caroline are these Primes."

"Terribly true," she nodded. "But what you just went through almost never happens." She pointed at one of her ears, pierced with a light blue stone the same color as my crystal. "From birth, Aspectu and Tactus wear protection. It's in the interests of all Five Families to do so."

"Why am I just now hearing this?"

"That question is just one part of a much larger mystery."

"Does everybody know this? All the artists in Skysill Beach?"

"None of them. Only the few I've told myself. How do you feel?"

"Powerful. Olympic."

"How do you feel about Caroline?"

The buzzing was gone. The underwater echoing had cleared away. I felt steadier than I had in days. I thought about Caroline once Veronica brought her up. Caroline—it was a name without a judgment against it. A word without a history. How I felt about Caroline, I discovered, was uncluttered and a little bit grateful. A storm had taken the house away. But the foundations were there. Where, maybe, something new could be made. I didn't need to hold her. I didn't want to sleep with her, live to old age with her. I *liked* her. It felt completely different. Manageable and not exhausting.

"I feel pretty okay about her," I decided.

"Well. Congratulations."

Veronica seemed to be withholding information on this outcome, but I was perfectly satisfied feeling this way about Caroline. Veronica's eyes were dry now and black as wells. I struggled up onto the couch, she stood and speculated at me.

"What happens if I take this off?" I asked, fingering the necklace.

"If you ever take that off," she said, "you will die. Either searching for her, or, more likely, finding her."

"I could just put it back on if—"

"You would never put it back on."

"Where is she?"

"She was convinced to put on her own crystal."

"She went through what I just did?" I thought about my cloud of bad sorrow.

"She would have searched you out and found you if she had not worn a necklace. And with proximity to her, your own crystal would have failed."

"I want to see her, see if she's okay."

"I don't think that's wise right now."

"Why?"

"The severing... the neutralizing process is always harder on one of the two Primes severed. In this case, it was harder on Caroline."

"Is she crippled or something, or brain-dead?"

"She's as healthy and whole as you."

"That sounds bad. You said you'd take me to her. I want that."

Veronica gave me a look resenting all my inconveniences, and then sighed. "Perhaps we should get it over with, sooner rather than later." She stood, and I scrambled, and I followed her into the elevator. A big jacket appeared, but Veronica shook her head. We descended alone.

"So, these large employees," I pointed above me as we dropped.

"Hmm?"

"Are they *sighted*?"

"No."

"But they work for you. Everybody here does."

"Yes."

"And you're going to make me just come out and ask."

"Am I?"

"Are you, like, super wealthy? Like, some kind of continent hopping plutocrat, with a mysterious agenda? That involves me somehow?"

"I am."

"Why are you running a paint store in Skysill Beach?"

"Sometimes the only way to study zoo animals is to become their keeper."

The elevator opened before I could complain about the analogy. The floor looked familiar. I ran my colors up, found soup spotting the carpet going left. I went that way and Veronica followed.

I kept expecting my feelings for Caroline to spike. Since the first moment I'd met her, laying on the sidewalk in front of Psychic Touch, there'd been a tweaky sharpness to all the things I'd thought and done around her, and those had burned hotter and higher over time, fed by an accelerant of obsession. But the neutral crystal had put the fire out. Not only eliminated the flames, but restored the forest. Caroline. My could be friend. Queen of the Past.

"She's psychic," I said softly, as Veronica and I followed Caroline's tomato tracks down the hallway. "Is that it? Are Tactus psychics?"

"No," Veronica said emphatically. "Caroline is psychic because she *isn't* fully Tactus. Cross breeding between the Five Families produces psychics. The combined senses. *Sensus simul,* you asked me about it. So Caroline is at best *half* Tactus, yet Primes—a full blooded Tactus and a full blooded Aspectu—only full Primes connect as you two did."

We'd come to a doorway in the hallway where two XXX jackets stood. The trail ended here. Veronica stopped me when I went for the handle.

"Before you go in, there's something more I need to tell you about Caroline. She went through the same violently sorrowful ordeal you did but..."

I heard voices behind the door, one consoling, one unhappy. Then a cry of anguish. It was Caroline. Veronica waved back the jackets who'd moved to keep me away from the door. A second later I was dashing down a short hall into a sizable suite. The drapes were drawn and the light came from a single standing lamp. I found Alison, seated beside Caroline at a table, her hand on Caroline's shoulder while Caroline squeezed her elbows into her sides and sobbed.

"I just can't believe it," Caroline cried. Her face blotched with tears of fury. "I never expected..."

Then she heard me and spun in her chair, livid sobbing. A silver chain hung on her neck with a blue stone. Her fingernails scissored the hem of her blouse.

"What happened?" I asked.

"What's he doing here?" she howled.

"Is everything all right?" I asked.

She jerked a step toward me, shaking her head.

"I can't have him here," she cried around the room. "He can go or I'll go!"

"Asher," I heard Veronica behind me, "it's...we must leave..." but by then Caroline was close to me, sobbing wrath.

"Are you trying to put me back in the hospital?" she screamed.

"Hospital...no, I mean...what?"

"Everything we saw, lies and lies and oh god I *won't* have it all *like* that again!"

"Caroline," I said, "calm—"

"I won't have it!" she cried.

"Okay, I..." I stammered.

"I'm not crazy, it hurts too much—move let me out *get out!*"

"Wait," I pleaded, "I don't—what happened to you I know, but what we had—it felt like painting again, what we had. I'm broken, I know, I felt it... too intense and crazy, but we can—"

"Don't you even *try*," she snarled, hands balled and hard. "You asshole—this is me! I'm not getting sucked back! This is *poison*, fucking get out get out *Get! OUT!*" she bellowed and I couldn't move fast enough so she spun around me down the hall. Alison followed. I wanted to go too but a big jacket stopped me. All my strength was gone.

"What'd you do?" I cried at Veronica. "Why's she like that?"

"I didn't do it," Veronica said. "I tried to warn you."

"Warn me *what*?"

"There is repulsion and attraction between the Primes," she explained. "Like a magnet, yes? In cases like this, neutralized too late, one of the pair orients in opposition. Nothing could have been done."

"In American, Veronica! What are you saying?"

"Caroline's Tactus antagonism toward you dominates her feelings now."

"Tactus antagonism? That's what this is?"

"At least you are both alive. Be thankful for that."

"But... I didn't do anything! It doesn't make sense!"

"Nonetheless."

"How long will it last?" I asked. She shrugged. But she made her guess pretty clear. The range was, a very long time to forever.

I was on the floor by then, so exhausted I hardly had energy for bewilderment. I had indignation and sadness but those I dialed away, bringing the color down. Or tried. I found changing the colors didn't make a difference anymore, as if my emotions were uncoupled from color after all these years. Free range emotions. Go where you want. And, I realized, I hadn't *stormed* or gone *Gray,* despite Caroline's distress and fury. Things kept getting less reliable for me.

"I'm sorry," Veronica said.

I waved her off. "This won't last. I don't care what you think. I need a drink."

"Yes. Come with me."

Elevating back up to Veronica's alcohol, the last of my strength drained away. Then I sat on her couch observing atmosphere out her sheets of glass. She poured me something clear. "Get some rest," I heard her say. "I will see what I can find about Whitney Lamb. We must discover what the umbra eye is doing in that painting." It sounded like she'd moved on already. I felt like I hadn't. After a minute her voice put my brain to sleep and then I leaned back on her cloud fabric and let the rest of me go too.

CHAPTER

SEVEN

I woke up hungry and couch bent. There was no noise so I lay a minute pretending to sleep, letting my thoughts loll out. I felt the neutral crystal, degrees colder than the skin of my chest. I wondered if Caroline's crystal felt cold. I didn't want us returning to Skysill Beach with a raw wound between us. And for some reason, despite years of evidence to the contrary, I thought a good way to clarify things was would be for me to explain them to her.

Did I even believe in Tactus antagonism? Behind closed eyes I tried recalling what Veronica had said about Family Tactus, realizing she hadn't said much. They did something with *touch*. I recalled that being psychic meant Caroline was half Tactus, half some other Family. *Sensus simul.*

The possibilities made me nauseous. I opened my eyes. The sun still shone bright in Veronica's sky tower. Early afternoon. I'd slept maybe three hours. A full meal was spread for me on a low table, somehow done in absolute silence. I took a pickle in one hand and a sandwich in the other, suddenly starving.

"You're awake," Veronica said, to startle me, a few minutes later.

She took her phone from her ear, caught half-cocked, and came to face me across my lunch.

"Where's Caroline?" I chewed.

"Good, you've eaten," she said, though I hadn't really. She gestured to employees in several jacket colors who swifted everything on the table out of sight, plates and tablecloth and the rest of my sandwich. Veronica stage managed impatiently. I'm averse to management in all its varieties, and I was still hungry.

"I need to talk to Caroline," I told her. "I want my sandwich back."

Veronica looked at her watch.

"Caroline's in Skysill Beach by now," she said. A carved wooden box was stage managed into her hands, and she lowered herself down across my empty table. She looked tired.

"I brought her here," I protested, "you can't send her away without telling me."

"Tell you? No one tells you anything," she snapped, "I assumed that was the way you preferred it. I gave Caroline a car because she asked, I didn't *send* her anywhere. Now..."

"She left because of your necklace," I spat, "before I could talk to her!"

"You're lucky you're alive," she shot back, then I saw her make an effort, and put the carved box on the table and focus on that, before something came out despite her grownup restraint. "Perhaps you might try a touch of *gratitude* some time," she offered.

"Are you kidding? You don't know me, you've got no idea what my life —"

"—oh yes yours are the deepest wounds, aren't they, no one—"

"—you have a lot of nerve—"

"—bloody hell! Do you think you're the only person who's suffered loss?" She struck the table, the only violent and the least premeditated thing I'd seen her do since I met her. She was tired, and furious, at the end of some rope I frankly couldn't care less about. "You are not the only one suffering, not the only person who made sacrifices, the entire world does not *revolve* around you, *dammit* Seamus stop acting like a *child!* I expect more from you!"

She slid her box to the center of the table. "Now! In this box—"

"Whoa-ho your box!" I slammed. "Who's Seamus?"

She stopped moving.

"What?" she asked.

"You called me Seamus."

"I... did I?" She watched the air stir between us a few seconds. Her hands came up to her face. Then, quietly, she got out of her chair like she had teacups stacked on her head, seeing things somewhere else but looking down at me. I thought maybe she was about to start talking like I wasn't there, since people had been doing that, but instead she balanced, slowly, to the couch, and sat, her hands to her mouth the monkey way, the one who won't say what she thinks.

"Oh," she monkeyed after a moment. "Oh. I see." She spent a moment staring, then nodded, and she looked even more exhausted, and I cared even less. "Well that does explain it. How very tiresome." It caught her throat like it was about to close and choke her. She turned away a minute and turned back. "It's possible I should apologize to you."

"You can try, those don't usually work on me."

"I'd avoided the idea, you see. Obviously I should have seen it. From the entire town of entitled children, *you* are the one who pushed every button. From the moment you came into the store with your insufferable bravado."

"Is this the apology, or we're skipping that?"

She reached to put a palm on each of my cheeks, which I let her do because she moved so slow it was hard to dodge. Her black eyes moistened. She blinked. She shook her head. "So... obvious. Very well. Let's start our relationship over again. And I will try to treat you as a person I've just met, with no preconceptions about your selfishness. Shall we start over?"

"I feel like we'd just make the same mistakes. How about tell me who's Seamus?" I didn't really want to know, I was just feeling belligerent and she was sensitive about Seamus. Because Veronica had taken Caroline. She claimed she hadn't, and pretty clearly that was true, but I'd decided to feel aggrieved like she'd done it on purpose because I needed some kind of satisfaction from this conversation. There's no explaining myself to myself sometimes, which is why I rarely try.

She thought about my Seamus questions and about exactly what she was going to tell me, the exact words and specific stresses she would put on them. She seemed like she wanted to get this part right.

"Seamus was my son," she said. Then she said, "He died some years ago. You are like him. In some ways. Apparently."

"Okay," I stopped her, "I don't actually want to hear that. That's triggery territory for me. But there are explanations you owe me. Since you want to start our relationship over, maybe tell something about these *light powers* you've got. Splashing soup around, mind control, god knows what. So I guess light powers exist, which is fine, it's less weird than some of this stuff happening. But then I wonder, what's the part you're not telling me?"

"I haven't told you anything," she reminded me. "And it's a very confusing question. You may not be good at asking questions."

"Why haven't you people taken over everything? *Compulsion*, you could take the fucking world. In my experience people take the advantage they're born with, and fuck everyone else."

She looked at her wooden box. She *said* she wanted to start over, but really she just wanted me to do what she wanted me to do, and I didn't think she wanted me asking these questions. I reached into my shirt and pulled up her crystal. Her eyes got worried.

"You should leave that be," she said, the way you'd say to some-one, *don't pick that scab on your exposed artery.*

"I'll wear this," I agreed, "but you have to fill me in. I've seen you control people. You say there are other ones like you, which I'm trying not to imagine. Why don't you take over, if that's true?"

"You assume we *haven't* taken over," she observed. She watched me. "How would you know? But we have not. You are right. Very good, Asher! This gets us closer to the heart of things." She looked at her box, but decided to wait. "Perhaps there's hope for you after all, which I say in the least condescending manner imaginable, because I'm taking a different attitude in my relationship toward you. Why do Aspectu and the rest of the Five Families not seize control and rule the world? We certainly could."

"And?"

"It's complicated. Perhaps we should have a cup of tea while we talk. Nothing for you? I'll have a cup."

A cup of tea came over. She took it without looking. She was excellent at tea, really skilled. I had no choice but waiting.

"There are three things," she said finally, after her thoughtful swallowing, "which limit an Aspectu's power to fabricate. The first, the simplest—most cannot fabricate at night. Only while the sun is up."

"Yeah? I saw you do it at night. You kept that Fenestram dancer from kissing you."

"I am a relino. Only a few of us have the capacity to fabricate at night. Relino hold a night charge."

"Why not conquer the world in the day?"

"The second limitation—geography. Fabrication is tied to our longitude of birth. A strip around the globe, plus or minus fifty miles north and south, and beyond that we weaken."

"Take over the city where you're born. In the daytime. What is it you're not saying ?"

"Some have tried daylight revolution. It brings... the third limitation." She did more work on her tea, very methodically tasting and thinking about tea and all the ways tea has helped the world. Finally she remembered me. "Aspectu, and to some extent the rest of the Families, have been, through history, hunted. By one vengeful predator."

"A predator."

"An atavistic force which has stalked us down through time. A… ghost."

She watched, waiting for me to point out the obvious.

"Ghosts don't exist," I said, cooperative. "That's what everyone says."

"One ghost. Only one. His name is Aeternus."

I had a superior kind of feeling. It doesn't happen often. Here we were, talking about things I was most qualified to have opinions about.

"Just Aeternus," I said, toying with the sensation. "Just that one ghost exists. Huh. So, what's this *Aeternus* look like?"

"He is never seen. A ghost *cannot* be seen."

"How do you know he's a ghost if no one's seen him?"

"For eons, through lifetimes, thousands of generations, Aspectu have felt his hand. We know him as the eternal ghost. He is ancient. He is all that remains of a time, in the very beginning, when ghosts did exist."

"Really. Where'd the ghosts go?"

"They perished in a war. So it is thought. At the hands of man. Millennia ago, ghosts and humans fought. Nothing is known of that time but that fact. We are prevented from seeing more. But after the war, ghosts were gone. And humans remained."

"Humans won? The ghost war?"

"It would seem."

"And you're saying Aeternus is still pissed about it. Not that I believe he exists."

"No one knows what he thinks, or why he does what he does, and he does exist."

"So what's Aeternus got to do with holding you sparkle fingers back from world conquest? He sucks up Higher light?"

She finished her tea. Her hands drifted to her mouth again, like the monkey, and she talked that way, very quiet, very still.

"He culls us. If an Aspectu fabricates for personal power, Aeternus will take her. At times he takes us for no reason at all. If we are not circumspect, we disappear. Those who are taken always look the same, when found. Aeternus disassembles them, spreads them out, experimentally, some say. Sometimes even trying to put his victims back together again. Endlessly looking for something. Through all time."

Sometimes I get an idea by accident. Like this time. "Hey," I said. "Your ancient tattoo. That's got something to do with Aeternus the vengeful?"

"The umbra eye—the ghost eye. That is Aeternus's sign."

I didn't see any way around it. Samantha, the forgery, the ghost eye—circumstances conspired against me so I had to confess some things. Fortunately I have years of experience sounding like a lunatic and it hardly bothers me at all now.

"I see Samantha," I said out loud. Veronica squinted, not understanding. I egged myself on. "The dead girl. Damely's girl, the one who wanted The Dancer's Kiss bought. Her name's Samantha, remember? I see her as a ghost. She's a girl shaped... floating... she's made of Higher light..."

Veronica waited as I fumbled along and then eased down into silence.

"You have seen a ghost," she said.

"I've seen half a dozen, just in the last few days. No, I must be exaggerating. I hope I'm exaggerating, I mean, that feels like too many ghosts."

"You are quite serious," she said. I nodded. "Have you always thought you saw ghosts?"

"Well, sneaky little dig. I don't *think* I see them, trust me, I see them. They tell me to do things. I have to find things for them."

"I see."

"And no it wasn't always like this. Ghost vision just started a week ago. When I saw Samantha's body. So now, with this Aeternus thing, I thought I should put that on the table. Maybe I made a mistake bringing it up."

"It was not a mistake." She decided a thing with millionaire clarity. "It cannot be a coincidence. Are there ghosts here now?" She swept her arm around the sky tower. The amazing thing was how suddenly she was willing to take me seriously. I wasn't used to that. Usually the longer people know me, the less willing they are.

"No ghosts right now," I said. "So far, I see them when I find dead bodies, which is something else that's happening more. So you tell me. You're the ghost doctor. What's it mean?"

You could tell she wished she knew how to answer that question, though she still probably wouldn't have told me.

"I do not know how to answer that. But I know some people who might."

"Let's go," I said, standing. "I like answers. This is the kind of thing I could get used to."

"We cannot go until tonight. After dark. When no Aspectu can track us."

"Aspectu... I mean, Aspectu are *our* side. Right? Or is there a side?"

"There are *many* sides. Aeternus has servants everywhere."

It struck me then how little I knew about her. I was taking a lot on her word, which goes against one of my most basic principles, not trusting anyone or ever doing anything people want me to. She did seem to own expensive real estate, but other than that she was a sparkle finger enigma.

"So what are you, anyway?" I asked. "Like, president of Aspectus Anonymous?"

She pushed her wooden box to the middle of the table.

"I am *relino*—a tapper." I saw another complicated explanation coming and it made me wish again for my sandwich. But sometimes information comes this way, in obnoxious streams, and you just have to suck it up and listen.

"All Aspectu are born sealed," she told me. I nodded, eh, go on. "That is, able to *see* Higher light but nothing more. Aspectu must be tapped before they can fabricate light. Tapped like a barrel of rum. You see? Opened. And here! We've come at last to our purpose. This is the reason I followed you to Los Angeles. Your eyes. We need to tap you."

She pushed her carved wooden box out on the table for more convenient viewing. I did not appreciate it.

"I say we leave my eyes out of this. It's confusing in there as it is."

"We have to find your root. Find the Higher color most native to you. It will help us understand what's been happening." She tried to open her box, but I held her arm.

"Ix-nay the ox-bay, Veronica. Not doing it."

"Asher. The Brazilian men, the ball of seven, now ghosts, we must—"

"We must nothing," I told her, and stood, suddenly, feeling claustrophobic. "My eyes are off limits, forever, end of discussion. Got it? Look, I've got things to do. For one thing I need lunch. Thanks for the one pickle, by the way. I've got to go find Whitney Lamb, then get back to Skysill to talk to Caroline."

"We found Lamb already," she said. "Whitney Lamb. His office was closed. His neighbors say he's been missing a month. But we found him, an hour ago, at SoCal Medical, where he's had, I'm told, a stroke."

"He hasn't been missing for a month." Just arguing for arguing sake now. "He checked in twice at the lawyer's in the last three weeks. With his assistant. Did the assistant go missing too?"

"Well," she said, "according to the people who knew him, Lamb did not have an assistant." We looked at each other, it was a little spooky, then my stomach growled.

"Would you like to come with me to the hospital?" she asked.

"I'd go," I said, "if you get them to bring my sandwich back and I'll take a vodka."

"Poor dear. Let us get your sandwich."

A crew assembled around her from hallways and doors as we headed for the elevator, then we were going down and I ate my sand-wich while we dropped, and I was not sorry to leave. We hit the lobby and the crew members delegated to evaporate on errands did so. Veronica and I glided out to her car and let her driver get us onto the freeway. Being in Veronica's world was frictionless. Everybody got out of your way. It meant I was able to finish my sandwich.

Up in Veronica's ivory phallus it'd been easy forgetting I wasn't in Skysill Beach, but now buildings I'd never seen, unknown entrances and unknown homeless people and angry graffiti began flashing the windows. I found myself wondering, again, why no Fenestram painters ever left Skysill Beach? The only ones who'd left that I knew about, my parents, had never come back. Had they come to LA? We passed side street apartments leaning so far out they were part of traffic, and freeway oleander with seabirds, and cinnamon haze over inland mountains, and I wondered, did my parents ever come here? To drive on this freeway? Had *anyone* I'd ever known ever seen what I was seeing out these windows?

The shriek of a siren past my door warned me about the hospital. It was nothing like Skysill's hospital. This seemed like the mall that ate the doctor's offices. It had to be dense with injuries and sickness and people shopping for gifts and food. Now I was noticing them, the many ambulances made me reconsider the wisdom of going in with Veronica.

The driver steamed to the curb and stopped. Veronica looked at me. I didn't move.

"Come," she said.

"I don't think the best place for me is a hospital," I said.

"Ah, of course." I kept getting the sense that she was filtering snark, now, whenever she said anything. Like flipping through some index cards to see which comment was least stinging. This time she got a card from someone else's deck, someone sincere. "You've had to spend enough time in hospitals recently."

"No. What?"

"Well, Celine being..." she saw my face and stopped making words but she looked like it was too late.

"You mean Tante Celine?" She nodded a little bit. "You know Tante Celine?"

"I do. I shouldn't have said anything."

"What do you mean, Celine being *what*?"

"Oh, dear." She tightened her lips like this was something she had very little time for, but had gotten herself into, and would be careful never to get into again. She had very expressively tight lips. "I believe you need to speak to Celine," was the best she could do after all the expressivity.

"About *what*?"

"I'm going into the hospital now, are you coming?"

"No I'm not coming."

"Why?"

"Because fucking dead bodies turn me into a garden gnome! I shouldn't be anywhere *near* a place like this. I don't know how close I have to be, or...yesterday it happened twice, and now I'm falling asleep on couches because it's *exhausting*. What the hell are you saying about Celine?"

"Your aunt is sick." You could tell that was all she was going to say. "You need to speak to her yourself. I will return as soon as I can." She looked me over, turned to her driver. "Dwayne, I'll call when I'm ready. In the meantime store Mr. Gale somewhere free of dead bodies."

We all went our mission directions. Dwayne took me a few blocks away to an upscale shopping complex where they'd be sure to clear the dead bodies out or it'd affect business. We waited. I did not leave the car. I asked Dwayne if he knew anything about Celine but he stared into his sideview mirror and grunted. I felt like I'd tarnished our relationship when I'd tried crawling back between his front seats. I missed my phone.

Forty minutes later Veronica called and we swooped back to pick her up. Night was coming by that time, and she stood out in the pickup area in her white clothes. I saw someone mistake her for an orderly and ask directions.

Then she was in the car, buckling, and we were on our way. I decided not to give her the chance to refuse to tell me anything else about Tante Celine. But I saw how the relationship between us was. There were information tiers, and I was not at the top.

She had other things to talk about anyway.

"What did Judith tell you about Lamb?" she asked. "Anything?"

"She uses him when she has art come through LA."

"Whitney Lamb is a vegetable. Brain dead. But not because he's had a stroke."

She paused to think about Whitney Lamb.

"Well, what did happen?" I asked, irritated that she'd stirred my curiosity.

"Lamb's been glowed," she said. "Someone used *compulsion* on him for too long, or too intensely, and burnt his mind out. His skull glows *compulsion* in his hospital bed. You never see this. A very gifted Aspectu, born within a few hundred meters of the longitude where the act was attempted, could glow a person this way. The doctors will be unable to explain. A clever way to dispose of someone, just a medical anomaly."

"You're saying someone did that on purpose... oh..." I saw it. "The apprentice he wasn't supposed to have."

"Yes. An Aspectu."

"Lamb supposedly goes missing, but he shows up a couple of times at the escrow office with his new assistant, and now he's full of *compulsion*. Could an Aspectu control someone with *compulsion* without other people noticing? Even up close, like at a reception desk?"

"Yes. Except for tapped Aspectu, no one would know."

"And keep it up for a month—remember, he made two visits, weeks apart."

"Eventually the victim would begin to glow."

"It doesn't make any sense," I said. I listed my problems using my voice, which is a bad habit I can't break and sometimes sounds like complaining. "Look: The Dancer's Kiss comes in, the escrow people don't know it's forged, they store it and contact Damely. She gets

Lamb to look. Our Aspectu glows Lamb to go in with him. And keeps him glowed. Why *any* of that?"

"To glow Lamb like that you need brutal intent, and great strength. Maybe we're dealing with a psychotic, perhaps torturing Lamb was the only point."

"Or maybe the point was stealing the Dancer."

"Steal a forgery?"

"No one but me would have known it was forged."

"But why come twice to steal it?"

"Maybe the first time's a trial, or something didn't go right. But it wouldn't be hard—you sparkle the guard out of the room, you pop the canvas, replace the drape, it might be months before anybody notices."

"But the picture wasn't stolen, Asher. Not the second visit or the first. It's still there!"

Then it came to me. I'm bad with linear thinking but wild leaps of logic are a specialty.

"That forgery," I said, "was only finished a few days ago. Less than a week."

"And?"

"I'm this forger. A few days ago I'm still in my studio, copying, but copying *what*?"

She was impatient. She spun palms up, pretending mystification.

"I'm not a painter, Mr. Gale. What are you saying?"

"I'm saying," I said, putting it in place as I talked, "it went this way: the authentic version of the Dancer gets shipped from Italy. The escrow house receives it and contacts Damely. Three weeks ago our Aspectu comes in with Lamb—steals it—copies it, then two days ago comes back and *unsteals* it, but leaves the forgery and keeps the original."

"Ah. Of course. Now you've stolen it, but no one even knows."

"Something else, too; Niccolo Filippi was *sighted*. To forge the Dancer you'd have to *see* sub shade color like a master. So on top of being a thief, our psychotic Higher light slinger is either working with—or *is*—a master painter. I'm saying there are almost no *sighted* painters who could pull that picture off. It's that good."

Veronica seemed inclined to agree with my theory. But it didn't make her any happier.

"All very interesting," she allowed, "but still. The important point, the missing point, is the umbra eye."

"What is it with you and this eye?" I asked.

We rode in silence while it got darker and I waited for her to answer but she never did. Finally her watch made a chime

"Sunset," she announced. She leaned forward. "Dwayne. It's time. Quickly, please."

Dwayne put his foot down. The big car sprinted out.

"Where're we going now?" I complained. "I'm feeling whisked from place to place and taken for granted."

"There is an Auditus inholding in Los Angeles," she told me, checking her watch and looking out the windows, making sure the sun was really set. "If anyone can give us insight into ghosts and the movements of Aeternus, it will be them."

CHAPTER

EIGHT

Dwayne cleaved us a path through headlight traffic, an automotive force of nature. I looked out the window and got thirstier and less comfortable with each halogen interchange we put away. Los Angeles at night became a landscape of hilltop silhouettes, tiny lights in banks against invisible stars, freeways chopping at the feet of everything.

"I need a drink," I complained, though no one cared, which often happens. We ramped off our freeway, crossed a narrow aqueduct, then we were slipping down an avenue of darkened beauty shops and dollar stores. The feet of the hills were close to us here, the porch lights draping down the slope almost to our fenders.

I spotted a sign, a door, a stool on the sidewalk under neon.

"Dwayne," I announced, "pull over."

Dwayne looked in the rearview. We both saw Veronica shake her head.

"I need a drink," I said. It came out like a warning, which Dwayne didn't like.

"This isn't the time," Veronica told me.

"I think I know when it's time to drink. I'm an expert."

"No stopping."

The bar, friendly and full, blurred away. Veronica returned to her phone. I started smelling an unpleasant, familiar gas in her oiled leather interior, a smell that reminded me of Waylon—a fog of wealth, getting results by asphyxiating other people's options. A lack of options, asphyxiation, a lack of balance and understanding—at least I was starting to feel like myself again.

"Let me out of here," I said, pulling at the door. "Here's another bar."

"We've nearly reached the inholding," Veronica said.

"Look," I reasoned, "Veronica, let's you and I just pursue our separate agendas now. That makes sense right? You go buy another skyscraper, I'll go get loaded. I have a lot of things I should think about, I need to get drunk so that doesn't happen."

"But our agendas are *converging*, Mr. Gale. I think a partnership is the wisest course."

"My last partner," I recalled, "died under his Hockney. It's safer letting me out."

"Listen to me. This Auditus compound might be the only chance you're ever given to help your ghost. Presuming you do want to help her. And presuming she exists, of course. Don't you want an expert opinion?"

"Those always come down against me so no."

"The Auditus have studied the umbra eye. The ghost eye. Think, Asher—just try, I know you're very busy—but think: this forgery appearing, and with it the umbra eye, connecting you and your ghost to Aeternus, who is himself a ghost. It is not a coincidence. Not at the very moment Aeternus is making his presence felt in the world again."

"How can I explain this?" I wondered to myself and her. It was a real challenge, since I usually don't bother explaining anything. "The key to functional insanity, like I've got, is staying disciplined about your delusions. And this eternal ghost, killing you Aspectu down the annals of time? I don't know. I feel like I have bigger problems. Personal ones."

As I said it, we passed another bar. They had a lot of them here, doing me no good.

"I believe Aeternus had a hand in killing Whitney Lamb," she argued on, relentless and exhausting, the way they always are. "So Aeternus *is* involved in the issue of The Dancer's Kiss forgery, and that makes him a personal problem of yours."

"Like I said, I have a lot of problems, your ghost can take a number. Presuming he exists. You're really not letting me out?"

She was not. I scanned the interior of the car. Like riding inside a beautifully sewn glove. Not a hint of fresh air. I kicked the panel in front of me to see if it was hollow. Dwayne threw me a bad look.

"This is that kind of car where there's booze, right?" I asked her.

"I need you lucid."

"You're decades late."

After that, all I could do was ride. We left behind any chance of bottle service by peeling up a side street into hillside residences. The road wiggled, got smaller and became a private and carefully groomed fingerling. The regular residences priced out. Our paved way twisted around a high precipice where I saw LA, farming its roads and houses in shining fields that vanished toward the distant, black sea.

A minute later we rolled up to a hilltop thick with trees. The road dipped under the trees and ran along a ten-foot stone wall that curved and tracked the hillside. Finally, Dwayne parked at an unlit curb overhung with oak, a postcard portrait of LA lights off the downslope side. A little portico was recessed in the stone wall across the road, a dozen yards ahead. Veronica unbuckled.

"We're here," she told me. "Keep your voice down while you are inside."

"No. Dwayne can take me back now. Right Dwayne? Get me to the nearest bouncer?"

"Don't be ridiculous," Veronica said. "Asher, are you hungry? Is that what this is? I have some nuts in my bag..."

"Listen to me," I ground out as she pawed her purse, "I do not want a partnership with you. I don't want a friendship. I don't want to be your intern or your project. I want to go think about my failings, maybe lose a bar fight, things that don't involve you. Dwayne drives me, or I can walk."

"I need Dwayne."

"Fine."

Veronica and I climbed out opposite doors and met at the rear of the car. It was cool, up on the hill, above the dark carpet of carbon dioxide smothering the lowlands. And above everything, always, the Higher borealis swept contrails through space. I looked down the road. It would be a longish walk.

"Why must you be so *obstinate*?" Veronica demanded.

"If I only knew," I told her, "maybe I'd be better at it."

At that moment the portico in the stone wall opened and four silent figures stepped out. All four had hair cropped short and robes of red and yellow and no shoes. I twisted extra brightness into the scene so I could flesh them. Three gave back no expression and stood unmoving, but the fourth, a small pumpkin of a shaved friar with soft and bloodshot eyes, swayed, and tapped her fingers and didn't try to hide her impatience or the dangled fifth of whiskey she held.

"I changed my mind," I told Veronica, "let's go in."

She hadn't seen the monks. I took her by surprise. She wasn't used to how adaptable I can be. In a beat I passed her and was approaching the monk quartet. "I'm Asher," I called, "does someone know where I can find a fifth of whiskey?"

I noticed the short monk disappearing back inside the portico and weaving down a path through dark foliage. Pointing Veronica out to the remaining monks I called, "I'm with her," then went after the whiskey girl.

Coming through the portico I felt my ears pop. Suddenly

someone turned the volume down. It was like walking into an empty movie theater, sound just flattened.

"Hey," I called to the girl as she ducked in and out of trees.

She turned and held up her bottle like a statue of alcoholic liberty and with a finger to her lips she blew a boozy, "Shhhh."

"I'll give you a hundred dollars for that," I pointed as I got to her. She bit the cork, spit it out kind of piraty, and took a pull and handed it to me.

I swallowed, feeling grateful. "That's all I've been asking for," I explained.

"So everybody's heard," she whispered with what might have been an eye roll or she might have been pretty drunk. Her whisper was full and perfectly clear. She held a finger to her lips another time then took the bottle back and diagonaled off through shadows on paths, and I followed the bottle. We went across a greensward, I kept wondering if she was going to fall over but she never did. We went under dark tropical trees and past some kind of midnight monkey god palace. We saw only a few other monks.

The farther we walked, the less I heard, and I was certain it wasn't my imagination, which hardly ever happens. When I tilted the bottle I barely heard slug-slug-slug. And it wasn't just my footsteps and my drinking—nothing sounded *anywhere*. Not with the silence of forests or empty rooms. It was surface of the moon silence. I clapped several times and heard nothing.

"Something's wrong with my ears," I said. I heard my voice conducted through the bones in my skull, but nothing else. Whiskey girl ignored me by not turning around.

Then I heard a slurred, "Quit yelling's not a *forest* fire." It was a clipped whisper, five inches from my face, though she still hadn't turned. I stumbled, surprised.

"What are you, a ventriloquist? Hey whiskey girl," my shout went nowhere. "Are you doing something to my ears?"

"No. Shut up. Mine'name's Nella," she ventriloquized backward while climbing some tall stone steps. I waved my hand in front of me, just out of instinct, in case there were invisible people, but it was just her voice. She sensed the wave somehow and backhanded the bottle into my palm like a relay runner, never breaking stride. She had coordinated shoulders and amazing backward aim for a person with a drunken style of walking like hers.

I had my eyes cranked way up for extra light but no idea how Nella was navigating. She never missed a step. I followed her under an arch where vines dripped, and past some stone bleachers and saw we'd come into a wide outdoor amphitheater. Nella sat on a bleacher bench. She put the bottle at her feet. I put myself on the other side of the bottle. We both looked out at the grass.

At least a hundred silent, shaved monks gathered there, motionless in garbage light thrown by the city. Nothing else lit the field. They were pairs, and each pair sat on a square few yards of yellow blanket.

Then, from somewhere came the sound of a bell. Once it started, it trailed on and on, fading. And suddenly Nella stung me on the arm with a sloppy backhand and pointed outward, to the other end of the field, to a pair of monks in robes now standing and facing each other. One had his hands on the shaved head of the other.

"Made it," Nella whispered. Though she sat to my left, her voice floated between my eyes. "Shh. Raylynne's Answering Osric."

"Which one's Osric?" I asked. "The one dressed like a monk?"

"*Shhh*. See? Raylynne's the Ask, Osric's the Answer. Just listen."

She dismissed me. She took the bottle and hit it, facing hazily toward Osric and Raylynne and the other hundred on the field. She passed the bottle to me and her eyes dropped shut for long seconds at a time, unfocused, and it might have been alcohol but it seemed deeper, like a lack of practice using them.

Out on the field, both monks now had their hands on the other's head. Nothing happened. Nella started nodding. And then a gong sounded, and one of the two monks got a little paper out from under the corner of the yellow blanket and handed it over, bowing. Then there was just the gong, in the whole impenetrable nothing of silence surrounding us. It spread a golden net of sound.

Nella left her eyes closed until the gong faded out.

"That's't for tonight," she sighed. Osric and Raylynne stumbled off the field, looking exhausted, and the other pairs went back to whatever they were doing. This time Nella's voice came from my left, from where she sat, and that became the direction I looked, and then I had the feeling I was just looking around in exactly the directions someone wanted me to look. I could smell her now, clothes, body, a day or more drinking. At least my nose was still on the job.

"So," she whispered, disinterested but loaded and genial, "information. I've gotta fill your holes. That's t'assignment. What're the holes you need filling?"

"I'm all holes," I shrugged. "Information goes straight through me. But you have the bottle, tell me anything you want."

Nella snorted and hit me with another backhand, which did not feel pleasant, then leaned her head back with her mouth open and stared at the sky, starless from LA ground light, the way turkeys do when they want to drown in a rainstorm. I thought maybe she'd passed out.

"This's's noisiest city," she whisper-lolled after a minute facing the missing stars. Her voice came from the sky above her. It was a great trick. Her lips didn't move, as far as I could see, and how do you talk with your head bent back that way? "Don't hear how people live in it, you know? The endless sound's, like, *batshit crazy sounding*."

"I hear nothing at all," I whispered back. I can whisper. I'm adaptable. "I don't even have ringing in my ears. Are you doing that?"

"It's the sound'ome."

"The soundome?"

"Sound. Dome." She pointed up. "You *are* holes." She laughed. This time I dodged the backhand. "Sound dome keeps's city noise supp... res... sed. Protection too. Battery. Anyhow here I'm." She shrugged, like I might be interested or maybe not, she didn't care. I knew the feeling. "My Answer got food poisoning, I told'er *do not eat the prawns,* and that's why I'm drunk but they asked me to, hey meet that noisy boisy, so what're you most stupid on?"

"Who answered the food poisoning? What's that mean?"

"Tami." She pointed at the amphitheater. "Ask and Answer pairs. All those ones. I'm'n Ask. Tami's my Answer. She's sick'n I'm here with you. Gotcha?"

"No."

"This's training exercises for'n up... coming deployment. Any day."

"You're what, ninjas?"

"Listening teams." She drank again.

"That makes total sense but I have no idea what you're talking about." I took the bottle back. I tried to lose interest in her story, but she'd been assigned to talk about the field of monks and she kept doing it.

"Every Ask guards and cares for her'r his Answer," she slurred. "Food'n water, wash'n dry, piss'n shit. Now it's making sense?"

"What's wrong with the Answers so you have to nurse them?"

"Nobody's *wrong,*" she whisper snorted. "The Answers'r down hearing."

"Are you the clearest drunkard they could get to fill my holes?"

She snorted yet again and backhanded me a third time while I was blinking. She had a loopy style, it came in sideways and kept catching me by surprise. My arm hurt.

"Okay," she said, "here's for your holes—you know energy? Energy never destroyed—right? Conservation'f energy. Thermo... namics. Right? Changes form, but not destroyed. Not ever. Right?"

"Oh, conservation of energy," I said. Like it was all coming back to me.

"Sound waves'r energy, propagating the universe, gotcha? Sound goes into forever because conservation of energy, right? Softer and softer, fading and fading, but never gets destroyed. Sounds dinosaurs made? Still bouncing round the world. See? That's what an Answer listens for. Old sounds. Information. We get facts, figure things out. Archeology maybe spying. Maybe that's not my problem."

It took me a minute. It was too foreign a thing to come clear fast.

"No shit," I whispered finally. Apparently I was interested after all. "You see the past in sounds?"

"Not *see*," she derided. She weighed several things in both her hands. "More for your holes, Aspectu boy. Auditus got lots'a shit, echolocation, three dee spatial. Weapon sound. Audible sculpture—like the umbra eye. But under in here? Sound dome in here? All we do's prepare Ask'n Answer pairs for battle."

For the first time in my life I wished the teacher I'd been assigned was less drunk than me.

"You listen into the past?" I said slowly. She nodded. "And hear things that happened?"

"Listen for *one* thing that happened—because's hard, focusing so deep, an Answer mind holds one question at a time, carries it down, farther farther, hearing older older. Ask connected way up above. Steady tracking the question, keeping the mission, she's the only one can get'er partner back, Asking the right question out loud."

It was almost as outlandish as my own outlandish ability *seeing* ultraviolet light. Veronica called them Five Families. But they seemed more like five species. I drank and stared out at the monk field.

"How long's an Answer helpless, listening like that?" I asked finally.

"Depends if the thing they're tracking's easy, could be days, sometimes it's months'n you could get a mission, go down *years* for old'nough sound. That's rough."

"You're saying missions."

"You betcha, Aspectu boy."

"Don't call me that. Say Asher."

"Ok whatever you want *Mr. Gale*," she said, and in the middle of the sentence her voice changed to Veronica's in a disturbingly perfect reproduction. Nella cracked up at my face. I'd had enough experience to lean away so her backhand went wide and she toppled, then looked up aggrieved at me.

"So what's your mission?" I asked as she climbed back to her seat. I asked mostly to distract her, so she'd stop hitting me.

"Don't have one yet," she shrugged, "but once Tami's up it'll be the same one everyone's getting." She dropped the last of the alcohol down her throat. She motioned to the field, the sky, the world. "Only one mission now for all of us. Find'n umbra eye. Figuring out'bout Aeternus. Same's your mission."

"That's not my mission. I haven't even decided Aeternus is real. Let me ask you this—you know anything about a ghost girl who goes around carrying a cup?"

"Ghosts'r gone, died in the ghost war. Focus on Aeternus."

"Screw Aeternus," I said. "What's he got my ghost doesn't?"

"Listen me, *hey*," she roped me around the shoulders and leaned into me, round and bald and intimately, collegially drunk, and whispered, "I like you how you drink, but you're'n asshole. Don'be'n asshole, man, too many assholes everyplace. You know's true. An everybody hears, you don't wanna *teacher*, or a *friend* or a *partner*, *but*, keep getting rid *those* kind pretty soon only people left are *enemies*, an' *believe* me Aeternus's is enough enemy. For all us. Gotcha?" She burped. "Now you gotta go." She made her voice come from behind me when she said that. I turned instinctively to see nothing there, and felt confused, which was not atypical.

"Where?" I asked, turning back and sounding plaintive from the advice and voices issuing places unexpectedly. I didn't feel like I'd had enough to drink. Then I heard fairy bells, soft and sweet.

"Follow the bells, Aspectu boy, they're waiting for you."

So I did. The bells took me deeper into foliage and they got worried if I had to sit down at all. "Fuck you, bells," I muttered, no sound, but then clarified, in case Nella was listening, "and I mean fuck you as a compliment since I'm not an asshole." Jingling pathed me under arches and up viney hillocks and then stopped me at a long, genteel burrow, rock-carved into the hillside, no door, just a stoned in hall leading in to a distant, dimly lit chamber. An open mouth.

I paused a moment on the lip of that hole. I didn't like the look. Things were getting more confusing and unsatisfying, now there's a mysterious tunnel in a hillside—you didn't have to be a rocket scientist to see there'd be more LA problems in that hole. We had problems in Skysill but in LA they had lovers short circuiting to death, people with their brains blendered. I preferred my Skysill Beach problems, which are, I tend to over-analyze and I also under-analyze and I'm no good keeping cars. I'd gotten used to those problems. I felt unprepared in LA.

The bell fairies, getting tired of my introspecting, rang out and lunged, fed up with me. I considered flipping them off but it didn't seem worth the effort, they were just bells. I followed them underground.

The walls of the tunnel were cold, hewn granite, but when I reached the end I found lamplight and a small office, like a bank waiting room, carpets and footstools and weak lamps casting shadows, like they didn't care one way or the other for light at this branch. A door across the room opened and a monk stood, holding it wide. I know an invitation when I see one, though usually I turn those down.

"Come, Mr. Gale," I heard Veronica, just a few inches in front of me. "I'll introduce you."

The inner office was more velvet finery and flavored tobacco shadows and mellow wood administering its empire where the sun never sets. And more very weak and badly placed lights. Veronica used an uncomfortable looking, high-back chair, and was holding a present in birthday wrapping as I came in. She put it aside and stood.

"Asher Gale, meet Kuparr, one of my oldest friends, Baton of Angels Inholding."

Kuparr was the height of a floor lamp, with an overhung brow as sharp as my elbow and white eyebrows like thistles. Under that were eyes hanging three quarters closed. His white hair hung to his hips. I thought maybe he'd once been an old man softly amused by the world's antics who now wasn't amused by anything. He bowed. I resisted doing it back since I didn't feel flexible.

"Nice catacombs," I whispered at him. "You have problems with bats?"

"You see, Kuparr, what he's like?" Veronica whispered. She turned to me. "Kuparr assigned a girl, an Ask, to bring you up to speed. Did she fill you in?"

"Yeah," I said, "like a Ted Talk. I admit to lingering questions."

"Please sit, Asher," whispered Kuparr. His whisper came in ribbons of forest calm, but I resisted that too.

"I don't want to get too comfortable," I said, "because that makes me uncomfortable. I followed your ring tone to your lair. It's been a long day. I haven't had enough to drink. Am I kidnapped? What're we doing?"

"You have many questions," Kuparr said, agreeing, though with what I couldn't tell. "It is said, the questions we ask rule us, but the answers destroy us."

I looked over to Veronica. "I don't have energy for poetry. Does it make more sense after he's warmed up?"

"I will be direct," Kuparr whispered, and there was steel in it, which is a very unexpected thing to find in a whisper. "You have seen ghosts. Tell me how it happened."

"That's a confusing story."

"What do you know of the umbra eye?"

"I know nothing of it."

"Did you recognize the eye when you saw it painted?"

"No. Maybe ask an ophthalmologist these questions."

He nodded. He turned to Veronica. "You are right," he whispered to her. "I hear no lie. Only confusion and a certain..."

"Intolerable hubris?" she suggested.

"Self-loathing," he offered. "Yearning."

Kuparr and Veronica regarded me like a taco truck price list. I disliked it.

"Veronica says you know more about ghosts than I do," I said to Kuparr.

"About ghosts," Kuparr observed, sad, "there are only questions without answers."

"You believe they exist, that's a start."

"I believe one exists. There is only one. Perhaps the things you see are not ghosts? This we know: ghosts existed alongside humans in a time so distant it is no longer even audible. Mankind and ghostkind went to war. Afterward, the ghosts were gone. Only Aeternus remains."

"If mine aren't ghosts, I want my money back," I said. "Let's compare, see if this sounds familiar. Mine are Higher *light*. They come in a pose. They're always holding their hand out with a ghost picture, a ghost ring, something. If you take the real picture to a psychic you know, and she reads the past from it, the ghost gets to go on to, you know, wherever the next stop is."

Kuparr and Veronica took a moment to have a conversation I wasn't allowed to hear. It was just me and the bone sound I made clacking my teeth just to have at least a bone sound.

"Asher," Kuparr told me after that, "I want to explain to you the nature of the umbra eye. But first I need to explain Auditus art."

"Picture tells a thousand words," I said. "I'm a visual person, just show me. Also, whatever the monks had for dinner, I'll take leftovers. Veronica doesn't really feed you on her kidnappings."

"I offered you nuts."

Almost instantly a monk came with a bowl of gruel, absolute ambrosia, as good as any gruel I ever ate. I chewed, waiting for Kuparr's art lesson. When he had my attention he started by disagreeing with me, which settled me into my sweet spot.

"I cannot show you Auditus art," he began. "The Auditus craft siglium. From sound. You walked through several siglium on your way to my office just now. Only Auditus create, and only we perceive, siglium. They are three-dimensional auditory sculptures. A skilled artist can make a siglium that lasts a hundred thousand years if sourced in the deepest sounds of the environment where it stands."

I raised my hand politely. Some gruel dropped. Veronica rolled her eyes. Kuparr called on me.

"This umbra eye," I said. "I remember Nella boozing me. The umbra eye's an audible sculpture?" I felt okay drawing this all out with more questions, as long as they were going to keep feeding me like this. I'm pretty simple to work with if people put in any effort at all.

"Yes," Kuparr agreed, very solemn and slow. "The eye is Aeternus's sign. He has left it, planted it, a flag, if you will, once every fifteen hundred years, going as far back in time as the Auditus can hear. We know of 507 umbra eyes scattered over the globe. We're confident many, many more exist. We traverse their histories, searching for clues. But Aeternus clouds his actions. He is... ghostly and impossible to know."

"Every fifteen hundred years?" I asked. I motioned to the serving monk that I'd like more gruel by licking the bowl and tossing it to him. I kept the spoon. "What happens every fifteen hundred years?"

"All we know," Veronica whispered, "is every fifteen hundred years Aeternus conducts a bit of a slaughter."

She shook her head, like it was inconvenient and vexing, this slaughter. I don't know how she pulls that off. "Every fifteen hundred years Aeternus falls among the Five Families, killing, vanishing people, searching and laying waste. The slaughter culminates in some mysterious ritual, or game, or judgment. Some call these culminating events his quorums. At each quorum, every fifteen hundred years, he plants an umbra eye. Going back to the beginning of audible history. Hundreds and hundreds of thousands of years. And farther than that."

I got a sudden, chilling idea. The investigator kind. "Is today..." I whispered, "is this the fifteen hundredth year? There's a slaughter coming?"

"No," Kuparr whispered quietly, which is another funny thing you can do when you control exactly what other people hear. Some of your whispers are quiet, some are conversational. "It's been just over five hundred years since the last quorum. Almost one thousand years left in the cycle. But something is stirring. There are unmistakable… signs."

"I've been saying it for *years*," Veronica snarled, "but the Fabrica council refuse to see—patterns, activity, violence we trace to Aeternus. Attacks, people vanishing. Dissected and spread. He is preparing."

"So hey, five hundred years ago," I mathematized, just to show I'm well rounded, "that's about when the Dancer's Kiss was painted." And then it hit me. I'm hard to hit but sometimes it happens. "Wait. Aeternus's last quorum," I whispered slowly, "the one five hundred years ago, the High Renaissance—what was the date, exactly?"

"Aeternus clouds the exact dates," Kuparr told me. "All we know is the year. 1492."

I made a guessing face. "The umbra eye Aeternus planted that year was found in Florence. Right?"

Kuparr's eyes went from three-quarters shut to all open for the first time since I'd come in the room. He nodded.

"The thing is," I explained, mostly to myself, "Niccolo Filippi painted the original Dancer's Kiss in 1492. In Florence. The years match up, the umbra eyes match. The location matches." I followed that up with some context, which I'd recently learned could be an important element of a work of art. "From the design of the painting, religious iconography, it's likely a celebration. Maybe a ceremonial depiction. I wouldn't be surprised if it's your quorum in 1492. Why a dancer, I wonder?"

"The Dancer." Veronica stared. "Tactus?"

"Could it be?" Kuparr muttered into his whisper, another thing it appears you can do. He exchanged a look with her. "Depicting the Families?"

"What's this?" I asked. You really had to stay on your toes around these people. They had a code or something.

"Family Tactus, the family of touch. They are represented by the Dancer," Veronica told me. "Just as Aspectu are represented by the Painter."

"But why only Family Tactus at this quorum?" Kuparr asked. "Why just Tactus?"

"Maybe there are other paintings." She turned to me with a question. It was disconcerting. "Could there be other paintings?"

"You'd often see something like this as part of a series," I told her.

"Kuparr," she spun to him, "do you understand now why you must consider deploying to Skysill Beach? Everything points there. These Aspectu painters collected like cattle, the umbra eye appearing on this painting, depicting a *quorum*...Skysill Beach is a nexus. We need an Ask and Answer pair there, for years I've been asking! We must hear these secrets out—you must understand now!" A thread of fury actually made its way through her whisper. Kuparr getting sloppy? Maybe Veronica knew the trick.

Kuparr closed his eyes and stood. He stayed that way for a moment, then left his eyes closed and went past me to a small wooden stool where he sat. If his eyes had been open he might have looked deep in thought, but the way he was he looked like an elderly sleepwalker. He worked the muscles in his jaw, once or twice he faced blind toward Veronica, then turned away. I got the sense he was having at least one other conversation. Veronica saw it too. She likes being in on all the conversations so she wasn't happy. These Auditus all had multi-track minds, I'd started thinking.

Eventually, our little umbrella stand of a monk sighed and lidded up his eyes.

"By speaking this," he said, with a note of deep formality, "I terminate their mission."

I saw Veronica startle. I liked seeing she could do that. Humanized her.

"You're saying," she whispered, "all this time they've been there?"

"I'm feeling left out again," I observed, "and I'm still hungry."

Veronica took a breath so she could start another round of explaining things to me. I bet she was as tired of it as I was. "Kuparr has an Ask and Answer pair in Skysill already," she said. She looked at Kuparr. "For how long?"

"Twelve years," he whispered back, "twelve years they have been there, since Skysill first appeared as an anomaly. Remember, it was I who brought Skysill to *your* attention. The pair have been there, cut off, searching. Obviously, I could not speak of them."

"Obviously's not the word I'd use," I said, "you people—"

"He could not speak of them," Veronica interrupted, cutting right to the answer before I could snark up a good complaint, "because swimming *deep* in sound, as an Answer must to go back so far, any merest perturbation creates ripples, confuses the record. A mention of their names by anyone who knew their mission. Or a mention of their mission. Ask and Answer pairs must be embedded and forgotten, never spoken of. If this Answer has been submerged so long— twelve years! extraordinary!—the journey must have been deep and far indeed."

Kuparr nodded, rose from his little seat, went to a wooden cupboard to retrieve a leather dossier, and dropped it on his desk.

"They will have heard me within one minute," he said, "but I'll send formal notice. He will not want to return if he hasn't found an answer. Pierre, the Answer in Skysill Beach... he is the strongest we have ever seen. The finest of his generation. My protégé. After twelve years, he, of all people, will have learned something. Something..."

We all seemed to notice it at the same time—the *not silence*. Veronica spun to face Kuparr. I had a moment of dizziness as all the mute sound reappeared at one time like an elevator door opening on a raging party. Even muffled underground the difference between absolute silence and regular silence was huge.

"Hey," I asked, "do you guys hear that?"

"The sound dome," Veronica said, full volume. "What's happening?"

"The dome... collapsed?" Kuparr puzzled out, his eyes still closed. He was far away. Narrating. "The wardens are silent." He opened his eyes. "We are under attack." He stood suddenly.

"By whom?" Veronica asked.

His eyes opened and flew to her, baffled, fearful. "Aspectu," he said.

"At *night*?"

Beneath my feet there was a thump, a blow conducting through stone and packed granite. One of the useless lamps began rocking.

"Stay here," Kuparr told us abruptly.

He took his monk assistant and ran out the way I'd come, through the antechamber, down the hall, and I watched while the thick doors hung open, and I heard screams, far away and high.

Only a few seconds after the doors closed I noticed my hands clenching into fists, and Higher light flooding the room, and I jerked my stiffening body around to see Samantha.

CHAPTER

NINE

My ghost body popped from my flesh with a snap like I'd pulled my foot from deep mud. Momentum lofted me up between my shoulder blades, and then I floated spectating over my crown of hair. My ghost eyes were locked, my ghost neck wouldn't turn, but I made out Samantha hovering peripherally to my right, and Veronica pacing in front of both of me between a standing globe and a wall map, not noticing any of the ghosts she shared the room with.

The floor shuddered again. Something blasted our hillside. This tremor knocked the globe over and sent the ball of continents rolling.

"It can't be Aspectu, the sun is down!" Veronica shouted to no one. I realized she'd been shouting for a minute or two. The globe rolled past her feet. She stared at it, then at me.

"The sun's been down for hours!" she insisted, waiting for me to admit it, like sun tracking was a responsibility I'd failed at. My flesh was frozen in exactly the pose of insouciant bewilderment people are used to seeing, which meant Veronica had no idea she wasn't looking at me when she examined my flesh eyes. Veronica was a deeply conventional person in many ways, I thought, a little smug.

"This is ridiculous," she complained, kicking at the globe. "I'm going to go see what's happening. You wait here. Do you understand? Do not leave the office!" She was getting the idea at last that I might not be paying attention.

"Maybe I will," I ghosted sullenly, "and maybe I won't."

"*Mn ghh aaa m grss,*" my flesh body gargled out.

She invested several valuable seconds considering my monosyllables, and how I'd keep wasting her time if she kept talking to me, and during those seconds the floor bounced again, the most violent shake yet. She yelled about me being infuriating—for once I agreed with her, but I didn't know what to do about it—then she rushed out the doors and down the hall the way Kuparr had gone, and just as the doors closed again a flash of *crush* flushed the hallway walls. It shot down the burrow from the opening on the surface. Veronica faltered. The door closed.

Another convulsion ripped the floor. My flesh body tottered. He was in a lot of trouble—he'd already been drunk and now no one was steering him. I had horror movie feelings watching him teeter back and forth as the floor racked, but he didn't go down. When the floor steadied I remembered the puppet master game. I walked him toward the wall map, then winched him around to drop into Veronica's overstuffed chair. I hoped it would keep him out of the way.

And all the while I moved my flesh body, my ghost body pivoted, automatically pointing where flesh me stood.

"God dammit Samantha!" I ghosted at her off at my side. I watched my flesh mouth hock up noise, like *grgh grndgrf lmambamnn!* If only I could see her face, I thought, I'd really lay into her, since even dire circumstances like this don't affect my tendency to fixate on trivia. And then I remembered, if I wanted to see Samantha while I yelled—and I *did*—I had to get my ghost oriented that way.

It was a great pleasure having a project so intensely personal but meaningless, like moving your ghost around. First, I thought, I'll need to transfer out of my ghost body back to my flesh body. How had I done that earlier? I'd skipped from corpus to other corpus.

Like... this, I thought, and with thinking it felt a kicking off sensation, a pushing the wall in a swimming pool feeling. Just glide over.

Once I pulled myself aboard flesh me in his chair I had a critical look at ghost me.

He hung five feet from Samantha, off to the side, six inches from the floor. Steaming up Higher translucence like that he cut a more imposing figure than flesh me, no doubt of that. *Dominion* wrapped vivid mummy lights over the surfaces of both ghosts, who each watched my drooling flesh in the chair with their unblinking intensity, like they'd discovered a celebrity overdose on a street corner.

I could see her now, I couldn't yell at her, not from flesh me. So I tried rotating ghost me in place like a top, to turn him toward her, but he didn't swing on that axis. Ghost me would never ever face away from flesh me, it was one of his stupid rules. I shuttled him farther back, through a desk and chairs, and he liked doing that okay but from that vantage I only got a view of Samantha's back. So I swung him around behind flesh me like a tetherball. He disappeared past my shoulder but I had a sense of his position and I lined him up so from back there he'd be looking over my flesh shoulders at Samantha. Then I kicked off again, to the ghost side of the pool, and hoisted up.

Darkness was everywhere. I panicked until I realized I'd pushed ghost me into the rock wall behind the chair. I'd hung ghost me in stone hillside. I jumped back to flesh me, yanked ghost me closer— just by feel— jumped back and from there, finally, looked at Samantha.

It'd been a lot of work setting it up. In the end it wasn't worth the trouble. My dissatisfaction with her faded in my generalized dissatisfaction with the rest of my life.

"You really know how to crash a party," I ghosted at her. My flesh body went yowling away, pronouncing gibberish. He looked like he might bite his tongue. Samantha didn't disagree about party crashing. In fact, in general, Samantha kept all her opinions to herself, assuming she had any. In most ways she was the best, most accommodating company I'd ever had.

"So you know these people?" I asked. "These Auditus out there? Is that why you're here?" Another giant fist slammed the ground and rolled the globe Veronica had kicked farther into the room, under a rattan footstool.

"Seriously, Samantha what's the *deal*? Why are you *here*?" I pleaded it out. "I mean let's do each other the courtesy of not pretending this is a coincidence, you appearing here—in Los Angeles—the moment there's some unexplained attack by Aspectu. I mean right? It's not a coincidence? I don't think it's a coincidence. Or it's your thing now you just pop up? It's inconvenient! You're there in my office, you're at the psychic dormitory, you don't say why, and I keep splitting into two bodies, I have to get together which, *by the way,* it's no picnic doing that, it's bathing in a bucket of hell."

She accommodated me by not speaking, and holding out her goblet full of holes.

"Okay yes I know. You have your goblet, I know you're a ghost, blah blah, you wish you weren't, maybe—I don't know what else you'd be, if you stopped being a ghost, have you thought about *that*? —you have problems, but why this pop in thing? Teaching me a lesson? Yes I probably haven't been at my genial best recently, maybe somewhat shittier than usual, is that what this is? I mean I haven't been shitty to Caroline, but maybe other people, I don't think I was, I hope not, man that's a mess, you know who I mean? Caroline. I barely know her, a few days and all of a sudden we're—I never pretended I'm not crazy, you know, what do people want? People and ghosts? And also do you think we should be worried about these explosions?"

Complaining to Samantha had a clarifying effect—I clearly saw I'd lost track of time and that Veronica hadn't returned, and that we'd been or currently were suffering an attack of some kind, and it started to bother me. I thought I'd like to know what was going on.

When you're incorporeal, it's easy to lose track of things like battles, Veronica coming and going. Time.

"So listen, moving ghost me around do I have, like, a *range*?" I ghost asked her. "How far can I move this ghost body away from the flesh one? You see where I'm going with this don't you—what if I moved ghost me up through the ceiling and up through the hillside so he was up there somewhere and then I slipped up into him, could I get a look outside? Is that something you can do? Samantha? I'm going to try it."

Slipping from my ghost body to my flesh body was now a second nature feeling. I pulled ghost me in front to see what I was doing. I tried raising him, I was happy to see that up was an axis he recognized and he stayed feet down, pointing four feet above flesh me. Getting him places was effortless, like orienting a flashlight around. If he was behind me or in a wall I couldn't tell what the flashlight was lighting up but I knew it was doing something.

With a push, my ghost slid up through the ceiling and disappeared, and after a small interval of blind levitating I stopped him, kicked from flesh, touched down in ghost, found total darkness and hillside. I needed a few round trips like that, but I got ghost me up, into the open, floating above a slope of chaparral, looking over the Auditus compound, and beyond that at the sweep of cityscape—a ghost surveying the City of Angeles.

Through whatever thread of connection it was that held my flesh and my specter together I sensed, far below, an overpowering urge to throw up. Ghosts are not immune to vertigo, it seemed, they just pass the feeling along to the part of the system with a stomach. There was no closing my ghost eyes and waiting for it to pass since ghost eyes don't close. Not that I would've closed them if I could. There was too much to see.

It was a Higher light show.

From behind a low hump of hill there rose sizzling shafts of *compulsion* which grew and faded and cast shadows in sickly shapes through the jungle trees. To my left a pocket of foliage and fortification opened into a plaza where *wander* and *crush* pulsed, where monks with poles and fists whirled, striking everywhere, in a frenzy to hit enemies I couldn't see. Several fell even as I watched, flattened horribly by an unseen force and spreading bloody on the stones.

Below me was the burrow opening, and light from the entrance spilled the path, and a hundred feet away from that I saw Kuparr with his hands funneled to his mouth, standing in a circle of monks facing him. His body convulsed—I had the impression he shouted though I didn't hear anything—then my body in the cave shook as a blow struck the hillside, flinging gouts of turf.

A smear of *crush* appeared at the edge of the Auditus circle and then a huge stone lofted from a temple building, tinged with *crush*, flew through the air slow and easy, headed toward the monks. Kuparr oriented his cupped hands to the stone and convulsed and fragments blasted off it but it floated on. The monks ducked, some scattered, then the massive stone stopped lofting and dropped, loco-motive fast, to crush several monks, including Kuparr, and below me in the office my flesh ears registered another thunderous blow.

I spied Veronica near the monks, crouched among tall bushes. She was deploying her own *crush,* attempting to slide monks out of danger, but when Kuparr was crushed she stood and cried, or seemed to, her voice outside the range of my flesh ears below ground. The stone rose again to drift toward Veronica and then, where Veronica had been standing was a flash of *wander* and she wasn't standing there, and another *wander* burst directly below ghost me, and Veronica staggered into view and down the burrow.

Suddenly a star of *dominion* split the darkness above Kuparr's remaining monks. It dropped into their midst. It was so bright my ghost eyes lost track of the details. I'd never seen *dominion* like this. It was brutal. Relentlessly bright, it exposed the cracks in the world everywhere for the few seconds it stayed, before it flashed out of existence again.

The monks had scattered. I saw a woman run through the battle site, leap the crushing stone, come up the path—a redhead in dark clothes. There was a flash of *wander* around her, and another flash below me, and the redhead appeared at the burrow mouth and flung herself in. Far away I heard a voice calling my name. I pushed down and rammed back into my flesh body.

Veronica was bent and screaming into my flesh face where I sat in her chair.

"Asher! *ASHER!* My night charge is finished, we have to run—now!"

She didn't look great—in fact she looked grey as driftwood and she could hardly stand, but she was trying to pull me up on my feet.

"Helloooo…?" hollowed a voice of playful menace from the hallway beyond the closed office doors. Veronica went into overdrive getting flesh me out of the chair. I couldn't tell where she wanted us to go. As far as I could tell we had an armed and dangerous Aspectu lurking in the only hallway we could take to freedom. We were stuck.

"Helloooo, anyone home?" called the voice, coming down the hall, nearer and nearer.

Veronica gave up on flesh me, turned toward the door, but it looked like desperation and not a plan. I pushed ghost me through the closed doors and into the hall , then jumped to him and from there I saw a girl, long red hair, face streaming wet like mermaid death, doing fatal curiosity at our door, closing the distance down the hall.

I had to get mobile. I had to get my bodies back into one place. My flesh body sat behind the door, out of view, but it didn't matter. I was good enough at the trick by this time, I could ram his eyes crossed and pin them, just by feel, and when I did it my ghost body got sucked back through the door, heading for flesh me in his chair. Rotating in the air as I came, flying backward so I slammed my flesh where he sat trembling, his hands clenched in psycho fists, his face a silent scream, so two bodies slid to cohabitate the one body space. The pain started.

Heat burned me in strips, head over heels, but I squeezed, hands and eyes, and forced the bodies together so they started to fuse. The heat grew, I was molten hell scorching agony. But the bodies did fuse, the Higher colors of my ghost went out one by one, bottom to top: *choke-compulsion-reason-crush-farewell-wander-bleed* until the only thing left was a shining ball of *dominion* around me. Burning. Melting. Flesh.

My body fell from the seat, crying out, onto its knees on the floor. Veronica turned. The *dominion* cloud expanded around me, through the floor and the wall and the ceiling, and the pain passed a threshold, where it defined me. Now, I thought. Now! Go, I thought! Unpop! Go down my arm!

But it didn't go. It wouldn't move. The *heat* grew. The *pressure* rose. And I thought, I hadn't been holding anything in my hand this time. No keys. No phone. I saw it. No place for *dominion* to go. The agony, impossibly there was space for more agony, went inward, deeper, eating, and soon I'd be a pillar of *dominion* and pain and die. My flesh hadn't taken a breath in a long time. It couldn't. I was going to pop and end like a light bulb.

The office doors blew in off their hinges. They bounced over the floor like playing cards and slammed and shattered the far wall, a shimmer of *crush* sleeting the air from the opening.

Despite it all Veronica heard me, turned, bent where I'd fallen.

"*Asher*," I heard her, "*are you…*"

She touched my shoulder.

That's when *dominion* made its move. It shot up past my shoulder blade, out my back, a high-velocity exodus—the heat eased, my chest released, I gasped a breath as a ball of *dominion* flowed out of me, not down my arm, but up through Veronica's palm.

I heard her gasp. The entire pounding heat of *dominion* ran up and disappeared into her, filled her, and I lost track of it. I looked up, both of us confused, and suddenly her eyes narrowed. She changed from haggard-last-gasp zombie to aviator-alert action lady in half a second, I watched as both her eyes crossed *outward*, toward her ears. It was sickening to see. And in her hands there formed balls of *farewell,* and a dark bubble of *farewell* distended out around us, sudden as cannon smoke, and it froze. Like we were in a cave. We watched the rest of the office through an opening in the cave, far away.

The redhead nosed into the office. Dainty as a hunting panther. Sweating. Wondering when the fun part would start again. She prowled to a stop on a whicker carpet.

"Come oooout," she suggested, "come out come out, wherever..." She slow turned. Drew her gaze over us. Didn't see us. She looked straight at our little doorway in the black. She wiped sweat off her cheek with the back of a finicky wrist. After another turn she shrugged. Then she backed toward the door.

Veronica began to tremble. Her breathing came with guttural effort. Her crossed eyes were slits. I tried to sit up, but she kept a hand on me, to stop me moving. I didn't like the look of our dark room, though. I felt like the darkness was coming closer. It reminded me to check my fingers. It would be a hell of a time to go *Gray.*

The redhead got through the door and another explosion of *crush* lit the hallway, and the ceiling above the door and the rocks above the ceiling in the hallway came down, the entire hillside dropping in. Veronica groaned out, our dark little room went away, dust billowed, we both fell forward, gasping in swirling debris.

I crouched on my knees and ankles, but only because I lacked strength to fall over onto my side. I spit grit and slobber. Veronica looked at her hands, laying on her back, in amazement. Then looked at me. "What in the name of heaven have you done?" she faltered out.

I wanted to tell her what I'd done, it was a pretty interesting story, but what stopped me was another flood of *dominion* firing up to my left. Another ghost! Before I even looked I felt my hands clenching. My brain cast around—grab something, my brain told me. Get something inside your fist for *fuck sake NOW* but it was too late, poor brain, and my hands were curled, tight and empty. No keys, no phones, no steering wheel to drain the *dominion*. Maybe I'd just stay this way.

Ghost me popped out. Flesh me knelt on the floor so ghost me appeared torso deep in the floor behind him. Our heads aligned. From the edge of my ghost vision in the direction of the *dominion* glow I saw the ghost of Kuparr swirling Higher.

"Tell me!" Veronica was sitting up now and demanding answers of flesh me. From my ghost I puppet mastered my flesh face toward her so she'd think I was listening. "What have you done? Why was I... able to do that?"

I stood flesh me up. He was tottery, but he did it. Good boy, flesh me. Partly I just wanted to see if I could, because if I had to stay a ghost—no way I was going to do the *dominion* squeeze again without something in my hand—I thought I should work my flesh body out a bit, get him limbered.

"There's a new ghost, so, yeah, I'm stuck here," I ghosted at Veronica.

Mmanggumassndruphhhht tobl, flesh me spit at her. Veronica got ready to shout at me. I puppeted up one of my flesh body arms and waved the fisted hand, miming to her, *stop—a train is coming!* It got her attention. I puppeted both his arms wide, miming *wait here while I think of something!* She cocked one eyebrow. I puppeted up two bent arms in front of me to charade *two words*, and then one arm, for *first word*.

"What the hell are you doing?" she wondered.

I puppeted *never mind that one start over*, then held up *one word*, and pointed a fist at my ear to do *sounds like*.

"Are we playing charades?" she asked. I puppeted a fist *on the nose*, then repeated *sounds like.* Then with club hands I put a bread slice in and levered down a handle and waited and caught what popped up and ate it, and Veronica said, "You are eating toast."

I didn't know how to mime *you might be a judgmental megalo-manic but you are some world champion charades player* so I just did *on the nose* again.

Then I repeated *sounds like.*

"Sounds like toast?" She stared at me. I made flesh me nod. I could tell she already had it, from the way her eyes darted the room. She said, "Ghost?"

I had fleshy nod more, then made him walk a straight line to ghost Kuparr shimmering beside his desk, which wasn't second nature yet, all the puppetry, but I felt like I was getting better. Flesh me looked almost natural once I got his arms to swing opposite his legs. I stopped him beside Kuparr and puppeted up a club arm to point.

"There?" Veronica said.

I got my ghost close to Kuparr and then Veronica and I stared at Kuparr, though only one of us saw him. Kuparr had in his extended hand the leather dossier he'd taken out before the Aspectu attacked. Other than that he was just an ordinary ghost, with *dominion* in Higher cat's paws patting the other Higher colors into Kuparr's shape, keeping him tied in place with a tendril above and a tendril below.

Veronica waved her arm inside Kuparr. She said, "You're claiming a ghost is standing there? Is that right?" I puppeted a big nod.

Veronica expressed skepticism—who could blame her—so I puppeted fleshy up to Kuparr and leaned him toward the ghost so he bumped, chest to chest. Then I puppeted flesh me's feet back, but kept him leaning, so if you couldn't see the ghost he looked like he was leaning his body on thin air. Veronica walked through ghost me to get a better look—not pleasant—and waved her hands under flesh me's hands and under his chest where Kuparr supported him. Then I puppeted him back upright. I could see Veronica starting to believe. For show and training purposes I had flesh me fold slowly down over Kuparr's outstretched arm with the dossier, and then had him raise his arms and legs and float in the air. I wished I could make him say *wheee.* Veronica gasped. Flesh me slipped off Kuparr's arm and fell onto the floor, and bounced like a mannequin in a hurricane.

"Yes, fine," she said, "I believe you." She watched flesh me stagger back to his feet and reached an arm to help. I was the first one to speak.

"What now Kuparr?" I ghosted at Kuparr, which sent flesh me yodeling and surprised Veronica. "You're expecting me to take your dossier to Skysill for Caroline, I guess? Well let me tell you Caroline's not really in the picture anymore, so what do you think of that? And *honestly*, why is this even my *responsibility*? Plus how are we even supposed to get out of here with the door blocked? Maybe you think I can squirrel my flesh body up over those rocks in the doorway but I don't think so, he'll break his neck. There's no fucking way I'm crossing my eyes, Kuparr, I'm telling you. I've had enough. I'm thin from it."

"What does this ghost look like?" Veronica asked after flesh me had babbled to silence grunting saliva. She was fascinated by him. He was her new favorite experiment. I puppet charaded: long hair guy, short guy, guy who owned this desk.

"The ghost is... Kuparr?" Flesh me did *on the nose*. On the desk lay Kuparr's dossier, and I had flesh me scrape that off the desk into his fists and posed him like Kuparr was posed, and Veronica guessed it right away. "Kuparr is holding this?" *On the nose.*

She took the dossier. The leather was smooth, cracked—a used looking case. Leather ties held in shut. When she undid them we saw a variety of sorted papers. The top page had an address, somewhere in New Mexico. Veronica thumbed them, shaking her head. But then she stopped shaking because she'd figured it out.

Each page had a single address, in the center, and nothing else. "These are the mission files," she whispered. "The deployed Ask and Answer pairs. In Paris, Sidney..."

She turned a page and stopped.

"Skysill Beach," she said. She showed the paper to flesh me, but he didn't care. She turned it back and read out the address, "478 Skysill Canyon Road, Skysill Beach, California."

As soon as she said it, a change started in the Higher light around Kuparr. It got brighter. He now had both his arms at his side, no longer holding his case. On his face stretched exactly the same expression he'd had before, with less of one thing, more of another, so it was almost gratitude. *Dominion* began its million car pileup flashing Higher light rampage, and all its spinning, and brightening, then explosions to sparkles, and finally the fading. The tendrils of *dominion* drew up and down, pulled away, returning wherever they'd come, and Kuparr was gone.

I found myself in my body. Simple, fast, two of me jump-cut together. I went to my knees. All my youthful vigor and strength was gone, and I'd never had much to start with. I took deep breaths while Veronica watched.

"You're fucking amazing at charades," I gasped when I could speak.

"Yes. A childhood spent not speaking the local language. Are you... normal?"

"Jury's out. Kuparr's ghost is gone. I thought you said Aspectu can't sparkle at night?"

"Most cannot. Only certain... and even then, very few could perform this kind of wholesale, wanton destruction."

Veronica was staring at her hands.

"When I touched you... something came into me," she said carefully, thinking back. "Like standing in midday sun. And I could fabricate. And then, after a time, it ran out, as if I'd used something up. I was able to put us into a *wander* co-incidence. It should not... be possible."

"There were three Aspectu up there," I pointed outside above. "The redhead, another one doing *compulsion* over the hill, and another one battling monks by the wall. They were all doing Higher lights."

"It felt like... you were a *battery*?" she wondered to herself

"It happens when I come back after being a ghost. I get filled with something."

"What?"

I pictured the *dominion* star that appeared while the redhead was flattening monks, but I didn't have the energy to get into *dominion* with Veronica.

"Is being a battery a thing?" I changed the subject asking.

"It most certainly is *not*." She thought about it, and thought something she didn't like. "None of what they did should be possible... unless... maybe there was someone like you. Powering them out there."

Veronica seemed to be making other realizations too. She made realizations fast, her face was an engine for that kind of thinking.

"If you truly saw Kuparr's ghost... if he has perished... that will be devastating," she reached for better words but got throat stuck, stood holding the paper with the Skysill address. "This will all have been a waste unless we find this Answer pair and hear what they have learned."

"I always thought it was Caroline," I said out loud, having my own realizations. "I thought it was: I brought her an item and she made the ghosts go away. Now I think it's me. I make them go—I learn whatever it is a ghost wants someone to know. Sometimes there's a psychic, and maybe they congregate around her because she's the best chance they have, but sometimes I just hear it... like this address... it's not her it's me."

Veronica lost interest in my realizations. Who could blame her, they were pretty esoteric. Instead she started picking her way through the rubble in front of the door. I was still recovering from trans-spectral gymnastics, so I just watched. At the impassible door she looked up. I did too, and we saw it, a glimmer of stars. The whole hillside had collapsed and there was an opening that led up and out.

"How do you even do that?" I asked, coming to stand beside her, meaning ruin a tunnel.

"*Crush*," she said. "The color concerned with heavy and light. Gravity."

"Impressive trick."

"You have no idea."

She stepped up on the pile, agile as a goat, climbing toward the slit of night sky, while I struggled after her, not agile at all, at the end of a long day just continuing to get longer. She stopped when her head rose through the hole, perched on a lip of stone. I waited while she squinted and assessed landscape. The dark air flowed down on me, cool and dry.

"Are they gone?" I asked.

"Yes. The police will come. There's a fire down the slope. We need to be away before anyone arrives."

With that she slithered up and out onto hillside and I followed. Standing beside her I recognized the view from my ghost surveillance, the light pools of LA, the inholding spread below us. Veronica headed downslope, very carefully. I saw the fire.

"Where are we going?" I demanded. It's just the tone that comes out naturally. I can't help it. "The way we came in?"

"Dwayne will meet us at a gate near the bottom of the hill," she said. "Hurry."

"You know, it's occurring to me..." I started, and then we came up on the body of a monk, crushed beneath a grey temple stone, as a roach beneath a heel. The kind of thing that pushes me *Gray,* except in this case a ghost floated beside him, holding a book by Anne Rand.

And snap. My hands curled and I popped out a ghost. My new *chroma storm.* I know from experience you can't be *Gray* and *chromatic* at the same time. It hurts a lot, and then you just can't, so why even try? But once again I had nothing in my hands. Why hadn't I thought ahead and grabbed a rock if I was going for a walk on a battlefield?

Veronica hurried away, oblivious, slinking through cover in the dark. I revved flesh me up and started puppeting him furiously after her, falling behind as he stumbled on roots and his own feet. I'd only recently learned to walk him at all and skulking was beyond his ability. Veronica turned the corner of a shattered stone temple and vanished, then reappeared looking for me.

I got around the corner myself and suddenly I dropped into one body. I bent, held myself on my knees, breathing hard.

"What is it?" she wondered, not saying what she'd really meant, which had been, what is it *now?*

"Dead body," I panted out. "We passed it. Ghost."

"I saw the body." She gave the night around us an appraisal. "I'm afraid there may be more."

"If there are dead bodies," I advised, "slow down, it means I can't talk, or walk fast, because I'm steering long distance. Because I'm a ghost. Ok?"

"*You* are a ghost? Or you *see* a ghost?"

"Both. Apparently it wears off when I'm past a certain range." I said that with more confidence than I felt, just to get her moving. I wanted to get as far away as I could, as fast as possible.

She nodded and led us down the path, parting branches and scanning the sky. I palmed a stone and followed.

Soon we came to a path and I thought it seemed familiar, then a little archway with vines which I recognized as the entrance to the amphitheater. The first thing I saw, coming into the open, was that Nella wasn't benched anymore. She'd left behind the empty bottle. The second thing I noticed was dozens and dozens of dead bodies out on the grassy field. Each attended by a swirling Higher ghost.

And the next thing I noticed was the back of my own hair from eight inches away.

"Oh jesus fuck," I ghosted. *Manna manna phhussev*, my flesh mouth whispered.

On every yellow blanket on the field lay a dead body, and all their skulls glowed *compulsion*. Among those prone figures staggered fifty living monks, tripping, sometimes making noises, falling, rising and veering off. I watched a monk very near us trip on the monk at her feet, struggle for a moment to rise, then lay still. A ghost rose from the body.

"What is this?" I ghosted. *Shhlemp nnrornn dphtire*. Veronica's voice shook when she spoke.

"This... is beyond horror," she moaned. "Cruelty beyond... the Asks have all been glowed. Just the Asks. And now the Answers..."

"*Mnnganaam?*" flesh me demanded.

"The Answers are forever sundered," she whispered. "They have no way back to the present. They are lost in sounds past."

"*Wnnughman?*" flesh me wondered. "*Shwemph?*"

"Within hours," she told me, because there could really only be one question I'd ask, "the Answers will begin to die, one by one. Some, the strongest, those who truly know themselves, may last a day. But as they settle farther and farther from the present, falling deeper and deeper... waiting to be Asked back home... eventually they fall too far. The sickest torture. Unspeakably cruel. Meant, I think, to send a message."

The little moon had come up, a daub of orange tarpaulin positioned near the horizon, and it cast unwelcome light into the soup bowl of ghosts and dead monks below us. Some of the bereft Answers let moans up into the sky, but most tottered, drifted, silent. I watched one Answer trip on a yellow blanket, and saw the little paper under the edge flutter free. She lay motionless. A moment later her ghost whirled Higher.

"And I led them here," Veronica whispered. I was happy to be a ghost that moment. I didn't have to think of anything to say. I could feel anything I wanted. Which was the worst kind of mixed blessing. Not that much of a blessing.

I puppeted flesh me after Veronica to the edge of the field and stood with her until, with a deep breath and a backward glance, she stepped onto the grass to cross that field of death.

"*Huunh,*" I demanded. She ignored me. I had no choice but follow —she and Dwayne were my ride. I stepped off. We picked our way around bodies and spiraling ghosts. In the middle of the field flesh me came face to face with an Answer. He was less adrift than the others. He almost seemed purposeful. His eyes were filmed with devastation, and distance, but he tried, a lot of mouth work, to get words out, then seemed to lose track of me. He turned away. At his feet I saw a slip of paper, and read: *You are an Answer, so give yourself now: what did Master Kuparr have for dinner ten days ago?*

Veronica had made headway while I'd stopped. The last thing I wanted was to get left in this field of death, and I hurried flesh me along, until we were out the opposite side of the field, and I started down a stairway carved into the rock, following. Eventually I rejoined my flesh. Now I heard sirens coming, and smelled smoke.

"That's just…" I said, waving behind me. Veronica paused to scan the sky.

"Yes," she said. "Aeternus."

I felt it coming then. Just like with Waylon. Veronica and I had a bond. A horrible thing. I couldn't ignore it, which is very unusual for me, there's hardly anything I can't ignore.

"Okay," I admitted, "I guess we're partners. I guess Aeternus is real. He's a very bad ghost. Because that back there… is there a plan?"

"Wait until morning, return to Skysill Beach," she said.

"But the Answer pair there," I said. "Shouldn't we get back as soon as possible?"

"We need sleep. If I am going to lead these Aspectu to the last Answer in North America, I will do it in the daylight. When the field will be level."

We got to the wall and exited the inholding and I was surprised how happy I felt when Dwayne sluiced up. We were moving before the doors closed. Dwayne knew his business. Veronica's car floated smooth as a Pacific tide. We left the flashing emergency lights behind, and got on a freeway. I started dropping sleepy in the leather. Veronica on her phone was arguing with people in a language I didn't understand.

I want to go back to Skysill Beach, I thought. Back to Caroline. No that can't be what I want. That will kill me. Then my eyes closed.

CHAPTER

TEN

The sky was still dark and the air had a desert chill when a phalanx of hotel security hustled me from the elevator on the ground floor and scuttled us through the lobby of Veronica's hotel empire state building. The phalanx loaded me in the back of a black Suburban very like her other Suburbans or maybe the same Suburban, complete with Dwayne as driver. He eyed me in the rearview. I tried to let him know, with just my eyes, how happy I was to be getting the fuck out of Los Angeles.

During the night I'd woken several times feeling the cold of the neutral crystal like a menthol nail on my chest. I felt it now. I didn't like it. It was a reminder of something I'd failed at. I get tired of those. While I was disliking my necklace Veronica was outside the car issuing last minute instructions to a group of whatever they were, scribes or ninja spies—who could tell with these people? Veronica was taut and jumpy and kept glancing above and around, until a hotel ninja ran up with a small box and she seized it, turned, and leapt into the car.

"Go, Dwayne," she commanded. "Time is of the essence."

Dwayne knew what that meant—we went fast. Veronica opened the box and took a new phone out, then handed it to me.

"We'll need to stay in contact." The phone was on but had no bars. "The danger is growing. Pieces are beginning to move."

"I'm not learning a new phone number," I scoffed.

"I had your old number transferred."

"Don't you need permission for that?"

"Not if you own a cell phone company." She pointed to my new phone. "The account will process in a few minutes. Try not to lose this one."

"I didn't lose the last one I melted it. Cell company. Exactly how rich are you?"

"Richer than you can imagine. Not nearly rich enough."

"I don't get it," I complained. "Why are you in Skysill beach running a paint store?"

"Because no one else is qualified, Mr. Gale. With one exception. And he died last night."

"Kuparr," I said. She didn't nod. She didn't have to. She looked tired and sad and I felt a dangerous throb of sincerity when I said, "I'm sorry about that."

Sincere's a very risky position for me. But my world was slip sliding. The only *storms* I had these days were ghost ones. Which meant maybe I was free to feel sincere about anything I wanted. Which felt like, at best, inconvenient.

"Kuparr's loss will have devastating repercussions," Veronica was saying. "We must make good use of this final gift." I noticed she'd taken out the paper with the Skysill address, was holding it like a precious talisman. Veronica was remembering.

"I had heard of him, Pierre." She spoke to herself. "It was Kuparr who saw—before I or anyone else—how important Skysill was. I should have guessed he'd place his prodigy there. People spoke of him in amazement. An authority on the umbra eye. The things he would hear for us one day. The secrets he would reveal. Now he may be our only hope."

"Hope for what?"

"Showing us our enemy at last." She pointed her scientist eyes at me and the subject changed like a magic trick. "What do you mean your phone *melted*?"

"It's a thing that happens."

"Try communicating complete thoughts. You might surprise yourself and like it."

"Okay, it's a thing that happens when I see a ghost. I guess I'll just say it. It's going to sound fucking crazy. Are you ready? When a ghost comes, I pop out of my body, and then *I'm* a ghost. It's a different kind of *chroma storm*. And when I cross my eyes and squeeze to get my ghost body and my flesh body back together something builds up in me... an eighth Higher light. I call it *dominion*. The *dominion's* got to go someplace to get out of me, so it goes into whatever I'm holding. That's when phones and keys melt."

"There are only seven Higher colors."

"Beg to differ." She raised her eyebrow. "Now you'll explain how science works."

"Yes. Ordinary humans have three sets of rods and cones to process color. Homo Aspectu have four—as do hummingbirds and a few other animals who see ultraviolet light. Technically, we are tetrachromats. But within the ultraviolet spectrum there are only seven wavelengths of color. You only have receptors for seven."

Arguing with people like her, the ones who are right because they've thought a lot of it through in advance, is useless. Usually I do it anyway, of course, but I was out of energy. After a small silence, she reached to the floor and raised her beautifully carved wooden box, and the subject had changed again. It was a little hard to keep up. Probably that's how she made her money.

"We need to tap you," she told me quietly. "We must."

"The eye thing? Listen to me—my eyes are off limits."

"We must find out what you are!" she insisted. "These people are extremely dangerous. They clearly know more about us than we do about them. You must be able to protect yourself. We have to find your root!"

"You go opening my eyes, you don't know what the fuck you'll find, so no—end of discussion!"

My voice had gone loud enough to get Dwayne's attention. He cleared his throat and rolled one of his shoulders to show how thick and limber he was.

"It isn't painful," Veronica insisted. "Not for you."

"Drop. It."

She sighed. My new phone chimed. The sound I'd been waiting to hear. Active messages.

"Finally," I said to the car at large. "That's probably Caroline..."

But it wasn't. Seven notifications were texts from Amelia, and one was a message from Tante Celine. I ignored Amelia because that's what she'd expect me to do, and listened to Celine.

Her voice was just a small sail, stirring in the faintest breeze.

"Dude, this is... Saturday night. It's Celine. Hey I'm shipping you down some canvases. It's all your old work, what's stored up here, and it's half the stuff I've got from your mom and dad. It's all getting picked up Monday morning and dropped at your house. Before you call to say anything—I'm not going to change my mind. This is your life, Ash. You gotta try to own it. If there's someplace else you want it sent, call me tonight and tell me, but don't say the garbage, and don't say Amelia, she's already got her half. So remember..."

I stabbed pause. "Wait—what day is this?" I asked Veronica.

"Monday, darling."

I called Celine at home and got her machine.

"Hey," I started, with some heat, "what the hell? I don't want my old paintings. Or my mom's or dad's you know that. I can't even get *into* my house, don't send anything, it's locked and I lost the key and I'm not near there. Just throw the paintings in the trash!" I hung up. Then I listened to the rest of her message.

"... what I said, I'm not keeping them. I'm not giving them to Amelia,

I'm not throwing them in the trash, dude, you have to take them. You have to..."

I paused again and called in another message.

"Fine," I messaged, "if you're not... just send them to this office, the office of Asher Gale, it's in the Bradley..." I wrestled out one of my cards, "it's 1577 Beach Front. Third Floor. Number 2. I don't understand why you're doing this."

I hung up and unpaused her message to get the end. "*...take them. Also, there's some things I gotta tell you and Amelia. Strange things, I don't know, maybe I should have told you years ago but I promised... I don't know. Anyway. Don't forget, dude. Monday morning.*" Then she coughed a swamp and the message stopped.

Veronica was looking out the window pretending she hadn't heard. I texted Amelia—*what's going on with Celine?* But knowing Amelia's morning routine, which didn't start until the afternoon, I wasn't holding my breath. I turned to Veronica.

"So how'd you say you knew Celine?" I demanded. She gave a small sigh, as if just remembering she was in a car with me was enough to break her.

"I didn't," she evaded.

"But you do know her," I recalled for her. "You told me, you said she's sick."

"She comes to the store for glaze," she said. "We've become friendly."

"Tell me what's wrong with her. You owe me that much."

"I should never have mentioned it." But this was one of the responsibilities that came with partnerships, and she was a person who confronted responsibilities. You could see it. One of her few weaknesses. "Well, it is too late now. Celine has lung cancer."

"Celine." It was meant as a question but didn't fool Veronica. She waited. "Are you sure?"

"I only know what she told me."

"Told you? Nobody told *me*!" Veronica looked vaguely sympathetic, or maybe one of her shoes was pinching. "Why wouldn't she tell me?"

"Did you not notice? Coughing? She's grown much weaker?"

"I mean... things sometimes get past me. I have a lot on my plate."

"Well," she shrugged, leaving her opinions in plain view, "sometimes one must ask, you know, before one is given the truth."

I sent Amelia a text complaining about Celine.

"I'm sure she's fine," I said to Veronica. "Or they'd have told me."

Veronica wasn't committing one way or the other on that. She had too much on her plate.

The sun wasn't up but the sky was yawning light east of the turnpike Dwayne wove us around. He took all the express lanes, pumping the breaks, and I waited for Veronica to complain about getting thrown around but she was preoccupied and worried, taking calls in foreign languages. Once or twice I heard the name *Pierre*. She seriously wanted us in Skysill as the sun came up, she prodded Dwayne if he slowed.

I couldn't tell if LA ever ended—the enthusiastic concrete of the place was endless—but an hour after we'd left the hotel we peeled onto a new freeway cutting west, up the backs of coastal hills, and the quality of light gathering over the hilltops was suddenly familiar. Ocean light.

Skysill Light.

Another fifteen minutes brought us up and down the father side, past the train tracks and a train starting north, the same one Caroline and I had tested out for public sexual misconduct. Then the sun broke the horizon, and Skysill came into view at the bottom of an alluvial valley. The Pacific Ocean eating the edge of the continent. The ribbon waves.

Dwayne kept the speed up. The tourists were still sleeping pina coladas off so we made good time. Again and again I felt myself reach for my new necklace, stop halfway, drop my hand. Veronica noticed and said nothing and didn't need to say it to make her position obvious.

"We should arrive in fifteen minutes," Veronica said.

"Let's drive by Caroline's on the way," I suggested. "I mean Psychic Touch, not Three Paths. I think we should check on her."

"No, we have to hurry," Veronica said. "The sun is coming up."

"Let's just look in at her shop. Or maybe it's closed. I can leave her a note."

"She will not want to talk to you."

"She'll want to talk. Believe me. You have no idea what went on between us."

"It will not matter."

"Oh?"

I showed Veronica my new phone and I showed her me, dialing it. I listened a few rings.

Caroline picked up. She didn't say anything. Everyone in the car wondered what was going to happen. I guess including me.

"Hi, it's Ash," I told her. "I'm getting back into town, just wanted to check in." It didn't sound like me. After two or three seconds her voice, sleepy, came back. "What?"

Veronica wasn't listening, very pointedly. I bent away from her. This wasn't one of my best plans, I saw. Just the only one I had.

"You left before we got a chance to talk," I explained to Caroline.

"I know that."

"So have you... there's this necklace. I was wondering. You're wearing one?"

"I'm wearing it."

"Is the crystal always cold? Every time you touch it?"

She combed the silence. It took a moment.

"It's always cold," she told me. "It's cold right now."

"I keep touching it. I can't stop."

"What do you want? Why are you calling?"

"Get together? Talk? The thing that happened in LA was weird and I want to clear up..."

I curled tighter around the phone, wishing I'd waited to make the call, feeling suddenly like it might not turn out the way I'd predicted to the car at large.

"You know the worst kind of crazy?" Caroline asked finally.

"I know a few different kinds."

"The worst is wanting what never existed."

"Okay, look, let's skip what happened in LA," I hurried. "I'm just calling to make sure we're still friends."

"We were never friends."

"Right at the beginning? I thought we were. Before it got complicated."

"We were opposite poles the second we met. We short circuit."

"We got a little trapped in a room of crazy, but we escaped. It's just us now."

"I'm real glad you escaped the crazy room, but I didn't. We barely know each other. There's been enough damage done!"

"I was never trying to damage you, I — "

She lost patience. That's what happens to people I talk to.

"I'm not saying *you* damaged me but *there it is,* there's *damage!* It's not going away. Whatever happened, to me, to us, it's done. Stop calling. I'm not like you, Ash."

"Well no don't be like *me,* that's a horrible idea."

"If you care about me just stop calling."

"But these necklaces... how're we supposed... you know, I didn't want any, like I didn't..." I was trying all my explanations, but then the situation officially exceeded my verbal capacity. They all do, sooner or later.

"Please," she said. "Don't make me hang up on you."

I heard longing like ice in her throat. Heard her waiting for me to get on with it.

"Okay," I said, "whatever you, you know I'm not trying to hang— okay. We'll just... go separate ways. No hard feelings. I'll fade into your past. You fade into mine."

"Oh my god don't make a country song out of this Asher. Just say goodbye."

I wasn't thinking fast enough. She waited quite a while. Finally she did hang up.

The car was full of people looking other directions. Even Dwayne seemed uncomfortable. It was the one bright spot in the whole situation.

"I am sorry for this, Asher," Veronica said. "Tactus and Aspectu. You're better off far away from each other. To tell you the truth, it is unexpected she'd speak with you at all."

"So what's all your concern for Caroline, anyway?" I snarled. That's the way I do it when I'm confused. I know it's not attractive. "Why've you been *consulting* her? Why so interested?"

"Why am I interested?" she snapped out. "Look around you for once. Here in the middle of this massive, terrifying collection of untapped Aspectu, there is also a hillside district of psychics. Why do you think he's done that?"

"Who?"

"Aeternus of course! I've been *consulting* her because I am trying to discover what horrible fate he has planned for them. For all of us. But the psychics are impenetrable. They will not say a thing to me. They will not let me into Three Paths."

"You're not missing much. It's like a huge hippy sanatorium."

"You've been in?" I shrug-nodded. "How did you manage that?"

"Just my charm," I told her. "You know anything about a broken Path by the way?"

She didn't. We rode another moment in silence, while I thought about Aeternus. Apparently psychics couldn't get any information about him. But what about the Auditus?

"So Aeternus's last quorum in Florence, five hundred years ago. How come the Auditus don't just listen back in time and figure out everything he's doing with the untapped?"

"Because the record has been expunged. All sound from that location, at that time, has somehow been eliminated. His quorums leave no historical record. Just an umbra eye, and a plug cut from the fabric of the past."

Dwayne yanked us left then, away from the ocean, and we began to wind up Skysill Canyon. The sun had come fully over the back of the coast hills and the sky was clear of fog. Veronica got fixated on the map screen in the front of the car Dwayne was following. I watched out the window. The last time I'd been up this road I'd come to question Felicia in her little firetrap cottage.

We slowed, Veronica peering upward at the sky out the windows. Calculating the high ground. Defensive positions. We pulled to a stop along a curb under spread elms. The neighborhood was still. Dwayne rolled all the windows down, and started taking deep breaths through his nose, like smelling the wonderful morning air, but not like he was enjoying it. I heard only birdsong and the wash of far away surf. We were all looking across the street at the house where Pierre lived.

"Hey," I said. "I know this place."

Past the spreading elms on the sidewalk was a white picket fence and just inside that was a border of rose bushes circling a lawn. In the middle of the lawn was a tree, and on the tree hung a swing. Twenty yards beyond that, poised on the hillside, a shake bungalow waited, its arms crossed, surveilling the street impassively.

"I pulled a friend off that swing last week," I said. "He shows up the strangest places."

"Who does?" Veronica asked.

"Homeless guy. You're not going to know him."

All three of us were out of the car then, into the ocean damp air, crossing the street silent and fast. Veronica surveyed the route, glancing sidelong at trees, shadows, cars, the air above it all. Dwayne kept focused on the little white gate. He unlatched, pushed through, stood for a moment absolutely still, inhaling, then motioned us to follow.

The yard felt very exposed to me. I started wondering, what was I even doing here? None of it was really my problem. I had ghosts to put to rest and goblets to find, I had girls who no longer wanted to talk to me even though I'd never done anything to deserve that. My own problems.

I remembered these windows, dark, drawn shades under their porch. Dwayne was all confidence and speed, up into the shadows under the porch roof. It was better than lurking by the swing so I followed Veronica up. The porch was mossy river stone. Neglected redwood chairs had coastal grime coating them. Years' worth.

Veronica kept watch across the yard. Dwayne knocked. I had no idea what my role was. So, no different than usual. Just unusually dangerous seeming.

"I don't like this," Veronica muttered. "Something isn't right."

Dwayne knocked again, then tried the door but found it locked. Veronica traded places with him so he watched the trees and she addressed the knob. I watched her cross her eyes to the outside, I saw a sleeve of *choke* form on her arm, she gripped the knob, and the handle just came off. Inside the house I heard the other handle hit the floor, and bounce. She pushed. The door swung open.

"Hello?" she trilled, very British, like someone's aunt visiting from the palace. No one answered.

"Come inside," she told Dwayne. He went in first, taking deep breaths. I stood on the porch practicing ambivalence, but a few seconds of that was all the training I couls stand and I went inside too.

We found an empty living room. Classic craftsman bungalow, low beams, small windows, plenty of nooks. The smell was thick, like undisturbed tombs just before they get disturbed. Dust frosted the floor, the shelves, and not a stick of furniture. It was exactly what none of us expected.

"Nobody's been here in years," I guessed. I hadn't been asked. Someone had to say it. "Is this the right address?"

"This is the address," Veronica said. She turned to Dwayne. He closed his eyes and drew more air through his nose. His lids flashed open. He spun. We followed him down a dark hall. He had a certain way of moving, like you'd want him with you in a bar fight.

He stopped at a door near the end of the hall and pulled it open. We saw a staircase descending under a silver chain. He grabbed that and lit a bulb, then stepped in and down. Veronica went after him.

I filed after her, reluctant. I was starting to have a feeling, a deep, disturbing suspicion, the kind you hope, you really hope, isn't true.

Dwayne reached the bottom of the stairs. He stopped. I couldn't see much. But then, watching Veronica's face, I guessed I probably didn't want to.

"Good lord no," she whispered. She and Dwayne stepped forward and my deep suspicion made me follow them. The air was even more crypty down here. Cool. Dry. Pungent as a cupboard of tubers and gourds.

It was a body, I saw, as I came through the doorway. Or rather, a skeleton. It sat in a chair, with its head up, held that way by I know not what. Enwrapping its thin shoulders and bony legs were the yellow-red robes of a monk, stained, the way the floor was stained, with what had once been wet. It was desiccated, dehydrated flesh. It was gruesome.

Too late to run. I tensed for the ghost. Seconds passed. All I saw were dust motes and bones. Belatedly I looked for something to grip in my fist. Bodies were everywhere these days. This kind of surprise wasn't an outlier anymore, I needed to come to terms with that. Maybe I could wear a ring, brass knuckles—something in my fist. But I guessed that this body was too old for ghosting, because nothing happened. All I did was stare.

Veronica took small steps into the room then stopped. Behind the bones in the chair was a pile—clothes, books, personal items. On the floor in front of the chair spread the same yellow blanket I'd seen on the field in LA. The one the Ask and Answer pairs spread when they were sounding out the past.

"It's the Ask," Veronica said, her voice flat. "He's been glowed, like the others."

I looked where she pointed. Faint as peach fuzz a thin layer of *compulsion* still crowned the top of this gruesome, skin stretched skull.

"This happened a long time ago," I whispered, putting events in chronological order, as I'm sometimes forced to do.

"If this is his Ask," Veronica sounded numb, "then Pierre is dead too. Somehow the pair were discovered. And removed. Tortured first, and removed."

"The same thing as Kuparr's monks. Glowed with *compulsion*," I told myself softly, as I bent to a pack on the floor and sifted keys, a few coins, a wallet. "Why all these clothes? All this personal crap? Did they have him clean the house and pile everything before they killed him?"

"They probably kept him alive here for days, possibly weeks. It all must have happened soon after the two of them arrived. A decade ago. It looks as though they never even moved in. But to glow him, to keep him here while his Answer drowned in a mental prison... this is sick. These Aspectu knew exactly who Pierre was, and where to find him. And they wanted to watch him suffer before he died."

"So where's Pierre's body?" I asked. The deep suspicion I'd felt was growing.

"Elsewhere in the house, perhaps. Or fallen over a cliff into the sea. Pierre's body, disconnected from his mind through his Ask, might wander a few hours. He wouldn't have gotten far."

I flipped open the wallet in the pack.

"Aldous Levi," I read. The skeleton Ask.

"We must go," Veronica announced.

Now my suspicion had become a full-fledged investigator feeling. A hard-to-believe-coincidence kind of feeling. I pushed through the pile of clothes, books, portable personal effects. *Pierre,* I found myself muttering, *where are you?*

"We should go," Veronica insisted. "The longer we stay, the more likely they are to find us."

"There's just something," I said, dropping a case of sewing

supplies, "I mean, what if this Pierre... I mean you said he was a prodigy. The strong ones last longer, right? Could he still be— "

" —no. No one is that strong."

Dwayne stood close to her, inhaling, and began urging her up the stairs. I had no desire to stay with the skeleton alone. But something held me. This Ask, a *compulsion* zombie... deep down, all his training, glowed up but maybe still wanting to protect his Answer. His only job, like all those in the field. Osric and Raylynne. Osric handing... my gaze went to the blanket on the floor. Veronica and Dwayne got to the top of the stairs.

"We're leaving, Mr. Gale," she called.

I drew up one corner of yellow muslin. I saw bits of paper. So Levi'd been working, right up to the end. Even as his mind was stolen. He'd secreted bits of Pierre's life, piece by piece, under the cloth. On a credit card I saw Pierre's full name: Pierre Laghari. Beside that a library card. A ten dollar bill.

A driver's license.

I raised the license. I knew what I would see.

Shipwrecked eyes. Deep open heart. Bottomless willpower.

Peter by the Beach.

CHAPTER
ELEVEN

For a moment I got disoriented and not just the usual kind I can drink to eliminate. For a moment I felt like all of Skysill—all the world I'd known—was on a lazy Susan and someone had spun it. The spokes of my life didn't match up to the old holes.

Peter by the Beach was younger in the license picture, his beard neat, his hair center parted. He was thirteen years older than me by birthdate. But by the time I'd met him a decade ago, he'd aged centuries, become the beach dweller I knew. Like petrified wood, a new object, a different form of him.

I'd chased him away from his own swing! They'd killed his Ask, they'd sent him wandering, but still he came here—trying to understand what had happened? To return to... the world? For years we'd stumbled down the same sidewalks and the same back alleys, we'd enjoyed the same lack of company. I'd thought he understood me in a way other people hadn't, but I'd never wondered why. And all along he'd been this Auditus prodigy, severed from the present. Lost in the past.

I caught Veronica and Dwayne in the dusty living room. The door hung open. It had no handle. It moved as the breeze dictated. I knew the feeling.

"He's alive!" I soft shouted.

"Who?" Veronica asked.

"Pierre. The Answer."

"I told you…"

I held out Pierre's license. Peter's license.

"I know him. That's *Peter.*"

She looked, flipped the card, tapped her palm while looking into space and then shook her head. "Impossible. There is no way he could be alive."

"He figured out a way."

"To what?"

"Stay here. Hang on. Hang on to whatever it was he heard. He heard something. He wants to tell us."

"An Answer's heart *stops beating* Asher. It just stops."

"I'm telling you it's Pierre. He's alive. His heart's bigger than you think."

"You're claiming he's still alive, in Skysill Beach, after a *decade*?" She sounded partly filled with scientific curiosity and partly outraged by the mere suggestion and partly exhausted by me and all my claims. Dwayne was tense in his position at the door and no more pleased having me along than ever. He clearly thought the safest course was leaving, if possible without me.

"And I might know where to find him," I told Veronica.

She did make decisions fast. You had to give her that. It's a millionaire skill.

"Dwayne, we'll take the Suburban," she instructed. "I think the inconspicuous shopkeeper disguise has to end. They must know we are here. They know too much."

Dwayne started protesting but she stopped him. "No. Make sure it's safe, then we go."

First Dwayne nonverbally blamed me for all these changing

plans and dangers, and then, while Veronica watched, he stepped out onto the porch and started inhaling.

"What's *with* him?" I asked her, feeling jumpy. "All this breathing freaks me out."

"He is Sapor," she said, tapping her nose. "They are prized as bodyguards and drivers."

"Like show dogs," I suggested. She didn't deny it. "He's smelling danger, that's your story?"

"He is smelling the probable future," she said, quietly. "Sapor process the olfactory world in gestalt. Every chemical cue in the environment at once. From that, they build an image of the very local future. Just as Auditus process sound waves to build an image of the past."

"So, basically, they just guess things that might happen."

"Sapor do not guess. They *know*." When she got a text she looked down.

"Oh yeah?" I wondered as she read it. "Does Dwayne *know* I'll say this? Angioplasty?"

Veronica sighed again and held up her phone, and I read the text from Dwayne. It said, *dickhead is about to say, Does Dwayne know I'll say this? Angioplasty?* I looked out where Dwayne was ignoring me. It was pretty convincing.

When he was confident the very local future smelled safe enough, Dwayne led us down again. We were almost running, which I thought made us even less incognito, but these two were the professional sneaks. At the car he tucked us in. He knew exactly how confused I was going to be in ten seconds.

"Where are we going?" Veronica asked.

"Doesn't Dwayne already know?"

"He's not focused on you."

"We're going downtown to the Bradley Building. So, this Sapor fortune telling, is this like the psychic thing? The Path Before?"

She shook her head. A little puzzled. Like she'd found a stock market problem that wouldn't quite break her way.

"You know the Paths of time?" she asked. "That is surprising."

"Yeah, everything I do's a surprise," I agreed.

She frowned. "What psychics do on the Paths is fundamentally different from what the Sapor and Auditus do. Psychics literally travel inside the medium of time. They move within it, or on it, time the universal continuum. Sapor and Auditus use rare physical senses and brain structures to decode information in the physical world. Psychics are not decoding anything. They move in an entirely different world."

"So are psychics a different Family?"

"They are a subset of the Families, arising from breeding either of the Primes—Tactus or Aspectu—with one of the non-prime Families."

"Breeding them? Nice. So, either Tactus or Aspectu and *then* what happens?"

"Cross Tactus or Aspectu with Auditus—a psychic on the Path Behind. Cross either with Sapor, the Path Before. Crossed with Nidor, the Path Beneath."

"What about Tactus and Aspectu together? What's that breed? Canaries? Contempt?"

"Aspectu and Tactus cannot breed. That union is always sterile. And even with our neutral crystals, the two Families tend not to interact. There are always dangers."

So my sorrow vision of Caroline and I with a family—never more than a frankly ridiculous fantasy—had officially blown away in the wind. Tactus and Aspectu and never the twain shall meet. The relationship I didn't have with Caroline kept getting simpler and simpler.

"So... Pierre," she asked, as Dwayne ran a red light. "He's real? He's a friend?"

"Yes."

He's one of my very few, I did not say. It was all less pathetic that way. What I felt at that moment was complex and full of blood and motion and loss. Full of no longer knowing Caroline, failing Samantha. It was me wanting vengeance for Peter by the Beach, for what'd been done to him. I wanted someone to pay. But I didn't bring any of that up. Vengeance is more grandiose than my usual look, it hangs awkward on me.

We slalomed up to the Bradley Building. We'd thoroughly abandoned understatement by then. Veronica had Dwayne wait with the car. I'd given Peter the office key but I knew he'd never lock the door. Not a monk in his condition. We made it to the elevator. I was feeling anxious. But eager. I felt eager to start doing something, for a change.

"Fair warning," I told Veronica as we rose. "This office where we're going, things keep happening to me there; seeing ghosts, or I get assigned something, maybe an assassin comes, I don't know, keep your eyes open."

"Ghosts are outside my purview, Mr. Gale. Assassins I can help with. Shall we?"

I stepped out into Asher Gale's hall. I flashed Higher, just out of habit, and a claret and island-sunset shirt with Phil inside shocked me motionless. He was teetering our direction down the hallway. He saw me.

"Hey Asher Gale!" he shouted.

He balanced toward us holding an aluminum busboy tray with two stacks of white salad plates and a tower of dessert bowls. I already saw the problem he was going to have. He still wore his glasses and had the same sweaty nose. I stopped to watch it. I couldn't help myself.

"Who's this?" Veronica asked softly.

"A kind of hall monitor they have here," I told her.

Phil's bowls were piled precariously but it never paid to underestimate Phil and his ability to balance things on a tray. In seconds he'd reached us. Indignation fogged his glasses as they slipped lower. He twitched his nose, failing to put the brakes on.

"What do you have to say for yourself?" he demanded at me.

"Nothing that'll make a difference," I admitted. "Phil, Veronica.

Veronica, this is Phil. Phil owns a business carrying things down this hallway on a tray."

"Don't give me your attitude, *mister*," he spat through dishes. "Don't pretend everything's normal."

"I'm not pretending," I assured him, "all this actually is normal—hard to believe isn't it? By the way what are we talking about?"

"We got eviction notices! Like you didn't know!"

Phil was tilting his face farther and farther toward the ceiling to keep attached to his glasses, and finally Veronica reached a finger in and pushed them back up, which surprised me but not Phil. I mimed her the question, *what is with that shit?*

"I help those most in need," she admitted, a little embarrassed. "Those with disabilities."

"You know who *didn't* get a notice taped on his door?" Phil demanded, including Veronica in the question now that she'd declared herself his ally. "Asher Gale! That door right there! Look! Not evicted!"

Phil's phone started ringing, he danced his bowls back while deciding what approach to take with his call in his pocket. I shot a look at the two doors within view, saw yellow forms taped below the numbers. Then I sidled for Asher Gale's door, which did not have a form on it. Maybe Peter had removed it. Veronica followed me. Phil decided to come too and brought his pocket of ringing phone with him.

"We know," he accused my back as I moved. "Dale, your neighbor in 3? Finances by Dale? There are *city records*. So we know the trust that runs this place, the corporate address is your office! We know it's you evicting us. Where do you want us to go? If you kick us out on the street we'll be homeless!"

"Peter's not here," I admitted to Veronica as I reached the door.

"Are you listening?" Phil demanded. "What are we supposed to do?"

"How can you tell?" Veronica asked me.

"He likes opening this door for people," I said.

"I may have to call a tenant's meeting," Phil threatened.

Veronica raised her fingers and crossed her eyes and told Phil *shhh*. Sickeningly familiar *compulsion* sparkled a discharge between her knuckles and Phil's lips and he stopped talking and looked puzzled. I felt a little sorry for him.

I stood before the door a moment. Please, no ghosts, was what I thought. Then I went in.

Everything was morning sleepy and self-satisfied inside, and no one was there. I flashed Higher, dialed the saturation, all in a heart-beat—no Peter, no ghosts, no sign of violence. Veronica slipped in after me, and after her came Phil, drawn in and still puzzled that he didn't want to talk. I heard the elevator ding behind me. I stepped past in and let the outer door close.

"It's fine," Veronica said to Phil. "Speak."

"This is the biggest *office*," Phil murmured instantly, turning on his heel with his tray in amazement. "You could put a whole food court in here." He put his tray on the reception desk and his hands on his hips and then pulled out his phone. "I'm calling a meeting."

Veronica turned from Asher Gale's window of inland hills. She had that particular kind of hopeless look that people in The Charles can't ever get rid of.

"We'll find him," I told her.

"He won't be any help to us."

"If you'd ever seen him clean a windshield you wouldn't say that."

Phil was on his phone pointing to the back of Asher Gale's office and expansive downtown view and extra wall space where all the forgeries were hung. "I know!" I heard Phil exclaim. "He could put a commercial kitchen in here."

The office door opened. For a moment my heart quickened. Then I heard a voice, and a second voice answering, and then through the door came a man with weeping willow sideburns wearing a blue work shirt, carrying a clipboard. Behind him came a work-shirted assistant who wore a baseball cap and carried a bubble wrapped canvas. Behind those two came a third man wearing blue coveralls, sweating and carrying another wrapped painting. Celine's shipment.

"Delivery for Asher Gale," said the weeping willow leader while showing me his clipboard. "Is that you?"

"Would it matter if I was someone else?" I asked.

"No," he reassured me, "it's okay, just sign. Where do you want these?"

"No one wants those. Leave them in the street."

He thought about it. He noticed the empty real estate in the back of the office. "I'm Cliff. How about we stack everything over there and you can sort it when Asher Gale shows up?"

Cliff didn't wait for me to agree, due to his professionalism. Instead he pulled his subordinates to him and outlined the plan. They left for more paintings and he started unwrapping bubble plastic.

"Transport only," he said, "we reuse all this."

And then he stopped. His eye had been caught by one of the many forgeries in Asher Gale's gallery. He stepped closer, like he couldn't believe his eyes, his forgotten plastic bubbles trailing, and he stopped in front of a Thomas Cole forgery: luminous river flatland at the base of a high hill, the background all in storm. Fantastic forgery. All the ones in Asher Gale's office were highest quality.

The office phone rang and Phil answered it, which seemed wrong but who was going to stop him? Veronica, who'd taken a seat by the windows on one of Asher's club chairs, told me, "It's very busy here, isn't it?"

"Like a city park," I complained.

Phil hung up Asher's phone. "The board has agreed to meet!" he announced. "We'll assemble here, read the minutes and errata, then discuss our options."

Cliff came to stand beside me. I noticed a gleam in his eye.

"That Cole landscape," he pointed with his clipboard, "that's a really amazing piece."

"It's fake," I told him. "They all are."

"Yeah," he laughed. "The Pissarro? Amazing. My guys are going to *love* it. I mean, we might not be artists, but we see this shit every day. So we know. Do you mind, could we take a few minutes and soak it in?"

"Take anything you want. Take the landscape, I don't want it."

He laughed, he was really starting to like me. His underlings sweated up two more canvases and then Cliff pulled them to the wall and they got busy analyzing a Casper David Friedrich fake where an inspiringly dour man looked out at fog on a rock. They started arguing whether modern civilization had lost the connection to nature required to understand one of the Romantics like Cole. They had strong feelings pro and con.

A woman came in wearing medical scrubs. She was from the third floor, Phil told me, and her name was Ambrosia. Phil outlined to her how I was responsible for everyone's evictions. Then Dale of Finances by Dale came in. He had a Santa Claus beard. Dale was speaking at the tenant meeting and had some notes. I asked what tenant meeting? A couple of people dressed for square dancing or a rodeo came in. Phil waved at them while he toured Dale and Ambrosia through Asher Gale's office and then checked in with Cliff and his guys analyzing the forgeries. Phil was an extremely attentive and thoughtful host. Someone with a boom box started up some Israeli pop. A party atmosphere swept through, sudden as a flash flood.

Veronica appeared at my shoulder where I stood cultivating confusion.

"This soirée of yours is wasted time," she said. You could tell she thought less of me for having a soirée under the circumstances.

"I told you it's this office," I protested. "I don't know these people."

"We've run out of leads. I suppose it really doesn't matter. And we were so close."

"What are you talking about," I objected. I had the feeling she was somehow blaming me for the investigation coming up short. She was definitely blaming me for the soirée.

"I'll admit I'm under-qualified here," I told her, "I mean, you're the multi-national capitalist, but we do have leads, we've got a dozen leads. Like, whatever Aspectu glowed Peter's Ask here in Skysill are probably the same ones who glowed the Asks at Kuparr's, right? The same bad habits. It's no leap thinking those Aspectu also glowed Whitney Lamb. They went to all that trouble *just to forge* The Dancer's Kiss. Right? Everything leads back to The Dancer's Kiss. Why's it so important? Who was Niccolo Filippi—I don't know *anything* about him. What else did he paint? Who was the person that was selling the Kiss to begin with? Why *now*?"

She took a moment to finger her phone. It was ringing. She ignored it.

"You have a flair for this, you know?" she said.

"Yeah. You're good at changing your mind and owning things. We all have gifts."

She held her finger up to ignore my compliment and answer her phone, turning away from me to speak. I backed against the wall, wondering if I should stay and wait for Peter's return. And then, inspired by my long list of leads, I got a better idea, which involved getting away from Asher Gale's festival headquarters. I slipped out the front door as someone came in with a tray of sandwiches and a cooler. Phil called to them. Someone took the receptionist monitor off the desk and started a food table. They were beginning a call roll. I put a Post-it on the door: *Peter, if you see this, I know you're an Answer. Don't go anywhere. Remember there's booze. I'll be back. ASHER.*

After walking ten minutes to the train station parking lot, I started setting off car alarms testing my key—I couldn't remember what my current used car looked like, and I was surprised when I found the one the key fit because it wasn't the kind of car I pictured myself owning. I opened, eased in, shook my head at the sad handful of melted phone I'd taken from Three Paths, still pealing out a steady *dominion* nimbus.

To get to Lady Damely's, first you veered inland at the car wash, then you angled up. She lived elevated, like the rest of them, in her case on a hill above downtown overrun with historic oaks and waxy succulents. Through a gate her lane ran under oak shade to a white gravel roundabout where a stately manor house stroked its Colonel Sanders goatee. The house was ringed with Grecian columns, for the air of authority it gave and to hold up the eaves of its double-decker porch. Pines and palms and eucalyptus circled, wild as wolf packs, but the house held them back easily with its powerful columns.

My car coughed and gouted smoke after I turned it off, but I ignored it and ambled toward the front door, partly blocked by a catering truck and an extra phalanx of columns. I took the steps and handled the knocker. I did it again and the door pulled open, not wide enough to get through, and a voice I didn't recognize floated out.

"Yes?" An elderly man, the thick necked kind that once played football in nothing but a leather helmet, inspected me. He had white hair dyed auburn and white gloves, and was dense with cold arthritis.

"Hi," I tried it cheerful. Why not?

"Yes?" he repeated. "Can I help you?"

"You must be Damely's man," I told him. He neither confirmed nor denied. "She talks a lot about you. I'm Asher Gale, I'm here to talk to Damely. Lady Damely."

"Deliveries in the back."

"No I'm here to talk." He didn't believe me. "How about this. I've got an outstanding invoice that needs to be paid. Authentication services."

"Billing issues are handled by post."

"I don't think that's still a thing. I need a face. Not yours."

"Card?" He extended a tray.

"I'm out of cards," I was surprised to find, though he didn't look surprised. "Will you get me Lady Damely? She's got to be in there someplace. You should make her wear a buzzer."

We both looked behind him, through his foyer where one wall had Impressionist marvels and the other walls displayed antebellum nonsense, and in one corner a bundle of balloons looked eager to be decorative, if only someone wanted them.

"For heaven's sake, Charles," I heard Damely scold, "let Asher in." And then Lady Damely sallied up behind Charles, eyes fixed on me.

"Why on earth are you standing in the door?" she wondered. I stepped into the house, smiling at Charles. "That will be all," Damely told Charles. He wasn't convinced it would, but he animated away. Damely watched me like the last example of a vanishing species.

"You've come about the invoice," she said. "You could have used the post."

"I don't know how that works. Plus I have other questions."

"What was it *like*?" she marveled suddenly, in soft horror. "Los Angeles?" She suppressed a shiver so she could really feel it. "What... did you *find*?"

I tallied them up. "Forgery, dead people, traffic, lots of bars but hard to get to."

"I see," she inhaled at Los Angeles, relieved she'd never go. "I have no idea how you did it. And The Dancer's Kiss, we were so certain of its provenance. How did you discover it was forged?"

She asked a fair question.

"It was... new," I told her, "but mostly, I recognized the forger. I've seen a lot of forgeries, and whoever painted this was fantastic. It's funny, you don't find *sighted* forgers. They stand out."

"Well, I am grateful for your services. What do I owe you?"

"Nothing. Our policy's the first forgery's on the house."

"How unusual."

"Right? Here's the thing." Time to chase my leads, so maybe Veronica would forgive the soirée and flagging investigation. It felt unusually proactive. I didn't particularly like it. "You remember when you came to Asher Gale's office? You said you wanted the Kiss for your collection. Nicola Filippi's an artist you're familiar with?"

"Oh yes." Her eyes got a little wistful. I noticed sounds deeper in the house, someone pounding, loud voices calling back and forth. "Filippi did five paintings in this Kiss series, you know. Two are lost, it is thought, The Alchemist's Kiss and The Musician's Kiss. For years there were rumors of the third, The Dancer's Kiss. It was said to reside in a private collection. Overseas. And then Samantha came to me with the auction. It was so exciting, because of course I myself own the final two, The Hunter's Kiss and The Painter's Kiss."

It's humbling how many answers are just sitting there in the obvious places, if you only bothered asking. Ask often enough, you might save yourself a lot of time and energy. I tried it.

"These two other paintings... do you have them, by any chance?"

"Of course," she cried. "Here in my collection."

"Any chance I could see them?"

"Of course!" she repeated in her enthusiasm, hooking glove laced fingers on my elbow. "I cannot tell you how pleased I am to finally have you."

She navigated us through her hallways, gracious as a riverboat captain, keeping to the middle of passages and pointing out the sights. The thing you could say for Damely was, her taste in art was a lot better than her taste in manservants. The canvases, thick on every wall, were wide ranging, mostly western, and if not masterpieces then still mostly minor miracles. She had an eye.

"Please excuse the state of the house," she told me as we swept along. "If I seem a bit distracted, we are hosting an event this evening—understaffed, I fear. But for your errand, I will take time. Nothing makes me happier than sharing my Filippis with young painters!"

"Okay. But full disclosure, I'm not a painter."

"You see, Asher," she espoused, ignoring me, "if we are blind to our past, our future will forever be veiled. If the art we do in Skysill is to advance, to progress, as all art must, we daren't forget our past—and Niccolo Filippi *is* our past. Such rare technique, such narrative force, such absolute command of the surface—one can only imagine what he might be painting if he were alive today. Sometimes I fear we are stagnating, in comparison to those who came before. It brings me such joy that your generation shows this renewed interest in Filippi—it gives me hope for the future!"

"Yeah, you stay hopeful. It's good for your digestion. But I don't think Niccolo's going to see a resurgence of interest. Just my sense of the market."

"I would not be so sure. There is your own interest, and of course Samantha's... poor child, so young, and who knew so troubled? Filippi seemed a passion for her. Then there was the other boy. Do you know, he spent weeks here, copying both Filippis? Then that terrible fire a few days ago. And I'd just seen him at the Nagato! Oh, life is short, Asher. One never knows what the future holds. We must live to our fullest while we can. Don't you agree?"

I noted investigator alarms struggling to ring—distant and sluggish, since ringing takes so much energy. While I noticed them, Damely led us under a beamed lintel into a great room where blue bunting was having itself draped on walls.

"Someone copied your two Filippis," I repeated, "and there was a fire?" I felt disjointed, confused by the alarms. "What fire was that?"

"You must have heard," she remembered for me, while at the same time approving the fold of some crepe paper and pointing out a table to be turned a quarter inch, "surely you heard, a home in the Seacliffs burned. I understand a number of other people perished along with the young man—whose name I cannot remember. Age does brush out the fine details. You will see."

Damely took us through a kitchen where a barge train of cheese platters held us up, and I clarified as we waited for them to pass, "A house burned in the Seacliffs. Do you mean Roman Sutherland's house?"

"Yes, that's the fire that killed the boy! I heard the bodies were simply dreadful."

"His apprentices died. You're saying one of Roman's apprentices was here copying your Filippi's?"

"That is right. Perhaps a year ago."

Then a man with a question about a folding chair distracted her and I ate cheese from the platters going by—the alarms burned up blood sugar pretty fast—as I sifted new pieces of information; fires, apprentices, Niccolo Filippi.

Damely averted the folding chair crisis then ferried us across the kitchen and paddled us into more private waters, and we slipped among couches, through a grand library, and finally she tilted us down a staircase, a waterfall of marble and ivory. We sluiced out into a cut glass and chrome gallery where a private collection, even more notable than Waylon's, gave off genius from every wall. I didn't have a chance to gawk. Damely moved to dock us, checking her watch. We entered an alcove where pin spots on metal poles lit two Flemish masterpieces and Damely unhanded me. I drifted to a stop in front of the first; The Hunter's Kiss.

In composition, The Hunter's Kiss mimicked The Dancer's Kiss, though it might have been the other way around, who knows. Here a brooding figure lay on his back looking up while another man, facing down, obscured both faces with a kiss. This time, instead of the lithe leggings of The Dancer, the figure on top—The Hunter—wore leather breeches and a cape. In place of The Dancer's curling streamers, the Hunter held a glinting knife.

The obscured figure, a languid king taking fealty, had a tattoo of the umbra eye on his chest. It was brilliant. And it was a total fake.

The brushed paint was less than a year old. Barely oxidized. I thought maybe I should have taken more cheese. My brain wanted blood, I wobbled, I gripped the light pole—shocked, I suppose, because I'd finally identified the forger who'd left a trail of counterfeit through my life the last few days. I should have seen it long before: The Dancer's Kiss, the forgeries in Roman's gallery, the sickening forgery in Samantha's office, and here, The Hunter's Kiss, right in front of me—all of them in the same hand, by the only *sighted* forger I've ever come across.

"The guy down here forging this painting..." I started, but Damely jumped.

"What do you mean *forging*?"

"Call it whatever you want. That painter—was his name Julian? Sharp looking, matador hair. Maybe a heroin addict?"

"Heroin? I wouldn't know about that. But the rest, yes that's the one! So charming. So knowledgeable. We chatted about the High Renaissance like school girls. Such a terrible loss. He had a bright future."

"By any chance did you see the copies he made?"

"I did. They were *extraordinary*. Side by side they were indistinguishable from the originals—and I know these paintings as well as anyone who ever lived."

My estimation of Julian went up and down at the same time. He was the most astonishingly talented defiler of art I'd ever met. But he only seemed to know one trick. Here and up in Los Angeles, he'd forged a Filippi, then swapped it with the original and walked out. He'd done it so well he'd fooled Damely. It was hard to believe. She'd been staring at it for a year. Why couldn't she see forgery?

Damely had the air conditioner too cold. I felt lightheaded in the little burial chamber of Filippi fakes. I went to wrap my arms around my shoulders, to shiver a little—but I couldn't move. I couldn't let go of the pole I'd leaned on.

My fingers were dead curled. *Dominion* swirled behind me. I yanked, but the pole was screwed tight, held floor and ceiling. A ghost grew in back of me and I went *chromatic,* so easy now, easy as falling into a pool, to find myself in air, facing the Hunter, looking past the back of my flesh head. I swung ghost me around to face behind us. There was Samantha.

From my ghost I watched her curl, spun in place, all Higher light with *dominion* sheep dogging it, pushing and building and keeping her up. Her cup seemed to beam even brighter, with even more *dominion* spilling out, and the holes more fully formed. The whole cup *insistent,* somehow.

"What's the *deal*," I screamed. It just came out. I didn't really blame her, I hoped she could tell. "You showing up like this just makes a spectacle—you, your goblet, you come out of nowhere and turn me into a puppet—it's very frustrating!" The ghost yelling set my flesh body off, anvil toothed and snapping, it wasn't dainty and Damely didn't welcome it. All she saw was flesh me growling out electrified cat spasms and yanking her pole. The real action was out of her view.

"Okay, wait," I ghosted, once I got my spectral equilibrium. I snapped fingers in my head, because that's all I had, and said, "Here you are, *again*, and... I get it. There's a pattern. There has to be a pattern. It's Filippi. Right?"

Damely heard flesh me saying, "*chocopreen herrgnes wnnnananam tor fffflnn?*"

"Oh, dear," she gloved her pinched lips, "is it one of your fits? I suppose we must call the paramedics."

"*NORGGGMA!*" flesh me insisted, wondering how she knew anything about my fits. I puppeted his free arm in a calm circle to stop her calling, then made other shapes suggesting she should lean on the wall and give me a minute while I talked to this ghost, which she did.

"You were at that office," I went back to guessing at Samantha, "when Damely came and first brought up the Dancer's Kiss. Now here you are with the Hunter's Kiss. That's the pattern, the Filippis— or wait, *is* that the pattern?—you showed up when I found the mural Julian painted, the one in your old office—so is the pattern *Julian?* Things forged by Julian? Look, he killed you with *compulsion,* I get it, but I already know about Julian so if *that's* what you're trying to tell me you can rest in peace. Even though...you must know I know about Julian. Right? So, that can't be it. I know there's a pattern. What am I missing? Something in the picture?"

I poured back into flesh me and stared at The Hunter's Kiss. The hearth shadows on the stone floor echoed the scene in The Dancer's Kiss, the candlelight so well conceived it almost flickered, both the Dancer and the Hunter works of shocking depth and verisimilitude, both in Julian's hand. High sacred Renaissance. I could see Damely's

Hunter had been forged a year earlier than The Dancer—Julian'd been on a forging spree. I was sure he'd done the other Filippi here, the Painter, though I was dating a light pole and couldn't sidestep to confirm.

"But then wait a minute," I told Samantha. "The Dancer's Kiss was completed, like, four days ago. I mean dates do confuse me, this could be wrong, but... something's wrong with the dates." I noticed Damely, leaning on her wall, urging an intercom into action with her cane.

"Remember?" I speculated to Samantha. "The fire where Julian died was six days ago. But Julian, let's say we think it's Julian, checked into the escrow with Whitney Lamb *three* days ago and replaced the Dancer. So...what, did he go to LA after he died in the fire? Probably not, and yes I see what you're thinking Sam, you're saying what if Julian's not dead? Which would explain this *date* mystery but that raises a lot of *other* issues we have to think about, you know. I mean look, my strengths are introspection and getting drunk, not reasoning, but if Julian *didn't* die in the fire like you're suggesting, then what about those bodies they found? You have to account for dead bodies, Samantha, that's how investigations go. I don't get it. So why are you here? What's the pattern? *Why do you keep popping into my life?*"

Then Samantha did a thing she'd never done before, that I didn't know ghosts could even do, although I might have guessed—she traveled. Or anyway she stopped being where she'd first appeared, behind my flesh body, and reappeared halfway out of the wall, half visible, right where The Painter's Kiss canvas hung. I saw her past the edge of the ornate frame, half in the picture, half in the wall, split down the nose and giving me one eye. She could have traveled anywhere. This was the only time she'd ever moved. She'd put herself in the center of a picture. A message. It was ghost charades. My best game.

"You're saying it's the Painter? Look at The Painter's Kiss? I can't, I'm stuck, Sam, and that's actually *your fault*, so how... fine, I'll do it. I see what you're thinking, but all I'll say is every time I do this—it's not like a relaxing beach sunset is what I'm saying. If you'd just disappear, I'd snap back into one body the easy way. No? Fine. I see how it is."

I didn't bother to sit or bend flesh me, I left him tied on the pole and crossed his eyes, squeezed so *dominion* sponged out in a pond and pain kicked off. I ramped the pressure and ghost me suck-slipped into flesh me, but the bodies weren't connected and pain baked agonized screams out of flesh me, trembled him while the Highers sizzled away and left us in a bulb of *dominion* lava. It infused both my bodies, the ghost and the flesh.

At that point I had to get rid of the *dominion*.

Down my arm toward the pole I pushed it, worrying my reputation would suffer melting Damely's house, noting, even through shivering agony, Caroline's influence—here I was worrying about my reputation—Damely's house being so vulnerable and old and not up to much melting.

Using self-control that I never knew I had, or maybe it was self-respect or something else I wasn't familiar exercising, I heat forged ghost me *into* the flowing river of *dominion*, like a fish in a rushing stream, and then I was inside me, piping down my own arm, hitting the pole at the border where *dominion* seared the metal and I watched the pole unbinding into a puddle onto Damely's alcove hardwood and I added some kind of tint to the thing the pole was—*dominion* my brush and my paint—and changed the metal pole to something better, that could suffer what came, absorb *dominion*. Which it did.

And then it was over.

My bodies snapped together and my hand unclenched the infused pole which now blazed *dominion* like some ripped star. I fell, knees to hands, gasping drool, then collapsed to the floor on my side and rolled to my back in the drool and spread my arms to locate anywhere comfortable and failed.

Damely issued a last instruction to her intercom. She tottered over and stood looking down. Something about our positions felt familiar.

"Can you speak?" she asked.

"The ghost squeeze," I mangled, not saying what I meant, "I'm not puppety."

"You speak! Oh, what a relief. Listen now. The paramedics are coming. They say you must not move."

"I'm not broke... I'm a fine, cherry on top," I wheezed. "This is totally normal."

"I'm sending Charles down. We've had a kitchen fire and there's a tapenade emergency I must see to." She regarded me. "You'll recover?"

"I'm totally normal go tapenade, stop the medics, keep your man off."

She wasn't persuaded by my arguments. People seldom are. The floor was cold on my back. Damely's footsteps faded up the stairs. I looked back over my head across the wall where half of Samantha still stuck out.

"There's no pattern," I accused. "You appeared at the Auditus compound, when the attack came, so how's *that* fit? And you were there when the Monarchs posed together at Three paths, how's *that* fit? It's not Filippi, it's not Julian. I give up. I have to leave before the paramedics get here."

From far above came the sound of sirens. It drove me sliding to my knees, crouching to my feet, damp from bodily fluids and barely holding things in place. I grabbed the pole for support and felt *dominion*, churning and infused, and let it go quickly to stand on my own.

When I pushed away from the wall I noticed Samantha had vanished. Typical. Running off just as the authorities arrive. I started for the door but shot a glance at The Painter's Kiss as I passed. Also forged, I saw. Composed to echo the Dancer and Hunter, stone floor, candles, gold leaf, one figure above wearing an apron stained with paint, kissing a tattooed figure.

The sirens wailed nearer, but I stared. I stared at the pattern I finally saw.

In LA I'd seen The Dancer's Kiss, with the figure on top gripping handfuls of colorful ribbons. In The Hunter's Kiss, the figure gripped a gleaming knife. But in The Painter's Kiss, the figure on top, bent low to kiss the man with the umbra eye, held a goblet. A glowing goblet. A goblet full of holes.

Samantha's goblet.

CHAPTER
TWELVE

Paramedics rushed the alcove and found me staring, shocked dumb by art—a condition they must have encountered before, considering what passes for art in this town. They urged me into a wheelchair, firm and professional, an arrangement I resisted from habit but then surrendered to after remembering the stairs and the long hallways between me and Damely's front door. Why work harder than I had to? I thought I'd use the time to plan my next move, which shows my disarranged thinking since I need more than a single wheelchair ride to plan anything. As we spun a squeaky exit from the tomb I snapped a picture of the Painter's Kiss. And the goblet.

My bearers chaired up the steps as confident as art gallery sherpas and at the top I found Charles, bearing a tray.

"Madam Damely says *goodbye,*" he said, making it clear it was a message from him, too. He served me a plate of tapenade with a selection of crackers. "She hopes you will return when you are recovered." I took the snack and tried not to appear grateful. With someone like Charles, that's a slippery slope. But it's hungry work, slipping back and forth inhabiting your bodies—in fact, Investigation and Authentication in general is a lot more work than I'd ever have guessed. So I ate, and let them roll me.

They convalesced me all the way to their van, where I handed them my empty plate and demonstrated a miraculous recovery. They told me they were legally obliged to disregard the miracle and transfer me to a gurney in the van, and what did I expect them to do with the plate? I said donate it to a food bank then showed them they'd injure me more trying to take me than by leaving me, so they powered away down Damely's dusky lane, taking her plate.

Their sleigh ride hadn't refreshed me. I had too much information. I felt it would go to waste unless someone more complicated than me used some of it, and I went for my car. When I reached it I saw the passenger window broken. Glass had fragmented all over the passenger seat. It was the perfect end to a perfect afternoon of seizures. Someone had stolen... what? Nothing was missing. No, the melted phone was gone. Maybe I'd invoice Damely.

Pointing my detuned car back down the hill with one hand, I juggled up my phone and called and got Veronica's message with the other. I wasn't unhappy leaving a message. Partnerships are still purely theoretical for me, I don't know what's expected. But talking in my car to basically myself is something I have plenty of experience with. I set the phone on the dash and made observations.

"Veronica this is Asher. Remember how you and Kuparr wondered if there were other paintings like The Dancer's Kiss? Well there are. Damely's got two of them. I just saw them and they're both forgeries. One of them has the goblet in it. At least now I know who our forger is, it's Julian, one of Roman Sutherland's apprentices, supposedly burned in a fire though I can't make the dates fit. I'm thinking Samantha maybe found something out about this goblet— she's the ghost holding the goblet, remember—and Julian found out and killed her in a weirdly gruesome and inefficient way. I don't know what's going on but I'll tell you what, this guy Julian's fucking crazy. So now he has a bunch of these Filippi originals. Maybe that's connected to your ghost eye, and ancient old ghostly Aeternus.

We've got to figure out this goblet. You're helping me, I really have to find this thing, every time Samantha pops up I freeze and I don't like it. Texting a picture of The Painter. The goblet looks... I'm looking at it now and..."

By then I'd hit the coast highway. I pulled off at the Chevron with the car wash and two fingered the Painter photo. In the aftermath of my miraculous recovery and the rest of the tapenade and seeing the photo texted to Veronica I began thinking maybe the Painter goblet wasn't the same as the goblet Samantha had. They were similar, pretty similar, but I couldn't decide if they were the same, and I started to suspect they were not.

I knew the sidewalk Samantha occupied. I could find her and compare the picture with her ghost goblet. It would mean swinging in close to Caroline, but at least I'd have a really good excuse if she saw me. I'd probably stop at The Charles first, for fortification. I remembered to end my call with Veronica and got my car pointed out of the parking lot. Then I saw Peter.

At first he was nothing but a white blur on a ten-speed bike, dodging up a side street, and then I lost him completely, but I'd seen where he went. I jammed the pedal down. Not as much acceleration came out as I expected. It was disheartening thinking my car might not be able to catch someone on a broken bike, but I slalomed around a corner and up the side street where Peter had gone and spied him again, three streets from the beach and heading south.

I chased him back and forth. We ended up circling the Civic Center, once I even got out of the car and yelled his name when I thought I saw him down in the outdoor amphitheater. More than once I'd come across him at the Civic, splashing though fountains. Sometimes I wondered if he slept there. Maybe he liked catching the occasional production of Mame.

But finally sunset rolled up off the water and I had to admit he'd eluded me, on purpose or just through Brownian motion. At least I knew he was alive. At least that. On the chance that he wanted to make a few dollars washing windows, I looped down to the 7-

Eleven, where I didn't see him but paused my search long enough to microwave a burrito and pour a cherry ice.

I ended up near the boardwalk, a spot called Pier 9 where Skysill's homeless gather at night. I'd sometimes end up there if *Gray* for more than a day or two. The unpredictable visitors and sporadic violence at the pier appealed to *Gray* psychology. The homeless collect food and services around Pier 9—I'd taken advantage of them myself because the *Gray* is very practical. This was where I'd always pictured Peter spending the night. I did a drive-by, spun the dial on my *sight,* but found no sign.

The encampment did remind me of another call I wanted to make, though. I pulled over, surveying for ten-speeds and Answers. By this time, just by mental jumping and free association, I'd more or less shifted from my plan to check Samantha's goblet to my plan to dial my phone and sit drinking watery slushy watching two guys try to light an aluminum bench on fire.

"What," Hennessy answered.

"It's Asher," I said. "How've you been?"

"I gave you phone instructions," he said. "Never calling was my instruction."

"I don't remember instructions very well, next time text them. I'm calling about a crime, by the way."

"A new report, or from your expanding collection?"

"I mean I have a *question* about a crime. It's that arson up at Roman Sutherland's."

He listened very carefully for two seconds, then observed, "Arson was not the report."

"Well, here's the thing," I told him, "I'm parked across from Pier 9, I'm thinking about your detective friends grilling me the other night about five missing homeless people, presumed dead or murdered I got the impression, and over here it occurred to me, there were also five disfigured bodies pulled out of that fire up where nobody reported as arson. Five missing homeless. Five bodies up there. That's an interesting coincidence right?"

"The burned bodies got ID'd," he said, reflexive.

"Who by?" I asked, quick and breezy like calling for the score when you get to the bar. If Hennessy knew the score he kept it to himself.

"Recall I told you," he slow warned, "concerning cop work, *do not do it?*"

"There's a guy, Hennessy, a guy named Julian, one of Sutherland's apprentices, I think he might still be alive and he's a violent psychopath, a murderer, and a forger. I think the police should look into it."

"Gale. You come out of this one of two ways—never calling me again or arrested and beaten. Can I be clearer?"

"I'm just doing my civic duty, reporting crimes."

"Do it elsewhere. Europe. Circuses. Not. My. Phone."

"Okay, Hen. I get it."

"Do not call me Hen."

"I won't call you Hen. I won't call you. Not if I can help it."

"Never call me. Associate with fewer crimes." He hung up.

After that I spent a few minutes watching people I'd seen asleep in various parks over the years, until I'd swallowed all my ice. And then, since I thought Peter might return there, and because I couldn't get into my regular house, and because I lacked energy for other ideas and I remembered it had a convenient mini bar, I drove to Asher Gales's office in the Bradley Building. I knew no one ever locked it. I got inside, didn't turn on lights, carefully did not look to the gallery end of the room where two generations of Gale family artwork collected moonlight.

Instead I took cushions off the window chairs, arranged them in the inner office on the Admiral's floor at the foot of his desk where his ensigns slept, refilled my vodka bowl, and went to sleep. And did not dream.

The smell of French roast in the morning woke me.

The last time I woke smelling coffee I'd blacked out on a McDonalds bathroom floor, so I jerked my eyes open ready for action. I found soft sunlight falling on my chest, my chest sideways on chair cushions just where I'd left it, on the Admiral's floor.

When I sat up I saw a man in the Admiral's open door in a wheelchair. He had coffee in one hand and it steamed, and greying hair and a tan arranged around a pretty attractive smoker's squint. In his lap was a tablet. He tapped that with the stylus in his other hand, browsing. I'm noisy sitting up and he noticed me. He stopped tapping to sip coffee.

"How come you're here," I rubbed my eyes, "isn't this supposed to be somebody's office?"

"It is, yes." He drank coffee again. His lips were something, extremely confident how they handled the lip of the cup, but he had other business here than sexy lips. I saw that right away.

"Asher Gale?" he asked. Very organized. "I'm Victors, of Cardsworth Victors Williamson." He wheeled in and handed down a card. "You got our calls?"

"Oh no you don't," I said, leaning against the desk, "I see what this is, listen to me, no investigations! They don't do investigations here, use the bar, get drunk if you want then go down the hall for a Hawaiian vacation but leave me alone."

Before I'd finished pleading, Victors had dropped his card on the desk and ignored me again in favor of tablet tapping. I felt like he'd been ignoring me all along. My problem was I couldn't lock that outside door because then how would Peter get in, but if I didn't lock the outside door look at the other problems that showed up. What was I supposed to do?

"I'll just be a minute," said Victors with tap tappery.

"Take all the time you need," I offered. "Is there a bearded guy on the floor in the other room?"

"Not that I saw," he told me, a little bit slow because he had one of those dual-track-minds where people can talk to you and you can work out other problems on handheld devices at the same time, jsut slightly slower. "I'm almost ready."

"Use the desk," I said. "Think of this like your own office."

"It is mine... I... suppose..." he drew the words out, two-tracking me along.

"I like a guy with your confidence."

"Give me one... there." He showed me the tablet. He held up the stylus. "I've signed and dated. Your turn."

"I don't know what day it is. So, no."

"Here, this is the trans...oh. Oh, I see. Yes, I'd forgotten," he laughed, a soft sound, he did it mostly because he enjoyed the soft sound. "Waylon said you might... that is, he led me to expect something like this, should this sorry day ever come. I take it you haven't read the documents? We mailed them."

"I don't open any mail with my name on it."

"Also email. And voice messages?"

"I'll be honest with you, I can't get my mail, it goes in a slot in my locked house, your voice messages were probably on the phone I lost, and I don't think I have an email address."

"That's fine," Victors said. He really was confident if that's what he thought. "I can fill you in. I can be brief. Would you prefer to sit somewhere else?"

"No one ever falls off the floor."

"Very briefly, then: you are one of two named co-trustees of the de Hory Institute. The de Hory Institute is a vehicle Waylon Goodman created to pass certain assets to you. On Waylon's death you are to take sole trusteeship. In the event you are unwilling or unable, those obligations devolve to Cardsworth Victors Williamson. Our participation is fully dissolved, however, pursuant to Article 5, with your signature here. Is that clear?"

"I'm trustee of what now? I never gave permission for that. No again."

"You may decline to serve," Victors said slowly, agreeing with something I'd said though I had no idea what. "But you are named."

"Waylon did this you're saying, he—what assets is he trying to pass?"

"This building for one. Find a list in Addendum 2."

"The whole Bradley Building."

"The same."

I liked the floor less, suddenly. I was unsettled by the familiar touch of it. I rose and saw we were out of vodka but had gin but found what I really needed was coffee.

"Let me ask you something," I turned to him.

"Yes?"

"Would you mind sharing your coffee, trustee to trustee?"

He made a gear shifting gesture with the cup after thinking for two seconds, then when he handed it to me it was hot and perfect and three-quarters full. Holding it focused me. I tasted too much sugar but drank anyway while Victors watched.

"The evictions in this building. That was you people?" I asked.

He nodded. "Whether you are trustee or we are, evictions are the obvious first step. These tenants pay... well, it's rediculous, and frankly a little too obvious. There's a clause in the Bradley tenant lease where transfer of de Hory trusteeship triggers a renegotiation or termination without prejudice of all leases in the building. Out with the old and in with the new. We chose eviction because these particular tenants are a liability."

"I don't know why Waylon would try any of this."

"As to his motives... well. I knew Waylon for decades. He was a man of many interests, but, I believe, a lonely man. It's not mine to speculate, these arrangements are sometimes irrational, but acts of emotion... well. I know he thought very highly of you. He never told you?"

"He might have, who listens? What happens if I don't sign?"

"Cardsworth Victors Williamson become sole trustee. Though there would be separate documents for that. I don't have those ready, I didn't presume I'd need them."

"How long's it take to get those?"

He used one track of two to think something about schedules while the other track looked me over, a little bemused, before he said, "One day, maybe two days."

"Awesome. You get the new documents, take the building, text when you're ready. Text, I keep telling people. Will you?" He told me of course. "Okay, look I've got an errand on a sidewalk on the other side of town, but if the receptionist comes in, try to get him to drink some water. I worry he gets dehydrated."

I grabbed a fistful of Asher Gale business cards retreating. They'd been handy in surprising ways this week. Some fell to the floor but I left them. I rode my caffeine deficit down three floors to the lobby thinking I'd had a very close call. I'd understood the relationship Waylon and I shared to be based on reciprocated disdain, leavened with contempt for each other or ourselves. Finding out he'd thought highly of me was a shock I couldn't process. Being the target of millionaire affection is the most dangerous of all. They can't help it, they kill what they love—like Waylon, working these landlord schemes to poison me with ownership responsibilities. Doing it all from beyond the grave. Terrifying. They're basically unkillable.

Morning air, cool and ocean peppery, calmed me outside. On my way to my used car with the broken window I passed my used car with the melted key, my very first one, abandoned in street parking. It was ticketed and tire booted. We take parking very seriously in Skysill Beach. More seriously than murders and thievery, I was starting to think, maybe because the city makes better money on parking.

I knew Samantha lived outside Psychic Touch on a sidewalk on the opposite end of town. I got a breakfast burrito from the counter where Caroline and I had forgotten breakfast burritos days earlier, then ate as I wheel crawled block by block down coast, through commercial Skysill Beach stretching like a birth canal of *compulsion.* Signs in *compulsion* along the highway framed art as something for consumers, instead of framing it as a fucking risk, because you can't sell risk. It's a sore spot I guess. Eventually I left the high charms of downtown and as I drove toward the psychic district things got shabbier and the Higher signage less emphatic. By the time I finished my burrito I'd come to a stoplight two corners from Caroline's shop.

Waiting for the light to change, I glanced up, and above an Italian restaurant three blocks down I saw sparkle-spreading *dominion* in the sky. Maybe it'd been there all along—I *had* been looking mostly at my burrito. But it seemed new. It swirled high and tentacular, a whirling sky bound tail that rose and went beyond the sky, wide at the base, and narrowing. An upside-down tornado of Higher light.

The Italian restaurant stood on the same block as Psychic Touch, which was around a corner, and my best guess put the tornado on top of Caroline's store. And while wondering what it meant and observing that my life had a relentless kind of pacing—all the time these days, one thing after another after 26 years of comfortable ennui—I felt my hands twitch. I ripped them off the wheel just in time to avoid getting fastened to my car. They curled into clubs.

I *stormed,* popped out behind the driver's seat looking at flesh me facing right where he examined the sky, with *what the hell* frozen in his grimace. Previously, seeing ghosts had been the trigger for these new *storms*. But there were no ghosts here. Just this massive funnel of *dominion*. What, I tried to picture, is Samantha doing over in front of Psychic Touch to blow this ghost light into the sky? My stoplight went green. The guy behind honked and gestured, apparently it was life or death for him to get to the restaurant parking lot.

No way to drive *chromatic*, I'm not that coordinated a puppet master, so I planked flesh me around to open the driver's door, and he couldn't do it with a fist and I had him use an elbow. I was sorry how spastic he looked I was hurrying. I tossed his feet and leaned him out and stood him up, then jerked him sideways to shut the door to stagger him through honking car threats up onto the side-walk. He stumbled and looked drunk but I kept moving him away from the *dominion* storm, hoping to get us out of range. When I remembered about working his arms and legs in opposite directions he started almost looking normal.

Fifty feet we shambled, seventy-five, a hundred, then a hundred fifty feet from the car, underneath an elm in front of Sea Spray

Antiques, the *storm* blew out. It happened without transition. Once again I owned and operated a single body. Behind me I saw no *dominion* funnel in the sky.

So yes. Driving a car to see a ghost, *knowing* that ghosts gave me paralyzing seizures, had been a badly conceived plan, but I put very little of myself into my plans so I didn't feel too bad. The important thing, I felt, was to ignore the past and get my used car back. I went into Sea Spray Antiques and purchased a palm-sized bronze turtle, originally from the estate of Rudyard Kipling, I was assured, and absolutely invaluable to the right collector. I picked it because it was easy to hold in my fist. That's the way I held it walking back toward the stoplight where my car waited, looking up for the *dominion* funnel, which soon reappeared.

I *stormed,* popped a ghost, puppeted flesh me to a comfortable bench where I sat him and crossed his eyes, then sucked a breath and squeezed, like a human vice, furnace tight.

It went faster this time. Ghost me slid to co-occupy flesh me, the agony of compression started. Flesh me screamed and drooled on the bench but nothing could be done there, a quaking corpus of free ranging *dominion* formed around us, terrible heat crushed in and *dominion* superconducted down my arm, through my hand, and into Rudyard Kipling's turtle. The turtle would have melted but I changed it out of reflex, made it deeper than it had been, so it held all the light without changing.

My fist always opens at that point. This time it did not.

Instead I *stormed* again. Popped a ghost, hung behind flesh me, watching him sweat soak, seized weirdly sideways, my poor human body really was taking a beating. The bronze reptile in his hand was now slamming out *dominion.*

I'm nothing if not a creature of habit, so from ghost me I tried it all over again; crossed flesh eyes, squeezed bodies, screamed on the bench—all his noise had drawn a small crowd on the sidewalk— bubbled *dominion* out then shot it down my arm. The charge filled the turtle again. But not the old turtle. The old turtle got pressed out into flesh me's lap. In his hand was a new turtle, exactly like the old one, both copies now beaming *dominion* like little shot-glass rockets.

The pattern was getting kind of obvious, even for me, but I tried again. I have a well- earned distrust of the obvious, plus I couldn't think of anything else to do. This time the loop went even smoother and faster: squeeze, scream, mint a glowing turtle, then *storm* and pop out the back of my head. A family of turtles was growing in my lap.

My expanding crowd of admirers skittered back when I puppeted flesh me standing. He moaned. One mom told her daughter to run back to the car but she herself stayed behind because she had me on video. Many others did also. It was my fifteen minutes.

"Happy memories from Skysill Beach!" I ghost snapped, and flesh me sneer-yelled *ggrandd dacan moose prunphla tcoo* and spit at them. They cleared a path when I started him down the street. The gridlocked drivers had lost track of me by this time, so instead they cursed each other and the crosswalk pedestrians and were just confused why they couldn't go anywhere. Flesh me fell into his walking rhythm and soon the tourists forgot me so they could go back to buying the art they didn't know they were going to want. I headed for the Italian Restaurant where Psychic Touch would come into view. When ghost me swung around the building, I could only stare.

Rank after rank stood ghosts, motionless, scores, each one contributing a single *dominion* tendril up into the sky where they braided and combined and became the tornado. Every single ghost pivoted to face me.

Having a ghost track your every move was by this time a perfectly natural feeling. But this pale field of sunflowers tracking me like their star startled me with eye force. I saw them spilling into the road, halfway inside buildings, cars and tourists bayoneting through them without consequence. Many in the new ghost congregation wore robes. These, I realized, were the Asks and Answers. The ones I'd watched die or seen the bodies of in LA, glowed dead on their field, all gathered here in thick chaotic rows to form a Higher cloud that concealed the rest of the block.

The nearest ones were spaced so I could steer flesh me among them. It was like entering a forest of spectral Christmas trees. The first monk I came to had straight transparent hair, eyes that bulged, cheeks that sunk. In his right hand he held a vacuum cleaner. Each ghost had its item, like they always do, a book or a model airplane or scissors or a telescope. They all watched me get sad, knowing what I was supposed to use the objects for. I'm lucky responsibility has so little hold on me, or I would've turned and run. Well, stumbled.

"Excuse..." I said, sidling flesh me past the vacuum monk, who turned, all the ghosts turned, like clock tower angels they tracked me move among them, "I just need to get..."

I was stopped, pressed against a lady monk with a crew cut holding out a wedding gown. Beyond her crowded a screen of ghost bodies, tendrils twining. Flesh me could go no further. I had him push a monk holding a bird feeder but that bird feeder weighed a million pounds and the ghost weighed a hundred million. They stood too close. Too thick. Flesh me could go no farther.

By that time I'd moved him too far from where ghost me hung puppeting, so I jumped into him and reeled ghost me up behind, then swung my ghost in front, thinking maybe I could use him to scout a path, like Lewis without Clark, and the moment he hit another ghost, that ghost went bouncing and slamming away, hitting other ghosts who bounced and spun too, like pool balls ricocheting.

So I could wield ghost me like a bat. Apparently.

After that I jumped from one me to the other using my ghost like a plow to nudge a path forward because I was trying to be respectful of the ghosts. Still they slid into the road or through the sides of buildings to dissapear. I didn't know if that was bad. And always they pivoted as we went, facing flesh me.

Eventually I got us up to Empty Nest Furniture. A half dozen ghosts congregated in the 1960s themed family room Tim had set up to block the morning sidewalk, bean bags and lava lamps and dayglow tables. Within Tim's invisible walls, the ghosts looked almost normal. I swung my own ghost through the den like a feather duster, cleared a path—then finally I saw Samantha.

"Have you seen all these ghosts?" I asked, because who could actually tell what any of them could see? I was just making conversation. Were they all thinking things, in their minds, the way I was in my own ghost body? Did they wish it would stop?

Flesh me was exhausted and he tremble-shimmied like a two-stroke engine so I pressed him back against Empty Nest Furniture to keep him out of the way. He never looks comfortable, but with his snot stained shirt and the shivering tendons in his neck it was more noticeable than usual. No way to relax him. You could stand him, walk him, sit him down, but relaxing him was impossible.

"I'm stuck in this *chroma storm,*" I ghosted to Samantha. "I can't escape, it's crazy, I saw your tendril up there and it popped me out, I can't get back. I'll have to go out of range. I keep making turtles. I have a theory which is there's too many ghosts. Right? Every time I escape a *storm* from one ghost I get sucked *chromatic* by another one. I guess I should test. Because science. It's just a little bit agonizing, that's all. You don't care. Whatever. I'll try."

Squat down I puppeted flesh me. I crossed his eyes, I squeezed, I had the agony. I blew *dominion* down my arm into my keepsake and I watched another Rudyard Kipling turtle fall off my fist and hit the concrete, and then two more followed, like squeezing *dominion* turtles from a tube. Flesh me was hunched, beaten, straddling a puddle of fluids. A customer coming out of Empty Nest Furniture with a straight-backed chair offered flesh me an uncomfortable glance. Most other pedestrians ignored him from as far away as they could get.

"That's all I can take," I ghost groaned to Samantha. "Look at flesh me. Back down on Caroline's sidewalk. I hope she doesn't see, god he looks terrible. Don't worry he's been through worse, I'll get him some juice and he'll be fine. Listen, I saw the Painter's Kiss. I saw the goblet. And, you know, I'm not sure your goblet's the same as the one in the painting and that's why I came. If there's dozens of these goblets it's a bigger problem getting you released from this earthly plane or wherever you ghosts are going—what if I tracked down the wrong goblet? I want to compare. I'm going for thoroughness. I've had limited success with that in the past so don't expect too much, there's a picture on my phone..."

My phone was in flesh me's pocket, his hands were fists, it took delicate puppeting to knead and side palm the phone up. When it emerged pancaked with two fists, I knuckled the password and tapped the app and twice I dropped it. My screen cracked. Flesh me would never be a brain surgeon, but eventually we had the Painter goblet zoomed and I puppeted the phone up, two hands, faced him at Samantha then poured myself into him.

The things you take for granted having only one body. But at least I had both goblets in sight, digital and ghostly. And I knew what to look for. And I could clearly see the ghost goblet didn't match the painted goblet. For one thing the lattice of holes surrounding it was more delicate and larger than the digital. Overall Samantha's goblet appeared simpler, shorter, less ornamentation and flare.

"Does this happen to you," I asked Samantha, seeping back into ghost me, "where every time you ask a question you get ten answers and five of those are just more fucking questions? It doesn't seem efficient. So now it seems like part of the awesome treasure hunt you have me on is there's more than one of these goblets with the holes, whatever they are, the lattice, and Julian's involved and so is Aeternus. Is that right?"

A wind blew in off the beach that I couldn't feel. The morning wasn't warm, but none of us ghosts noticed, and flesh me had goosebumps but felt nothing. Holding his cracked camera up he looked like a crazy paparazzi. Passersby swung wide. You couldn't blame them.

"All I really see is Julian," I complained to Samantha. "Julian everywhere. Your goblet's tied to him. It was Julian who forged The Dancer's Kiss. Julian's supposed to be *dead* but how could he be dead and do all this forgery, is he that good? I think Julian has Higher light powers. I think he might be part of that crew glowing people. But forge anything at all, he can do it, he's really brilliant. And he's a psychopath, I know he tortured you to suicide because something about the goblet you have, you found out something, I don't know. I think he tried breaking Peter—it had to be him, but a decade ago, because the operation's the same sick—and then somehow Peter survived. And by the way I'm looking for Peter so if you see him…"

Nothing's easier than talking to ghosts. They provide endless undivided attention, which addicts like me are always hungry for. Flesh me was all spooled out slobber and tongue pain. A baby in a stroller gave him a sympathetic look and got hurried away, but it didn't stop me.

"Something else about Julian," I complained next, "something's wrong with his forgeries, they're *too* brilliant. I mean think about it. Damely's staring straight at one for a year, why can't she see it's a forgery? He didn't even disguise his style like he does in Roman's gallery or in the mural he killed you with. Hey. Do you think Roman has one of Julian's personal canvases? Roman's got to have at least one of his own apprentice's signed works, right? So god dammit I guess I'm going back to Roman's again. There's something about Julian's painting. It's just, it's *disgusting* at Roman's and…"

Pedestrians toured a path around flesh me roaring his gibberish. Two ladies holding hands skittered all the way over to the curb where ghost me hung, and one lady passed inside ghost me and stopped there, which transgressed every personal boundary I'd never before had—though I'd heard other people talk about those things— even though I knew it just didn't matter, because as a ghost you get what you get and you don't get upset. I did feel like it was time to get off the sidewalk.

My alien occupant stood a minute watching flesh me. She lamented to her friend how homeless people were everywhere and discounted the chance flesh me would ever get the treatment he needed, then when flesh me stopped gibbering and wasn't amazing to watch anymore she exited ghost me and took her partner to stare at Caroline's store. She wondered whether all psychics were frauds or if some were actually insane and believed what they told people. Then the couple sauntered off, grateful for, and confident about, the reality they'd picked to live in. I turned my attention back to the ghost in front of me.

"Sam I'm leaving," I ghosted. "Can I ask a favor?"

I didn't wait for her not to answer. She continued to provide the attention I craved. I tried pointing to Psychic Touch with my mental powers, which didn't work.

"As you can see—maybe you can, maybe you can't—Caroline and I aren't going to have anything to do with each other, whatever we had was short circuiting us. We found out what we were feeling wasn't real. We really started falling for each other but it wasn't real, can you believe... so that's over. So I'm wondering if you'll keep an eye out down here. You probably see her all the time, in and out, do you see her? Did you know she's a Monarch? So badass, Queen of the Path Behind. I have a feeling things are really precarious up at Three Paths, although who am I kidding - I find it precarious everywhere, so maybe it's just me. I heard one of the Paths is broken, I don't think anybody likes talking about it, and the thing I'm worried about is these *ghosts*. They're everywhere out here. I think they're here for me but this can't be healthy for a psychic. Spirits of the dead thicker than happy hour? Even though she doesn't believe in spirits of the dead so that's on her, I honestly thought we had a connection but it was just self-destruction. And it doesn't matter but she actually liked the ridiculous shit that happens all the time around me, which is all my life is, ridiculous shit. That's why we worked. She *liked* it. Anyway I shouldn't stay. I hope she doesn't see flesh me, shit, come on, get up." I puppeted him to his feet. "I guess we'll go down and talk to Roman but listen, Sam, don't get your hopes up. None of this plays to my strengths, your goblet and Julian and Aeternus, and I'm doing my best, but historically speaking that doesn't always mean a lot."

I poured back into flesh me and spent a minute in him with his frozen eyes on Psychic Touch. A tall monk balanced an aquarium sideways halfway through Caroline's dark front window. She might be inside, I thought, in her shop right now, in this crazy hurricane of Higher light, with dead people all around. Thirty feet away. It felt wasteful. I wondered if she was thinking of me. I hoped she wasn't. I only knew, wherever she was, whatever she was doing, she had a cold blue crystal against her chest. If she ever took that off I'd feel it.

You can't get ghosts to heave self-pitying sighs. It's one of the things you don't value until it's missing. I could only puppet flesh me back the way he'd come. He was bumping ghosts who'd continued pinballing, slower and slower, circling back in to press Psychic Touch like it had specter gravity. I swung ghost me and cleared us a ghost groove up the sidewalk.

We didn't get far before a pedaling rider was pacing us in the bike lane, balancing as slow as a circus artist. He wore a once white waiter's top and some once white pants and when I saw him I yanked flesh me to a stop. Peter.

Peter halted his own progress, still balanced, then stepped down and wheeled up on the sidewalk, gazing intently at flesh me.

After a flurry of body switching I got flesh me facing Peter with my flesh arms wide in greeting, which was weird, and I'd stashed ghost me behind flesh me with myself inside ghost me to watch Peter over my flesh shoulder. I don't know what it says about me, in these fifty-fifty situations, I was finding I preferred being the ghost, not the flesh.

From that vantage the scene was a disappointment. Peter and flesh me both appeared in need of medical attention; unwashed, vague of gaze, torn, confused. Peter's shoulders hunched under a frayed schoolboy backpack, hair a shipwreck, eyes inflamed, body thin as Halloween branches.

"I've been looking for you," I ghosted. Flesh me told him *hwahh nasawnnnna phhahha.*

"Celery season soon," Peter shrugged, soft basso profundo. "Eat them in salad to digest your sacrifice."

I made flesh me put his arms down. Peter met him eye to eye, an intent kind of inspection, but Peter's eyes were shifting fifty directions a second and he seemed desperate. He tipped foot to foot like trying to remember where gravity started. His backpack jingled.

"Peter, I know what happened to you," I ghosted out uselessly. Flesh me spat *nmmmaph gggggghaguna vynupphhhun paao!* "I'm stuck, I can't talk right now, I know about you!"

"The dead eye is here," he told me. "They go back infinity. It's the dead eye."

"I'm so sorry Peter." Flesh me went, *gammall moshibats*

"Our secrets are inside-out, like strawberry shirts," he moaned. "But don't put the socks inside out. That's a slippery slope, bad socks."

"Tell me how to help," I pleaded, trying to see behind his eyes. "You're trapped, right? Are you coming back?" *Manata an wanna flabbrnn tin shhhhnockle beaney?* asked my flesh mouth.

Peter leaned close, an inch from flesh me. I poured in to meet Peter's eyes. I was sure that somewhere inside, a spark struggled. A candle, lost in the not-present, a mind, lofting mad sentences, steering a body—who knew how—in a battle to deliver his final Answer. His beard stirred sideways in the breeze.

We shared a seaside moment. The present continued past us, incomprehensible.

"The rats eat peacocks in their dreams," he lumbered, a secret for flesh me alone. "But they never fly. They never feather. The rats can only run and run and run."

And then, shaking his head, mumbling celery, rats, socks, he wrestled his ten-speed back onto the bike lane and straddled it and launched away. I couldn't turn fast enough to watch him go.

A moment of insufferable humility passed. Neither Peter or I had a clue. It was quiet enough humility for me to hear the phone in flesh me's pants ring. I puppeted it up since I was expecting one of several calls from Amelia or Celine or Veronica but not Caroline, but it was none of those. Roman himself was calling. It went to message. He'd left several other messages. A text came up as I watched.

"Asher. I need to speak with you. Come to the gallery. NOW."

I'd been going there already. Now my visit was going to be mistaken for cooperation. I didn't want to get that kind of reputation, but under the circumstances there wasn't much choice.

CHAPTER

THIRTEEN

The featured canvas in the window of the Gallery of Light and Shadow was a fleet of sailboats bathed in sunset pathos and it stopped me outside the gallery door and I stared, a little sickened. This was Roman's authentic work, a Sutherland original not yet fed through his reproduction machine. I didn't like it but I still felt sorry for it, like a baby they were preparing for slaughter. To the shoppers crawling the square, however, it was simply more of what they loved. An elderly woman paused beside me. She was warm and knowing. We examined the sailboats together.

"Roman is just *magnificent*, isn't he?" she asked.

"He really is," I told her, trying reverse psychology on myself. "I can't wait to get inside and see all the rest of it."

"I came to buy a painting yesterday," she confided, "and now I'm back to buy lunchboxes for my grandkids. I can't stay away." She gave me the Sutherland fan club arm squeeze then hurried inside to spend money. Since I'd come that far already I followed her, and like falling into a toilet, the first of Roman's three interlinked galleries swirled around me, coating me in drama. Recessed lights soothed us with brothel shadows. The sound of whispering cash registers lulled us. Pin lights showcased all the masterpieces, and *BUY BUY BUY BUY BUY BUY BUY* circled *compulsion* on the ceiling. Eager patrons spiraled thick in there, getting milled like dandelions in a rock grinder.

The elderly woman buying lunchboxes stood before one of Julian's reproduced Sutherlands. I recognized his hand, the subtlest trace, from all his earlier forgeries. This one depicted an entire night-time city lit by candles. Now that I recognized it, Julian's hand was everywhere here, just traces. Roman's four other minions were also represented, but none was in Julian's league.

Under the second archway, and into gallery two, it was more of the same; Julian, first among five liars. I snaked between pliant buyers, confirming over and over how Lady Damely's forgery had been Julian's style, but got no insights into how or why she'd missed it. I was impatient for something real of his, something authentic and unforged to answer my questions. I hurried toward the final gallery.

Beneath the arch to the third space I stopped and stared. Across the dim room, in his little wall cubby, drinking coffee I could smell from where I stood, Roman sat, tailored in silk. He was talking to Hennessy, who was tailored in cop. They leaned toward each other in casual conspiracy. Roman, seeing me, held up a finger, indicating I should wait. I pretended not to see the finger and jumped back under the arch, wondering—what did Roman Southerland and Hennessy have to talk to each other about? In my mind Hennessy had been *Waylon's* cop. Maybe it was a kind of timeshare arrangement.

And then because of my tendency toward mental darting from one place to another, especially when I'm confused, I started wondering about the odd painting I stood facing, called *Garden Prince Portrait #4,* where a prince languished in a decaying conservatory.

I'd glanced at it passing, but it wasn't Julian's—it was minion number three, or so I'd thought. But now I saw that *Garden Prince*

Portrait #4 had something of Julian after all. It took a minute, but I realized that the figure of the reclining prince *was* Julian. He'd modeled it, sharp brows, pointed glare, someplace better to be than some decaying garden. Roman had painted Julian, and then the image had been reproduced as many times as it would sell by minion three. Dizzying. Twisted.

"Imagine my happiness finding you anywhere near me," said Hennessy, who'd come very quietly, with eyebrows battened, to my side. A human the size of a Stairmaster should make more noise when he moved.

"I'm guessing Roman asked me here because of you here reporting him things," I speculated, "probably from my call last night that wasn't about arson. Am I right? You can't be surprised I'm here."

"Nothing surprises me."

"See, I'm the opposite, *everything* surprises me. We're opposite twins. Are we adorable?"

There were amusing things he wanted to tell me which I looked forward to hearing, but then he stopped himself. He gestured at Roman's coffee cavity where Roman had a phone to his ear, and said, "Sutherland wants you."

"Maybe I don't want Sutherland," I proposed, though talking to Roman was the only reason I'd come and everyone knew it. Hennessy responded amused.

"I think you are not that stupid," he said, then prowled off toward the cash registers.

He had no idea how stupid I was. Part of me wanted to prove it. But instead, I slid out into and across Roman's lair, watching him conclude his call. While he talked he indicated me sitting where Hennessy had. I did, and reached for the little cup Hennessy had left, and sipped, momentarily quiet, like a baby with a rattle.

While Roman waxed obsequious to his microphone, assuring someone something artistic, I scanned the forgeries on his walls. His most dramatic masterpieces hung in this gallery. Half of them were

Julian's, because Julian's technical excellence made the most money, I guessed. In this inner sanctum Roman made his biggest sales. One painting that hadn't sold yet was *Sleeping Beauty,* where the redhead in a shadowed forest sipped something from a saucer to poison herself free of Roman's clutches.

It was minion five's work. Something about the redhead herself seemed like a forgery. It was getting hard to keep track of it all. Roman set his phone aside at last and pouted. His starry blue eyes and beard, his face of shadow and light, none of it was arranged in a welcome way.

"I am very angry at you Asher," he said.

"I don't mind that. Listen, I have some questions about Julian—" I tried, but he was ready for me.

"Listen to *me!*" he snarled. "You listen to me now."

He put both hands palms down on the table like he was keeping it from flying up and hitting me in the face. His shadow and light had a livid hardness I'd never seen before.

"I've always been patient with you," he reminded me softly, "generous, anyone would say it, but at every turn—*every turn*—you make yourself harder to help."

"I'll have to take your word for that. I'm trying to track down a piece of Julian's original work to—"

"Shut your mouth and listen to me you arrogant little prick! I want your *attention, my eyes, here,* are you listening?" I found that I was. I surprised myself. Roman hissed.

"Who do you think you are?" He pointed at his own face. "You think because I tolerate so much in the name of art that I'll tolerate *anything?* I will *not* tolerate anything that damages my *brand.* How many artists in the world accumulate riches, do you think? Vast riches, powerful influence, purely by making *art?* Very few. Vanishingly few. You could fit us in a phone booth. And right now I'm finalizing a contract, I'll tell you, with an entertainment company, which I can't name, but there are theme parks, hotels, they're expanding, and soon it will be *my* art, it'll be the *Roman Sutherland* brand that's the face of their company. I'll be the envy of every painter on the planet. And I've worked years, *years*—and now you, calling the police, raising questions about the fire that killed my apprentices? Destroyed a neighborhood? Took lives and livelihoods?"

His voice was very quiet. He leaned toward me like he'd leaned toward Hennessy, causally excluding any of the patrons, intense as a fusion reactor. I honestly hadn't thought he had this in him.

"The faintest smell of scandal or misconduct would undo this deal," he said. "This company chose my brand because I *fit*. Clean. Aspirational. And *that* is how my brand has to *stay*. So you will not speak one more word to the police, or to God himself, about this insane theory of yours. Julian did enough damage, even before meeting his fate in this fire. He was deeply unstable, violent, a madman really. I should have excused him long ago but his talent... he even influenced the others... I sometimes felt they were *his*, not mine. He infected them. And now, here I am. I've lost his brush at the very moment I need it most, a contract looming. It puts me in a very difficult position. I will survive this fire. I will come out triumphant, but the whisper campaign will stop! Do I make myself absolutely clear?"

Roman targeted me with his Mesmer eyes. All through everything he'd just said, some of which I'd even paid attention to, I'd been thinking about *Sleeping Beauty*. And now I'd figured out who *Sleeping Beauty* looked like. Roman was beaming fury. He was beautiful that way, like all the other ways, filled with swarthy alligator charisma.

"Roman, I think your apprentices—"

"Stop," he snarled, "this is your last warning. Do not bring up my apprentices again."

I wasn't going to be able to go straight in with this question. I tried it roundabout, which, honestly, is a more natural style for me.

"Okay, I'm sorry Roman. Let me say it a different way. No—I won't say it, I understand. You had a tragedy, and I'm sorry. But look.

After your tragedy... you must need new apprentices. The old ones are gone in the tragedy. Right? So what if I come paint for you?"

I'd taken him by surprise. For just a second.

"You paint for me?" he breathed. The change was a little sickening. "Oh, Asher. The two of us together—we could make so much money!"

"Do you think?" I asked, but my mind was on the portrait. I was certain the *Sleeping Beauty* redhead reclining on the wall was the same redhead who'd crushed Kuparr with a giant boulder in Los Angeles, and then come looking for us in our weird shadow in Kuparr's office.

So what was she doing in Roman's gallery?

Roman was excited. "The gifts you have Asher, you haven't even used... I know what you think of me. But you are wrong. Because what I think of *you*—all the years I've watched, waited, because you are something *new*. You're something new in the world of art. Something we have never seen. I can help you become a star."

People don't usually give me straightforward compliments this way. Not even in the old days. I remember them standing in front of my paintings, looking confused, lost, crying and laughing, but there was always a tinge of something suspicious, or fearful, in their comments to me.

"The boy in the hills," he mused, about me, it was clear, from across his coffee desk. "The boy in the hills was what we called you, it was all we had at first, the boy who painted these... astonishing symphonies of Higher color. Your canvases smuggled down—your parents were so protective—we'd just stand looking, shocked. And then finally you came among us, after your parents vanished, and even with all your mental issues—some form of epilepsy is it?—I vowed I'd one day sponsor you. What you created... vortexes of reality, Asher. What you painted was authentic reality. In your work there was time and space and gravity... the world has never seen anything like it. I can make you successful beyond your wildest dreams. My only condition would be... tell me how you do it."

This is the one problem with going in sideways. Sometimes it comes back out that way.

"Do what, now?" I asked.

"Tell me how you paint. The power. The things you do with Higher color."

"You lost me," I admitted.

His blue orbs shined me, his shadow cheeks beckoned, he crooned, "Asher. Let's not play games. With my industry connections? I can make you fabulously, unbelievably rich."

"I already own four cars and it's a pain in the ass. I'll skip it."

"Real wealth changes *everything*. With the secret to your painting I can make it happen."

"Okay, sure. Whatever you want. So, you do want me to apprentice?"

I saw a flare of suspicion. Just a tiny flag going up inside him. It came from hearing me being agreeable.

"Why this change of heart?" he asked after a minute.

"Because of how much I respect your work. I want to understand how you do your portraits. I'd like to sit for you. Watch you work. I know you did Julian, the *Prince* in the garden over there. You do a portrait of all your apprentices, right?"

As I said it I pointed to *Sleeping Beauty*. He looked over his shoulder and nodded.

"I give them each one portrait and hang it in the gallery," he said. "The ones that sell. So they all can get a taste of fame. You see? It would be a partnership between us."

I still had coffee in my small cup. I finished it. Then I stood.

"Well," I said, "as always Roman it's been a razor thin slice of heaven. You really make me work to get anywhere. It probably makes me a better person."

"You're leaving?"

"I am. Thanks for the coffee, it's the best in the city. If you put a drive-through in that wall and burned all these paintings, you could make an honest living."

"The apprenticeship?"

"I'll call your people."

I headed for the exit, wondering how I was going to get around now, to the places I hoped to need to go. My most recent used car I'd abandoned in the middle of an intersection. I thought maybe I'd get one more at Arroyo Automotive, or if maybe he sold bikes I'd do it that way. I went past the gift shop cash registers. Patrons followed ropes to the checkout counter. Sixth in line was Hennessy, waiting impatiently, with Sutherland postcards and a Shadow and Light snow globe. He didn't see me leave. Outside, I stopped beside a potted palm.

Five minutes passed. I filled them thinking how bad a plan mine probably was, and then Hennessy came outside carrying his shopping bag of Sutherland keepsakes, blinking the sun and the *compulsion* to buy out of his eyes, looking puzzled at the little bag of art products he hadn't known he wanted to buy. I stepped up beside him.

"I hope he gives you the cop discount," I charmed, then segued, like I can, smoothly into my bad plan, "hey, the boss says I should—he has me—what's her name again, the redhead apprentice?"

"The Genth girl?" he said, still looking confused. It wouldn't last.

"Yeah, Cindy," I nodded.

"Britta..." he told me, and a penny rolled in his mind, hunting ninety nine cents. I had about a second before he got his change.

"Britta Genth, that's the girl he said," I agreed, then jerked my head at the gallery, "so the boss says ask you—where is Britta now?"

"The boss? The boss says ask *me* where she is?" He looked back at Roman's gallery, where only one of us actually had a boss. He had his dollar now, and it pissed him off. His face twisted to me hard. "Her location is the *morgue,* as she is dead, which Sutherland already knows. Do you think this wise, fucking with me?"

"If it was I probably wouldn't do it. So, Sutherland a great boss? Pay you good?"

I don't try to burn bridges, but it's hard to avoid. It just seems to happen. I'm used to it by now, but other people are always surprised. Hennessy wasn't surprised long. He bent very close. I smelled his mint breath and wondered what it would be like to kiss him.

"My *boss*," he growled, "is the police commissioner. Remember?"

"Well okay, but don't tell Roman," I thumbed inside, "it'll break his heart. He thinks you feeding him my private police reports makes you his bitch." Look at me, Hen. Lighting matches. I can't fucking help myself.

"Oh, Gale, oh I am a bad friend but as an enemy, I am worse. This game you will regret. Believe me."

"I believe you. I regret almost everything anyway. Roman really does want me to paint for him, you know. Since his apprentices are all so dead. I'm just asking his current employees their experience, before I accept his offer. He pretty reliable with payoffs?"

The thing with burning bridges is the ecstasy of saying goodbye. Lighting them, watching the smoke rise, though it was novel doing it sober like this. And since a half burned bridge is a hazard for everyone, I always make sure I raze them to the ground. As a public service. Hennessy understood.

He tightened his teeth. What could he do? Or anyway, what could he do here, considering Roman's likely brand guidelines about beating customers in public in view of the shop. I smiled, I showed my most charming innocence, and I walked away. After you burn them it's good to leave the area as fast as you can.

I thought of going across the street to Asher Gale's office but remembered the lawyer who'd come this morning claiming Asher Gale owned the whole building. I wanted to keep learning about Britta Genth. Landlording was just a horrifying distraction.

I scratched up my shattered phone while I walked and I called Veronica. She answered after maximum rings, sounding vacant and soft.

"Yes," she said. In her background I heard street sounds.

"It's Asher," I introduced myself. "Listen, I need an address from your card catalog."

"I've just left the office."

"It's important."

"Is it?" she said in her drifty voice. I'd never thought of her as the day drinker kind of millionaire. She was full of surprises. "Important to whom? I have a car waiting, to drive up the coast, to clear the cobwebs."

"Have you been drinking?"

"Possibly, though it doesn't really help, does it."

"If you're good enough it does."

"I'm afraid... I'm afraid I may have made a mistake."

"Could we stick to my subject—this is my call—I've got a name and I need an address. Remember our partnership. It's important. I said that."

She sighed. After a minute I heard keys, a door, a little bell, and street sounds became empty paint store sounds.

"So?" she said in the silence. "What is it you want?"

"See if there's a Fenestram record for a girl called Britta Genth in your cardboard boxes."

"Who is she?"

"One of Roman's apprentices. An associate of Julian's. Julian's in the middle of all of this, forging away like a printing press."

"I understood that the apprentices were all dead."

"Dead doesn't mean what it used to. And I think... she might have been involved in the attack on Kuparr's compound. I'm just crossing some t's."

"Kuparr," she sighed, a sift of breath.

A realization came slowly, me juggling concepts I'm frankly awkward with. I tried out some of my new sincerity. "Kuparr was a friend of yours. I'm sorry about all that. That's why you're going drinking and driving? That... dead people... drinking definetly helps *that*."

"If this is you expressing concern it is unnecessary and off-putting."

"Agreed. I'd just hate seeing you do the thing where you blame yourself for shit that isn't your fault. Although I encourage you to drink either way. You're frendlier.."

"I led a pack of Aspectu killers straight to Kuparr's door," she said, soft and loose, "and once again, I failed to... well, there's sufficient blame for everyone, I'm sure." I heard her cupboards open and boxes sliding. "Britta Genth," she murmured under her breath. "Yes. Here she is."

"Anything stand out?" I demanded because I lack patience.

"Not that I see. Britta Lynn Genth. Range of *sight* through *bleed.* Other than that... well, she isn't a Skysill native, she was identified at NYU fifteen years ago. You see a few like that every year."

"How about Julian? Julian Donner, can you look him up?"

After more filing she found him.

"Nothing unusual here. He *sees* to *bleed,* also not a Skysill native —identified in Italy twenty-five years ago."

"He must have been young. They snatch him from kindergarten?"

"And... their birthdays. Both the same... the same date as... "

She sounded confused. I had very little time for that. "Maybe they're psychotic clones," I suggested. "Are there addresses?"

She texted the addresses. I thought maybe we were done. But she kept talking.

"You are not wrong, by the way," she breathed to me. "I miss Kuparr I... but I have a different reason for driving out of Skysill Beach. I do so at least once a day."

"What's the reason?" I cooperated, like I was learning to do.

"To make certain that I still can. I still do not know how or why the Aspectu in Skysill are prevented from so much as *thinking about* stepping outside the city boundaries. If Aeternus traps me here with the rest of you, I must know as soon as possible."

I wished her good luck escaping the city, and she told me be careful creeping around houses of people supposedly dead, and we partnered off in separate directions. My problem at that point became choosing which address to creep first. Julian's or Britta's? I choose Britta's since only circumstantial evidence suggested Julian was alive, while Britta I'd seen walking around smashing boulders on people.

Satellite mapping found her jewel box style party house angling for sun and watching ships right on the edge of Aliso Canyon. Trestles braced it out over the sloping ravine. It was leagues beyond the class of any stipend housing I'd ever heard of. I doubted Britta earned millions apprenticing in Roman's sweatshop, so maybe she was an heiress.

Below the house I saw the trails that branched and wove the canyon bottom. Aliso Canyon isn't a place I visit sober, and I'm familiar with a whole community down there who share my feeling. Sometimes the *Gray* takes me, long term, and when that happens I almost always find my way to Aliso Canyon. The things I've done *Gray* I prefer not to dwell on, but it does get me around.

My Lyft dropped me on the ridge across from Aliso on a broken strip of blacktop popular with coyotes and hikers tripping crank. From this side of the canyon I planned to surveil Britta's house. If anyone was home and saw, I'd just be an anonymous canyon crackhead. The memory of Britta's massive boulders flattening monks was more and more in my mind. I thought a ravine might be enough distance to keep me safe.

My ride backed away up the road and I slid down the trail to find a position to lurk. One hot and dusty minute later I was missing the hat I wasn't wearing and the water I hadn't brought. My plans seldom include water or hats. I don't like carrying shit around.

Soon I was hunched in half shade beside a rock peering at Britta's living room windows. I dialed my *sight* up, past technicolor, all the way to Higher color, so the air effloresced, the sea hues and coast flora blew open like hyperspace and I jumped. Since I'd begun seeing ghosts, going full-spectrum this way no longer summoned *storms,* but it was extremely distracting. After a few minutes I dialed it down to a modest glow.

Britta's cocktail perch stayed boring the entire following hour. I watched a lot of curtains and patios and places to mix and swallow drinks but no people, no signs of people, and at the end of the hour I lost patience. Sweat stung my eyes, and the trails outgassed dust in clouds. I coughed and admitted to myself I wasn't stakeout material. You need a better developed attention span for stakeouts. So I stood and slalomed the chalky path to the bottom of the canyon. I picked my way past beer bottle pyres and through condom fields and stopped on the other side, near an oak that was guarding graffiti rocks. There I panted, then started climbing toward Britta. I might lack an attention span, but I make up for that with my spirit of poorly conceived exploration.

I came to a wooden fence bisecting the hillside and scaled it without grace. Deep shadows covered me on Britta's side. Above me her pool hung—engineers had convinced the city to let them suspend a swimming pool in a wooden deck a hundred feet in the air. I got under it, tied to the hill with cables, counter-sunk on beams. A lot of work for one pool. Up through the scaffold forest I struggled, until I found an access ladder, and by that time I badly wanted out from under all that water, so I went up.

The ladder emerged onto the deck in front of an iron railing just a yard from the lip of the pool. There was nothing but canyon air behind me. I rested for a moment. The pool water was sprouting algae. The grass of the lawn was wild. I took these as signs the place was uninhabited and it gave me confidence, which is my least reliable state of mind.

There was a gazebo mothering some chairs in the shade and I made for that. Halfway to it I saw, from the side of one eye, refractions of *reason* unfurling up off the swimming pool. I turned. And there was Britta Lynn Genth, coming past the side of the pool house.

She wore a cloud of *reason* around her body like a cotton candy sundress. She wasn't looking my direction but out toward the ladder I'd just climbed. I studied her for fractions of a second. She'd definitely modeled Roman's *Sleeping Beauty*. She didn't look sleepy right now. She looked irritated.

She saw me then, and froze. One heel hung in the air. It was the thing you'd do coming into a room where people were sleeping, if you'd just made a noise. Motionless, considering me carefully, her irritated expression changing to interest, she then slowly put her foot down, waited, side-stepped, and watched me watch her.

My gaze shot around the patio looking for boulders, then returned to Britta.

Her *reason* glow went out.

"I think you can *see* me, can't you?" she asked.

"Britta Genth," I told her slowly.

"You're the Gale boy," she said. She had locked-in green eyes fitted close, shepherds for her thin nose, Renaissance lips, skin mottled ginger in shadows and hair in red waves. "You're *tapped!*" she said, like—oh, *now* I get it!

"The funny thing," I told her, "is how many people think you're dead. But you're not dead. Are you?"

"When did you get *tapped*?" she asked, stepping toward me while a little irritation returned to her face. I backed as she advanced, feeling unprotected.

"Anyway it's been a pleasure," I told her, continuing to retreat, a glance back, then, "can I get out this way?"

"I don't think so," she smiled.

Many things happened in the flash of a second—she raised and thrust her palms together and crossed her eyes away from her nose and *choke* in a nimbus rose on her shoulders, to radiate off algae water, then *choke* exploded down her arms. Out her palms. In one solid beam. At me, but it didn't reach me, because a globe of *dominion* snapped up and started absorbing it.

As *dominion* englobed me, my body froze. Not a *chroma storm* freeze, or *Gray* chopsticks frozen but full-body seizing like nothing I'd ever felt. It was death cramps, like bones might break if it went on too long, and it did go on, the whole time Britta's *choke* beamed out, until her eyes narrowed, her pupils reappeared, her head tilted sideways in anime confusion and she dropped both hands. She phasered off and my body un-seized and I fell to my knees.

"What was *that?*" she wondered, with a touch of wild mania I hadn't noticed until now. "What kind of ball of seven was *that?*"

"A ball of who? Is this what you did to Peter?" I gasped.

"Peter?"

"By the Beach?"

"I'm suddenly fascinated," she admitted, not in reply to my question. Again she beamed me, this time a rod of *compulsion*. Again a *dominion* globe formed around me, fending off her light, and my kneeling body froze, and started crushing itself. Britta passed her beam to hold it in one hand and tapped her teeth with her other fingernails. She moved around me, beaming me motionless, her white socket eyes pointed out the sides but somehow still seeing, just not seeing what she expected. Again she cut her beam.

I slipped from my knees to my face on the overgrown grass, sweating palsy. It was cool there. She could do this to me in full view of everyone, if anyone was watching, because no one else would see anything at all. Her eyebrows signed delight and consternation.

"Whatever this invisible ball of seven is," she said, laughing, growling, "it's not going to help. Where's your root, hmm? Only five colors left, little Gale boy. You're weak in one. Let's get this over and find out which."

She took a deep breath. Even shivering with strain on the soft ground I could see that beaming took some kind of energy from her. But it was energy she was giddy getting rid of. She threw her palms at me and out cracked a beam of *reason*, and *dominion* sphered up and my muscles froze, pulverizing my bones. I couldn't breathe, one bicep over tightened, it was ripping, I wondered if I'd be whole when she'd beam off, but she didn't beam off—after *reason* she shifted to *crush* and kept pouring. I felt a tendon pop in my shoulder and then Britta went Higher still, from *crush* to *farewell.*

Then I noticed a funny thing happening—it was getting hard to see the Higher light coming off her hands.

The saturation all across my field of vision faded.

And I was *Gray*. And everything felt very different. Very *wonderful*!

What a relief. I hadn't done this in so long. The last pale color left the world, and everywhere a smooth greyscale landscape spread, and it became a thing of no effort for me to align the stress in my limbs, even in my seizure, to work the levers and pulleys of me and save my muscles from breaking my bones.

I felt *unbelievable*!

The hilarious thing was the smile that wanted to spread on me that couldn't actually appear because I was in a seizure! So *funny*. I felt the sun on my left arm and warm wet where sweat kissed my lips, those things were fantastic. My eyes were frozen on Britta but that was perfect because she was all I *wanted* to look at! There were hundreds of amazing changes happening on her face, she was getting tired, she was getting upset, she was having a really great time, she was insane. I loved it. I loved it because that's the way I felt and I imagined how astonishing it would be to tear her face from her skull, could you get it free in one rip if you were fast, probably not but *something* was going to happen, it was going to be *amazing!*

The only Higher color I could see now was *dominion* and that was not a pleasant sight, there was something upside down *seeing* Higher color while *Gray*, a brain twisty wrongness, but nothing could be done until Britta stopped beaming. I was patient. I had my inside smile. And finally she turned off. I guessed she'd cycled through all of her Higher colored beams and she was shouting in frustration, "Where's your root you motherfucker," and then, instead of falling over feeling beaten and squashed I bounced up, happy, curious, and full of destructive ideas.

I ran at Britta.

I ran so fast I laughed at myself, so fast I crossed forty feet in a freakish blur which felt *astonishing* and surprised Britta who had no time to do anything but throw her palms wild, just as I got to her, my hands reaching for her face, and I froze because she beamed me even though I couldn't see it. For an instant I was a race car with the steering locked, I spun out of control toward the deck, the precipice, but going so fast she couldn't track me with her beam so my body unfroze and I found myself in a fifty mph tumble which it took quick thinking—I *loved* it, nobody thinks as fast as me *Gray*—then I dug palms into pool water that geysered and bled off momentum, then I hit the deck and rolled to the railing and rebounded! I spun, howling happy.

Britta'd been knocked to the grass as I passed, I saw something different in her eyes now, unfocused and frightened, which was so *fantastic,* I wondered what it would feel like to be her, to know she was about to have her face torn off, and what it would feel like if I popped her skull between my fists instead, it would feel awesome!

"Wait there," I laughed.

"Fuck you," she yelled and I watched—it was *extraordinary*—her eyes crossed outside and suddenly she lifted off the ground! If I hadn't been *Gray* I would've seen Higher colors flowing probably but I was *Gray*—thankfully!—so I power kicked in one long bound and braked so I looked up, directly below where she'd gone blast-off, to see her face peering down getting its confidence back. She rose into the air and I flexed my legs and my feet and my hips and back and *jumped!*

Even I was surprised how high I jumped. Britta floated dozens of feet from the ground but I hit her in mid-air, a little sideways because she tried adjusting when she saw me coming, and—it's so funny—once you leave the ground you lose leverage, it stops mattering how fast or strong you are, you're just a big leaf! I sort of flailed and snagged her foot, just as she beamed me, I couldn't see but I knew she'd done it because I froze, and I couldn't squeeze my hand any tighter to see what it felt like snapping an ankle bone. It was *fantastic*!

We hung floating in the sky, me locked onto her foot. She started gasping and I wished I could laugh but I couldn't move! You could tell she was almost out of whatever it was she used doing what she did—beaming me with one hand and floating us both up took a whole lot of *something*—and I knew after she ran out both of us would smash to the ground but before we hit I'd pull her close to me and break her neck—what would *that* feel like?

But it turned out she had enough to land us. She did it on the grass rough enough that my grip came off of her ankle but I did feel her foot snap. *Amazing*! She screamed. I rolled away and suddenly I could laugh again because she wasn't beaming. Oh, so great!

She was done, done, done, even though she tried thrusting her hands out I flashed sideways then circled all the way behind her *so fast*—even if she still had any beaming left she'd never be able to hit me, she wasn't fast enough, she didn't even know where I was! It was hilarious!

I watched her from behind for a second to enjoy hide and seek before I twisted her neck like carrot greens, and then on a hillside down-canyon where ordinary houses lay in rows I saw a incandescent *dominion* star flare, which was ugly and I wanted it off. I recognized it from the night at Kuparr's compound. And then, around me, my *dominion* sphere clamped again and I froze. Something was beaming! It wasn't Britta! She didn't know I was behind her! I didn't mind being frozen, it felt interesting, but I hated the *dominion* everywhere. The distant *dominion* star expanded out, broader and brighter and at the same time the sphere around me got thicker and harder, fighting something off, and I felt less and less happiness. Higher light in the *Gray!* It was obscene.

Britta turned to face me, struggled to her knees. I saw her eyes cross to the sides and then I heard a rumble behind my back and suddenly the gazebo was crashing me from behind—like the boulders!—and it came apart in chunks but lofted me all the way to the edge of the pool again. Whatever was aiming the other beam lost me as I flew so I landed and stood, smiling, halfway onto the deck.

Before I could run at Britta again something chopped the deck in half.

I found myself on the outer portion, peeling away out and over the ravine and starting to head down. There was a roar. Some invisible beam was cutting the pool and the deck to pieces with me on it! I tracked the line of the cut to the distant *dominion*—and while I did that Britta caught me—she caught me, good shot Britta!—with some beam or something and I seized again and the deck got hit again and *again* with invisible razor lances cutting everything up, somebody really did not like that pool, and then it was pitching in, collapsing down and in and sucking me. Britta kept me frozen. She had great aim! I went blind when a million gallon waterfall shifted into my unblinkable eyes, and a steel strut forked me so my body spun crazy.

I plummeted toward the canyon floor out of Britta's sight and unfroze.

Then, falling, I had the very amazing challenge of not getting slaughter crushed by wet, plummeting, ragged debris. I pushed off a quarter section of tumbling pool through the air toward another section, weightless, everything grinding, timber buckling. Maybe this wasn't going to be so hard. I'd learned how midair made you slow and weak so I aimed for a slab of plunging deck to get leverage but then something behind—a splintering beam, it felt *amazing*—raked my spine, folded me out of the air, everything spraying water, dark springing scaffold, no room to twist, it hit the back of my skull and I went fuzzy. I lost where the bottom was. It had to be close now. I wasn't going to live. So hilarious!

Headfirst—

FOURTEEN

I came awake the usual way, in bilateral pairs: thumbs and big toes, all the joints and limbs, until I was conscious enough to wish I hadn't started. Jostling. Bouncing. Dark and chilled. I pulled open my eyes. Night. Moving. Upside down. Sirens.

"What... threllahh..." I gasped. I felt a shoulder in my folded stomach. Blood spikes in my brain. Someone carrying me. The moment I spoke the rhythm changed, I was shifted, shoulder sloped and dropped, felt warm gravel under palms. Palms that shook. Blood on them.

Still in the Canyon, lower than I'd started. Not *Gray*. Fucking hell what? The *Gray*. It's never, *never* been like that, that fast, strong, determined on destruction. What was happening to me? I focused... on a figure trooping off down the trail. Head forward, a little bent. White pants. Rat beard. Thready daypack and everything blood-stained.

"Peter," I called. My voice broke. The night air damped sound. Peter kept walking.

"Peter!" When I shouted, it felt like my head blowing up. "Hey!" And I wondered, do I really need to shout?

"Pierre," I whispered. "Is that you? Are you okay?"

He stopped. He turned and met my eyes. His voice rumbled the canyon, "I cast the line too far. All those years ago. Since then it's been snagged on roots."

"You're covered... in blood," I ground out. And I thought, hazy, that's not his blood. That's my blood.

"The condo board killed my family," he shrugged. "Now I'll have to join the marines."

"The last time I saw you, I was a ghost," I explained. "That's why all I said was gibberish. Do you know what I'm saying?"

"You can travel in a boat made of water but you have to be a very good swimmer."

"That's right. I don't know what that means. I know it means something. Right? I'm... so you're okay. It seems like... maybe you rescued me? The last thing I remember, I was buried, passing out."

"Don't say Volkswagen," he told me, placating. "It's not confusing."

"If only that was true."

He tilted his neck then and his face flopped to the sky, and he blinked dark glassy eyes at high stars. When he took a breath he shook, and a stick dropped from his beard.

"Everyone takes the endless," he subsonic rumbled up, "turning corners they keep forever. They have spiders, build airplanes, and everyone finds forgotten *nothing*."

Dirty tear trails starlit his cheeks. It occurred to me he'd probably heard everything that happened to Kuparr. Supposedly Pierre could hear from Skysill to Los Angeles if you so much as said his name. He'd heard the battle. Would he recognize it, though? Did he know his people had all been slaughtered?

He was done with me. He ducked some mesquite and headed away, and I heard him basso singing. It settled into the bedrock. Went everywhere. *It's just another manic Monday, I wish it was Sunday, 'cause that's my funday...*

"Thanks Peter," I croaked at his back. I had no strength to go after him.

Carefully twisting behind me I saw helicopter lights and a firetruck emergency at the site of what had once been Britta's suspended pool, a half a mile up the dark canyon. Just to hear how unlikely it sounded, I tried out a theory that Peter had coincidentally been in the canyon already, and just happened to see me under several tons of debris, and pulled me out without really knowing what was going on. But I suspected Peter must have heard Britta attacking me. He'd come to find me. So what did that mean?

All I knew was how he'd left me—aching, though without broken bones I decided, and with a concussion. Anytime they knock you out it's a concussion... or concussed people just think that's true... loopy. I waited. After extended listening to night predators and my moans I decided I'd try standing. After that I walked, down hill, kept to shadows, didn't stop until an hour later when I stumbled out onto the coast highway. I felt I couldn't take another step. I needed to lie down. I found my phone still worked though, and I got a car. With my house locked, and me being unwilling to go to Amelia's all bloody like this, and because nobody other than Amelia would've let me in, really there was only one door left.

The hired car dropped me at the Bradley Building, which welcomed me into its dim marble lobby. Asher Gale's door wasn't locked when I got to it. I limped through, found the floor in front of the Admiral's desk and the thrown cushions, and fell. I slept.

Nothing woke me in the morning—I did it myself, hungry and raw-headed and alone. My bruises felt deeper in sun light. I reached a bottle from the bar—gin—and had some, which in no way helped, so I tried more. I surveyed Asher Gale's premises while my aches took liquor. The premises had a charm. No one ever cleaned. I liked the low stakes in that. There was also the bar and the open door rule that left you no way to lock yourself out, which I found appealing. I sighed. I didn't remember until too late not to take sighing for granted.

Going down in the elevator I scheduled another car and noticed some of my tongue was missing, and I had a loose tooth. I was poking the tooth with the tongue when the elevator opened on the lobby. On the far wall, near the hydrangeas, there were mounds of clothes and dishes and birdcages and a saddle and pictures of tigers all arranged around Phil and a few other people including Dale from Finance by Dale and Ambrosia in medical scrubs from Asher's reception party. The square dance couple were there. Everyone looked at me.

I headed for the front doors.

"You look beat up," Phil offered. He leaned elbows on knees, holding a bowl of mango slices. He had dark circles under his eyes. "You should take a taekwondo class."

The observation stopped me. I guess it's not that hard to do.

"Taekwondo particularly?" I asked.

"Yeah. That's the best one," he told me. He looked at my clothes and noticed me seeing his mangos.

"You ought to go to a clinic," said Ambrosia. "Your head's bleeding like shit."

"I'm fine," I told her. "It's mostly just skeletal damage."

"Eat some if you want," Phil said, raising his bowl.

"Hey," Dale complained, "don't feed him. That's the guy!"

"What's it matter?" Phil philosophized to Dale. "This is what happens in the jungle. Powerful animals push weak animals out, weak ones find a new a biosphere or die."

"It's too sudden," said the rodeo lady, "where will people square dance now?"

"The rich eat the poor," Phil shrugged again, "that's the way it's supposed to be."

His grip on his bowl looked precarious. I helped him with it. He offered me a plastic fork and a paper plate. I took the fork and started eating from the bowl

"Believe me, *I'm* not the rich," I told them, chewing, "I'll be kicked out of here as soon as I sign their papers. You can't work with these people."

"Do you know where you're going to go?" said the rodeo lady.

"I'll probably buy another car," I guessed. "This salad is great."

"Island fruit," Phil sigh-bragged. He rooted in a box and held tropical shorts and a shirt wrapped in plastic to me. "Old merch from my store. You need it more than I do."

"Change clothes right away," Ambrosia encouraged, "and check for lacerations."

I returned Phil his salad and fork and took his clothes to the stairwell to change, because while *I* don't have a sense of decorum, I do have a sense of other people's decorum. My old clothes, bloodstained and ripped, I dropped onto the stairs. I took everything off but the cold, blue necklace.

"Just go find a different building," I shouted from my changing room, "what's the big deal?"

The rodeo lady yelled, "We can't afford anywhere. Nobody makes money in this town but *art* galleries. So stupid. The Bradley Family is dead."

I reemerged fully Hawaiian in short sleeves and buttons. The rodeo lady was crying. Dale patted her quietly. Ambrosia came and taped sterile gauze behind my ear and reminded me that bloodstains come out with hydrogen peroxide. Then my phone chimed.

"That's my car," I announced. I felt I owed an explanation.

"Been great knowing you," Phil sallied.

"Has it though?" I couldn't help wondering, and he shrugged one last time. I exited the lobby and entered my car and let it take me down to Fenestram Paint. As far as I knew there were no ghosts along that route but I still felt jumpy. I had post-traumatic ghost syndrome.

I arrived without a haunting. The little entrance bell sang when I went in. Paper and acetate smells plumed. The place was crowded. I saw Dwayne standing in one corner, breathing and scanning. He didn't wave hi. Veronica stood at the register pushing buttons and issuing commands to a teen beanstalk. I high-hand waved her over the backs of two or three artists I was disappointed to recognize in line and she waved to say *wait over there*. The artists in line turned. I ducked into drafting supplies. A few minutes later she found me loitering near mechanical pencils.

"Busy in here," I complained.

"Hmm. You're very colorful," she told my island clothes and bruises.

"You'll never guess what happened to me."

"Did you lose your cage fight in Maui?"

"Roman's apprentice dropped a swimming pool on me."

She tried to picture it. "She had a crane?" She didn't seem concerned enough.

"Not from a crane," I hissed, "she did it with sparkle fingers! Britta Genth is one of *you*. How come you didn't recognize her when we saw her in Kuparr's command center? This is the apprentice girl. I thought everyone came in to Fenestram Paint for Higher supplies?"

"The woman who attacked us is an apprentice? Roman's people find supplies elsewhere, or I would have recognized her. Julian I knew from social gatherings, but I don't know the others. Roman kept them closeted."

"I don't think that was Roman. I think it was Julian. He's a closeting kind of influence."

"You say—Britta, was it?—attacked you?"

"Yeah. With light beams. You ever hear of getting attacked with light beams?"

Her face ceased working on the many other problems which had, until that moment, been more important than whatever I was likely to say, and it focused. Her black eyes fixed on me.

"Beams?" she said. "*Lances*? That is how Aspectu duel. Did the lances hit you?"

"No. I got a thing, I don't know what, a light shield."

"There! A ball of seven! Yet those cretins refuse to believe me."

"Are these cretins I know, or is it new cretins?"

"The cretins do not matter. We disagree about many things." She shook her head at me, like maybe I should be sent to my room. "How is it possible? Unless you've been tapped, you shouldn't be able to shape a ball of seven."

"I shaped a ball of something. It was pure *dominion*."

"Yes. Your extra color. Which I do not believe is a color."

"Believe whatever you want. Look, I'm here because I changed my mind about your eye thing since getting jumped by the psycho sparkle girl, and beaming everywhere fucking hillsides sliced up, it leaves me... just do it. Tap me. Let's even the playing field. I want beams of my own. Do I get beams?"

New information was coming at Veronica pretty fast. Shields made out of light she didn't believe in, tapping me, a mysterious Aspectu apprentice. She put her hand to one temple and lidded her eyes, not drunk, but definitely suffering. I liked seeing it happen to other people. Veronica got things back in hand faster than I'd ever managed, though. She'd weighed the pros and cons.

"It is about time," she agreed, mentally accelerating, gaze fully stable.

"You guarantee this won't fuck up my eyes? They're barely working as it is."

"Tapping creates a passage. What is inside comes out. Your eyes are unaffected. There's one very important condition I do have, however. Once tapped, I will exercise a degree of control over your abilities. For everyone's safety. But you must agree. Think of it as an internship."

"Is that real," I said, suspicious, "an internship?"

"Yes. I'm afraid it's non-negotiable. Your consent in required."

"Fine whatever," I told her. "Intern me. It can't be worse than getting beamed."

"Very well," she nodded. "Follow."

She signaled the cashier teen—he seemed better self directed than taking Veronica's directions—then had Dwayne follow us at a distance. She took me out the back door of the Paint building and we hurried across a narrow lane, and on the other side we went in the back door of someone's house, into a mudroom where a washer and dryer had once been. Without slowing she led us into an empty kitchen and through an empty living room, blinds drawn, heading for the front door.

"What goes on in here?" I echoed from behind.

"This is a shortcut," she told me.

"Whose house is it?"

"Mine."

Then we were out the front door and I had a view of a rocky point, some ocean spray, and across a frontage street from us, bird-cage houses rowed up to view the water. I followed her across the street up the steps of the nearest house. She worked a key, we stepped into an open floor great-room devoid of furniture. Ocean bluffs were framed through what would have been a kitchen if there's been appliances. There was a staircase leading up along one wall. While she locked the door, I made observations.

"You own this too?"

"I bought them all together. And those to the right and left. Defensible space."

"Money's no object."

"Not for what I am buying."

"Which is?"

She took us toward the staircase. We pulled the banister toward the second floor.

"I'm buying whatever time still remains to us, Mr. Gale," she said. "The ghost is the only thing that matters. He's rising again, a thousand years early. If Aeternus can't be stopped then all my money is useless."

"I don't think I've heard you this upbeat before."

"Perhaps if you paid better attention."

"I've tried that, I don't notice a difference."

We reached the landing on the top of the stairs where a hallway went past three ocean-view rooms. Sea light came through two doors and the last door was closed. I could see we were headed for the third door. I got a pang, because why is it always the mysterious, closed door?

"Is something the matter?" she asked.

"You probably have a plan."

"I do."

"I just... I hate plans with me in them, they're too unpredictable."

She faced me. I noticed she looked tired, her pallor less subtle than usual, her lips hardly bothering to be bloodless. Her eyes battled bloodshot. Her face was fierce, drawn in a way I'd never seen.

"My calling—curse, gift—is to tap Aspectu," she told me, quiet. "I am a *relino*. I stay in Skysill Beach because of the many thousands of untapped Aspectu here. Understand—anywhere else on earth an Aspectu child will be tapped the moment she comes of age. If left untapped, an adult Aspectu's mind will eventually break. Skysill was quarantined, somehow, so, until a decade ago, no one knew there were Aspectu here at all. But you are here. All of you untapped. Living peacefully, perfectly adjusted. The Council should *all* be investigating, but as you can see, it is only me."

"The council."

"The Fabrica Council. Idiots."

"I should've known there'd be a Council. Shadowy cabals. It's perfect for you."

"The Council is too inept to be shadowy. They are *cowards*." Her lips did a snide dance, but her eyes glared fury. "I described it, do you know? I described the experience you and I had in Los Angeles. And can you imagine what the Council told me?"

"You and I had an experience? I don't remember."

"Aspectu attacking after sunset! The power you transferred to me! The council refuse to act or even *believe*. They insist I'm imagining it, because of my... it had only been five hundred years they say.

There are a thousand years to go before Aeternus's rises again. But the signs are clear!"

She'd stepped down the hall to stare through an open door at salt beach spray, and some gull shrieked, and it deepened the furrows in her face but made her look younger, and looked like it hurt.

"The reality is, the eternal ghost terrifies everyone," she told the sand and the light. "And the Council wants to hide, but you cannot hide from facts; more than two hundred years ago Aeternus came to Skysill and seeded a group of Aspectu painters. He grew them here. He keeps them somehow, untapped but thriving. And the only way we can fight Aeternus right now, that I can see, is by tapping his pet Aspectu. Shall we?"

Me getting tapped, I noticed, had morphed somehow into us fighting Aeternus. I wasn't in love with the idea. But Aeternus and Julian were connected, and Aeternus and Peter were connected. And Samantha. Aeternus was the ghost behind everything I hadn't been enjoying.

I followed Veronica as she used up the hall.

The open rooms were empty. Wide windows showed a hundred yards of dune, then a cliff of lippy succulents, and below that thundered waves on rocks, and far away a distant centimeter of cloud on ocean. Possibly a storm.

Veronica opened the third door to show me a different setup: two chairs and a wooden table holding her carved wooden box. The walls shimmered dust motes of Higher color. The air smelled like orange blossoms.

"This your lady cave?" I asked, following her in.

"The ceremony requires light," she told me. "Light from the sea or from elevation."

"So now it's a *ceremony*?" I complained. Ceremonies unnerve me and are boring.

"Sit," she said. "Look at me. Listen."

Veronica said this pointing at the chair facing the windows. I sat and looked the room over. Floor to ceiling Higher light bounced around, the surfaces coated with something I'd never heard of. I felt like I was inside looking out the window of a giant microwave.

"We're skipping a month of preparation," she instructed. I saw we'd come to the part where I'd be given instructions I'd fail to follow or remember. I don't know why people bother. "We can take a few hours now and go over terms, expectations, so you feel more secure."

"Skip that," I told her. A nervous tension was building. "Start anytime."

"Put your hands on the table then, palms down," she told me. I did it. She sat in the other chair and opened her inlaid box where in gleaming blue silk were cushioned seven opalescent, delicate glass figurines—forms infused with reflectives, so each figure gave back one of the seven Higher colors.

There was also a small disk—like a beverage coaster—in such a deep matte black it had an antiglow. It pulled light in. I spun my *sight* wide but didn't catch a photon from it. Veronica placed this coaster carefully between my palms on the table.

"We already know you have all seven Highers," she told me, with a hint of apology that didn't inspire confidence. "One of those seven is your root. Through your root we will tap you. These figurines represent the Higher colors and their powers," she nodded at her box. "Take each as I hand it to you, and set it on the black pad. One figure will pulse. One other will burn. When the second figure burns —we call this the purgation—you are tapped."

"Burns?" I wanted to take my hands off the table. "That's why I said no explanations, they never help."

"It does not burn. The purgation is happy. And painless. How is that?"

"One figure pulses, with another there's a purgation that's painless?"

"You see? Pulse and purgation. Almost as though you were paying attention."

"I feel like I'm doing all the work. You're just showing off your glass menagerie."

"The figures play their part equalizing body chemistry. The Nidor make them. But my part is...intense. *Relino* are very rare. When I do find your root there will be a reaction. Higher energy will be released —a paroxysmal multi-variant purgation—and when this purgation of light emerges, someone with sufficient capacity must absorb and return it, in an instant. Few are prepared to take so much light. Of those that are able, most fail the training. The remainder are relino."

"It gets more complicated and weirder the more you talk. Just do it. My arms are tired."

She touched the box and a *choke* webwork danced from her fingers to a thin drawer, which slid open. She took out a half-circlet of silver and diamonds that spotted the walls, the paramount jewel a glitter globe repercussing Higher light. It was a lot. She fitted the circlet over her brow, pressed above her ears to pin it on her fore- head. Her pale skin and white hair had ice goddess glimmer. I watched both her pupils cross the wrong way out, then she dropped her lids.

"I get a headache watching that," I offered.

"It is a side effect of gathering *light*."

She reached a hand into her box and lifted a translucent glass shape. When she held it closer I saw a human heart, the size of a matchbox—anatomically accurate, I thought, though I'm no cardiol- ogist. A gleam of *choke* waved from the glass.

"Take it in two hands," Veronica said, voice soft.

I held it with my fingertips and it reminded me of every other tiny glass heart I'd ever fingered; cool, smooth, light, with aortas. The back was flat because that's where you mounted it on your shadow coaster. Veronica let me get familiar, then she started talk- ing, eyes closed.

"*Choke*," she announced, rote like pledging allegiance, "first Higher color, form of a *heart*. Concerning: *accumulation* and *dissipation*."

She put her own hands on the table. She straightened her back.

"I am prepared to take the light," she said. "Place the figure."

Slow as certain death I lowered the heart, not remembering why I'd decided doing this was a good idea. A paroxysmal purgation seemed like a misleading name for something that wasn't going to knock you unconscious. Veronica looked relaxed though, slow breathing, Higher crown all peacock brilliance. Fuck it, I decided. I dropped the *choke* heart and held it *click* to the lightless coaster.

Nothing happened.

Efficient as a dealer collecting cards Veronica pulled the heart off the table, still white eyed, and lifted the next figure from the box; a straw of glass the thickness of my little finger, twisted into a knot, reflecting *compulsion*. Veronica held it out and I took it with both hands. I learn fast. I'm monkey trainable.

"*Compulsion,*" she announced, smooth, emotionless, "second color, in the form of a *knot*. Concerning: *attraction* and *opposition*."

She put her palms down, leaned back, toned out, "I am prepared to take the light."

I hardly hesitated this time, probably because I learn all the wrong lessons the fastest. I probably have a learning disorder. I snapped the little knot onto the coaster fast as an empty shot glass, and nothing happened again.

Then Veronica did open her eyes. I saw her pupils cross back in toward her nose and she pointed them at the glass knot reflecting *compulsion* from her dark-matter disk. The eyes rose and considered me.

"What'd I do?" I asked.

"This is interesting," she told me, though I wondered if her way of using the word wasn't a little sinister. "9999 times out of 10000, we get a pulse with either the *choke* heart, or the *compulsion* knot."

I sighed. Already something wrong with her plan. I tell them, they do not listen.

"What's it mean for me?" I asked.

"Your paroxysmal purgation, when it does come, will be... magnified. More dangerous."

"Maybe let's take a break."

"No. No stopping—somehow you and Aeternus are connected. You must be tapped. We cannot let the sacrifices of others be in vain."

That seemed like a lot of pressure I didn't deserve, but I decided she was mostly talking to herself. She inhaled, sent her pupils away, shut her lids. She cleared the knot from the black coaster, and from the box she lifted an eye—a perfect statuette in glass, with lid and pupil reflecting *reason*. I monkeyed it into my fingers.

"*Reason,*" she said in her lecture lady voice, still smooth but not quite emotionless, maybe from all the talk about sacrifice, "third color, in the form of an *eye*. Concerning: *transparency* and *obscurity*."

Palms down, she pronounced, "I am prepared to take the light."

I snapped the beady little eye right down, fast and easy—by this time it was a habit. It clicked, nothing happened, Veronica snapped her eyes up, speculated them narrow, then crossed them and cleared the table and lifted the next figure; a glass measuring spoon in *crush*.

I took it from her.

"*Crush,*" she said, but now her voice had an edge. Her hands did a little brace on the table, an unconscious thing. I half expected her to call it off, whatever we were doing. But she took a breath and her voice got smooth, and she announced, "fourth color, in the form of a *teaspoon*. Concerning: *vast* and *infinitesimal*. I am prepared to take the light."

I clicked it down but there was no light. Her eyes darted open. She failed with a keeping-things-calm expression. She tapped one finger on the table, no longer even pretending smooth or emotionless.

"Why so worried?" I asked, worried.

"No reason, just thinking out loud..." she said, and seconds ticked by.

"Your thinking out loud needs practice," I told her. "I get a vibe. This is dangerous?"

"Yes."

"To who?"

"Who do you think?"

Then she counter crossed her eyes and closed them and took the next figure from the box—a tiny theatrical stage with curtain, broadcasting *farewell* from buried facets. Veronica barely waited for me to take it before speaking.

"*Farewell,* fifth color, in the form of a *proscenium.* Concerning: *beginning* and *ending.* I am prepared to take the light."

There was sweat at her temples now. Her hands on the table flexed and she clenched her jaw. Everyone in the room had the picture. Something was going to happen. We knew it.

But nothing happened, though I snapped the little stage right down on the disk. Veronica hissed a tight breath, didn't open her eyes, speared the space clear and held me another figure, a gossamer frigate under sail, glazed *wander.*

Her crown had grown blinding, I realized, though I couldn't remember when it had happened. I dialed my vision back to keep from being dazzled blind. Veronica passed me the sailing ship. Two colors left, and supposedly we still needed both a pulse and a purgation.

"*Farewell,*" she said, clear voiced again, direct, almost resigned, "sixth color, in the form of a *ship.* Concerning: *here* and *there.* I am prepared... to take the light."

She claimed to be prepared but it was hard to think she didn't have doubts.

"Are we sure—" I started.

"Do it."

I gave it some thought which didn't help, then I did it. I knew it wasn't a good idea.

Nothing happened. Veronica shuddered.

"I feel like there's something you're not telling me," I complained.

"We've come to *bleed*," she said. "Those with a *bleed* root are... dangerous. What *bleed* concerns is dangerous. Those Aspectu tend to be a type. And in this case, we've not even seen your *pulse*... so the purgation will be... the pulse and purgation will happen at once. It implies power that simply isn't... practical."

Her temple sweat was gone. Her boa eyes fanged the back of my brain and held me.

"Under normal circumstances," she admitted, "the only thing to do would be kill you."

"That keeps coming up," I complained, "what'd I do everyone wants to *kill* me—"

"But we cannot afford to kill you. We are fighting the ghost. We must proceed."

"Let's stop."

"No."

"I want to stop. I'm leaving."

"If you leave, I will kill you. You are too dangerous."

"Well apparently this might *already* kill me, so I'll take the chance."

"No, Mr. Gale. This might kill *me*. I believe the chances are... high."

She closed her eyes. I saw her pupils counter cross. She passed me the only figure remaining in her box—a knife, viciously serrated, the handle studded, the whole grim thing reflecting acid bright *bleed*. I refused to take it.

"*Bleed*," she said softly, "final color, in the form of a *knife*. Concerning: *destruction*."

"I quit," I said.

"No," she said.

"Destruction? *Bleed's* the power of destruction? I totally quit, Veronica, come on!"

"I am prepared to take the light."

"Game over."

"Yes," she said.

She lifted one hand. Over her knuckles a trace of *compulsion* river danced and shot at me across the table. I felt soft nothing hit me in the face, a whisper or kiss or ice age. Aspectu are supposed to be immune to *compulsion,* I objected to myself. But suddenly I knew: I'd follow whatever orders Veronica gave me.

"Take the knife and place it on the black," Veronica whispered. Her forehead refractory was in total Higher overdrive. "Do so now."

"You're fucking *crazy*," I said, and did exactly what she told me.

CHAPTER

FIFTEEN

A shocking silence tore the room.

And nothing else happened. Seconds passed. Veronica's eyes opened to sweep the walls and ceiling where nothing had also happened. Nothing anywhere.

"That was *super* shitty," I said, "you *compulsioned* me? You said that wasn't possible!"

"It's possible because I'm tapping you and we're synched. The question is, how is the rest of this possible? How can you possibly fail to have a root color?"

"This isn't the first test I ever failed," I shrugged, "don't take it personally."

"This wasn't a *test*. Every Aspectu alive has a root!"

The stress of almost murdering Veronica, and even worse doing exactly what she told me to do without being able to stop, twisted me jumpy and cortisonal and mind leapy, and sent me trying out this conclusion and that one until I came to the conclusion that Veronica was either avoiding or had decided was too hard to believe.

"You left a color out of your test," I said. "*Dominion*. Maybe *that's* my root."

"Whatever *dominion* is, it is not a Higher color. It can't be your root."

"You admitted you don't know what's happening. Maybe..."

"You cannot shoehorn extra colors into the rainbow, Mr. Gale, you're a painter, you know how it works! There is no *eighth* ultraviolet color."

"Then what's *dominion*? How come I'm the only one who sees it? Whenever I s*torm,* I get filled with it. I think it should be part of your test!"

"It is *not a test*! As for *dominion,* I'm afraid... you know more than I."

Neither of us liked the idea of me knowing more than anyone.

Since she had no idea what was wrong with me, she pretended to ignore me and began boxing her toys. There was hot sweat in the air. Her windows had no sliders. What the hell kind of beach house was this? After she packed her figures she took off her tiara and the sparkle went out of the room. Then I got one of the ideas I'm sometimes burdened with.

"There's a *dominion* star," I said, quietly. "I've seen it a few times now."

She closed her box, distracted. "At the Auditus inholding."

"Yeah. When I saw the star up in LA, it flew around, recharging Aspectu the same way I recharged you, so they could sparkle at night. Yesterday I saw it again, only this time it sliced a swimming pool into pieces saving Britta. There are Aeternus connections... this star's connected to those Aspectu, connected to Julian, connected to your ghost..."

"Mr. Gale. Focus."

"I guess I'm saying, all the ghosts I see are glued up with *dominion.* They *shine.* So I'm wondering what some ancient, malevolent ghost—like for instance the one *you're* obsessed with—would look like? Do you see what I'm driving at?"

Veronica did not like my driving. Even I found it fast and reckless. Unfortunately, that's the only way I do it.

"You're suggesting," she murmured, "that this... *dominion* star... it might be a single, extraordinarily bright... ghost?"

"Maybe. Maybe they get brighter the more ancient and evil they are."

"Aeternus."

My face had a relieved look which meant *you said it not me.* There were lots of things wrong with my theory, I knew that. For one thing, it fit all the available facts, and that almost always means I'm looking at things wrong.

"Is that how Aeternus rolls?" I asked. "He goes around, recharging Aspectu?"

"No one knows."

Despite the refractive walls and saltwater glare and beach sun out the window, the day felt suddenly darker, and threatening. Veronica felt it too. She pulled her arms in, and inspected the room, a reflex.

"If this is true," she breathed, "if Aeternus is here, I have to convince the Fabrica... you can find your way back to the store?"

"Five living rooms that direction," I shrugged. "Maybe there's a bus."

I left her, I just wandered downstairs and across the street the way I'd come, not at all happy, wondering what these new ideas meant for me personally. Because, if that star was Aeternus, what did it say? About me? I had my own problems getting filled up with *dominion.* What was I?

These thoughts were so distracting that I returned through two different living rooms and in the back of the paint store before remembering there wasn't any reason to go back to the paint store. I didn't have a car parked in front. I didn't need paint. I found, slowing to a stop in the frame and mat aisle, I had no idea where to go next. That's when the bell on the door dinged and Amelia came in.

She scanned the aisles, saw the line, the teen cashier, put her hands on her hips and narrowed her eyes, then saw me. I hadn't thought to hide. I didn't look the way she wanted, though I find I seldom look the way they want and you'd think they'd be used to it. She came toward me slowly, then stopped, glanced sharp, right and left, down oil paints and specialty papers, then suddenly at my hands. Fists? Chopsticks? Is Asher *Gray? Storming?*

She grabbed my arm and dragged me into watercolors.

"Are you crazy?" she hissed.

"Yeah," I said. "Why?"

"Are you painting? Are you trying to have a *chroma storm*? What are you *doing* here?"

"What do you care—I go any place I want—what are *you* doing here?"

"Oh my god. This is a paint store. I'm a painter. The Gala Lumina's coming, people are having problems getting Higher paint... what are you wearing?"

"Christian Dior. What's it matter to you?"

"I sent you *ten texts*."

"No you didn't."

"*Look*."

I checked my cracked phone. "Oh my battery's dead," I nodded.

"You have. To charge. Your phone. Oh my god you're so irresponsible."

"It's not *my* phone... it didn't come with a charger... *you're* irresponsible."

"If it's not your phone why are you..." she noticed the tubes barreled in display cases around us, pivoted mid-harangue, "... seriously, you're not painting are you?"

"Why would you even ask?" I snapped.

"What are you hiding?"

"Me hiding—how about you? How about we talk about Celine?"

I saw her freeze when I said it, and it was the first satisfaction I'd had since she'd started talking, but it faded instantly, thinking about Celine. My satisfactions are all like that.

"How come nobody told me she's sick?" I demanded.

"How did you find... ?"

"So you *have* been hiding it? That's so fucked up—Celine did raise me, you know, just like you, but you don't mention 'oh the person who raised you's in the hospital?' You don't tell me? *Why?*"

"Ash," she stopped being mad Amelia, the way she can, on a dime. I preferred mad Amelia to sad, but now it was too late. "Are you seriously asking why? Why we wouldn't tell you? Because why do you *think*? Your... the *chroma storms,* the *Gray*—we never tell you anything."

"What?"

"No one tells you anything, Ash! You must know that. I can't believe I'm even saying this, you might *storm* from my tone of voice."

"What do you mean? *What* don't you tell me?"

"Anything! Things going on. People coming, leaving, painting, gossip. Graduations. Shopping trips. Babies—oh my god *babies*—you'd *storm* a week if anybody had a baby! You can't handle anything. That's just the Asher we've got. We love him. But we never tell him anything. We *can't.*"

"But you don't tell me Tante Celine's sick? Because I'd *storm?*"

"Yes. My god, Ash, I've seen you fifty hours out of your mind sleepless crazy—and then the *Gray,* you vanish for a month, six months, we don't even know you're alive—do you know how many times you've come *this close* to jail? Of course you don't, it's a blur to you. Roman, Damely, somebody saving your... plus *come on.* Admit it. You prefer being in the dark. It's simpler. You don't have to be responsible if you're in the dark. How could you be *responsible* if you never *know* anything? It's very convenient."

It was a very painful and confusing argument to be having in the watercolor section. It was the confusion that kept me going.

"What are you saying, I *like* nobody telling me anything?"

"That wasn't fair. I'm sorry. It's been a shit fest of a week. That wasn't fair."

"How long has everybody, or nobody...?"

"There're so many things that can go wrong, Ash, we keep you as safe as possible. That's why we didn't tell you about Celine. We didn't want to lose you. But you seem... you're not *storming*?"

"I don't *storm* the way I used to."

She grabbed my hands, squeezed, a deep physical test, the only test I ever felt like trying to pass. Amelia's test of my state of mind.

"I'll just point out one thing," she said, glancing around now, and wondering how loud we'd been arguing, "you never *ask* anything. If you asked, I'd tell you. I wouldn't *lie* to you."

She frowned, smiled, and everything between us was forward facing once more. The Gales confronting the future. I have no idea how she got so good at that.

Her smile faded, though.

"The truth is Celine's really sick," she said, one eye on my hands. "It's... cancer. How much do you know? It started with lungs, and, you know... brain, bones."

"And? Is she getting better? What do the doctors say?"

"Ashy. No more doctors. She's... you're sure you're okay?"

"Yes, stop," I said, "I mean, I'm fine, go."

"What else is there? She doesn't have much time... so she's home."

"You really weren't going to tell me?"

"I don't know. We could lose you for *years*, what am I supposed to do with you?"

"Never mind. I get it. I'm a burden, but you love me. I feel the same way about you."

"Okay. I'm going up there in a few minutes. You should too. If you think it's safe."

"Of course I'm coming."

"You drive up ahead. I need a few things here."

"I don't have a car. I mean, I have I don't know, half a dozen cars at this point but various reasons I can't use those."

She decided not to ask—maybe it's a family trait—and instead she frowned at the cashier, checked the nearest aisles, noticed

Dwayne loitering near the measuring tools and frowned harder, then finally shook her head.

"I wanted to talk to the owner," she said, "but I can come back later."

"You wanted to talk to Veronica?" I asked as I started us out of the store.

"You know Veronica?" she asked, surprised.

"She shows up places you'd never expect."

She sighed frustration at my allusive style of conversation. And then, just the way I like it, she left me alone, though she did make me quick charge my phone in her car. She drove us up the dusty hills, and soon the sea was spreading behind and beneath us, and then it was flashing into view and away through branches, and then, before I was ready, we'd rolled in under pine shadow and slowed, tires crackling cones in a bed of spongey needles, where Celine's 70s beach Chevy had its own hollow, dusted with an inch of yellow pollen. Unused for months. If I'd noticed, I might have asked.

Amelia was out before me because I have trouble with her seatbelt. Then my Hawaiian shorts were free, the pinecones slipping underfoot as I went after Amelia toward the yurt, into the tang of vanilla pine bark, the buckthorn musk, the nursery rhyme I hummed:

Mommy's got three,
Daddy's got four,
But little baby Asher,
Has got one more.

Because I'd slowed, recollecting my rhymes and childhood smells, Amelia stepped into Celine's first. I heard her scream. In a second I was up on the porch, through the door, the mudroom, to find Amelia bent over a figure, white feet, white hair, nightshirt—Celine on the floor, in her empty main room.

My eyes clawed light from heavy shadow, everything curtained darker than a coffin. The solar was out again.

"She was just lying here," Amelia moaned.

"Is she...?"

"She's breathing."

Tanta Celine looked cold and pale, skin translucent as ghost water.

"Help me lift her to her room," Amelia said.

"How come she's alone?" I demanded, positioning.

"She wants it this way."

We carried her. She weighed as much as a tattoo. We laid her in her bed. I went outside to flip the breaker. The electric needed work. That's what everyone said. Then back inside, hitting the living room light, then into the bedroom. I reached to inch Celine's curtain back but Amelia stopped me.

"The light hurts her eyes," she said.

There was no place to sit. "What can we do for her?" I asked.

"Just be here."

For a while we watched Celine in bed, watched her breathing, sometimes shallow and light as a bird, sometimes deep-sea dive breathing, once a minute. And then, as though she'd finally remembered where she'd left her keys, she pulled a gasp, whipped up her eyes, and took the scene in.

"Ashy," she coughed, soft moss.

"Hey, Celine," I bent down. "Hey."

"Dude," she said, "dude, what are you wearing?"

Amelia snorted.

"It's a pretty complicated story," I hedged. "I'll get you some water."

"I don't need any..."

"Everyone needs water," I told her and turned for the kitchen and Amelia handed me the glass of water Celine already had beside her bed.

"*Fresh* water," Amelia nodded. I wondered how many times a visit she did this herself with the water. If there's nothing else you can do, at the death end of things, when they didn't know what they needed, you treated the people you loved like pets. I wondered if what you were supposed to do was get used to it. I hoped so. Living with it unchanged for very long was going to be intolerable.

I don't know how long I stood at the sink, remembering Celine; her laughing, her singing Hotel California and spinning wet clay like a tornado, and the missing pieces of me she saw and tried to fill with pieces of her.

The sun was lower. It looked like feelers of a storm out there, building over Mineral Beach. Amelia came looking for me.

"Ash," she asked, "everything okay?" The *special tone.*

"She's so sick," I ignored her. "How didn't I see it?"

"The last few days she's gone really fast." She had her shoulder against mine. We stood at the sink as we had so often growing up. After a minute she gave me a little pull, said with a puzzled tone, "Anyway. She wants us. She has something to tell us."

The curtains were thick and the lights were off but two candles had been lit in the bedroom, carving hollows and dancing the shadows of crystals and dream catchers and ceramics around. The lines at Celine's mouth pulled hard, a tooth stuck on a lip, dry as a chalk-nub, but the smooth skin around her eyes was braced, alert, focused.

"Amelia says you know about me?" she whispered as I came in.

"You're sick," I said.

"You're not *storming?* Is it true? Are you better? Ash?"

"I mean, I don't know if better's the right word—how are you feeling?"

"Dude. Not the best. But if... if you're okay hearing it... there's something I want to say. Because I love you both. Both the same. You're my kids."

Celine closed her eyes and rasped, collecting energy. Amelia had tears in her lashes.

"It's about your mom and dad," Celine said.

Suddenly her voice sounded strong, as strong as it had years ago screaming hallelujah and mescaline dancing. And for me, light froze

—that's the way it seemed. The candle photons stopped. For just a moment. Because my parents.

"What about them, Tante?" Amelia asked, low and curious and careful.

"A secret I promised. For you two. I never saw the point. But for Katerina… anything she asked. To keep you safe. Now maybe it's safer that you know."

She looked at us, blinking to keep eyes clear.

"You know why they left," I begged her to be saying.

"No—why they left? Nobody knows…" She began to cough, deep body stiffening, blood on her lips and a moment of panting—she waved us back. Drank water. Started again.

"It gets more and more like a dream. How they loved each other, like a fairy tale, your parents. From the moment they met. You see, your father and I had… Marlon and I were supposed to get married, but then Katerina came. Everything changed. Everyone knew. It's hard to explain. It was like… they read each other's minds. It was beautiful. And she was… she was everything. But you know. Nothing's perfect? Marlon and Katerina tried for years, but she could never get pregnant. Oh, they wanted kids."

She took water again, Amelia and I like rabbits fixed on a wolf. Run. Freeze. The difference is nothing.

"So she asked me," Celine continued. I had the feeling she was asking our forgiveness. "You see? The three of us were already, I mean Marlon and I had… they asked me to help them. It's strange to think of it now. We went way up, deep in the woods. Katerina and Marlon and me. We left as soon as I started to show. Oh lord I was so big! My god. And we came back down with you. It was what they always wanted. A baby."

She stopped, long enough for Amelia to whisper, "Tante Celine, what are you saying?"

"You're mine, Amy. I love you so much. You're my daughter. I'll never be your mom, Katerina's your mom. But you're my daughter."

"But," Amelia looked. At me? World upside-down? Amelia went, "You never told? You hid it from us? But why?"

"It's all clustered up, dude. I'm sorry. It's funny, the closer I'm... the weaker I get, the more I remember the love. The less I care for those... stupid promises..."

Amelia shook her head. "Tante... are you sure? I mean, you're saying..."

"That Marlon and I made you? I'm very sure."

"And then what?" Amelia whispered. "They kept trying for six years and you had Ash?"

"I'm sorry Ash," Celine said, turning to me "But I don't know who your mom is. Another secret they kept, this one they kept even from me. When Amy was five they left again, and came back nine months later with baby Ash."

"Ash and I have different parents?"

"Moms I think. Marlon got me pregnant so I assumed Katerina couldn't have kids. You look like your dad, Ash."

It was dizzying. The words filled out around us in the little room and rose in piles, a transformative stream, turning me into so many new things. Half brother. Semi-orphan. Love child.

"They loved you both *so much*," Celine burled. "Loved you like the end of the world. Your mom—whoever brought you into this world, Ash, Katerina was your mom, that's the way she loved you—and so I promised her. I couldn't say no. She made me... her gift..." Celine's words were slurring. She'd come to the end of what she'd marshaled. It was too soon. Too soon.

She fumbled at her neck with a chain she always wore, under her clothes. She'd never taken it out, I'd never asked to see, but she pulled it up now and from her mouth a few last sentence pieces spilled, soft trust, promise, as the chain came out.

A crystal hung there. Thin, blue, cold. Like the crystal I wore. Like Caroline's.

"Celine," I said, squatting to be sure, "where'd you get this? Tante Celine. Your necklace—where'd you *get* this?"

"Katerina…" she told me, words like smoke, "Katerina said he didn't need it, not anymore, she gave me the necklace to… so I could think straight… around her…"

Celine's hand opened, her breath ramped, bird bright, she sank back, eyes lost, mouth open. Unconscious.

The room went as silent as the shadow of a candle, until Amelia stuttered into dead air, "Do you believe any of that?"

It only took me another moment to figure out where I needed to run. Then I was on my feet. Celine always left car keys under the driver's seat. I went for the front door.

"Where are you going?" Amelia pleaded, following. "Asher! Where are you going?"

"To talk to a psychic I know," I yelled back.

CHAPTER

SIXTEEN

The air on the hill was colder now and blowing wetter, though not wet enough to clean Celine's windshield. I mashed a handful of pine needles and cleared the worst of it. The car hadn't been driven for I had no idea how long, but it took the key and guttered alive and I peeled around, off the hill. I felt glassy. You never realize how much you rely on the mother who abandoned you until you don't have her anymore.

Katerina Gale—my not-mother. Something in me resisted the idea. I yanked the wheel, poured the car down the grade too fast, grinding thoughts. Not our birth mother. She'd been married to our father, that much everyone agreed on. But in some ways, she'd never belonged here. She didn't have a file in Veronica's cardboard box. She'd had a neutral crystal from somewhere—a crystal she, or my father, supposedly no longer needed, though I'd been told you had to wear those forever. Neutral crystals were required for tapped Aspectu in Five Family society, protection from Tactus primes and vice versa. So before I'd been born, Katerina Gale had to have been familiar with Five Family society. So... she'd been tapped? She was Fabrica?

Halfway to the beach I pulled a hard left, going too fast, and then for three miles I rimmed through mid hill neighborhoods until I got to the edge of the psychic district. A mile downslope the Pacific was brewing rain and wind, and there was a huge, surrealist globe of *dominion* pulsing, an inverted tornado of Higher crazy right where Caroline's shop lived. If I went any closer to that I'd *storm*. Thankfully, Caroline was not the psychic I was looking for.

Jerking the car around curbs and corners and past palm readers, scryers, tarot seers and fortune tellers, I roamed the dampening streets of the district not remembering where to go. *We Are Closed* signs abounded, like psychics didn't like working when it was getting ready to rain. Maybe it was a psychic holiday. But eventually the simple, squared adobe of *Madam Nikita Thomasonian: Guide in Spirit* appeared ahead.

The car lacked a functioning heater and a chill had settled in me. The storm billowed low, sealing around the hilltops chainlink grey. Palm fronds gusted above the street. I stared at Nikita's. Once I'd had doubts about her abilities, but at Three Paths they'd taken her seriously. And Nikita had given me certain predictions, the time I'd met her. Many of them had come true. One of those I now wanted to ask her about.

At Nikita's door the placard assured me *Walk-Ins Welcome,* but when I tried walking in I found it locked. I shook, knocked, pounded. A windy flurry wet the back of my neck.

"Nikita," I yelled, "I have to talk to you about... something you said..."

Behind me I heard gears, a chain spinning, and turning I saw Peter on his ten-speed—he never slept or ate, it seemed, just followed me from place to place. His hair was plastered wet, his shirt soaked and backpack sodden. He pedaled without holding the handlebars, with his head thrown back and his arms spread wide. He sped past Nikita's building and away into the wind and out of sight.

I ran to the street but he'd gone around the block. The wind blew hard enough I had to duck into the car. I was torn but I knew I'd have to leave Peter to the rain for a while. I only knew one other place I could find Nikita and my welcome there was uncertain, but I backed up, pointed Celine's rusty cruiser uphill and took it into rain. Up toward the ridge line where I knew Three Paths sprawled gothic. The road was slick. Celine lacked one headlight. But finally the high fence and three gates of the compound appeared. I pulled to a stop facing north where the road curved.

Water beat the dull drum of the roof. Even inside the car I tasted the tang of electric charge in the air. Far below, the sea crashed, dark. Lightning forked the waves, blasting Higher light around visible-spectrum motherlode yellow. It was still too far to hear the thunder. But I noticed a strange thing—there was *dominion* in the strikes. It left afterimages, mountains of light, valleys, ghostly illusions above the black rising sea. *Dominion* hadn't ever done lightning. Apparently it was leaking in everywhere now.

From the car I dashed through rain to the gates, *Behind, Beneath, Before,* with their silvered plaques and little thrones, and took the gate I'd taken the first time—*Beneath,* because I'm a creature of habit —then ran the convoluted path in my Hawaiian sleeves, blinking rain, hair in my eyes, navigating inexplicable corners, until I fell out onto the gravel courtyard before the dark, mirthless hulk of Three Paths manor.

I skipped the castle door, went right, down the wall of granite, blundering into the clearing then running through rain to the covered porch with its side door and little window.

The *Happy Birthday* banner was still up, despite the wind, but it wouldn't last. I crept toward the small window, cautious as a spy. It didn't pay to take these psychics by surprise, with the lax firearm etiquette they practiced. I did feel that a sanatorium full of psychics should be harder to surprise, though, or what was the point of psychic knowledge at all?

Suddenly Li Wei's shorn head appeared in the little window. The door swung violently open. I fell and scuttled back, but Li Wei was a step ahead and snagged my foot from inside the door and braced against the frame with both feet. He looked even more linty and stricken than last time but he wrapped his subterranean fingers on my ankle and reeled me. A dozen more just like him bobbed shaved heads in back, like cadaverous birds. You could see they didn't mean me harm. They just lacked social skills. I sympathized.

"Li Wei," I greeted as he pulled me into his doorway, failing to fix his pupils on my face.

"Get out of the rain," he wavered, sliding me over the sill. "You know the rules."

The others chirped. Four or five hands from at least as many people wiggled down, finger tipping, urging me stand, murmuring *stand* in case I needed everything spelled out, which I admit usually helps. I stood. The moment I'd stopped resisting I'd become strangely comfortable. The fingertips, the whispers, then the door closing behind me, people encouraging me into the midst of them.

"I don't know if you remember me," I started.

"I don't know what the difference is," Li Wei wavered, a sheet in a gentle breeze. "I don't know why the Path Before is broken. I don't know your middle initials. I know rules are rules, so get in out of the rain."

They clung in around me now. I didn't seem to have much choice.

"I don't know if you've seen Nikita up here at Three Paths today," I told them, careful about the question rule, which was the only one I was sure of.

"I know people who've seen Nikita," he said. "I don't know if *you* know them."

"I don't know anything."

He nodded, they all nodded, a moment later I was nodding too, it was soothing. I didn't feel that my investigation was making any headway but for a moment it didn't matter. For a moment I thought Li Wei had fallen asleep standing up. But we were all just balancing. I was getting numbed, pressed in the group. We glided forward on some cue in a flock. I let them group me out into the hall, murmuring about something delicious we were going to eat.

"I might be losing circulation," I mentioned to Li Wei. "I'm numb."

"Three Paths," he nodded, difficult to read. "The Paths can't find you here."

We went up stairways and up stairways and up until I thought we reached the top floor. The archways up there were small and numerous, like little hunting caves, mostly empty. We eased down a long hall to the end and some of us were able to fit under a particular arch and the group stopped, shifted me fingertip to fingertip, then out through the cell membrane they expelled me.

"You find lost idiot boy," Nikita congratulated Li Wei from among scarves below a 40-watt bulb. She handed them a snack bag. Hands eagerly snatched it, and then they were gone.

I felt more like myself suddenly. It hardly even qualified as a mixed blessing, considering the bruises and the wet cold confusion. Maybe a mixed curse. Nikita watched me. She must have seen I was hungry.

"Chips?" she said, drawing a jumbo bag from a wholesale box. I tore the bag open and ate a few handfuls to get my brain back in the game.

"You eat like starving dogs," Nikita nodded, eyes narrow in approval.

"So you just said, *chips*? So it's okay to ask questions on this floor?"

"Do whatever you like. What does it matter?"

"I went to your shop," I explained. "No one's down in the psychic district."

"Yes. Everyone stays at Three Paths now like frightened babies."

"I felt like Li Wei was expecting me."

"Yes. I saw you would come. Every day they are worse," she complained, "and I am not made of chips. But Li Wei will do whatever I ask, for chips. It's the Path Before, now their minds are rotten wet pumpkin brains. So. What is this important problem you are here for, eating chips like wolves are in your mouth?"

It's hard for me to talk about my mother. Whoever she might end up being. I honestly didn't know how to start. I always end up going sideways first, in these cases.

"Are you real?" I asked.

"Good question. Yes I am."

"A real psychic?"

"I am a crosspath, but I know truth when it appears on the Path."

"I believe in you. You said things. You said I'd inherit something and it happened."

"I remember. Great wealth. What did you inherit? I think real estate."

"A headache is what. See what I'm saying? I don't know why I thought you made it up."

"You are charming and a good eater but not so bright. Is not your fault. Go on."

"And you said you sensed a dark presence. You remember?"

"Gah. So dark it gave goosebumps, like someone on my grave eating my rat."

I was getting more confident doing it this way. Working up to Katerina Gale, working up to finding out—who was this woman who'd abandoned me, if she hadn't been my mother?

"Well there *is* a dark presence," I said. "He's very dark."

Nikita shrugged, watching me chew. "Pff," she said. "They think a crosspath like me makes everything up. I make up *very little*."

She held up two fingers a whisker apart.

"And you also said some things... about my mother," I choked out.

"I did."

"You said she had a message for me," I blurted, and now it came in a rush. "You said she was alive and she had a message. What was the message, Nikita?"

She spent a moment having trouble remembering.

"All *those* things," she said, recalling finally, "about your mother —*those* things I made up. The rest was good. I did not want to stop. I was on a good roll."

"No," I reminded her, slowly, jumbling some of it getting it through my teeth, "I mean Celine... the neutral crystal and, Katerina's not my mother..." the end of my tender hope had come, it was dead, but its corpse staggered on a few sentences from inertia, "... you remember, *mommy's got three, daddy's got four,* you took my hand and sensed my mother, who had a message?"

"Yes. That must have been my top idea at the time."

"You said she was alive."

"Hah! I said all this? I am very good. No, it was quite surprising to me so much was clear at all when I touched you since you had strange energies around, like magpies or frightening dandruff, everywhere, it was distracting. Nothing about mothers for sure."

"Why would you lie?"

"It is not easy being psychic. The dry times where you are blind. If people do not get answers from me they go someplace else. The internet tells them. They read a *book*." She rolled her eyes. "All the other things I just told you I did see, I did see them. Tell me this. What was it like when Li Wei brought you here surrounded by his flock of tweety birds? Did you feel anything?"

"Numb."

"You see? I am sorry about your mother. Mothers, you know. *My* mother left me for vultures to eat. She said she forgot where she put me, but she was psychic so please. You and I will drink vodka now."

While she pulled out another bag of chips and a bottle of vodka I practiced not giving up too easily.

"I could try asking a different psychic," I suggested to the bottle.

"Hah, no, there are no other ones." She poured, we toasted. "Everyone is here. Only Phyllis and Caroline and Jorge," she waved, indicating Skysill in rain down to the beach, "are still at work. The Monarchs are the strongest. But the Monarchs will not talk to you."

"Why?"

"Because of whatever you did to Caroline. Whatever it was, Phyllis and Jorge want to kill you." She found it amusing.

"Why... what?" I protested. "I didn't do anything, none of that was my idea."

"Too late. Remember the old goatherd saying," she philosophized, "you killed the goat, you eat the brains."

"I don't know how goat herding works, but I don't think that's right. Tell me who's a good psychic *other* than the Monarchs. I'll ask someone else about my mother."

"Does not matter good psychic or worst. We are all hiding at Three Paths now."

"From what?"

"From the broken Path."

Picturing all the closed signs I'd seen in the psychic district, I didn't need to ask, but I did anyway, "You're saying there's no more psychics down in Skysill Beach?"

"Just the Monarchs. Sometimes me. I am not so sensitive, a crosspath."

"Just when I think of something useful to ask a psychic they go out of business. What's this broken Path? Can I fix it?" I was feeling desperate. It's not the kind of idea that usually occurs to me.

"Pff," she snorted, enjoying the idea.

"Well what is it?"

"Is delicate," she equivocated. "We do not like starting the panic. We do not mention it."

"Try mentioning to me. I probably won't understand. I definitely won't remember."

She sighed and refilled our glasses. "*Time* is what is driving everyone here. Stupid boy."

"Say it different and remember how stupid I am."

"Time. Is ending. You see? You see the problem this makes for psychics? Some are already losing their minds. Is very terrible. I do not like thinking of it, pass the bottle. "

"*What's* the problem, now? One more time." I had a tip of the iceberg feeling. Like something bad I wasn't going to see until too late. She flicked her fingers at me.

"Eh. However often I say, it will not change the words. Time. Is. Ending. Coming to an end. The Path Before has been broken, now the end is coming close. There is a cloud of nothing. Think of it like, when Elvis died, but much much worse and then the world ends." To relax her I nodded like I understood, but she saw through me. "Every psychic knows this."

"Nobody tells me anything." She nodded like she understood the principal. Just then Li Wei and his headless horsemen appeared. They looked in Nikita's chamber. Nikita hid her chip bag quickly but Li Wei seemed suspicious.

"Hey Li Wei," I called to him, "I need a second opinion. I do *not* want to ask you a question."

That stopped him. That had to be like catnip for a psychic like him, in witness protection.

"Here's the thing," I said, "I just heard the news, about time, that time's ending. I'm a little confused. That's pretty typical, but Nikita can't explain it, maybe too much vodka or it's outside her ability. She says there's a *cloud of nothing* at the end of the Path Before where time ends, because this Path is broken, and I'd like to know what that means ex..."

Li Wei's eyebrows rose, his mouth dropped, and lamentations like hell doors creaking open came up his throat, and spread to the sunflowers around him, and then down the hall, a mad, rising, chorusing shriek, it was fear and rage and sadness and minds flayed. It went on and on and on and then whimpered out. Then Li Wei took his crew away from me.

"I hope you are proud for yourself," Nikita nodded. "That was very smart and mature."

I worked on the new vodka.

"So when is... when is time supposedly ending? Is that the right way to ask?"

"Eh," she balanced uncertainty from palm to palm, "three months from now? That is where the Path is broken."

We drank more. Now that people were telling me things I found I preferred the old way.

"Can you explain it once more, a different style?" I asked. "What the fuck? Is time... ending, you're saying time is ending? Are you sure you're using the word right?"

"Yes is right. What words do you want?"

"Ones I understand."

"Who knows what you understand? Okay, take this bottle tiny baby brain, listen to me, now, and drink vodka. Here are more words, good luck with them. Let me dredge my past for you. Yes, there I see, very gruesome. Like my grandmother said on the day I was born—also actually on many other days, it is one of the few things she ever said—the big-shot Path walkers, Monarchs of the Path Before, they once could walk the Path one thousand five hundred years. These were just the Monarchs, you know, not the feeble brains. Fifteen hundred years was the limit into the future. Who knows why. Anyway—you are paying attention?—yes, drink, listen. Five hundred years ago something changed for big-shots, who knows what. My grandmother was not a good storyteller, and also she drank, so a lot of this is nonsense. But. On that day five hundred years ago, when a Monarch Before walked the Path, poof, there was a cloud of *nothing* where the Path was broken five hundred years in her future, and that Monarch found out touching the cloud meant hyena brains. You know this saying, hyena brains? Crazy coo coo. Touching that cloud, where the nothing sits, made hyena brains. Since that time five hundred years ago the Path Before is broken. We get closer to that cloud of nothing every day we pass, we are almost in it now, the poof cloud, three months tops. Hyena brains everywhere. The cloud at the end of the Path Before, it will also cover the Path Beneath and the Path Behind so everything, past, present, future—it all will be poof! There. Time. The words of my grandmother. Vultures eat her memory. Has your donkey brain caught the picture?"

"What happens when time ends?" I was still struggling. The vodka was helping but I probably hadn't had enough yet. "I mean what happens to everything?"

"We will suffer. It will be horrible."

"Maybe it won't happen."

"Ha," she dismissed me. "Monarchs have seen it. Generations of them. Hundred percent. Li Wei used to be Monarch Before—then he touched the cloud, trying to understand it, and look at him—Phyllis is stronger, and less stupid. The rest of the chicks on the Path Before all have hyena brain now."

I nodded and drank and tried to decide how worried I should be. I decided I should be at least modestly worried, from the looks of Li Wei and his brain.

"Don't you feel maybe... people should know about this?" I wondered.

"Tell any people you want, I am sure they will believe you."

"So you're saying," I put one word in front of the other, the way I do when I'm about to make a plan, "that I can't ask any psychics if they know anything about my mother because there's no psychics working anymore, because they're up here getting numb to the Paths of time, because they're afraid when they touch the cloud at the end of the broken Path they'll lose their minds? You're saying time ends and that's the reason I can't find out about my mother?"

"Yes. Do you know your quirk where *everything* is about Asher? I like this."

"Thank you."

"Another reason the psychics hide is, the cloud is driving terrible time creatures down the Paths, everything extra dangerous."

"Time creatures?"

"Very terrible."

We gave our attention to the bottle. Eventually the vodka did its work and gave me the plan I'd been waiting for. I took out my phone. No connection, of course.

"Stand on that trunk, there," Nikita pointed. "There is reception. You are welcome."

The *end of time* problem was an important problem but it wasn't my problem. My problems were Celine's crystal, and who's my mother, and Samantha's goblet and Caroline and Peter, and seeing ghosts, and going *Gray*—I just didn't have enough space for *end of time* problems. This problem was the millionaire kind. So I jumped on Nikita's steamer trunk and dialed. The charge I'd gotten in Amelia's car might power one short call, I hoped.

"Yes?" In one word Veronica conveyed her unhappiness being bothered by me. "What?"

"Hi, oh nothing, just frivolously totally wasting your time, I've got nothing better to do."

"I happen to be in the middle of something important. Is this call important?"

"I don't know, is Aeternus and the umbra eye important?"

She was surprised I'd remembered all the nouns. It caught her off guard so I could go on. "I have to do this fast—battery—Aeternus planted thousands of sound sculptures down through time. Umbra eyes. Right?"

More surprise from both of us.

"Yes," she said.

"They go back every what? Once every how many years? How often?"

"Aeternus plants an umbra eye every fifteen hundred years."

"One thousand five hundred years," I mumbled, adding twos together, "and there's a ceremony, then the countdown starts over."

"A quorum."

"Yeah, the murder quorums. Okay, the last quorum was five hundred years ago, more or less, in Florence in the High Renaissance, when Filippi painted the Kisses. An umbra eye there in Florence."

"What is the point of this?" she demanded.

"The point," I explained triumphantly, officially passing the end of time problem to her, "is I found out a few minutes ago that time ends in three months. That's not an exact date, there's... "

"Plus or minus a week," Nikita estimated, opening a new bag of chips.

"So right around three months from now. Does that sound weird? It probably sounds really fucking weird but I'm actually strangely confident. Time's ending. You see it, right? The psychic thing—they walk fifteen hundred years into the future on the Path Before."

"Psychic thing?" Veronica protested. "Psychics absolutely refuse to divulge information to outsiders. You cannot glow them. Despite years of research I know almost nothing. And what does any of this have to do with Aeternus?"

"You've been confused because it's only five hundred years since his last quorum and Aeternus is running around preparing for a murder spree, a thousand years early, but I think that's happening because your ghost is, literally, permanently, about to run out of time. In three months, time *ends*. The psychics on the Path Before are all brain fried up here from touching this cloud of nothing—so what if it's this way: every fifteen hundred years Aeternus has a murder quorum. He has some psychic Monarch walk the Path Before, fifteen hundred years into the future, sees where the next quorum is, starts setting things up. Starts deciding which lambs he's going to slaughter. This goes on, thousands of eons, whatever, but after the quorum in Florence he looks ahead and finds a cloud of nothing five hundred years in the future, where time ends. So he has to move fast. He starts planning Skysill, right then, to get in one last quorum. You see? Aeternus knows about the end of time and I think maybe he's freaking out. Maybe it's a ghost thing."

I felt I was failing to pass the problem off to Veronica in any meaningful way. It felt like I was really making it more my problem.

"Time cannot *end*, Mr. Gale," Veronica insisted, "time is a condition of universal—"

"—yeah how much does anyone really know about time..." I was interrupting her but hearing myself talk over Amelia in Veronica's background and hearing Amelia say my name—Asher, why is *Asher* calling?—as I finished, "... about time, I mean time isn't very clear and is that... Amelia? What's Amelia doing there—where are you right now? What *is* this?"

"Your sister and I..." Amelia interrupted in the background again, sarcasting me, congratulations for picking *the least convenient* time to call with whatever crazy trouble I was in this time and then Veronica was back, "We are downstairs at the house I took you to this afternoon. You remember it? I think perhaps you should come also. It has to do with Celine."

"What," I protested, "I just left Amelia at Celine's..."

In the background Amelia started arguing something else and Veronica cut her off and then the battery died.

I shook my phone but that didn't charge the battery. I sighed. I'd had enough vodka to appreciate the good effects of sighing. I jumped down off the chest and returned to Nikita's table.

"I probably need to go rescue my sister," I said, and sat. Nikita refreshed my glass.

"Yes," she agreed, "always rescue sisters, or ghost vultures will haunt you."

I had to ask. "Have you seen... ghost vultures?"

"Of course not. Ghosts are gone. *Ghost vultures will haunt you,* this is saying from the old country."

"Exactly which old country is that?"

"Eh," she shrugged, "it does not exist since they changed the maps."

"Okay." I stood. "Time, I've got to go, so listen... if you happen to see Caroline... if you see her tell her I said be careful. Her shop is ground zero for the whole ghost universe right now. They're doing a crazy tornado down there."

"No I will not tell her. Make trouble with the Monarchs? No. Goodbye. Coming back, bring extra vodka, and I think pretzels. I am sorry about your mother sayings. But what could I do? I am just old crosspath, I have to make a living."

I left. The rain had grown to a torrent stepping off the porch. I gravel dashed the flooding Path Beneath to my car, my brain circling round and round, picturing Skysill Beach as I'd seen it mapped in the Historical Society: a two hundred year old preplanned community, which I now had the insane idea had been blueprinted in the High Renaissance to somehow imprison future Aspectu, a long-range plan the likes of which I could only dream, undertaken by a ghost who knew that the end of time was coming, determined to go on one last killing spree.

The thunder was closer now, lightning stroking *dominion* over surreal landscapes and in the glare of one flash in my streaming side mirror I saw Peter, speeding his bike through the downpour, his backpack clenched, a streak whipping down Three Path's winding access road. What could he be doing here? It took seconds of fumbling wet keys from a wet pocket and boating the car in circles, and by that time Peter was gone. Spies in the rain. Like any other respectable conspiracy.

Down on the beach I made out the ghost apocalypse fountaining atop Psychic Touch. I drove a wide detour, and that detour and Celine's failing wipers and uncertain brakes slowed me, along with the fading vodka, but eventually I skated off the hill and slid to a stop in front of Fenestram Color. Which was closed. I spun my *sight,* searching the dark windows. Nothing moved, so I drove slow, the long way, searching around one block and then another, in the deluge, for Veronica's beachy tapping room. When I found it I parked and waited. I saw Amelia's car. I listened to rain grind the rust on the roof. I wanted to give myself a chance to think of something better to do.

But a few seconds of procrastination later I picked Peter out of the dark, splayed prone on Veronica's gingerbread landing, a broken mannequin catching rain on his feet. I scrambled from the car and barreled across the lawn, wet coming sideways at me like a water park, wind pulling until I got under the little porch.

Peter was on his back looking up, a beard like tangled sea growth, eyes huge. I tried not to drip, bending to him.

"I heard that," he vibrated, softly, seeping rivulets. His clothes had been bloodstained carrying me in the canyon. He palmed a wet invitation to join him on the landing.

"It's safer down," he assured me.

"I have a different sidewalk for that," I demurred. "What're you doing following me around, or getting places before me, or whatever you're doing? Are you okay?" He looked much older, clean from the rain. Sun cracked and oily and lost.

"Sacrifice is all we have to prime the pumps," he barrel chested, weak. "The past is full of pumps. The past is full of pumps."

"Some of this blood is yours. Did you get hurt? We should get you to a doctor."

"The doctors froze my ovaries," he mumbled from his cavern, "so what's the point?"

"Why don't you come inside? Get warm? Are you hungry?"

I reached a hand to help him but he sprang to his feet and backed off the porch into the rain.

"Remember what I said," he pleaded, shedding water, hair striping his forehead. "We'll thread dead eyes back to the start."

"Remember what you said? Peter—come back!"

He backed across the yard, shaking, confused. I watched him stumble up the street. Maybe he knew a shelter this side of town. Maybe he had a friend with a tent.

When I turned back I saw his pack, fallen into the mud. I spun and shouted, then remembered I didn't have to.

"Peter," I spoke to the wind, "Pierre, I have your pack. I'll take it inside to dry. Come back for it."

Holding the pack, dripping mud, I pushed open Veronica's door. Rescuing, arguing with, or apologizing to Amelia would only take a couple of minutes, I hoped. After that Peter would come back or I'd go looking for him. The pack thudded when I dropped it by the door. Peter might secretly be a rock collector. When the door closed the storm became a whisper.

The ground floor was just the one large room, staircase on the right, a long kitchen island like a pier thrusting from the wall. Behind that a kitchen missing its appliances, and behind the kitchen, wide French doors holding back a dark storm. Most of the fixtures lacked bulbs, there was a patio table in the kitchen and no other furniture, and a fireplace with Grinch crumbs. The kitchen, under one bulb, held Amelia and Veronica at the table.

"Ah, Mr. Gale," Veronica noticed, like I was one more thing in her life to keep track of. My shoes squeaked as I padded toward them.

"You're tracking water," Amelia complained.

"Yeah, I filled them with a hose just now," I told her, "to inconvenience everyone."

"Wipe your feet! What are you doing here?"

"I go where I want," I kind of yelled, "and wait a minute is that Celine's necklace?"

It lay, curled in its silver chain, on the patio table between Veronica and Amelia. We all looked at it. Even in the half light it rang the blue of glacier ice.

"Veronica just told me you went to *Los Angeles,*" Amelia accused, changing the subject and pocketing the crystal, "are you *kidding* me?"

"You don't have any say where I..."

Veronica was about to start rolling her eyes at what she could obviously see was Amelia's basically pathological inability to speak a civil word to me, was what I assumed, but then she got a text, read it, and instantly stood.

"Stop!" she whisper snapped. For a minute we had no sound in the room but the sheeting of the storm. She spun to the French doors behind her, then to the rest of the room.

"Dwayne is warning me," she showed the phone, "something is

coming. This rain is washing out the scent, he can't get an accurate—"

The front door interrupted her, slamming open behind me. I spun. For just a second I saw only rain and darkness through it, before Dwayne rushed in, wet, unsteady, holding a handgun. He went from running to walking to stopped in the middle of the room in a few baffled yards. Around the crown of his head ran a flickering corona of *compulsion.*

And then, right after him, Britta came jogging in dry as fresh flour, with red locks salon perfect and one eye lidded by lunacy. For a second no one spoke because it would've wasted the stare down.

Britta's eyes crossed out the sides of her head. One hand shot a beam of *choke* at my chest which didn't hit me because a sphere of *dominion* engulfed me and held it.

I fell to my knees and then my muscles tightened like suspension cables.

"Thanks for directions, Dwayne," Britta snarl purred, "now shoot your face!"

Dwayne raised his gun.

"Stop!" yelled Veronica and counter crossed her own eyes white and arrowed *compulsion* at Dwayne's skull, "*do not shoot!*"

While Britta beamed me frozen—she'd learned to pin me—she surged more *compulsion* up the line to Dwayne with her other hand, and now Dwayne's head was lit like a magnesium flare.

"Yes *do it* Dwayne," she laughed. "Shoot her and *then* shoot yourself *now!*"

And he struggled to, but Veronica snapped whip ends of *compulsion* and shouted, "Do not shoot!"

And Dwayne's knees buckled while more *compulsion* bloomed a nimbus, spreading over him neck to crown, and Britta laughed, forest shrill, a hunting cry.

"Well okay!" she exulted, "I came for the Galeling but let's do this first—we'll glow Dwayne's brain to motherfucking *porridge*! Dwayne, shoot everyone but me!"

With nothing showing in her eyes but whites, I watched Veronica perform millionaire calculations—they all look the same working the costs—then suddenly she closed her fist and her *compulsion* beamed off, and Dwayne raised his gun, and Veronica smoldered two handfuls of *wander* and swung across her chest toward Dwayne pointing his gun at her, swung them like Dwayne was a door she was slamming, and he vanished in a *wander* burst. He just... vanished. Agonized frozen as I was, I still felt surprised.

"Well *that's* a solution," Britta decided after a moment. She watched Veronica, keeping me beamed, not even looking. "Quite a night charge you've got lady. So, Veronica Knight's relino. How inconvenient."

"Have we met?" Veronica was asking Britta but examining me. She couldn't see the *dominion* shell, none of them could, but she must have seen Britta's beam of *choke* pooling in a little half circle where my sphere held it away. And she saw me frozen on the ground, groaning.

"Britta?" Amelia said then, and stood from the patio table. Everything in me wanted to yell *sit down, this lady's batshit crazy* but I couldn't. Amelia was trying to understand, maybe to help, confused, "I'm... you're alive Britta? What's going—"

"Stay out of it," Veronica barked.

"Yeah, *Amelia,*" Britta howled.

Then she balled a mass of *crush* to flick toward Amelia and I saw the patio table in the kitchen crumple in rolls. I watched Britta sweep vicious, backhanded, and the table slammed Amy to the wall with a sound like a car hitting a deer and at the same time Veronica flung her own *crush* ball and deflected the table off of Amelia so it hit the other side of the room and lodged in the wall with a ripping thud.

"Little miss perfect," Britta laughed at my ssiter as Amelia slumped to the floor, holding a shattered arm, staring, shocked, as it flopped like a roll of dough.

"You're so lucky I'm not allowed to kill you right now," Britta said. She turned to me. "Is that what you are, Galeling? *Relino*? Then why didn't you lance me by the pool yesterday? You're so *young*—it shouldn't take a minute to burn through this night charge you've got."

Amelia, I was trying to cry out to her, bent forward and white with blood starting to soak her shirt. I had to get to her. Pain seared me. I jerked a hand to crawl. I shifted half an inch. I had to. Amelia. Bleeding.

A translucent Higher sphere flickered up around Veronica and instantly another surrounded Britta—a ball of seven, all seven Higher colors scaling and shifting—and the two began strafing finger light across the room, thrusting, prying, searching for roots, digging.

Every quarter inch I moved ran wood splinters through my spine, toward Amelia slumping, and then I felt the *Gray* begin to come. *No no no,* I groaned without sound. Going *Gray* would mean Amelia would be totally forgotten. The *Gray* doesn't give a fuck for sisters, or anything else. I forced myself to move. The colors slipped toward grey. I panned them back. Please. Let me get to Amy.

"You're very good," Veronica said, catching a Britta beam, "but I'm afraid not good enough."

"I drained you in LA," Britta sneered, "I'll drain you here."

"Los Angeles was your home latitude," Veronica smiled. "This is mine."

"Is that what you think? You think you know my *home latitude*?"

Veronica brought her two hands forward and now she bore in, full vibrating Higher *light* pipes, seven colors rippling waves and beating Britta. Britta fell back, her eyes got wider. But she never stopped beaming me. Please stop, I thought at her. Please. Amy!

"Listen Britta," Veronica urged, now there was a strain in her voice but her color was *bright* and Britta's was fading, I could see it, "that's your name, Britta? You're *relino* yourself..." smash her with *farewell*, "but your night charge can't last..." razor strip with *bleed*, "I doubt you have sixty seconds left..." jackhammer blows of *crush*, "there's just no way you win here."

Veronica lunged and Britta sagged toward the door. Still beaming me. I'd moved a whole inch. I felt a muscle rip in my side, and the *Gray* wanting out, and it was obvious what was about to happen.

"You're out of your depth," Veronica told her, "someone's using you Britta, let me help."

Veronica, confident as a doctor with a thermometer, had her hands out and open, while Britta's hands flashed around her body and Britta kept backing, color weaker—my shoulder dislocated. I fell on my side. Only a few more seconds. I could see Amy from here.

"Let Asher go," Veronica called, "whatever you're doing let him go and I will help you!"

Britta stumbled, screamed, glaring at me, "Where are you getting this *charge,* you little fucker? You're too young..." she looked at the door and shrieked at the top of her lungs, "... what took you so long *stupid fucking cunts?*"

Three more people rushed in from the rain, beaming Higher everywhere, undisciplined, wide-spectrum. And I slipped *Gray.* I couldn't hold it anymore. And Oh. My. God.

Suddenly I was bracing bone on bone, evening the muscle torque, making everything wonderful, free of pain. A cool, calm greyscale moonscape of a room settled down around me and it was *fantastic.* Britta still pinned me in a *dominion* shell, sideways on the floor, but the floor felt *awesome* against my hands.

Then she staggered, and for just a moment her beam died and my shield started dropping and I swung my leg, feeling so *happy,* before she screamed, "Lance him!"

Now it was easy to think straight. Why had I been worried about Amelia? She was boring. The new people in the room were the interesting ones. I recognized them from portraits in Roman's gallery. One had posed as a Fisherman with a goatee. Another as a New Mom. The third Roman had painted as a Serving Girl.

They were Roman's apprentices, risen from never having been dead to begin with—so *fantastic!*

Serving Girl flicked her hand and an invisible beam hit me—

everything Higher was invisible except for *dominion*—just as Britta's arms dropped, and my leg froze again. Tantalizingly close.

"Finish her," Britta screeched at Veronica. Fisherman and New Mom started pile driving Veronica, and good old Veronica threw her hands around, rotating wrists, not looking confident any more. I wished I could *laugh*!

"Who's got thirty seconds *now bitch*?" Britta panted to Veronica. Britta's hands were trembling, she bent on one knee. So close, but I couldn't reach her. Yet.

Veronica fell back, palms up, bracing them off, I could tell she was tiring and a wonderful desperation snarled her eyes, wrenching her hands one way, another, fending invisible arrows, face dull with sweat and *super fun* to watch! What would happen next?

"Use her up," Britta screamed, "do it slow. Hurt her. She's almost drained."

It was impossible for me to see what was really going on. All I saw was a lot of crying, cursing and hand pointing. Serving Girl pinning me with her pointy finger. Britta looked nearly unconscious from fatigue. What a mess! Veronica went to a knee. They crowded close, Britta glared hate, Veronica no longer holding up hands to push things away, just hollow-eyed and desperate.

I had the strangest sense that I could hear Veronica talking to herself, it was confusing and awesome! Hear from all the way across the room? Fantastic and strange, the sounds in the room shifted, went backgroundy. There was something familiar in the effect. There was almost silence.

I heard Veronica doing apologies, personal whispers, "... *my fault*." Hilarious and mysterious! What was going on with sound?

A drunken lady voice issued two inches from my face. I knew that voice.

"You people'n deep shit," the voice whisper boozed.

Veronica panted back. It was like a conference call. "Nella?"

Her head came up. She was about rubbed out, clinging by fingers, it was *fascinating*! She blinked, "How many are you?"

"Jus me, stop'n *listen*," Nella slurred. So many surprises. None of the apprentices could tell we were having a conversation, it was *amazing* fun. All the apprentices wanted was to strip flesh from Veronica's body and kill me or try to kill me and that's what I wanted them to do! Come on! Let me go!

"Asher, listen," Nella boozed, "*you gotta open the backpack*! Get that? Pierre wants you t'open'a backpack *Asher*!"

"Ash... can't... move... " Veronica groaned. Nella's voice was so urgent. *Ash can't speak either,* I wasn't able to shout, which was funny, not to be able to say you couldn't say anything.

"He wants you *use it Asher GO*!"

Fisherman was smiling a thick grin, Veronica was listing and honestly a beautiful shade of lime grey, a pre-death shade, even and smooth, but still somehow she was able to whisper, "Ash can't... I can't reach... just a few seconds left..."

"'Kay js'hold on," Nella warned, "distraction'n gonna sound shitty but..."

I saw her then through the French doors outside in the storm, battered like she'd walked from LA on foot, all pumpkin shaped in shiny soaking monk robes, and behind her lightning and *thunder*— she bowed her arms in a funnel overhead and braced, like grabbing the thunder, and pointing—the apprentices noticed, something sounded different and they turned, and Nella just monk bombed the fuck out of the French doors in a thunder cannonade of *destruction* like a prairie stampede, a ragged sound-hammer that hit and blew the glass in, and deafened me, sucking wind, rain, storm rage— disarray everywhere and New Mom, who'd been beaming me, had to duck, her beam slipped, I rolled to a squat—free, *Gray,* and picking targets. So many targets!

"*Lance Gale CRUSH the Auditus!*" Britta screamed.

I could hardly hear her, my ears were ringing, outside Nella flew in the air and slammed the beach, a rag doll, so *funny,* then god damn Fisherman got me, good shot Fisherman! But I was going to get them, they kept making mistakes, it was only going to take one mistake, all I had to be was ready.

In the chaos Veronica got to Peter's pack, wind everywhere, one whole side of the house missing, the kitchen smashed wet-dark and loud, they didn't see Veronica pull the backpack unzipped, and I saw *dominion* blast up when she did, just an ugly thing, Higher *light* in the *Gray*, and Veronica's face twisted. She turned the pack upside down.

A dozen Rudyard Kipling turtles scattered, and my twisted keys from Asher's office and my melted phone stolen from one of my cars, all belting out *dominion,* and I was the only one who saw it and I hated it—so *hilarious*! Veronica still didn't understand, but she reached for a turtle. I saw *dominion* swell up her arm and vanish. Her eyes widened. She looked at me.

Then she stood, and I thought to myself that Veronica's very adaptable and efficient and good at battling! Not as good as me. But good old Veronica, all of a sudden she was in control.

"Keep lancing the freak!" Britta coughed, not seeing Veronica's new turtle powers, while New Mom took over beaming me and the other two turned to Veronica. But Veronica was ready.

They found her standing. Holding amphibians. Pissed as shit and beaming them, I guessed that because they stumbled and seemed confused.

"I want to *help*," Veronica screamed, furious, and I thought what a boring thing to say that was. I could do a lot better if anyone would just *let* me.

"Britta! All of you, you're being controlled," she insisted, "let me *compel* you—"

"Kill her!" Britta screamed. "*Crush* her!"

"*Crush* her but there's nothing here to—" protested Serving Girl.

"—*bleed* the ceiling you fucking idiot *pull up the floor*!" Britta, screaming, "*you too!*" She pointed at New Mom "Lance Gale, *crush* her, she's got to be drained by—"

Before she finished, Britta collapsed, holding her head and moaning. Very suddenly Veronica had turned to her, a flick, must have beamed her brutally—it looked *hilarious,* Britta's head hit the floor so hard it bounced like a handball and even as she was falling Veronica was turning, fisting up more turtles, spinning with arms wide, she wasn't bothering to talk now she just ate *dominion* and whirled around and looked furious—now *that's* more like it Veronica let's get me *free!*

New Mom cried out, almost fell, Veronica bearing down, I'd lost track of who was beaming me but someone, I thought maybe Fisherman, another second and New Mom's face collapsed, my shield softened—it was New Mom's beam! I almost moved, I almost surged, I was *excited,* it was going to *happen!*

Fisherman reached desperate to the ceiling over Veronica and gashed the plaster like paring apart a swimming pool but Veronica sucked up more turtle juice and *smashed* the floor at Fisherman's feet, *staggered* him and *ripped* the floor up and *bolted* him sideways so he smashed Britta by the French doors. Serving Girl and New Mom the only ones standing, but fading, disbelieving and terrorized which I absolutely *loved* and Veronica relentless and screaming so *beautifully* ragey super violent with awesome palms out to each apprentice and Serving Girl reeled! She fell! New Mom cried, reached for her head, *she* fell, the beam on me was fading, my *dominion* ball of seven evaporating.

I got giddy, planning dismemberment, where to *start?* For a spotless moment things went calm. The last of my shield slipping off. Momentous stillness fell so there was only wind and thunder through the broken wall. The storm itself took a breath. I prepared to wield myself.

And then my hands curled into fists and I popped out of the back of my body.

"What the fuck *Samantha!*" I ghosted. The *Gray* feeling was gone instantly, because all the feelings were gone.

Samantha shimmered into place in the center of the room shedding orbital rings of Higher light, there were *so many* axises of influence crisscrossing in me at that moment I couldn't track them: the *dominion* shield fading but still holding me, the *Gray* and its violent eagerness waning, the ghostly *chroma storm* waxing—could I still be *Gray* if I was *chromatic*? Whatever part of me conducts my thinking didn't feel *Gray*, so I guessed the answer was no. One at a time. But part of me still wanted to be *Gray*.

Veronica, breathing hard, checked the apprentices, fast and smooth, then lanced Britta again making sure she was down, or maybe just pissed off. I saw the *farewell* beam jab, and a weak ball of seven rise around Britta, then burn away—and then Veronica knelt by Amelia, murmured something. A surge of *choke* engulfed Amy, and Veronica spun her gaze to me.

"These...turtles? Is this your doing?" she asked, exhausted, bloodied and sopping, singed like an animal who'd run through a rainstorm into a forest fire to a slaughterhouse where she found herself the only one still standing. Aside from me.

I puppet-pointed flesh me, *what about Amelia?*

"She is badly injured," Veronica panted. "I'm stabilizing her. We must move quickly. Can you speak at all?"

I shook flesh me's head, pointed where Samantha hung, then to my ear and did ghost charades: *sounds like toast.*

"A ghost is here?" she asked, checking the room. I puppet nodded. "None of these Aspectu are dead. So... is this someone you know?" I puppeted *yes, keep guessing.* "Is it Samantha?"

I was going to do *on the nose* but right then I noticed a swell of fresh *dominion* begin bubbling into the room. This was... so much *dominion,* like somebody'd opened a pressure tanked reservoir, pumping it in through the French doors blasted away in back of both of me.

I puppeted flesh me that direction. Then I slipped into him. And saw Julian.

He mushroomed nuclear *dominion* from an object he held, and floated down in the rain outside the kitchen, feet and knees, snarling mouth, to the beach. Perfectly dry. In his hand, emptying, forever erupting *dominion,* he held an object.

Samantha's goblet.

He blasted my body with a beam of *bleed* and my *dominion* shell flashed to catch it.

Veronica *bleed* lanced him, striking snakes, black eyes flashing.

His ball of seven snapped up, ensnared her beam, and he ignored her. I saw dope gleam in his eyes. He came off the beach lifting the goblet in front of him, blinding me, driving me with storm force out of my flesh back into ghost me, where I huddled, shocked. From there, like I'd put on sunglasses, the lights evened out.

The goblet. My eyes *saw* it, but my mind was scrambling. Julian had Samantha's goblet? From which *dominion* streamed? Samantha's goblet—what did it mean—useless questions, impossibly hard. Julian wasn't blinded by the goblet, the way flesh me was. He handled it with casual ease, the way I might carry a topped off margarita if I was totally drunk.

Even through the glare I was certain it was Samantha's goblet, not the one from The Painter's Kiss. It drew me. I felt it pull. Come closer. I wanted to touch it. I slipped into flesh me, endured blinding *light,* shoved ghost me out behind Julian where he was bending to hold the goblet to Britta's chest, and then retook my ghost body.

I was inches from the atomic blast furnace *light.* This was a real goblet he had, a blown glass cup, in yellow and red, filigreed and delicate with Latin scrolling under the rim and filled with *dominion,* or made of *dominion* but at the same time made of glass. I moved ghost me closer, still closer, until his ghost leg *bumped* the goblet, and when I touched glass—in my ghost—I saw a landscape.

Dominion had stippled allscapes over the world. A *dominion* landscape faint as gravestone pressings that slowly grew thick. The landscape was simple, it was mostly a mountain. Held inside my ghost in that kitchen I stood, at the same time, on a plain at the foot of the mountain. It towered over Skysill Beach, a ghost mount in *dominion,* a bulk overtopping any storm, ridging miles along the coast, flanks dense with woods, holding a stone peak high. And at the summit a finger of rock where an empty throne sat, facing away, alone, as much sensed as seen.

And I saw in the sky above it all, like a banner hung in stars, a *path*—a path of pure *dominion,* stretching from the stars, touching only the the ghost summit peak—only there, in all the world—to run along the cold rock at the foot of the throne and curl up again. Into a cloud of nothing.

I viewed this, this mountain, the throne, the path, all my thoughts leaves in wind, I was empty, until Julian stepped away from Britta and moved the goblet. When ghost me wasn't touching it, the *dominion* world collapsed in spectral strips and disappeared. Julian gave Serving Girl and New Mom the same goblet to the chest that he'd given Britta. Britta stood. She smiled.

Veronica still had her beam on Julian but she was looking at failure. She pawed turtles scattered at her feet but they'd been drained. She found the melted keys for another charge but I could see the situation was a one way street—and I try never to see that kind of thing. Julian had a generator. Veronica had batteries. It was going to be no contest.

Still beaming me, Julian gobleted Fisherman, and then all five apprentices were standing, recharged. Pivoting to Veronica, all at one time, they began to blast wide-spectrum ruination, and her shield quickly thinned. Julian did it too. He blasted a turgid beam of *bleed* as thick as my leg at her face and kept his *choke* beam on me, feather-light, but plenty to freeze me. They wanted me motionless. My reputation proceeded me. But they were in no danger—I was ghost *storming*, I couldn't be *Gray.* They couldn't know, of course. How could *any* of us know *anything*?

Veronica staggered. There was nothing I could do. The keys drained. Her ball of seven flaked in their pressure, a piñata in a sandstorm, and now she wasn't beaming them, she was reserving everything for defense, watching me, mouthing words I couldn't understand, because what am I, a lip reader? I barely read street signs. She only lasted five seconds. The apprentices poured in. She screamed, she fell, and she turned her face to me and I saw the patchwork of dead burned skin, an eyelid melted. Her shield gone. There's no gag reflex in ghosts so I didn't do it. *I'm sorry,* she mouthed, as the group turned on me.

For a few seconds they tried gang beaming, like they'd done Veronica. It felt to me like nothing. Julian was twitching his teeth, starry-eyed. He walked a circle around flesh me, pushing his hand through my *dominion* ball as the others beamed, watching the places where the light from those beams hit, spread, vanished. I understood —he didn't see *dominion.* That explained why the goblet wasn't blinding him.

They beamed and beamed and drained themselves and Julian filled them up and they were back to beaming and then he started getting impatient. I have no idea what took him so long.

"Stop," he ordered. But Britta kept going. She wasn't happy with Julian's idea.

"He's a thing," she snarled, "I don't know what he is but he's—"

"Stop lancing now," Julian told her. And she did it, like she had no choice.

And finally, only Julian's feathery *choke* tendril held flesh me in my muscle spasm, and I was so glad I couldn't feel my body in its ghost *storm,* because it looked utterly excruciating.

Then he stopped beaming too. The apprentices held their breath —especially Britta—but Julian just looked curious.

"Asher Gale. So. Let's see the moves," Julian suggested, crossing one needle tracked forearm over his stomach, casual but protective.

"*Asgghhha mmnnadah,*" flesh me suggested.

"If you think you can do it, take me," he offered.

"*Ghhro I cohntthhhh,*" flesh me admitted, and I puppeted his shoulders in a shrug.

Julian sliced a dopey path close to flesh me, the goblet in his hand a scepter painting the world *dominion.*

"You should have stuck to painting," Julian told him, while I watched. "That thing you used to do, you had something. Even I have to admit... but there's more than one way to change the world with art. I killed her. You figured it out. I killed her with a *painting*. A painting! Can you top that?"

"*Ohm orgnnoasm zzls tatnanggna,*" flesh me snarked.

"You once said you could identify my paintings," he said with tiny head rattles like it was the tightest, least comprehensible thing he'd ever remembered, and also like he was higher than fuck. "But what I do is so far beyond you. My... art. It's beyond *anything* you could ever understand. You're an arrogant pathetic little failure as an artist, and I want to laugh at that later. He'll be interested in... your invisible ball, whatever else, he'll reward me, we'll be... back together."

"Julian," gasped Veronica, and we all turned or had one of our bodies swung around to face that direction and saw her standing, leaning on the kitchen island to keep upright, charred like she'd just crashed a plane.

"Just go back," she husked to him, "into the *storm.*" She was husking at Julian, but looking at me. "Julian has no *dominion* here. Asher does."

"She stands," Julian observed, surprised.

"It's the only way," Veronica said, grinding the words out to me. "The *storm* will give us *dominion.*"

"*Brangh hgga susemannnblb,*" flesh me disagreed, it was a really bad idea she was proposing. She almost fell. Caught herself—a little forward, did it again—a stumble closer, and I decided she was probably right. It was probably the only way. Such a terrible way. Escape my *chroma storm.*

Making all those Rudyard Kipling turtles had left me adept at suffering excruciation, forcing flesh and ghost bodies together, collecting my *dominion* halo. But those times I'd been pumping *dominion* down my arm. This time I had nothing in my fist. The halo was going to infuse me and burn, burn like it did Kuparr's map room. It was going to hurt me then kill me, unless someone used it.

But in for a penny in for a pound, like I've always said but never really meant before, and so I squeezed, I viced ghost me and flesh me into one body, venting heat like a forge—heat, and sweat, and Crossing. My. Eyes. The apprentices glanced my way. Flesh me went to his knees. They were amused. Veronica staggered another step my direction.

My bodies congealed, *dominion* mummy-wrapped me but had nowhere to drain, so it started eating the things that made my body animate; electricity, hope, cells, enzymes, my willpower and my bone marrow and my purpose. My mouth dangled off its joints. I was screaming. I was silent. I strained a hand toward Veronica as *dominion* roiled around me. She stumbled one step closer and reached so we could touch.

Britta noticed. With a step and a kick she tripped Veronica. Veronica sprawled but kept crawling, white hair white clothes blood and fire torn, so Britta kicked her again, side kicked, and laughed. And then Fisherman joined her. Veronica clawed around them, stretching toward me as apprentices closed their pack and began kicking, and I lost sight of her. I was losing sight of everything. The *dominion* I wore like a superimposition, that I wore all the way through my body, ate me hollower by millimeters. I fell to my stomach.

No one saw Amelia crawl near me, cradling her shattered arm. They were watching Veronica. No one heard her whisper, as she dragged herself to me, shocked and pale, "Asher," like she'd done so many times before, like I was the one precious thing in her world, her one connection to anything that mattered, the only thing on her mind, and no one else saw her grimace and reach for me, just seconds away from atomic dissolution. I felt it the moment her palm dropped to my shoulder.

I felt the *dominion* packed inside me stir. Amelia gasped.

Her eyes counter crossed out the sides of her head. Nothing but white crescents stared back at me, her face confused, and the *dominion* was vacating me, a torrent of sweet release. It flowed into her. Into my sister. Like she was Fabrica. And then the *dominion* was gone. My *storm* was over. And I was *so* irritated.

"You're *tapped*?" I cough whispered, "you're Fabrica? God *dammit* Amelia *seriously,* you *totally* didn't tell me I mean this is fucking *ridiculous!* You don't tell me *anything!*"

She whimpered, trembled, white-eyes wide, "It's never... felt like —*what's going on*?"

"What do you mean?" I whispered. "Didn't Veronica tap you?"

"Yes, but this, I don't know what's happening," she was moaning in pain, "it never felt this..." One of the apprentices heard us and turned.

"Amy," I urged, "the thing Veronica did to Dwayne, with *wander*? You have to do it to Julian. Make him go *away*."

She recoiled at the idea, shook, groggy not from fear but like electroshocks going off inside. Like *dominion* overloading everything.

"It won't work, he's Aspectu," she whimpered. "Can't effect his body through his ball."

"Then the goblet, can you do the *goblet*?"

"Not without Veronica buffering... so dangerous... this is insane..."

More of the apprentices were watching now. Threat assessing. Intrigued.

"Try," I begged, and went to take her arm, but my fingers were flattened, "you have to vanish the goblet, it's our only chance!"

My fingers flattened?

The *Gray* took me.

I laughed.

Stood.

I ran!

I picked the closest one, Serving Girl, but all five saw me and all five started beaming, so I hit and flashed through beams I couldn't see like laser tripwires and missed Serving Girl because my legs froze a step, I tumbled, it was *fantastic,* not seeing the sparkle beams was a big impediment, like, it was super surprising how they worked together, in a pack—and next time I'd attack them totally different! Good job Aspectu psychos! So good.

They got me pinned.

Britta levitated the whole kitchen island in the air—it came free, rending wood and twisting pipes and hung dripping like a severed monster head, hovering over Veronica laying in blood on the floor, forgetting she was even there.

"I never saw it shape an *eminence,*" she said about me, and I felt how natural it was to think of myself as an *it.* "I don't think it *can.* It can't stop me, I can *crush* it with this—"

"—so that's the speed they were talking about..." Julian interrupted her, his face surprised how close I'd gotten to them, and then he himself was interrupted by Amelia screaming.

Screaming, crouching, flinging her non-broken arm to backhand the apprentices. Her black hair spread the air, spun dust and blood around a face abandoning fear as fury consumed it. I heard something *CRACK* somewhere— in the air, in the room, we all heard a rock shatter shriek.

"*The key,*" Julian screamed, at his hands, "*what have you done, what did you do!?*"

His goblet was gone.

CRACK expanded the sound I'd heard, between Amy and Julian, so the air rippled like a computer simulation of water, and in the middle of the room Amy looking *insane,* ripple waves rose around her, wind lifting, force gripping, everything going up, the roof peeling off and up like cat food dinner to expose the stars and shock waves *slammed* me, apprentice bodies scattered—but the beams.

Once they slipped not even Amelia's eldritch bomb blast could stop me—nothing might ever stop me again—no something probably would, it was funny to think about! I moved like the rest of the world was heaving in clay. Fisherman was tilted backward, hung in the air. I plotted a route from him, through the other three and up behind Julian. I could see the route would be a bloodbath.

I was happy to finally start.

In a half second I'd landed in front of Fisherman—he was looking the wrong direction and never knew I was there—and I kicked through his one knee so it broke backward bent the wrong way, because I'd always wondered what *that* would feel like—it felt like breaking a chocolate bar inside the wrapper—and then I stooped and grabbed a broken two-by-four from the ground and as I did I ripped Fisherman's throat apart with my fingertips which is when the bloodbath started. The slow, totally grey, ink soft low saturation capital letter Blood Bath.

The two-by-four I launched at Serving Girl. Momentum from that spun me into New Mom—who'd caught a glimpse of me and tried to raise a beam—good idea New Mom!—but I gripped her raised wrist and flipped myself and *yanked-down* the way you hear oil rigs drag off people's arms and New Mom's arm came off, caught clean and piston fast and adding thick, moon-grey blood to what was flying to all sides already.

The apprentices were confused! I was navigating Amelia's reality power pulse with ease but they were *bewildered!* So awesome! To reach Britta I passed Serving Girl, staring at the two-by-four piercing her stomach, and I pulled it out her back as I went, like a needle through a shirt, because I wanted something to swing at Britta— Britta was wily and had experience with me—she almost beamed me! But I let momentum carry me close. That's the strategy I'd thought up. Don't go around them. Be a bowling ball.

When I was too close to beam I got free, looped the two-by-four behind her back and pulled her into me and snapped her spine, *way* easier than I'd expected—I was starting to think I was just going to keep getting faster and stronger and it might never end—her spine felt so delicate and beautiful snapping I raised the board a few vertebrae and did it again and she slipped toward the floor.

The rain was sheeting into the house through the missing ceiling. Water and blood and debris piled everywhere in a masterpiece of storm wet ocher. Bodies lay around the masterpiece. But not Julian's.

Julian stood. He wasn't looking at me. His goblet was missing, it was *funny*, like fairies had snatched his baby, he gaped incomprehension and fury and fear.

"*This cannot happen now!*" he screamed.

He saw me coming but he wasn't fast enough to do a single thing. No one would ever be that fast again. I circled behind him. I pressed against his back. It felt *so soft*. I cinched his throat in the crook of my elbow and squeezed, and twisted, it felt warm, it felt easy, some of my best feelings.

I wanted to appreciate all the feelings, because this fight was sort of the culmination of the events of the day, and of the last few weeks, and either it'd be the start of something even better, or else after I broke him it would all be over, and if *that* was going to happen I wanted to really enjoy it.

"*He'll make everyone you love pay,*" Julian whisper strained.

And then—*wander* maybe, who knows, I couldn't *see* which light he used—my arm was empty. My perfect elbow noose roped nothing but rain. Julian wasn't there!

The storm came down and down on the floor and the rubble and piles while I stood figuring it out. I'd waited a second too long. Gone, and he'd taken the apprentice bodies with him. Veronica and Amelia were the only bodies left in water and wreckage. Neither of them moved. Nothing moved. So unexpected! I balanced on fallen ceiling beams, furious, astonished, frustrated, laughing gleefully—he'd escaped! He got away—oh well played Julian!

Then I turned. The French doors were open mouths breaking their teeth on the storm. I went through them out over the bluff and down onto the beach. And I ran, howling delight, feeling everything, getting ready for the end of time. I wondered what *that* was going to feel like?

CHAPTER
SEVENTEEN

I used, I drank, I ate and fucked and crawled the canyon of savage smiles and gave people fantastic memories wherever I ended up, it was all typically *Gray* and I did it for three days. A lot of it happened amidst the addicts of Aliso Canyon. Then I woke up.

It was the morning of the fourth day. I opened my eyes in wet shade under Pier 9 with sandals flapping on the boardwalk above me, and the *Gray* was gone. I checked my limbs and other features. I noticed I now wore unlaced hiking boots and a blue sharkskin suit without a shirt or underpants. Sometimes when I'm *Gray* I like buying clothes.

The first thought I had was, how long until The Charles opens? But the bar was miles upcoast and has iron clad *No Credit* policies, and my wallet had been in my Hawaiian shorts, lost wherever I'd changed to the new suit. My phone was there too, along with keys to whatever car I'd been driving last. Celine's?

I stumbled upright. I staggered out into clear sunlight and after-breakfast air, wiped sea drip from my face, crossed the beach, passed between kiosks and emerged on the sidewalk of the Pacific Coast

Highway running through downtown, where after ten wasted seconds of confusion, Hennessy spotted me from his cop car. Like you'd expect he would. He cut across the highway, lights flashing, then parked and got out to tower on the sidewalk. He no longer preferred me. He was a bridge I'd burnt. It came back to me in pieces.

"Get in," he thumbed his back seat with a lethal creak of belt.

"You're arresting me?"

"Would you like me to arrest you?" He stepped very close. Looked down more or less from straight above, and pinned me. "I should arrest you? Is that what you think?"

"I think, do whatever's most in the public interest," I told him.

"In your case," he said, low, "that would be illegal. So the public will continue to suffer. You and your mermaid pimp jacket will get in my car now, and come for questions."

"More questions? Jesus christ you guys, try google or something, leave me alone."

He clipped my head escorting me to my seat.

Soon after that I found myself fielding cop questions about a house that lost its roof in a storm, though nobody really believed it had happened that way, where my blood had been found—blood familiar to them from samples collected at other crime scenes—which led them to question how I got my current bruises and injuries. But I never remember those kinds of details. Since they never asked any of the right questions—how could they—I was able, in good conscience, to tell them nothing.

From clues dropped I gathered Amelia and Veronica had also given statements and forgotten similar details, which struck the police as an entertaining coincidence. So Amelia and Veronica were alive. I remembered I should have been worried about them much earlier in the day. I was relieved for a minute, and thought about calling, until I remembered how Amelia had been lying for years, treating me like an idiot, and now she was tapped? I took a childish pleasure in not calling at all, not telling her I was not dead. Plus I didn't have a phone.

Outside the precinct building hours later my desire for The Charles had grown but I had the same number of wallets. I wandered a few steps up the block before admitting the goal I'd set myself; the walking distance alcohol in the Admiral's bar.

In late afternoon sun the Bradley Building looked resolute and confident, but on the inside you realized that was just posturing. I crossed the lobby, stirring chaff from packing boxes. The sad leftovers. Riding the elevator up was exhausting, I wondered if I should have taken the stairs.

When I pushed Asher Gale's door open I found Peter sitting in the receptionist chair.

I remembered he didn't open the door anymore since his promotion. He wore his receptionist headgear and he held out a folder of papers like he'd known it was me coming in, which he certainly had.

"Some man wanted Cincinnati in his forest," he told me, brisk, referencing the papers, "but we only have syrup. It was fine. Take this list of famous elderberries."

Peter wanted the papers off his desk because he had a lot of work to get to, was what he'd left unsaid, so I shambled down the entrance hall and took the folder. Inside was not a list of elderberries. It was a set of documents outlining my transfer of ownership in the Bradley Building to a law firm. On the cover a note promised that someone would return at my convenience for the signed documents. Somebody did not trust me to get to the post office.

Peter began humming a sea shanty. He whisper boomed, like redwoods falling, and as I watched I realized something was going wrong with him. Now that he'd passed my legal documents, he stared toward his feet, rocked in the office chair, I could see he'd started collapsing from the inside. Maybe that had started a long time ago, but this was the first I'd noticed it. His hair had thinned—patches were coming out. His skin wasn't oily, but dry as a winter leaf. He had more bones and less of everything else.

"I'm so glad I found you," I told him. "Totally, absolutely, thanks for the turtles, they saved us."

"Tugboat watermelon highball," he muttered without raising his eyes.

I lifted the office phone, Peter tried to take it back but I snatched it away. I checked the dial tone. "I'm going to see if we can get you to a doctor," I told him.

"Don' bother, Aspectu boy," slurred a voice two inches from my face, which scared the shit out of me so I dropped the phone.

"Please don't do that," I pleaded into space while I scanned the back of the office, the piles of paintings in lunatic stacks, looked out the long wide windows where the foothills went humping into sun. On the rug in front of the windows, among the chairs in Asher Gale's sitting area, I saw a collection of the Admiral's bottles, mostly emptied, and around the back of one chair a hand hanging.

"Nella?" I said in that direction.

"Don'yell," she asked. The hand lifted a bottle that sloshed. "I saved all this for you."

I took the bottle and fell into the chair across from her. I drank and I eyed her down the barrel, doing two things at one time like I can when it's all going perfect. Her hair was less shaved, her golden-red sashed robes were beat to threads, but she was still as firm and round as I remembered and I still had the impression she was deeply involved in more than one conversation. Like I was being handled in a customer service queue. Not a bad feeling.

"How come you don't look like shit?" I asked when I finished swallowing. "Didn't you get...?" I beat the arm of the chair the way I remembered her body hitting the beach.

"Yeah," she remembered. "Veronica got'er something, melted phone'r something. Turtle? Presto. Fucking hard to kill'em Aspectu. You are."

"So that thunder blast you did," I wondered. "How come no one did that when you got attacked in LA?"

"Sound dome," she hissed. "Need'a high decibel noise or have a sound dome. Dome's like a battery. But fuckers... took it down.

Surprised us. Came at *night!*" I handed her the bottle. She really needed it.

"How long you in Skysill?" I asked.

"Why?"

"There's a bar I can show you once we're done here."

"I came for Pierre," she said, and peeled herself forward and looked around the back of the chair, we both did—looked at Peter trying to pretend to type something but running out of energy every few letters.

"He doesn't look good," I told her.

"Fact he's'alive at all... I don't know. After that night, Angels inholding, after everybody died... I heard him. Down here. I came fast's I could. He's the most... the best of us, the Answer every Ask wanted. Knows everything there is about the umbra eye. No Auditus ever went deep as he did. But he's just dying that's all."

"I'm not really a medical-help kind of person, but shouldn't we call someone?"

"Wouldn't matter," she shook her head and drank. "What he's dying from... he's misplaced, can't find it home. Lost alone *forever* in the past. Who knows how he's doing it? Nobody to touch'm, hear'm, tell'm he's real? Throwing messages up—anyone up there get em? Not sure there's'even a world any more. No idea. You can't fight forever."

"Can't you help him?" I tried not sounding hopeful, just an instinct, and she shook her head.

"I don't know what to *Ask*. The question he was answering when his Ask died. All I can do's listen, listen for him. I'll listen til he's..." She passed the bottle back to me with a change of subject. "So what's'th thing your freaky super strength? Kind of scary as shit. You are."

I never like to hear stories from when I'm *Gray,* like the story she'd just mentioned. I prefer letting those things fade into booze clouds. On the other hand, I felt like the *Gray* had taken a huge, terrifying, *much* more violent and unpredictable turn recently. So possibly

I needed an objective opinion about it from a person drunker than me.

"What did you see me do?" I asked, cagey.

"Heard. Did n'make sense, you're... fast... and more'n that? Super strong. Seem *crazy*."

"It's like... I get into a different body. But this time... " I looked at my hands. I felt thin, like this time the *Gray* had taken something out of me. I did not enjoy the feeling in the slightest. "A switch just throws," I said, and shivered, remembering. "I'm pretty sure... I think I killed some people."

"Ya *think*?" she snorted, "Jason Bourne much? Just a little light killing spree."

"Yeah. Well. You wouldn't believe the week I had. It just came out in a spree."

"I had'a week too," she drained the last of our gin. "Murdered field of Auditus... Kuparr..."

"Yeah," I empathized and drank. "Also I broke up with my girlfriend."

"Sorry."

"Yours is worse. She wasn't really my girlfriend. Also time's ending. Though that's not really my problem. And it's not a competition, but my Tante Celine, she raised me, she's super sick, so there's—"

"She died," Peter observed, typing up Asher Gale's memos.

I checked with Nella. "When he says something like that... ?"

"S'like..." she took a long time thinking, "deep inside's'got thoughts, sends them up, but he can't know where they go, he lost them."

"She died," Peter repeated.

The thing to do would be call Amelia, I thought. In case Peter meant something important. I didn't have Amelia's number so I borrowed Peter's office phone again and he didn't like it any better the second time. Stupid landline, there was no way to look up a number. But I looked up Fenestram Color using Peter's computer, which made him surrender his headpiece and sulk away to lie on the floor among the canvases.

Veronica answered.

"It's me," I told her. "It's Asher. I need Amelia's phone number right now."

There was silence. I sensed her updating various ideas about me being alive.

"Mr. Gale," she said. "We've been quite worried."

"Yeah, sure. So—you know Amelia of course. You *tapped* her. Didn't mention it to *me,* so *that's* something. So that's the person. I need her phone number."

"I'd be happy to get that for you, shall I make dinner reservations and have your pants pressed?"

"Will you get the number or not?"

She tried to text the number. It was confusing. I told her I'd use one of Asher Gale's pencils for it, like in Little House on the Prarie.

"We need to talk," she told me after I'd transcribed.

"We're so good exchanging information, yeah, let's do more of that."

"People are coming to Skysill, who... want to meet you." Her voice was not happy and wished it was being used to make different words. "The Fabrica are coming. The Council."

"Tell your Fabrica Council go suck a dick," I suggested. "I'm unhappy being a pawn. I don't picture myself a more important piece, I prefer not playing at all, is all. So...!"

It's much more satisfying hanging up on people on these old-fashioned phones I found—there's a serious visceral satisfaction slamming a receiver you never feel tapping a red glass circle.

I dialed Amelia using my pencil information. She answered crying. She didn't even know who she had on the phone—the kind of thing that once upon a time that would've run me *chromatic,* but not any more. I'd graduated. Now I did common suffering like everyone else.

"It's Ash," I told her when I got my breath.

"She's gone," Amy wept. "It was so quiet. I just told her... she's here, in bed..."

"Ames. Are you at the house?"

"I can't figure out how to tell anyone."

"I'm coming up. I'm coming up, hold on."

This call ended with a numb feathering, not a slam. Then I was turning to the chairs but Nella wasn't there. Peter and Nella were both on the floor, in late afternoon window light, Nella with Peter's head cradled. Her own head titled like a dog hearing whistles.

"Do you have a car?" I asked.

"No car talk softer," she said, two inches off.

"I need a car."

"Veronica's here in five minutes, take you up hill," the whisper moth said.

"*What?*" I whispered back.

"I just told her," Nella said. "Got a lot of conversations going. Asher I'm sorry, for Celine. You okay?"

"Check," I said.

"Then'nother thing."

She held up one hand, in front of her face and snapped. She tilted her head, like listening for an echo she wasn't hearing. "Skysill Beach's too quiet. Pretty sure's an Auditus here." She could tell I wasn't getting it. "Somebody ratted out Pierre and Levi. I think'e's still here. Or her. Smotherin' sounds. There's a big ass something missing. It's all too quiet."

Before I turned to leave, overfull of information, I watched a moment of her listening. Eyes closed. Listening to Peter. Listening to everything. Then I took the stairs down. They were no less exhausting than the elevator.

Veronica pulled up on the sidewalk, chauffeured in a tanky Suburban and waited, idling dinosaur blood with one door open. I made myself get in the back, across from her.

"Nella told me about Celine," she started.

"Listen," I stopped her, "I'm only here because I have no phone, no money, no keys, and no one else will take me. I don't want conversation."

She weighed the instructions, pulled her lip, then settled her pale elegance into black automotive leather. To look at her you'd never know she'd barely won a fight for her life in a rainstorm against a coven of psychopaths just a few days before. She scrolled her phone while the car raced up the hills, rich and poised. At least she had the idea speed was a priority. I glanced around, the car, the driver. Oligarch stuff. The silence went on.

"So no more disguises, no more little miss paint shop owner," I said. "Must feel great."

"Are we speaking then?"

"I guess it's time to come out and announce it, *I'm the millionaire! Here I am!*"

"Billionaire. Yes. The time for disguises is past."

"I don't have anything to say to you."

"Well," she shrugged, then went back to her phone.

"Hey Dwayne," I called to the front, "is it really worth it like this? Place to place for people but you're just a pawn? They tell you nothing?"

He ignored me.

"That is not Dwayne," Veronica breathed into her window glass, and I saw my mistake. Dwayne had been broader and more talkative. I pictured the last time I'd seen him, *glowing* like an oil rig, seconds before Veronica *wander* slammed him somewhere else.

"What happened to Dwayne?" I asked. The Suburban swayed, going fast around curves. Veronica took her time answering.

"She'd broken him," Veronica finally said. A cold, soft admission. "There was no other way, there was no way to save him. I had to stop him."

"Where'd you send him? Where is he?"

"He is nowhere. He is gone." She stared a grim challenge, *ask no further,* but the grimmer the challenge, the more I'm drawn to it. I'm surprised people haven't figured that out.

"Amelia did the same *wander* thing on Samantha's goblet," I said. "Did the goblet go nowhere too? Is it gone forever?"

She raised her palms, maybe yes maybe no, though she seemed to suspect maybe yes. Then she leaned in with an urgent idea of her own, "Asher, I know this is a difficult time, but you and I *really* must discuss—"

"*Shush*, shh," I hissed, avoiding a turn it into conversation. I peeled my face away but found myself wondering—what would happen to Samantha, if the goblet with her story really was gone? Was there any other way to release her?

We kept at our silence the rest of the drive. Pines rolled past, we hit ruts and raised dust that flowered sunset-red behind us. Before long the car was yanked stationary—and there was Amelia's car. Lengthening shadows framed us in the early evening, I jumped out, ran to the porch, then inside, and Amelia met me crying, pulled me into a hug, damp with tears like she'd come from the sauna.

All through the drive up, knowing what was waiting, I hadn't been able to think what to say, which is because there wasn't anything. A few minutes passed, the embrace softened, empty space went on around us—just the two of us, already it felt different—and then we went, without speaking, together to the bedroom. Celine's inanimate object body lay on the bed.

I ghost popped up behind my shoulders.

Celine's ghost, much younger than her body, greeted me inside an ultraviolet mixing bowl of Higher light and *dominion,* spun like candy light from the world beyond. She wore a polka dot mini dress, bouffant hair, she lacked all expression, and in her ghost hand sparked a neutral crystal necklace, in ghost powdered luster.

I puppeted flesh me down beside the bed and bent him to Celine's flesh face, then slipped into him. From that close she looked like a new person. So relaxed. Had she always been tense, alive? Just below the surface? To look this relieved when she'd left everything behind?

I didn't want her ghost disappearing to Psychic Touch before I could help. Down there, there'd be a gang of spectral monks to wade past on the sidewalk. I needed to get the voodoo gears rolling.

"I'm so sorry for your loss," Veronica said from the bedroom door. Amelia reached and grasped Veronica by the hand. It gave me a strange pang.

Sounds like toast, I charaded to Veronica.

"There's a ghost," she nodded.

"What?" Amelia said, spinning around.

"Yes," Veronica said, "Asher seems to see ghosts. I found this out in Los Angeles."

"But *what*?" Amelia demanded between me and Veronica. "Was anybody going to tell me?"

I puppeted flesh me standing, I steered him toward the living room, urging the others to come with us. I pointed fleshy out onto the porch, in gloom, and when we went beyond ghost range I was sucked back into my beast.

"I *did* tell you I was seeing ghosts," I complained to Amelia. "You choose to ignore it. Listen. You guys. Celine's ghost is in there, and she's holding her neutral crystal. There's something she wants us to know about it and then she can—whatever goes on—she's free to leave. So someone's going to have to read her neutral crystal."

Amelia pulled the necklace from a pocket. "*Read* the crystal?" she asked, but no one answered.

"I'll call Caroline," Veronica said, and started doing it. Amelia looked confused, which was a petty victory that I savored.

"Don't call," I said to Veronica, "Caroline doesn't want to be included in my problems."

"What's Caroline got to do with it?" Amy asked. She looked at Veronica. "Do you know?"

"Caroline's a psychic I'm not involved with anymore," I said to everyone. "Just to be clear."

"Well if not Caroline, then what do you suggest?" Veronica asked me

"Look up Madam Nikita Thomasonian. Down in the district. Let me talk to her."

Veronica dialed, then handed me the phone.

"Yes I am here," came Nikita, sounding rickety. "What is it you want?"

"Nikita. It's Asher. What are you doing right now?"

"Balancing on my trunk in the dark drinking vodka."

"So you're at Three Paths, were you expecting my call?"

"No, I sleep this way, standing like horses, many feet off the floor in mildew."

"I need your help."

"I will do it. What is it?"

"Come over and do psychometry on a necklace."

"I won't do it."

"What's wrong?"

"Here is safe. Surrounded with psychics. Only the Monarchs still practice outside Three Paths."

"Since when?"

"Tuesday."

"Well, the Monarchs are off the table for me."

"Come to Three Paths, bring pretzels."

"It's got to be here, Nikita. Please."

"Eh," she said, "rats ate my brakes, I need fluid, no."

"I can pick her up," Veronica said at my side.

"I got you a ride," I told Nikita. "A pretentious rich lady's going to send her bullet proof car over. Please. This has something to do with my mother, Nikita, or I wouldn't ask. Will you help me with my mother?" I was still thinking of Katerina Gale as my mother. That'd take a while to shake.

"Yes fine," Nikita sighed, after a moment. "Is very dangerous. I do not care. I am just old crosspath. Soon vultures will eat me. What difference does it make?"

Veronica sent her driver with directions. I returned to Celine's room and re-ghosted, then sat flesh me on a wood chair and positioned ghost me facing ghost Celine. Ghosts tended to start near dead bodies, but pretty soon they migrated. Maybe watching her would keep her stationary.

In the living room Veronica was serving ghost details to Amelia who was suggesting maybe I was just fucking crazy like I'd always been—ghosts?—but Veronica offered a spirited defense of me which was something I'd never heard anyone do. I wondered about Veronica and Amelia, what Amelia had gone through getting tapped, how they knew each other, but speculating other people's lives is exhausting, so I stopped.

I'm not proud how bored I grew beside the dead body of the woman who'd fed me and clothed me and loved me for sixteen years, it's just that ghosts are not exciting to watch, at all, and I'd been grinding hard while *Gray,* and ever since the elevator in the Bradley Building all I wanted was a nap. Celine's ghost never moved. Eventually I heard a new voice, imperious and elderly, so I puppeted flesh me to the living room. There Nikita stood in a sweater jacket so rough knit it was like Vikings had done it with swords, with bloodless white legs though purple shorts into clogs.

"Pajamas," she shrugged. I puppet pulled her outside to the porch, where night had come, and retook my body once again, an eel slipping into his tunnel. This time I felt a little thin, tired like I'd felt coming back from the *Gray*. I needed sleep.

"There's…" I had to clear my throat from all the mouth breathing flesh me had performed the last hour on his own, then I continued, "…there's a ghost here."

"Where. I do not see."

"I do. I see all the ghosts, they all come with an object, just like this one does, where the object's got a story and me hearing the story —one story was someone reading an address book—the ghost gets released from… they go on to ghost elsewhere. I assume it's better there. Anyway, that's why you're here. I need—"

"Yes, yes, I understand, I am not child. Where is some object with some story for me reading?"

"Amelia's—*ggrrrnaph stacot meeeltee, sphruph sholle*," I said after popping out the back of flesh me because Celine's ghost had followed us into the living room.

I puppeted flesh me back into the house, guiding Nikita to Amelia and miming to Amy, *give this foreign sweater lady Tante Celine's necklace.*

"No touching me," Nikita said to Amelia and Veronica, stepping away, "because psychometry, eh, is skittish like drunken dogs in the trunk of my car. Where is a table? Set it here. Put this crystal there, yes, now go away. Farther. Actually come back. Bring a chair. *Now* go away. Make a good space."

Nikita sat at the table in the ghostly, lava lamp afterglow that soaked Celine's front room, where macramé spider webs laddered and ceramics glazed Higher like pure veins in a gold mine. Nikita rolled up her viking sleeves. She hovered her thin arms forward, above the crystal on the table. Her eyes fell closed. She took several deep breaths.

I heard tires pulling dust to a stop outside. Nikita began to lower her fingers. Car doors slammed, footsteps dashed, up on the porch, someone yelling Nikita's name, and then Phyllis, agile as a lynx despite being many lynxes wide and a hundred lynxes dense, thundered in, yelling, "Nikita—what are you doing? *Stop now!*"

"Who..." Amelia wondered, as Jorge followed Phyllis in. He surveyed the room and his emperor-eyed face had disappointment. He took his ponytail to stand at one side of the door, he pinned those eyes on flesh me, who didn't notice.

"This is my business," Nikita scoffed, "what will you do, cut me off? This needs doing. I will do it."

"No, Niki, I'll do it," said a third voice.

I heard the voice and saw the girl at the same time. She stepped in from the porch. Flawless and exhausted, focused, purposeful, lacking sleep, she shivered me. In the light off Celine's ceramics, lit with mineral clarity, Caroline radiated things I wanted so, so badly.

This is not a person I'm supposed to feel like I miss. That was my very clear thought. I should not go without feeling or watching or listening to his person. The necklace on flesh me's chest sent a cold pulse, and that was as amazing as anything else and set my clear thought in stone—my zombie flesh sending signals my ghost body actually received. My connection with Caroline superseding everything numb. It was a little unnerving.

For a moment we all stood wondering what was next. Nikita leaned back from the table. Veronica and Amelia looking like outsiders. Phyllis and Jorge stared at me like everything was my fault, and they were psychics, so it was hard to argue.

"*Cllmmon treerrer,*" I had flesh me tell Caroline, and had him point outside, then walked him out through the door, while ghost me hung inside and watched Caroline decide to follow him. She assured Phyllis and Jorge he wouldn't kill her. They weren't so sure. Then she spun one hard booted heel and walked outside.

I was forced to pilot flesh me further away to escape ghost range, we ended in the trees, halfway to the cars, before suddenly I was one body again. A rush of sadness came up in me, a bouquet of sorrow flowers flesh me had been patiently holding, mammal feelings that are merely ideas when you're floating around as a ghost. I put these feelings aside. There would be time. I might not get another chance to say the things I wanted to say to Caroline.

Instinctively, through all our navigating, I hadn't touched her and she'd kept clear of me. The moment I got mouth control I started talking.

"I don't feel anything like I used to feel about you," I said while she watched. "Well, no, in some ways I feel *similar,* but not because something's making me obsessed with you. If I'm obsessed with you, and I'm not saying I'm obsessed, then it's naturally occurring. I'm in control. I don't feel insane about you. Just regular craziness. It's not what it was. Do you have any idea what I'm talking about?"

She almost considered it. She had wet lips in the evening air, they were distracting. I hoped what I'd just said was true.

"See," she observed, "this's what I love about you Ash. Your disinclination to small talk."

The way she said *love about you,* it expanded in my chest. Unbelievably light. Until there came a shocking cold pulse from the necklace. A warning. A slap. I gasped and grabbed it on my chest, and she watched.

"I do hate small talk, which is funny," I said, when I had my voice back, "because that's the same thing I love about *you.*"

I watched, I saw her shiver when she heard it, gasp, saw her hand reach to her chest, just below the line of her tank top, where her crystal hung.

"We should probably stop saying that word," she advised us after a minute recovering.

"I, for one, won't miss it," I agreed. We stood a body length distant, and evening flowed between us, quiet and dark. She drew a breath of evening and started speaking.

"I was crazy until I was sixteen, I was raving," she said in a dodging kind of voice, here and there like a butterfly. "All psychics have this stage where... mine was the worst anyone ever heard... anyway. Fifteen, sixteen years old, something changes... the crazy fades. The psychic comes out. You have to leave the crazy in the past. Sometimes that's harder than other times. And look, I had a chance to think this all over between us. It's so... screwed up. I can't go back to what we were. But I still... I want things from you, Ash. I just do. I just do. It's not healthy. And one part of me hates you, like the worst betrayal... it makes no sense. But the other part of me..." Her hand came up to her chest again, suddenly, and she gasped and she pressed her crystal, and looked a little weak. I knew how she felt.

"That's your distain for small talk," I observed, "I love that—I mean not love... okay, it might be harder than I thought."

"It's like, there's two versions of me," she groaned. "One hates you, the other... the other's the opposite. It's real confusing."

"Which one wins?" I quietly wondered.

"I guess we'll have to wait and see. But here's what I'm going to do. None of this is fair to either of us. I'm pretty good at compartmentalizing. I'm going to keep you in a box. I can't look in there. Whatever I'm feeling, you'll never know. I'm just going to carry the box around. Probably the rest of my life. It should be fine as long as I never look. Right? What do you think of my plan?"

"Fantastic plan. Super healthy. Hang out, but pretend we don't like each other."

"Yeah. Keep our distance, but you're sort of going to be my boyfriend."

"Right. And then just... like... never, ever touch."

"Or we'll die."

For three seconds we stared, until at exactly the same moment we burst out laughing—at the ridiculous, melodramatic and absurd idiocy of our plight. And then the laughter died because we felt horrified.

"We'll die," she insisted. "We have to be real careful, Ash."

"Careful's my middle name, that shouldn't be a problem."

"Ok. It's settled."

"Want to hear a theory?"

"A new theory or rehashing one of your previous ones?"

"You tell me." I started checking things off a mental list. "Nikita thinks I'm allowed up at Three Paths. When Li Wei bundles me up there I feel numb like he's cutting me off from something. When I was sixteen, I got suddenly less crazy—relatively less, the *Gray* isn't exactly peak sane—and on top of *all of that*, I see ghosts. What's that say to you?"

"You're complicated?"

"I'm psychic. Let me ask you, is there a mountain? A peak of granite? And a throne on top, a path that hangs from the stars"

From her face I could see there *was* a mountain. "Yes, but there's three thrones," she said.

"I only saw one, but okay, so the question becomes, if I *am* psychic, what Path am I on. Right? Because the Paths are Behind,

Below, Before—past, present, future. It doesn't seem like ghosts fit anywhere. So I was thinking, what if there's…"

It wasn't a thought I felt qualified to complete. I waited to see what the expert would say.

"What if there's a fourth path?" she whispered.

"Or something. Right? I guess it's nothing to do with time, it's like a… a Path…"

"…Beyond," we both said at exactly the same time, like the old train-trip days, and our hands flew to our crystals, cold pulses beat us, our knees got weak. We bent, staggered from each other, and only after a minute taking cool air could we meet each other's eyes.

"I'm pretty sure it's not supposed to work like this," Caroline complained, after we'd stepped even farther apart. "Veronica said we'd want to sort of… just, avoid each other."

"She says a lot of things. I haven't learned to trust her. I think she makes most of it up."

We leaned against separate trees and let night-deep pine into our lungs to get our hearts slowed. Caroline shook her head, unhappy at all the pieces that had no places, which I was very sad to see, that's supposed to be *my* disability.

"A Path Beyond?" she said, groping and fitting and testing. "But the Paths are *time*. Time's just past, present, future. Those are the directions. What other direction could there be?"

"Maybe we don't know enough about time. Here's what I *do* know—people seeing ghosts are psychic. It just stands to reason."

Footsteps approached from the house and I turned to find Phyllis and Jorge giving me the Monarch stink eye.

"It's fine," Caroline waved. "We're done for now. Right Ash? We should go see about your ghost."

Caroline and I practiced social distancing, me on the left and her on the right and the other psychic Monarchs in the middle, and we processed toward Celine's porch. We walked in a line. Phyllis was the least impressed with me. Not counting my own feelings.

"This was unbelievably selfish," she snarled. "You know how

dangerous it is right now? For psychics? She's a *crosspath*, she could stumble onto the Path Before, she could--"

"It's dangerous everywhere," I complained. "Explosions. Laser fingers. People going crazy. Football fields of people dying—I never wanted Nikita in danger but what am I supposed to do with the ghosts?"

"If Jorge hadn't seen what was happening..."

"Okay you two," Caroline eased in. "That'll be enough."

"What are you even doing here, Caroline?" Jorge asked. "I don't foresee any of it."

"I'm here helping Asher with a ghost problem," she smiled. So nice to see. So nice.

Right then we walked into ghost range and I popped out behind myself but kept on steering, like passing a glass of vodka from one hand to the other without spilling a drop. None of them even noticed that I no longer inhabited my body. I couldn't decide, was that a good thing or a bad thing?

Nikita and Amelia and Veronica had come to stand in the cool dark air and watch my dysfunctional drama, but the ghost had stayed in the living room where maybe she felt like she belonged and where she was, in my opinion, most convenient. When flesh me got onto the porch I stopped him and noticed how everyone watched him now. Like a celebrity with a gun, or a drunken bear.

Come on inside if you want to, I directed flesh me to charade, *just don't expect me to explain.*

I puppet pointed Caroline to the table Nikita had requisitioned, then I had flesh me move everyone back. Caroline sat before the neutral crystal. For just a moment her hand went to her chest, and her own necklace, she glanced at Veronica.

"Remember, I can only read an object one time. And I've never read anything like this so pay attention."

Then she closed her eyes. I puppeted flesh me to face ghost Celine, swung ghost me behind him a few paces looking at Celine over his shoulder, then I sort of slipped back and forth between them at random, watching. Waiting for Caroline in her reverie.

Celine had been a cook of simple, very odd food—food I've never seen anywhere else. Peanut butter spaghetti had been her big feast. From flesh me I looked straight through Celine's ghost to the kitchen where the spaghetti had happened. I thought of the time, I wasn't yet a teenager, when I'd gone *storming* in the middle of dinner. I'd taken her spaghetti in my fists and spread it on the walls, sobbing, sobbing until Celine had started doing it too, scraping it down when we ran out of room and painting it up again, continuing like that for hours while she *encouraged* me, told me *it's art, Ash, that's all we have. It's all just art.* And after the *storm* had passed, after I swam back to consciousness, the kitchen had been clean and she'd run out of peanut butter so she'd made grilled cheese. She'd kissed my head while I ate, and looked proud of me. Proud.

Caroline began speaking, though I hadn't seen when she'd put her hands on the dorsal blue crystal. I listened to her talk, I watched her eyes, sub-nautical spirits shifting under lid caps.

"It's a real simple story here," Caroline said. "Ready Ash?"

"*Jraphhh,*" flesh me agreed, which she understood.

"There was a woman in love with another woman. Celine, in love with someone, she didn't understand her love. It was like an obsession. The other woman had come, years ago, because she…"

Caroline stopped. She lifted her hands up, puzzled, but didn't open her eyes.

"This feeling's real familiar, Ash. Celine's obsession with this other woman."

"*Hmmm,*" flesh me said, which by coincidence perfectly expressed my feelings. Caroline put her fingertips back to the stone.

"The other woman came because *she* loved a man Celine had also once loved. Marlon Gale. The woman was Katerina. Katerina and Marlon were inseparable. Celine was beside herself—not jealous, just, like a fever. Then one day Katerina came to her, holding this crystal, said, *I'm so happy Celine, I don't need this anymore. Take it. It'll help you. But keep it hidden. And remember your promise; if he ever finds me, take care of the kids. Protect them. Promise.* So Celine promised. She'd do anything for those kids. And so she always wore the crystal. She always did protect the kids. She's always did. She loved them. That's the story. She loved the kids."

Flesh me wasn't crying but Amelia was sobbing. Caroline opened her eyes. And Celine started going around.

She expanded like clay slung on a wheel, inertial force bowing her out and out, lighting her up, lighting her in nuclear Christmas tree glory, silent screaming bright, pumping more and more of her, filling the house and the yard and the woods she'd loved and after that, in an instant, collapsing. Pinpricking. And she was gone.

The moment she left I retook my flesh and collapsed to the floor. I rolled on my back, moaning. My skin felt light, I felt like there was less of me, I almost felt translucent. Flesh me's throat had been tight —he'd been trying to cry but that was beyond him. I was on my knees before sobs took me.

Caroline almost came to me. I almost called her. But we're not fucking crazy. We're bereft on our islands, maybe lonely, but not fucking crazy. None of the rest of them found anything helpful to do. Phyllis knelt beside Amelia. Veronica gave Amelia a tissue. Nikita had fallen asleep on Celine's couch, which I understood, she was in her pajamas after all, and Jorge was standing by Caroline, watchful. Amelia and I finally helped each other stand, and stammered ourselves into a sort of balance.

"She's gone, Ash?" Caroline asked. I nodded. "Okay. Because there's something else. I just told you the Path story. But I took a few steps off the Path."

"You *didn't*," Jorge cried, and he sounded terrified.

"I had to," she said. "I saw it, you know how. This is real important. I wondered, who is Katerina talking about when she gives the crystal to Celine? Who's she afraid of?"

"Caroline," Jorge protested, "the Figura! You can't go off the Path like that!"

"It's done," Caroline shrugged. "I only took a few steps. Just to hear the one thought. I got her name, Katerina Ariana. That she was a dancer, but had a passion to paint. And here's the thing. When she said *if he ever finds me, take care of the kids,* she was thinking a name." Caroline looked at me. "She was thinking *Aeternus.* If *Aeternus* ever finds me, take care of the kids."

Jorge shook his head. "That's all? You left the Path for *that?*"

"Aeternus?" Veronica breathed. "That makes... no sense."

"Katerina was afraid of Aeternus? Here in Skysill?" Amelia asked.

Caroline nodded. We all waited. In case anyone knew anything.

"But what's it supposed to mean?" I pleaded. I looked from face to face. No one in that room had an answer. Which I found ironic, considering the people in the room—ironic, and deeply, bitterly disappointing.

CHAPTER
EIGHTEEN

I'd spent most of the next two days asleep on Amelia's couch. In my sleep there'd been dreams. I'd thought they were dreams. A choked off voice hissing, *He'll make everyone you love pay*. I wasn't sure who those people were, the ones I supposedly loved who'd pay, but it sounded like a bad deal for them. It sounded like something people would blame me for. I half-woke up repeatedly, over those days, each time in a sweat, each time to the memory of that voice. And when at last I'd come fully awake, I found that I'd been driven to one of the poorly conceived plans I resort to when I'm most desperate.

Julian was the one who'd made the threat, and he was the only one with an explanation. So the plan was I'd question him. I hoped to use the element of surprise—though I'd never used that before and don't know the first thing about it—and rely on the apprentices being out of the picture, and Julian being weakened without his goblet. I'd encourage him to beam me, full force, and pretend like I was going to die, while my ball of *dominion* absorbed all his energy. My plan was, then he'd be helpless. It was a pretty complicated plan. When I had him in my power, I planned to question him about

Aeternus. How things would go after that I didn't pretend to know. But I planned to use all my charm, so things would probably go really, really well.

But when I swayed up off Amelia's couch and checked my pockets I didn't have a phone, or keys or money. I searched Amelia's obvious bowls and shelves, in case they'd been stored for me, which they had not. I remembered I'd lost them going *Gray*. I yelled Amelia's name but she wasn't home. Yelling was tiring. It's frustrating to put that much work into a plan that you can't use. I found I wanted a drink.

That's when I heard a car, pulling to a stop outside. When I checked the front window I saw a black sport utility tank with Veronica getting out, so I twisted the lock on the front door closed and went searching for Amelia's liquor. In the kitchen I found a cabinet with her alcohol collection, which was one ancient, half empty bottle of vermouth. Of all the intoxicants, vermouth was the one I understood the least, and which had always tasted the most toxic, but beggars can't be choosers.

I was trying to twist off the cap when I heard the front door that I'd locked swinging open, and footsteps, and then Veronica stood in the kitchen. She looked brisk and organized, in that way that's so tiring. She watched me struggle with my bottle.

"How'd you get in?" I demanded.

"A key. You and I have a number of important things to discuss. "

"I hope that's not true."

"First things first, however," she said, and held out a factory fresh, no-fingerprints-on-the-screen cell phone. "You lost your phone—again—so here is a yet another replacement. Please take care of it."

"What are you, the phone fairy?" Her imperious tone put me off. It's my least favorite tone. "I'll get a replacement phone if and when I *want* a replacement phone, so keep your billionaire charity. Right now all I want is a drink of this vermouth poison. Then I'm going to find Julian."

She eyed me. "Find Julian?" she asked. "You are joking." I wasn't. "He will kill you."

"Not with a beam he won't."

"There are other ways a person can be killed, Mr. Gale."

"I'll take your word for it." A thought struck me. "Hey… now you're here, you do solve one of my problems, so lets both feel great about your visit. I need you to get Julian's address from your paint store boxes. Will you?"

"No. We have far bigger problems than Julian. Listen to me. The Council—"

"Oh my god, the Council," I muttered, "do you hear yourself? Look, you know what, I will take the phone."

She appeared relieved.

"We must stay in contact," she said, handing it over. "The situation has become very dangerous for you, it's no longer simply the Fabrica Council but—"

I held up my hand to stop her, so I could concentrate, which I think she appreciated. She'd logged into my personal account on her phone, because privacy, so I was able to search our texts. I wrote down Julian's address she'd texted earlier. Then I tossed her phone back.

"If you are determined to find Julian," she said, seeing the address on the screen, "then I will take you, to help keep him from killing you, but now we must speak—"

"No," I interrupted, "don't help me. Just mind your own business. If I want a phone, I'll get one, if I want to die I'll do that."

"You are *absurdly combative*… why… listen to me!" Her face grew just a little flushed. It was as much emotion as you ever saw from her. "Julian Donner is not our main danger any more. The Five Families have all come to Skysill, and now we must make sure you are not discovered!"

My first instinct was to argue, because it's true I'm absurdly combative, plus she didn't deserve anything better, she'd tapped my sister and not told me, hidden Celine's illness, probably many other billionaire manipulations, but I was still trying to work the cap off the vermouth and wasn't paying enough attention.

"What do you mean discovered?" I asked, by accident.

"The Five Families! They have come to Skysill Beach. Do you not understand? Nidor, Sapor, Auditus, Aspectu, Tactus, all together. Here. I had hoped to present you to Willametta and the Fabrica privately, to keep this among the Aspectu until we understood it better, but word of *dominion* has gone out and it is too late. There is to be a Conclave tomorrow night, an airing of grievances. The Families are in a furor. They have not heard about you specifically, but they have heard that Fabrica can suddenly wield *light* in darkness, just as powerfully as in daylight. It destabilizes the balance among the Families. This is what I had hoped to prevent. The Tactus in particular are threatened, and Skysill is now filling with Tactus. Since they have yet to hear about you specifically, we must keep you hidden. I will put you in one of my safe houses, when the Conclave is over we will decide what to do with you."

I gave up the vermouth, which was liquored tight, and took my frustration out on her. I'd barely been listening to anything she said but that never stops me.

"That's fucking ridiculous," I said, "whatever you were just saying—you're not *putting* me anywhere. But. I'll meet you halfway, because I'm naturally agreeable. Here's what I'll do. If you want, I'll let you give me a ride to Julian's house, because I don't have a car."

In her mind I watched her tabulate all the money and time she was wasting just having a conversation with me, and that decided her. The costs versus the benefits. She nodded, "Fine. I will take you there, but only if you let me accompany you inside his home, in case you do find him, god forbid, I can intercede. And after that, we must talk about putting you in one of my safe houses."

"No," I said. "So are we going now or what?"

Soon I found myself passing through downtown Skysill in her rolling vault, headed south toward Aliso Canyon. I encouraged silence in the car by not having anything to say. Veronica remained convinced I didn't understand all the peril I was in everywhere, but I refused to discuss it. Besides, I'd seen peril, thousand of times. I know when it's time to run.

"Remember," she insisted, "he may have lost the goblet, but he is extremely dangerous, the most dangerous Aspectu I've—ah, yes. The goblet."

The change of subject caught my attention. On her phone she found the picture of the Painter's Kiss I'd sent, and she zoomed on the goblet.

"The cup," she said, "my people have identified it. It's called a cage cup, or diatreta. These were the peak of the classical glass making art, a Roman invention."

"So Samantha had one of these?"

"Very unlikely. As I understand it, only a handful exist unbroken, in private collections. Samantha Goodman did turn up as the author of several scholarly papers about cage cups however. A rising star in that niche."

"A cage cup. Diatreta?" It sounded familiar. "I feel like I've heard that word diatreta.. so what else? Did they find anything else?"

"No. Patience, Mr. Gale. I have good people on it."

"Patience? Time's ending in three months," I complained, "in case you hadn't heard."

"Yes," she squinted. "So you have said."

"It's not me. Ask any psychic. It's a big deal. I'm not making it up." I decided I didn't like being taken so lightly. I deployed some facts, which isn't one of my strengths, but people respond to facts. I don't know why. "Do you know what *else* happens in three months?" I asked.

"Holiday shopping season?"

"Gala Lumina. Almost exactly three months, on the winter solstice. See? Time's ending, there's the Gala Lumina, there's the winter solstice. All together. What do you think about *that*?" I meant the question to sound triumphant, but it accidentally came out sounding like I really wanted to know what she thought.

"Ah," she speculated, "Lumina, the Fenestram rave, complete with Fenestram dancers. So many questions about Fenestram. Everywhere. So many questions." She considered all the questions as her car sped down the coast, shouldering aside tourist traffic, and I kept expecting her to answer some of her questions, but then we got to Aliso Trail and turned inland and I forgot what we'd were talking about.

After that I just let the car do its job. We hairpinned up to Julian's place, a California bungalow high on a flank of Aliso Canyon. The bungalow wasn't as big as the state it was named after, but not because it wasn't trying. It ate a whole hillside, a single story beach view daydream in eucalyptus groves with tennis courts. The smell of those trees hit me as I rolled from the car. Veronica climbed down and so did her new driver who I was calling New Dwayne because how anyone is supposed to remember the names I have no idea. Veronica stopped me before I could go through the gate and sent New Dwayne ahead, sniffing, and sort of stirring the air with his arms.

After thirty seconds he waved us down the path and went to the front door. That was locked, but Veronica flashed some *choke* and the handles dropped off. She sent New Dwayne inside, canary style, and used her billionaire patience while he inhaled, but I don't have that kind of discipline and I went in after him. She tried to stop me and seemed surprised when I ignored her. The dream voice had me unsettled. I was tired of being the one who paid. It felt like someone else's turn for that. Veronica sighed and followed me.

We stood in a long hall with a picture window full of ocean at the other end. The sound of the place was pure nobody-at-home. Echoes and no residents, no house cleaners, no flies, just furniture sleeping in rooms. Or so it seemed to me, but I get assessments like that wrong all the time. Just to be safe, I eased up the hallway like I was robbing the place. Whispery. Then we started searching. It felt tense, and the tension grew.

Opulence with coastal vistas came room after room. I had no

idea how anyone lived like that, you'd always be changing rooms to see if you were missing anything. It was a great house for parties. I pictured Julian and the apprentices, listening to music and practicing cult violence.

When I considered the apprentices, that's when I started thinking a little about what I was actually doing in the house and what was likely to happen, which is the stage where my plans always come apart, thinking. This time I thought about going *Gray* on the apprentices the last time I'd seen them, and what I'd done *Gray*. Carrying around the *Gray* felt a little like walking around with a bomb that could go off at any minute. I remembered my feelings of delight, smashing and letting blood pour everywhere, getting to Julian—I'd been basically unstoppable. I'd have killed anybody that night—the *Gray* had no sisters or friends—anybody, to get at Julian.

If he tried to beam me, I'd go *Gray* and start killing people and who knows how long I'd stay *Gray*? So why was I strolling back to confront Julian? Why had I let Veronica come? At the very thought of confronting Julian, I felt the *Gray* stir in my mind shadow, eager to save me and express itself.

I was following New Dwayne, who's sniffing and slow arm waving had both become more emphatic. And then he froze. He turned to the wall. Took a breath and closed his eyes. We were facing a stretch of the corridor that I now noticed was collaged with Higher paint fingerprints, palms smears, that someone had attempted to wipe clean, but not very diligently.

Veronica router crossed her eyes, and drew up fists of *choke* and infused the wall with ultraviolet light, that faded but for a rectangular seam—the outlines of a door, which swung in on its own. Lord of the Rings shit. I'd gotten used to ghosts, in fact I was basically taking them for granted now, but all the other craziness dumbfounded me. Through the door I saw a secret studio wing of the house, a whole art wing you could hide in plain sight because the rest of the place baffled your sense of scale. Veronica pointe New Dwayne in, and this time I let him go. He was the professional.

Just inside the door he stopped. He was frowning, and his breath had deepened. I felt the *Gray*, nibbling at the edges. The only way I'd be able to stop it was to *storm*. I needed something to hold in my fist.

New Dwayne waved us in and pointed to the spot he'd been standing, then moved deeper into the space, breathing slowly and carefully. Veronica and I stepped through. Inside were easels and racks of paint, a view of the sea, distant sand, sky and cloud. I reached for the first palm sized object I saw; a tube of *reason*. I felt better acting like I'd learned a lesson.

We were in a studio which Julian had filled with his own work. By this time I'd knew his hand the instant I saw it. Canvas after canvas was stacked or hung, most simply stored. There were works in progress and works completed, Higher paint and not, but each piece a triumph of sub shade. His work ranged wide, sometimes bold and provocative, sometimes intimate and beautiful, but always authentic. Authentic in every way that mattered. I found it brilliant, which made me doubt my taste, but then a lot of things make me doubt that. Veronica was unimpressed.

New Dwayne stepped back into the studio from a hall on the other side. He was worried. His arms were in constant, slow motion now. Veronica looked at him.

"Something happens down there," he said, pointing back where he had been.

"Yes? When?" she asked. "Should we leave?"

He gave her an unhappy shrug. "Go look."

The *Gray* was getting more and more interested.

New Dwayne led the way down a short hall, tiptoeing, smelling doom. We ended in a round gallery with no windows, cream white walls, and white filtered skylight. Here, a very unexpected collection hung: it was a gallery devoted to Niccolo Filippi. And not just High Renaissance work. There were Baroque canvases, Neoclassical, Art Nouveau, even Modernist paintings, period after period from the oldest all the way to the present. And in the middle of it all hung his

Kisses, front and center—all the originals, not the fakes. Each at least five centuries old.

"What does this mean?" Veronica wondered, staring at them. "Why are these here?"

She turned slowly, taking them in, reading the titles: The Dancer, The Painter, The Musician, The Hunter, The Alchemist. In each one, a different figure bent to kiss the same shirtless man, blocking his face, the umbra eye on his chest. All five of them brilliant.

I taxied to a stop in the center of the gallery. Some conclusion wanted to be made in my mind. I was resisting it, due to it being absolutely insane. I was palming the tube of *reason*, growing more unhappy, insisting that I had to be wrong. But I wasn't. And the thing that convinced me, the thing I couldn't deny, was the self-portrait. Veronica saw it too. We bent closer.

I knew it was a self portrait because it was a picture of Julian, in Julian's hand. He'd given himself a wry smile, and a palette in one hand, with sub-shade's of yellow. He'd put himself in a smock and a velvet cap and he looked across his chest the way Raphael or another Renaissance painter would have posed it.

"Julian. A bit pathetic," Veronica observed, "putting his own portrait here."

"All of that," I agreed. "The only thing is... that's not Julian."

She gave Julian's picture a good look. It looked like Julian to her. To me, too.

"Who is it?" she asked.

The obvious answer only required that you set aside everything you believed about what was humanly possible, so it came pretty easily to me. I knew it was going to challenge Veronica though. Two if these paintings had hung in Lady Damely's gallery for years, but then they'd been copied. She'd been staring at two forged Kisses for over a year, and hadn't she noticed they were in Julian's hand, not Filippi's? When she'd studied Filippi for decades? It could only be because Julian and Filippi had the same hand.

"It's too old," I pointed. "The oxidation—see, the lead-tin

yellows are falling off the spectrum?— bristle patterns say fox fur, Renaissance brush, so I'm guessing—and by guessing I don't mean guessing—this self portrait was done five hundred years ago. In Florence. By Niccolo Filippi." She was having a hard time putting it together, just like I predicted. Poor slow billionaire. I said it a different way.

"The rigged up junkie psycho we've been calling Julian Donner *isn't*. He's actually, somehow, the five hundred year old Renaissance master Niccolo Filippi. He's been living in Skysill Beach for who knows how long. Maybe it's our ocean light, but it might also be our heroin."

"That is not possible."

I shrugged, but I knew. He might have two names but he only had one hand, and he'd left a trail of canvases over five centuries to prove it. Julian was Niccolo Filippi. Alive today. There was no other explanation. And so I stood staring at the Painter's Kiss, speculating about the goblet, about how all of this started with a girl of light, holding a goblet, and then I found myself ghosting out the back of my skull. Very grateful to have something in my hand.

Because of course Samantha'd come. From behind me poured *dominion,* bulb-popping the gallery walls, soaking everything Higher. Of course she'd come. Because her pattern had been the goblet. She'd been leading me to something the whole time. Julian and the goblet.

I heel spun flesh me around to face where she floated, a Higher cyclone, a free-style color emergency. *Dominion* administered everything, all over her, pinched her off above and below, shaping up this Samantha ghost. She had her one hand held straight out to me, just as always. And there, cup curled fingers still pathetically cup curling, she held nothing. Nothing but empty space and a wisp of spectral light. Her ghost goblet was gone.

Her face lacked all expression, but still, somehow, looked horrified. Like she wanted to scream. Though that might just have been me.

And then, still embodied in ghost me, I felt a cold weight fade in. I turned him back toward the pictures, wondering what was happening. A new kind of cold filled ghost me, a universal, spectral cold. The color of light in the hallway changed, as if something massive had swung in above and cast a shadow, like clouds, like new planets. And since curiosity is my known weakness, I lofted ghost me up. Up though the ceiling, up off the hillside, and I saw it, over-spreading Skysill Beach and up and down the coast, the implacable slopes of a ghost mountain, superimposed, towering into the void.

I stared, and was carried toward the rock-bone crest of that mountain, up in comets and black atmosphere, where a Path hung from stars and a single throne sat, facing away. And I knew, perfect, authentic and true, that someday soon, at the top of that mountain, I was going to die. Maybe because I'm psychic.

The End of Book Two

THANK you for beginng this trip with Asher. If you'd like to leave a review or a rating here's the link.

https://www.amazon.com/review/create-review/?ie=UTF8&channel=glance-detail&asin=B0CFNKC3B4

Now enjoy a sneak peak inside Book Three: *The Shadow Waiting on its Throne*

CHAPTER ONE

AFTER SAMANTHA APPEARED and shot me up through my skull I found myself going a little fast, with momentum carrying me up the flanks of a ghost mountain out of control, which in some way felt like a metaphor for my life. Though in exactly what way wasn't clear. I usually can't tell.

Below me spread the hamlet of Skysill Beach, crowding to the sand in its cup of coastal hills. And floating up with no control I came to a realization, because I had all that extra time: in the same way that all ghosts had become my responsibility because I was the only one who saw them, responsibility for this mountain would fall to me. And you could tell it was going to be a problem. It was going to be exclusively a me problem.

It towered over Skysill. It cast ultraviolet gloom on all our malls and our beach umbrellas and art galleries and stoplights. And I'm against gloom, which some people might be surprised to hear. I like a beach that's blazing bright which I can hide from in a bar. In the past avoiding beaches like that has given my life a simple kind of purpose.

Up through gloom I power lofted until, coming fast, I saw the peak. It pierced the stratosphere, where I was headed. The bare ghost stone of it streamed out in *dominion* banners across the sky, like pinnacle snow off Kilimanjaro, while sheets of bare stone plunged miles before piercing the distant tree line—or whatever that line is. What am I a botonist? I'm a psychic.

From that height, Skysill was just an urban fingerprint dusted onto the coast. The California shoreline dimmed north, toward Los Angeles, and south to Mexico, in haze and cloud trail. Above me as I rose the stars appeared.

I went higher until I came level with the stone needle tip of that mountain. Miles away but as clear as a junkie's conscience I saw it. Sheered off. A high, lonely platform. Out of that platform emerged a throne, carved from the peak itself, facing away from me.

And I shuddered. I felt again a foreknowledge of my oncoming death. And not in my usual drunken way of foreknowing things—like when is happy hour over—this was very specifically psychic and horrible.

The thing with foreknowledge, I suddenly found, was it seemed a much higher quality of knowledge than any of my other knowledge. And I just trusted it as the no-question truth: I would die on that ghost peak, touching the top of that throne, in three months' time.

Then I ran out of momentum, and back down I started, with no control of speed or destination which, again, probably a metaphor. The moment I changed direction there came a shimmery shake in the air and the entire ghost mountain vanished. I had a moment of...

GET BOOK THREE NOW!

The Shadow Waiting on its Throne: The Book of Scent

AFTERWORD

This ends The History of Light, Book Two: *The Question in the Dancer's Kiss: The Book of Sound.* The History of Light series continues with Book Three, *The Shadow Waiting on its Throne: The Book of Scent.*

The Shadow Waiting on its Throne begins mere seconds after Book Two ends, as Asher discovers his new psychic powers in the realm of death. Though if he's psychic, he wonders, how come he never knows what's about to happen next? Soon he's trying to paint again while the Five Families run wild in Skysill, Aeternus stalks him, and even the Brazilians return. And to top it off, time itself is ending in three months. His sister, his parents, his girlfriend—even Veronica his billionaire—are imperiled, while Asher looks more and more like Skysill's only hope. And all along, in the background, a ghost mountain creeps nearer, carrying, high atop it, *The Shadow Waiting on its Throne.*

THE HISTORY OF LIGHT
BOOKS 1 THROUGH 5

— THE GHOST WITH A KNIFE AT HER THROAT: The Book of Sight

— THE QUESTION IN THE DANCER'S KISS: The Book of Sound

— THE SHADOW WAITING ON ITS THRONE: The Book of Scent

— THE SACRIFICE THE DEAD WILL MAKE: The Book of Taste

— THE CURSE AT THE END OF THE WORLD: The Book of Touch

ALSO BY KEVIN HINCKER

The Little Queen

The Einstein Object

A Debt to the Stars

ABOUT THE AUTHOR

Kevin Hincker writes speculative fiction for curious readers. If you'd like to join his mailing list, or find extra information about his books, you can signup, or just explore, at https://kevinhincker.com/

If you want Amazon to deliver you information about his future releases, such as Book Five of this series, go to his Amazon page, https://www.amazon.com/author/kevinhincker and click the "Follow" button in the upper left next to his picture.